I0763375

PAYBACK

TALES OF
LOVE, HATE AND REVENGE

A NOVEL

BY STEVE BASSETT

Ebook: 978-1-64184-204-4
Paperback: 978-1-0878-0033-2
Hardcover: 978-1-64184-181-8

I have decided to stick with love.
Hate is too hard a burden to bear.

Martin Luther King, Jr.
1929 – 1968

Impotent hatred is the most horrible
of all emotions; One should nobody hate
whom one cannot destroy

Johan Wolfgang von Goethe
1749 – 1832

"Vengeance is in my heart,
Death in my mind, blood
And revenge are hammering
In my head."

William Shakespeare, *Titus Andronicus*
Act II, Scene 3, Lines 38-39

ACKNOWLEDGEMENT

As a legally blind veteran, I owe much to the Veterans Administration for the completion of this book, the second novel of the Passaic River Trilogy, and the trilogy's first novel, *Father Divine's Bikes*. VA therapists and instructors in Tucson, Arizona, exhibited unbelievable forbearance teaching coping and computer skills to a garrulous man who refused to accept that his near blindness was changing his life forever. On board from the start, after visiting the VA Tucson facility, was my wife Darlene Chandler Bassett, founder and President of A Room of Her Own Foundation (AROHO), an invaluable resource for women writers and poets. Her uncompromising and often brutal editing made this final manuscript possible. Not enough can be said about the diligence and patience of Christine Cappuccino, who for ten years as my virtual assistant has been my eyes and ears.

CHAPTER ONE

By noon on Saturday, October 19, 1946, the sun had plunged through the grime and gloom of the air over Newark, and the city was basking in shirtsleeve warmth. Pleasant, but it had no effect on the two guys who earlier that morning butchered the corpse of a Hitler-loving swine, then packaged the pieces for afternoon delivery.

Mike tooled his 1939 Hudson Terraplane Coupe on a purposely circuitous route on his way to the city dump. Except for a few furtive glances, Mike ignored Frank who sat silently beside him in the passenger seat. There was no ball-busting during this ride.

During a spasm of bloodlust Mike volunteered the Terraplane for today's mission. He loved his Terraplane, inherited, along with his job, from his traveling salesman father who died of a massive heart attack while hawking men's suspenders and sock garters. The car was cherry red and Mike hoped it would be that way when it was all over. The sliding steel box in the car's trunk made their job easier for now, but Mike knew the clean-up afterward would be disgusting.

"We're getting close so let's just keep it slow as we go," Frank said. "It's all arranged. The dump's rear gate will be unlocked so we can slide in and out without any trouble. It can't be over soon enough. My gut's been up in my throat for the past hour. I know this is the third time, but the first two were never like this."

"We knew what we were getting into," Mike said. "We agreed that payback was due."

Mike and Frank were a matched set. Frank topped out at five feet ten inches. Mike at no more than five feet nine. They were of average build but fit and athletic. There was not a hint of Hollywood good looks between them. They were totally nondescript except for one thing. They wore their old army combat fatigues bearing the shoulder patch of the 42nd Rainbow Division that had liberated the Nazi concentration camp at Dachau. The patch's red, gold and blue rainbow crescent was an eye catcher, made famous back in 1917 by good old Doug MacArthur.

The Terraplane glided to a stop at the city dump's seldom-used rear gate. Frank jumped out and as expected found the padlock chain hanging loose. Mike watched as Frank pushed both sides of the gate open to clear the way. He thanked God the gate was wide enough to allow the Terraplane through without any danger of picking up scratches to the car's four-layered enamel paint job.

"Straight ahead about a hundred yards and then turn around that heap of junk and other shit on the right," Frank said as his finger followed squirreled handwritten instructions on a scrap of yellow paper. "Then we can't miss it. It's straight ahead and huge. Should be going full blast. We'll have to work fast. There's only one weekend watchman, but there's no telling when he'll be coming this way."

The heat from the open blast furnace door could be felt when they pulled to a stop a safe twenty feet from the hard-working behemoth. They jumped out and went to the Hudson's rear as Mike unlocked the trunk. They had already snapped on rubber gloves. He then popped a latch that allowed a large steel box to slide along rails out of the trunk and extend over the bumper. The box contained three bloody parcels. The largest was wrapped in a canvas painter's drop cloth, the two others in white sheets. All were tightly bound with untraceable hemp rope.

"Okay, let's get going," Frank said.

With great effort Frank and Mike hoisted the large canvas-wrapped bundle out of the steel box and carried it to the furnace door at arm's-length to avoid the dripping blood. "Don't want to drop this son of a bitch and then have to pick him up again. Ready?"

"Let's get on with it."

Sweating profusely, they waddled awkwardly toward the incinerator trying to make sure that their fatigues remained gore-free. With the blood-soaked bundle held at equal length between them, they rocked back-and-forth twice in order to get momentum, then heaved it into the furnace. Their speed was hampered by the Chaplinesque way they handled their grisly cargo. Next Frank tossed the smallest blood-drenched bundle into the flames.

Frank and Mike stopped in their tracks when a deep voice roared, "What the hell is going on down there? Stay right there! Don't you move! Else your asses are mine!"

They spotted a big black man hobbling towards them from about seventy-five yards away. They had been warned that a watchman could be a problem, and there he was coming their way.

"Let's get the hell out of here. We're finished, right?" Mike said.

"Nope, not yet," Frank said. He grabbed the last oblong and blood-drenched bundle, tossed it toward the incinerator and headed for the door on the front passenger side. At the trunk, Mike almost puked when he saw the red lake rippling at the bottom of the steel cargo box. He pushed the box into the trunk, slammed it shut and headed to the driver's seat. He turned the car toward the exit.

Once in his seat, Frank glanced to his right and spotted the watchman limping toward them still a good twenty-five yards away.

"Hold it mother-fuckers!" he shouted. "Ain't no chance you getting away!"

Mike hit the gas pedal hard grinding the gravel into a plume of dust as the Hudson sped off. It took only a few seconds before they swerved to a sliding stop at the gate. Frank jumped out, opened it and once the car was out on the frontage road, he covered any trace that they had gotten inside help. He carefully closed the gate, wrapped the chain in its customary place and clamped the padlock closed.

A frustrated Tom Candless could only stand and watch helplessly as the dust from the departing car caught the wind and eddied around him. It was the first time in his six months on the job that he had seen anybody while making his rounds. For a combat vet with a Purple Heart for a leg wound, it was a plum job.

His warning shouts were a bluff. Even at his top speed, he knew they would be long gone before he reached the incinerator. But they didn't know that.

With the city dump disappearing in the rearview mirror, Frank and Mike were breathing easier when a rousing rendition of *The Stars and Stripes Forever* wafted its way from nearby Rupert Stadium.

"Would you believe it, a fanfare from Johnny Sousa himself," Frank said.

"It's the Little Army-Navy game."

"Yeah, spoiled rich kids from two highfalutin military academies playing at being men," Frank said.

"Actually saw one of the games before the war, wore uniforms just like West Point and Annapolis."

"Hope they give *Bonnie Annie Laurie* a shot before we get out of here. It's my favorite."

Mike stayed well within the speed limit as he glided the Hudson past late arrivals hunting for parking spaces as close as possible to Rupert Stadium. *Careful now, can't afford any nicked bumper with all that blood swishing around back there. All we need is an honest cop nosing around.*

"There it is! They must have heard me," an excited Frank said as they finally got past the heavy traffic and were heading downtown.

"What the hell you talking about?"

"*Bonnie Annie Laurie!*"

Several blocks from the stadium, the heavy brass music from two marching bands was still loud and distinct. Mike momentarily lost control, his right hand jumping from the gear-shift knob in shocked reaction to the rich and exuberant baritone notes coming from Frank.

Her brow is like the snowdrift,
Her neck is like the swan,
Her face it is the fairest,
That ever the sun shone on.

"Goddamn, you should have warned me, my nerves already had me twitching."

"Mike, my boy, she's just the woman for you. It eases even the thought of the hereafter," Frank said with a smile affecting a deep Scottish brogue. "Did you know that the great Albert Parsons sang this lovely ditty in his Chicago death cell after the Haymarket Riots? A great man."

Her voice is low and sweet
And she's all the world to me;
And for bonnie Annie Laurie
I'd lay me down and die

“The Haymarket Riots? Never figured you for a Bolshevik.”

“No Communist blood, but a lot of anarchist from my dad.”

“Your dad an anarchist, doesn’t figure. He’s got a neat little meat shipping business, and the contacts to make it work.”

“You’re not a fucking babe in the woods, Mike. He had to do a lot of head-busting for the gangster-controlled meatpackers to get the nod. I know you think it’s just me and him, so here’s a couple of names for you. Tom Sioni and Gino Sambino. Two teamsters who don’t exist but get paychecks from Beagan and Son every week.”

Mike did not reply, focusing his attention on the traffic ahead.

“Nothing to say? Hope to hell you’re not passing judgment,” said Frank now agitated and defensive. “Can’t tell me the wop-gangster s don’t have a piece of your racket. They love fancy duds, the flashier the better.”

“Relax, I’m not judging you, your dad, or anything else. How the fuck can I after our year with Mister Rache.”

By the time they were on McCarter Highway both had lighted up and taken a few deep drags in futile attempts to ease the anxiety that had been building since the start of their bloody mission more than a year ago. But despite their involvement in three revenge-driven murders, they were still strangers.

CHAPTER
TWO

It was early Sunday, October 20, when acting homicide chief Lieutenant Nick Cisco padded his way to the kitchen to prepare another lonely breakfast when the telephone rang. His partner, Detective Sergeant Kevin McClosky, got right to the point.

"We've got another one," McClosky said. "At least part of one."

"What in the hell are you talking about?" Cisco said, knowing fully what it was all about. "I'm listening, but goddamn it's Sunday morning. Couldn't it have waited until I had a cup of coffee?"

"Nope. No way. The Third Precinct got the call from a watchman at the city dump," McClosky said. "Whatever happened and where it happened still don't know. Only that it was early yesterday afternoon."

"Do we have a stiff or don't we?"

"Well, yeah, at least part of one," McClosky said. "It's definitely connected to the two floaters we've been keeping under wraps."

Cisco took a deep breath, slowing everything down. "What the hell do we have? Give it all to me now."

"A couple of uniforms answered the call from the watchman. They got there just as the rats were sitting down for lunch. That's all there was, a sawed-off right arm. Here's the connection. Just like our two floaters, there was the same tattooed swastika and inscription, only this one said, 'Camp Siegfried 1938.'"

"Camp Siegfried? Where the hell is Camp Siegfried?" Cisco said. "We know about the other two. They were right here in Jersey."

"And there's the ring, exactly the same as the two floaters," McClosky said. "It all fits. What do we do now?"

"First, let's find out about this Camp Siegfried," Cisco said. "Okay, so we've got a right arm found in the city dump. What in the hell is going on? And where the hell is the rest of the body?"

"Barbecued, and I really mean bacon crisp, in that monster junkyard incinerator," McClosky said. "Here's the rub, it looks like everything but the arm goes into the oven. Seems these two guys spotted at the incinerator didn't want the arm roasted. Wanted it found. It was neatly tied in a white sheet and tossed on the ground not far from the furnace door. The watchman couldn't resist poking his nose in, cut open the bundle and probably came close to pissing his pants."

"What two guys?" Cisco said. "Give me all we know. I'll have to call Peterson. It's Sunday and he won't be happy."

"The watchman's all that we got right now, and he's not much," McClosky said. "He was making his afternoon rounds yesterday at about twelve-thirty, and he spotted two white guys going back and forth between the incinerator and a red car parked not far from the furnace door."

"Did he get a make on the car?"

"Nope, only that it was red and looked, in his words, 'kinda fancy-like.' The guy's a Purple Heart Army vet with a gimp leg, and says that's why he didn't collar the guys, who were about seventy-five yards or so away. He yelled at them, and they got their asses into that car real quick, and were long gone before he limped down to the incinerator. Then, as I said, he poked around and went back to the office and called the Third. That was around one o'clock."

"How long before the uniforms got there?" Cisco asked. "It was windy yesterday, and the wind plays hell with evidence."

"Just our luck, yesterday was the Little Army-Navy Game at Rupert and most of the Third Precinct uniforms were babysitting the rich snobs who rolled in for the game. It took a while to free up a car for the dump."

"Where's the watchman now? You better have him under wraps," Cisco said. "If that arm is a match for what we found on our two floaters, it's dynamite. And oh yeah, I hope that arm's on ice at the morgue."

McClosky ignored the question, saving the best for last. "I got the call this morning at six-thirty from Jim Murdock, the watch commander at the Third. The watchman's name is Tom Candless, he's with me here in the dump office. I haven't let him out of my sight. His boss, name's Stigman, is here too. As far as the arm goes, it's been a real zoo. The uniforms from the Third just stood around staring at it. Finally called Murdock, who passed it on to a plainclothes sergeant. We know him, Josh Gingold. It took an hour or so before the coroner's jokers finished their liverwurst on rye and finally got here. Took their pictures, wrapped the arm up and took it home. It's waiting for us now."

"Make it damn plain and clear that nobody opens his trap," Cisco said. "Grab Candless and I'll meet the two of you at the morgue. Maybe another look at the meat will jog his memory, and he'll come up with something new. On your way to Tomokai's parlor of horrors, stop by the Third and pick up Gingold's report. And Murdock, any problem there?"

"I laid it on thick, lied a lot, and threw Peterson's name around. Murdock should hold for a while, but I think a call from the D.A. will be needed to lock him up tight. You don't have to worry about Stigman, he's one of those City Hall hacks who'll button up for as long as you tell him, and I don't think Josh is a problem," McClosky said.

"Look, I just got up. Need a little bit to get my head around what you just told me."

Things were not going well for Cisco. He already had two bloody murders on his hands, and now this bombshell from McClosky. He had an estranged wife, a family who had disowned him and a sexual addiction he could not cure. Could it get any worse? Pessimism and self-recrimination, had been his companions since Palm Sunday when he attended high mass at Saint Lucy's alone for the first time in twelve years. His wife, Constance Sophia Margotta, walked out on him the week before and moved in with her family on South 10th Street. The word had not yet gotten around to the Ciscos when he took his seat in the family pew, their sidelong glances were more curious than accusatory. Before the day was over, that would change.

He didn't have the guts to be a no-show at the family Easter celebration that kicked-off Holy Week. When he arrived alone for the traditional feast at the Cisco home on Holiday Court, and without that huge side dish of antipasto that was his wife's specialty, it all went rapidly downhill.

"Where's that beautiful wife of yours? Not sick I hope." Angelo Cisco asked his son. "Connie loves your mom's leg of lamb. Smell it? My mouth's been watering for an hour," the elder Cisco crooned.

"I don't think she'll be here," Cisco said, reaching for the jelly jar of homemade dago red offered by his father.

Cisco wandered about more like a stranger than a family member as the afternoon progressed. Nothing quite compared to self-righteous Italian family hostility. The word got around fast. Cisco was a leper and without a Father Damian in sight. He was wrong, and his father made sure he knew that he was wrong, when he pulled his son aside on the front porch as he was about to leave.

"Couldn't keep your goddamned fly zipped, could you," Angelo slammed it out. "Grace De Marco. Knew you'd been fucking her, for how many years now? I kept it from your mother and I thought, no I prayed, that Connie didn't know. But no, you had to flaunt it, wave that cock of yours around. No shame, no goddamned shame. I want this fixed, you hear me, fixed. Don't come back until you do it. There's nothing here for you until it's set right."

Father and son were all alone on the porch. Everyone else had already left. Angelica was out of earshot in the backyard cleaning up. Her husband's white-knuckled fists gripped the lapels of his son's sports jacket. He pulled his son toward him until their faces were only inches apart. "I am ashamed. Until you fix it. *Non siete nessun figlio mio!"* Angelo's arm and upper-body strength earned during thirty-five years as a Port Newark stevedore was put to work. He shoved his son toward the stairs, where he stumbled down to the sidewalk barely able to keep from falling flat on his face. Nick recovered his balance, fought off a fleeting impulse for eye contact, turned and slumped to his car.

CHAPTER
THREE

Since April, there had been half-hearted appeals that were given a thin veneer of contrition when their pastor at Saint Anthony's, Father Peter Sullivan, tried to get Nick and Connie back together. They had tried, but there were no kids to act as natural buffers. For the past six months, he roamed their six-room house on Delavan, not exactly Elwood, one block to the north, but not bad on a cop's salary.

His self-loathing was lessened by Grace De Marco's carnal therapy. But these days it wasn't enough and he sought out a different kind of help.

The kid in the painting above the fireplace mantle was maybe thirteen or fourteen years old. The flowing collar of an obviously expensive white shirt fringed his neck and poked from beneath a black doublet-like jacket. It was the embodiment of privilege. It was clear that he wanted service and right now. Behind him several shadowy acolytes watched with bewildered approval.

Cisco operated in a world where cruelty, fear, and hatred notarized his paycheck. He only survived the dirt of Newark because of the escape his love of art afforded him. His beloved Diego Rodriguez de Silva y Velazquez supplied the artistic opiate with *The Waterseller of Seville*. He needed these interludes now more than ever.

Twenty years ago, even as a rookie cop serious questions arose about his profession, he started taking pre-law night courses at Rutgers, and chose Art Appreciation 101 as his first humanity elective. That opened the floodgate. Before he knew it, he had collected eighteen art credits. Sure, to please his family he still enrolled in pre-law and criminology classes, but his heart was never in it. Then Constance Sophia Margotta came into his life and there was a prolonged four-year courtship, not because of Connie, with whom he was deeply in love, but because he had so many goddamn questions about everything. He knew if they married, he would remain a cop, and his dream of getting an art degree would vanish. He couldn't paint or even sketch his way out of a paper bag, but he discovered that he had a natural talent for clear, distinct, and evocative writing. He saw himself as either a museum or gallery curator, perhaps even a newspaper or magazine art critic. It never happened.

Cisco got up from the living room sofa and straightened the *Waterseller*. He considered himself pretty close to expert when it came to Spanish Baroque art. Velazquez was his guide from the very beginning. Cisco had long questioned the existence of truth, then he found it in the sensual allure of Velazquez. Both worlds melded and how could they not. Velazquez had his humble *Waterseller*. Cisco had his Mike the Shoemaker.

"Quite something, isn't it kid?" the uniformed Cisco poached on the wide-eyed kid daydreaming as he peered in the shop window of Mike the Shoemaker.

"Been waiting three weeks. One more to go. Hope they're still there. Mom said she'll get them." The boy, probably ten or eleven years old, embodied Newark's North Ward in 1934. He had a kitchen haircut, most likely the mom's handiwork.

"Good luck," said Cisco, who was awaiting the results of his sergeant's exam and the end of his beat along lower Broadway. "How about the trophy, it's got everybody talking."

"Trophy, who cares about the trophy," the boy said. "Can't wear it, can I? Can wear *them* though. Won't need to pull the cassock over the shoes at mass no more."

Cisco looked down at the kid, not quite a redhead, but close. His plaid shirt and brown corduroys were clean but heavily mended. His shoes were falling apart, badly worn at the heels, and Cisco wondered how much stitching was left. Both shoes had black electrical tape wrapped around them to keep their soles from flapping. "Take care of yourself," usually empty words now spoken with concern. The kid shuffled away as Cisco entered the shop.

"Nick, long time no see! So, you've come in to shake hands with the celebrity," the impish, gray-haired Mike said extending his leather-hard right hand. "Something, ain't it? Didn't know nothing about it until I got a Western Union from some city out in the Midwest somewhere, can't remember which one. No matter. Said my shop looked great, my stitching was the best. And here's another good one, they said I knew what I was doing."

"Word gets around," Cisco said. "Hard times, nobody can afford new anymore. They're all getting them fixed. Congrats."

"The *Clarion* and the *Beacon* sent out a reporter and camera guy. Their stories are gonna be in this Sunday," Mike bragged. "We put the trophy in the front window sitting in the middle of my best jobs. Looks good out there, don't it?"

"Mike, I need a little favor," Cisco said. "You saw that kid looking in the window next to me a few minutes ago? Know him if you saw him again, if he came in with his mother?"

"Sure. Here every day looking in the window," Mike said. "Stays a little bit, and then takes off."

"I want to show you something. That pair of brown shoes. Probably too big for the kid but he wants them. No, needs them," Cisco explained to the befuddled Mike. "I want to buy them. Keep them in the window but nobody claims them, understand? How much?"

"The kid's got taste. A fine pair of bluchers. Needed tender loving care," Mike said. "A little more for this job, but nothing you can't afford."

For Cisco, it wasn't just this kid, an altar boy at Saint Michael's down the street. It was also what he had seen one Sunday at Saint Lucy's, his parents' parish on upscale Seventh Avenue near the park. It was high mass with a lot of standing, sitting, shuffling about, and kneeling. He'd noticed that one of the altar boys continually tugged at the lower rear folds of his cassock so that it covered his shoes. The few times the boy neglected to do so, Cisco noticed gaping holes in the soles of both shoes. The sock on the left foot was also worn away exposing skin.

Velazquez had his proud and haughty *Waterseller* who quenched the thirst of anyone with coin enough to pay. His badly torn leather tunic a defiant anthem. Three centuries later, Mike had his works of art beckon passersby, and he had a silver trophy to validate that the thickly-calloused hands and hammer-blackened fingernails had indeed created a utilitarian art form. Cisco wondered if there was not at least a figment of truth somewhere in all of this.

God, he was a fraud. What the hell was this search for an increasingly evasive eternal truth when he was fucking Grace De Marco, an addiction that worsened with no cure in sight. How could he say he still loved Connie while this was going on? Would this family rupture ever be repaired? He had no answers to any of this, and Velazquez might have momentarily eased the pain, but that was about it.

Doesn't seem possible things could get any worse, but they are, Cisco thought. *Mob murders with no solutions and our little rogue gang that's getting very dicey. We've kept it under wraps with three of the biggest publicity hounds keeping their traps shut, but for how much longer? And now we have Murdock and Gingold to worry about.*

On Saturday night, Gingold had slept very little since he was called to the macabre scene at the dump, a short nap on a bunk in the locker room was about it. He had never seen anything like it before, couldn't imagine it, and spent a lot of time on his report that ran for three pages.

It was just after six o'clock and he had just begun to relax when Murdock approached his desk, grabbed the report and started reading. "Jesus fucking Christ!"

"Couldn't have said it better."

Murdock reached across Gingold's desk, grabbed the phone and dialed homicide.

"Who'd I get this time?" he said, then recognized the voice. "McClosky, it's Jim Murdock, and we've got a good one for you."

Gingold watched as his boss picked out juicy snatches from his report. Murdock was on an expletive-filled roll and had just described the tattoos and ring on the severed arm when McClosky on his end pulled him up short.

"But I've got more, you wanna hear it or not?" Murdock said, then frowned and listened. "Peterson, you've got to be shitting me." He was getting an earful and didn't like it.

"Okay, okay, it goes no further, you don't have to draw me any pictures. Yeah, I can handle the uniforms, they'll keep their traps shut."

Murdock's face hardened as he nodded and nodded before hanging up. He was used to giving orders, and now this grizzled, police veteran was taking orders from a mere sergeant.

"Everything gets locked up. McClosky will pick up your report and no one else, and I mean no one else ever lays eyes on it," Murdock said, and with a grunt headed back to his office.

It was nine-thirty when McClosky arrived, poked his head into Murdock's office, and exchanged a few words before ambling over to Gingold's desk.

"Josh, long time no see," McClosky said, then got directly to the point. "You have your report finished?"

"Here it is, three pages, in duplicate. From what the boss said, you want them both. Do I get that right?"

"You got it right. Your star witness, Candless, is out in the squad car bitching and moaning. Taking him to the morgue for a final I.D."

McClosky turned and was headed out when he stopped and asked, "Do you ever miss it?"

"Miss what?"

"Center ring, the bright lights and all that goes with it. Turning in your gloves for a badge and the shit-end of the stick like this?" McClosky said, tapping the report. "Never could figure it."

"Not being a Jew, you never will."

After a short inquiring glance, McClosky turned away with, "Well, got to run, catch-up later."

It didn't escape Gingold the way McClosky had sauntered from Murdock's office to his desk. Josh knew Kevin well enough to know it was forced casualness, that something big was in the works. They were all violating police procedure, so why not take it one more step.

Gingold opened the lower right drawer of his desk and pulled out two small tightly-wrapped cellophane packages. They had either fallen or been accidentally kicked from the red car as it sped from the junkyard furnace. *Expensive stuff*, he thought, *too rich for my blood.* On each package, underneath the company logo was inscribed: *The best is always the best buy.* Below the slogan he found all he needed to know. One phone call to New York and some adroit detective bullshit would get him started.

He had two weeks' vacation coming and some sick leave. In his hands were two clues he wasn't about to share. They could be the key to a case that was obviously troubling some important people downtown. McClosky's uncharacteristic quirky behavior told him this coverup was not only big, but probably illegal. It didn't matter, Josh wanted in.

CHAPTER
FOUR

Grace De Marco never saw it coming, the instant that would change her life forever. The blow to her left cheek snapped her head to the right as she fell backward into darkness penetrated by tiny flashing lights. Her legs buckled as she tumbled over the sofa to the parquet floor. She was barely aware of what had happened, only that she was flat on her stomach, her head was ringing, and she had inhaled a dust ball into her left nostril. She cleared her nose amid a spray of mucus, and pulled herself to her knees, still not comprehending what had happened. She peered over the back of the sofa. John Fusina had returned to his cocktail, and when he saw her emerging head he smiled and lifted his glass.

John was third in a line of Fusina dentists who reaped the rewards that rotten teeth, inflamed gums, and impacted wisdom teeth offered. If there was a root canal hierarchy in Newark, the Fusina dentists were enthroned.

Sunday, August 30, 1942, was a ninety-degree scorcher, not the best for the job facing the photographer and young female reporter from the *Evening Clarion*. It was only two o'clock, but this was already their third assignment of the day. Theirs was the thankless task of collecting photos and caption material for next weekend's Sunday Magazine. Grace De Marco was to be featured as a war-time wife whose grit and charm pushed her into prominence usually reserved for men. As the Court Clerk's top assistant, she handled an ever-increasing workload with flare and expediency.

Her husband was not among the men and women shipped overseas for the duration. Family contacts had paid off when his dental degree earned him captain's bars, and a sweetheart assignment at Fort Monmouth. He made the forty-three mile trip home every weekend. That Sunday he played a late morning round of golf at Weequahic Park, and walked into the house while the photographer and reporter were in the middle of their shoot. He stood around, listened, watched and made little attempt to hide his annoyance despite his morning round of eighty-two that put fifteen dollars in his pocket. His irritation was compounded by the drenched shirt clinging to his shoulders, and the sweat trickling down his spine. *When was this circus going to end?* He had expected his usual martini to be waiting for him.

"I saw you move from that back desk in the middle of nowhere, to up front, and then to an office all your own," cooed the photographer, a courthouse veteran, as he positioned Grace for his final shots. "Nice to watch, and even greater to hear the sour-grapes from the courthouse good-ol-boys."

John was pissed. "How much longer with this?" he said. His forced smile failed to hide his anger.

The photographer, a stocky, crewcut redhead, had taken a dislike to Fusina the moment he walked into the room, and started huffing out twitches of annoyance, tapping his fingers on the mantle, and rocking while standing by the window. The redhead bore in for the kill. "I hope it was okay to call you Mr. Fusina. I looked over your wife's bio, and saw that you're a dentist, never was sure if a dentist was a doctor, so maybe I should have said Dr. Fusina."

"I hope this about does it," Grace said moving from her last set-up in front of an easeled still life of the Abe Lincoln bronze down by the courthouse, "Oh, perhaps you want a shot of me and John."

"Nah, got what we need, unless Trudy here wants me to get one." The photographer turned to the reporter, who shook her head. "Nope, got it all. We've got to get going."

Grace walked the pair to the front door, and then waved them off as their car pulled from the curb on Wilden Place, made an illegal U-turn and sped off in the direction of Ivy Hill Park. She knew she had made a mistake when she suggested a photo with John, fully aware that he would be seething if rejected.

Grace avoided John's eyes as she walked to the liquor cart in the southwest corner of the living room. His irritation filled the room. With three half turns, she removed the strainer top of the silver-plated Cobbler cocktail shaker. With a pair of tongs, she removed five ice cubes from a large glass lined chrome bowl, a gift along with the Cobbler from John's grandfather. Until her marriage, Grace had never mixed a cocktail of any kind. Her North Ward background included straight highballs, flavored brandies, every now and then some applejack, screw-top Roma wine, good old rock and rye for what ails you, and, of course, beer.

It was an incident that occurred only a week or so after Grace and John moved into the ten-room Italian Renaissance on Wilden, courtesy of the sixty percent down payment gift from John's parents. "What are you pouring, Johnny?" Rosetta asked her son, her voice stiff. This was a family that embraced the upper middle-class ritual they had earned, and the booze that came with it.

"Tanqueray, Mom, the frats at Temple love it," John said. "That's all they use."

"That might be true at Temple, but it's not for us," his dad said. "Look at you here, great house, new practice, and beautiful bride, a NJC girl at that. You can do a lot better than Tanqueray. It's Gordon's for you, triple-charcoal filtered, pure stuff to dip your onions in, makes the perfect Gibson."

Grace never forgot this admonition that was hardly fatherly, and precluded the need for any response. So, Gordon's it was, which along with two pickled onions and a whiff of Dolin Vermouth de Chambéry for a drink that Grace thought smelled nice, but tasted crappy. She developed a tolerance, and a sense of wonderment that she was now part of a family that kept track of how many times booze seeped through charcoal before it was worthy of ritualistic quaffing.

Her husband had moved from the window to the fireplace behind her without saying a word. She could feel his unremitting gaze, her discomfort increasing in lockstep with his silence. She measured out the Gordon's, added the vermouth, replaced the Cobbler's strainer top, swirled the ice cubes four times, removed the cap from the strainer, poured the contents into cocktail glasses, skewered two onions onto ivory swizzle sticks, and dropped them into the glasses. She gripped beveled silver coasters between her pinky and middle finger of each hand, picked up the Gibsons with her thumbs and forefingers, and turned toward the fireplace.

Like a waiting communicant her husband took the silver wafers from between Grace's fingers, and placed them on the fireplace mantle, exactly three feet apart. Grace placed the cocktails on the silver wafers, turned to John, and as always waited for him to take the first sip of the elixir. He raised his glass, inhaled and sampled his drink. His face was expressionless as he placed the glass back on the coaster and stepped forward.

Grace could feel the shock and pain at what had occurred suffuse into unfathomable disbelief. She wondered if the punch was real. Her thoughts were fuzzy and indistinct. Like a little school girl diagramming her first sentence, she tried unsuccessfully to place nouns, verbs, adverbs, adjectives, and most of all the conjunctions needed to piece it all together. With her fingers she found the proof that it was all real, an affirmation she still couldn't mentally accept. She felt around her rapidly swelling left eye, and how her cheek felt like a puffy balloon. The back of her neck and skull hurt like hell when she tried to move her head to the left. Grace knew she was losing it, and didn't care.

"Come on up here and join me," John beckoned. His smile widened exposing faultless teeth surrounded by full lips, topped by a well-tended Thin Man's mustache. "You've done yourself proud. Come on, join me, I won't bite." He made no attempt to help her. He took another sip and smacked his lips.

"You fucking son of a bitch! You goddamn bastard! You miserable prick!" Words she loathed in others were now driven by an uncontrollable hatred that couldn't be imagined only moments before. It was an outpouring that had been waiting for some time to surface. "You want me over there? Okay, you'll get me." She stood erect, walked from behind the sofa and over to the fireplace.

"Okay, it's over now. But the pressure, you know it's been building." With his glass, John gestured Grace to her assigned spot at the fireplace. "When I found those two cretins here with you, and what that punk of a photographer had to say to me, well it all exploded inside me."

Grace picked up her glass and threw her work of art in her husband's face, and smashed the empty glass in the fireplace. It was all happening so fast, without thought. She pushed past her husband to the drink cart, picked up the bottle of Gordon's, spun around and threw it at him with all the strength she could muster. He ducked and she couldn't believe it, he was still holding his cocktail. The bottle shattered as it hit the granite frieze over the fireplace, glass shards and gin cascaded over the mantle and to the floor behind John. Jagged pain engulfed the back of her neck and skull. She joined her hands, locked her arms so they were stiff and straight, and swept the top of the liquor cart clean. The beloved bottle of Dolin Vermouth de Chambéry spun into the window, fell to the floor without breaking, but left behind a three-foot spider web of cracked glass.

"Slow down, Grace, slow down. We can talk this out, we have to be rational." His features never crossed that subtle divide between disinterest and caring. "It was an aberration. I don't know what grabbed me. We'll talk it out, figure it out between us."

Grace was still in position beside the liquor cart. Unthinking she reached behind her for another bottle to throw at him, but came up empty. Debris from the cart was scattered at her feet. She stared across the twelve feet separating them, and for the first time really saw the mistake to whom she had been married for seven years. He looked the same, a compact and trim man just under six feet tall, with hairy arms, thick wrists and hands more suited for a dockworker than a dentist. He was strong, but except for the forceful way he put his strength to work in the bedroom, much of the glow of marriage had faded for Grace. When they married, Grace was a twenty-four-year-old virgin.

John was a craftsman. He knew just how much pain to inflict, how much force to use when he pulled her hair, and yanked her head into place. How much pressure to exert on her lower jaw when he inserted his fingers into her mouth and commanded, "Clamp down, bite hard, hard damn it, I said hard!" The first time she broke skin, she eased the pressure as her husband's blood sluiced over her tongue. "Don't stop, don't you goddamn stop." She did as commanded. At first, she wondered, is this it? Is this what it's all about? Her doubts faded as her pleasure increased. She gladly absorbed the pain when he grabbed her wrists, crossed her arms above her head, and held her helpless. She discovered prurient desires that both frightened and pleased. With her wrists crisscrossed firmly in John's hand above her head, she demanded, "Pull them, higher, damn you. Pull up hard!" Each additional inch of movement increased the pain in her shoulders. She loved it. The pain from the first penetration on their wedding night came and went quickly. How many more times that night, she couldn't remember. Every part of their bodies came into play.

One morning, as was often the case, they were at it at first light. Her clamped legs cramped forcing her to stretch them straight above his thrusting buttocks. The pain having eased, she lowered her legs only to have the cramps return, and force her heels down hard into the small of his back. A "huff" exploded in her right ear followed by, "Do it again, don't stop till I say so."

There was no thought of children, and they made use of every protective device available.

Sex had been the glue that held their marriage together, but was it really a marriage? John's punch and her rapidly swelling face erased the doubts that had been growing over the past few years. On that terrible day in August 1942, what had been passing for love disappeared forever.

Grace could hardly remember how she had propelled herself from the living room, and up the stairs. Once upstairs, Grace realized, and fully accepted, how coalescing hatred could be. She grabbed two suitcases from the bedroom closet, and somehow managed to go from room-to-room collecting personal items, treasured mementos, clothes, framed photos, and her faithful teddy bear. She pulled hangers of clothes from the large master bedroom closet, went to the kitchen to get three cardboard boxes, returned to the bedroom, and filled two of them with shoes and purses, and the third with hats. She kept waiting for John to interfere, but he was nowhere in sight. The man who a short time earlier knocked her off her feet had disappeared without a whimper.

She took her car keys from her purse, went to the rear of the house and drove her Studebaker to the curb in front. Still no husband in sight. She carried everything she had collected to the car, placed the suitcases and boxes in the back seat, and carefully laid the hangered clothes on the floor of the trunk. Grace reentered the house, went to the phone in the foyer, and called her parents. "That you, Mom?"

"Yes, Grace, I'm surprised to hear from you so early," Theresa De Marco said, sensing something wrong. "Everything okay? You and John are still coming for dinner at six, right? It's his favorite tonight, *osso buco.*"

"No, mom, just me. I'll explain when I get there," Grace said. "I hope dad's camera is handy and loaded. We'll need it."

Grace returned to the car, started the motor, and slowly drove away. She could sense John's eyes following her down the street. *That cowardly son of a bitch*, she thought, *he'll pay*.

CHAPTER

FIVE

"Damn, I'm glad it's William's last Army-Navy game. Love to see him play but hell, does it have to be a lousy trap like Newark?" Jason Cullan Tumulty III disdained as he carefully guided his Packard touring sedan off the Pulaski Skyway onto Delancy Street on its way to Rupert Stadium.

"You browbeat Billy out of our home and exiled him to godforsaken Bordentown and a second-rate military school. So, you can at least bury your pride once a year for the Little Army-Navy Game," Regina Anne Hodges Tumulty chastised her husband and got no reply, another one of her small but significant victories, more numerous over the years as she increasingly understood just where and when to puncture her husband's enormous ego.

Jason Cullan Tumulty III loved his brain. It was his obsession. Tumulty, even now at forty-two, still marveled at how well the grey matter between his ears served him in his chosen profession. He easily accepted his spot atop the most ruthless collection of brothers of the bar who were universally mocked and feared as their outrageous legal fees kept rolling in. The six-foot Tumulty had all of the armament, and then some, to define the classic Philadelphia lawyer. Stylishly muscular and graceful, with an engaging but not quite warm smile, good teeth, a multi-octave orator's voice and a salt and pepper dome, Tumulty got your attention. He could thank his promenade through ivied Peddie School, pre-law at Washington & Jefferson, and University of Pennsylvania's Law Review for papering over a quick temper and natural hubris.

Tumulty turned onto Wilson Avenue into bumper-to-bumper traffic. The entire cadet corps of their son's school and rival Admiral Farragut Naval Academy crawled by in buses to hook up with their respective marching bands already assembling outside the stadium.

He didn't have to look her way to know that his wife was savoring a triumphant smile as she leaned back contentedly next to him. Her Mainline upbringing and Bryn Mawr entitlement ingrained the belief that a lady never lost her composure during an argument, and that a soothing rebuttal opened the way to delicious condescension.

"Goddamn it, if our son had only cracked a book once in a while, he'd be setting his rushing records at Valley Forge and we could almost walk to the games," Tumulty's anger reached temple-pumping stage. "Instead, he milked his family name for all it was worth. Thought he could skate through anything, but my God, paying a freshman classmate twenty-five bucks to take his Spanish exam. Worse yet, getting caught at it and having his ass booted out!"

His wife had heard it all before and was ready with her dart. "I know, I know. It is all about getting caught. You don't pick up those big fees from guys who have gotten away with it. No sirree! Oh, and by the way, a big chunk of those fees came right out of this lousy trap, as you call Newark, from Nazi-loving moguls no less. Haven't forgotten, have you?

"And, by the way, did you see how our Philly papers have been throwing tantrums since the White House hinted it would go easy on German companies who play ball with us? Got to keep Uncle Joe, and the Russian bear on their leashes. Even mention M.L. Kraus by name."

"All of them, even the *Record*?" he said.

"Even the *Record,* and you can throw in the *Inquirer* and the *Ledger*. No coddling allowed. Even Fuddy-duddy Robert McLean, with a barely detectable pulse, was ranting at Truman from his *Bulletin* that *pampering gas chamber killers was obscene*. Gives you something to think about, wouldn't you say?"

"Think about? What the hell is there to think about."

"Jason, after more than twenty years, you know that your *holier than thou* pose has never worked with me. Your synapses and neurons have been snap, crackle and popping in that handsome dome of yours the closer you get to that M.L. Kraus booty."

Regina was on a roll.

"The blood-lust prose spewed by our hometown rags aren't lonely, forlorn cries in our journalistic wilderness," she said with a smile. "People want their pound of flesh. And there's no one better than you my Dearest One, when it comes to the courthouse butcher shop."

With their Packard at a near standstill, Regina reached over and began stroking the inside of Jason's right thigh, from crotch to knee. The growing bulge between his legs was proof once again that she had the magic touch.

Damn it, there she goes again, has it down pat, her bewildered husband thought. *First the painful barb and then her special brand of morphine to make it all good again. And she has it right, I can't get the Krauts out of my mind. No sense getting back at her, I'll just sit behind the wheel and enjoy.* He didn't bother to reply, his cerebral cortex having switched gears.

Back in 1942, he fashioned an agreement between the Treasury Department and M.L. Kraus that stalled the federal government's seizure of several of the company's pro-Nazi subsidiaries in the U.S. Tumulty had no trouble rationalizing his contempt for the plaintiffs he had represented. In fact, he was waiting with certainty for a call from Newark's federal court. The companies had agreed to convert their chemical and dye products to support America's war effort. He marveled at how easy it had been. One eye-opener was how strongly John D. Rockefeller and his Standard Oil interceded. At one point, Rockefeller might well have been Tumulty's second chair at the hearings, and a lengthy *amicus curiae* filed by DuPont attorneys warned that stripping Kraus of its industrial capabilities would only hurt America's war effort. Now that the war was over, someone had to decide what to do with this post-war loot, and Tumulty's law firm was willing and waiting. If the predictable pattern continued, more filthy lucre was sure to follow.

The Kraus family entourage fled Jersey right after Hitler's insane declaration of war leaving behind a retinue of crypto-Nazis to mind the store, and mend fences with the Treasury Department and posturing lawmakers along the Potomac. This bunch was led by Hugo Manfred Franke, a tall blonde, blue-eyed Prussian lawyer, with the rare ability to combine vapidity and arrogance without a hint of apology. Tumulty sized him up as a dangerous ass-kisser, happily mired in a corporate command structure that welcomed his fawning compliance to every order.

Representing the law firm of Dilberry, Tumulty & Benson, Tumulty ran into Franke for the first time in 1942. His job was to see that the government squeezed everything it could out of M.L. Kraus without completely dismembering it. The legal fees were enormous. The fact that the firm's founder, Everett Malcolm Dilberry, was married to a DuPont made it a cinch. A single phone call to DuPont headquarters in Wilmington, Delaware was all that it took to fatten the firm's bank account.

A week ago, Franke became more than just an unpleasant memory. In less than a minute, Tumulty knew something was brewing, but didn't know what. After a formal opener during which Franke oozed with phony collegiality, the Prussian said, "Well, Mr. Jason Cullan Tumulty, III, we'll soon be back in the arena, with luck as early as next week. It won't be long before you are Jason and I am Hugo. An easy agreement among friends, am I not right?"

Franke's voice dripped with confidence and a cynical Philadelphia lawyer was wondering why. "I think we can work up to it Mr. Hugo Manfred Franke," Tumulty said barely containing his contempt and added, "perhaps after you perform the impossible by explaining Wagner."

"A jokester, always the jokester," Franke said, exuding self-satisfaction. "I admire a man who can move so easily from the frivolous to the serious."

"Frivolous... Wagner is frivolous? Herr Franke, a slip of the tongue no doubt," Tumulty said, the tone of his voice mockingly stern.

Tumulty's remark was met with silence from the other end. He knew from his experience four years earlier that Franke could sniff out even the smallest negative nuances during courtroom verbal sparring. Did Franke's silence now indicate he was on the defensive? Doubtless he was aware of Hitler's words carved forever in stone, "Whoever wants to understand National Socialist Germany must know Wagner." Hardly frivolous.

"A bond, you see we have already formed a bond," was Franke's adroit recovery. "So with that, I offer you my home for the duration of the hearings, it could start any day now, so be ready. A suite has been prepared and is waiting for you."

"That's too much of an imposition," Tumulty said. "Who knows how long it will be. No, I think not. A generous offer, but it is too much. There are some good hotels in Newark, more than ample for me and my legal team. I'm sorry, but I must say no."

"I will not take no for an answer. Our home is large, and offers you much that you will never find in even the best hotels," Franke boasted. "It is in Forest Hills, the very best that Newark offers, very European. Remember, Jason, we are not so much adversaries, but colleagues chosen to piece together what has been broken."

"There's a bundle of money involved here, a big bundle," Tumulty said. "Collegiality disappears damn fast when all that green stuff is piled up and counted."

"Doubtless things will heat up, but we both know that our good friends at DuPont and Standard can easily cool things down," Franke said.

Tumulty knew that Franke was right. Ever since the 1942 agreement, he had danced around a mountain of unpleasant truths that the largest American companies had been reaping enormous profits as a result of their sweetheart deals with Nazi Germany, and to a lesser degree with Japan and fascist Italy. Nazi fighter planes and bombers could not have wreaked havoc throughout Europe without the tetraethyl lead fortified gasoline supplied by Standard Oil, DuPont and General Motors. Kraus' effort to develop a super chemical weapon were aborted when the war came to an end. Meanwhile, one of America's largest banks was illegally laundering millions of German marks into U.S. dollars. Tumulty realized that Franke's boast was a wake-up call. Nonetheless, without knowing exactly why, he decided to accept the son of a bitch's invitation. Why not view the enemy from within, perhaps over a glass of Riesling, one of his favorites that goes well with the pheasant he knew the Frankes would be serving at least once during his stay.

"Okay, Hugo, you've got yourself a guest," Tumulty said. "Only me, my team will be bedding down at the Robert

Treat. My firm knew this was coming so we booked an entire floor at the hotel."

"Dilberry, Tumulty & Benson, always one jump ahead," Franke's chuckle was condescending but not totally devoid of apprehension.

That telephone call with Franke was still with Tumulty as he tooled his car into the traffic flow on Wilson, then into the parking lot reserved for Bordentown Military Academy's followers brave enough to drive their expensive chariots through Down Neck Newark, one of the roughest neighborhoods in the city. He opened the driver's door and handed the car keys to a parking lot attendant barely old enough to drive. This was the kid's second Little Army-Navy Game and he hoped it would be like last year, a parking lot filled with winners and big tips. He circled to the passenger's side, and with a courtly nod opened the door for the expensively dressed woman who smiled at the gesture. One block to the east, the Admiral Farragut Naval Academy parking lot was a mirror image.

The two lots were destinations for caravans that displayed unabashed opulence, an annual spectacle that had locals gawking with envy and hate. Cadillacs, Packards, La Salles, Bentleys, Lincolns, flashy Town and Country Chryslers and Rolls Royces arrived from every Eastern seaboard state and then some. One bumptious swell from Farragut nailed the divide between young and old Newark with his vintage chauffeur-driven Hispano-Suiza.

"Can't drive. Never could. And probably won't never," a craggy, bent Negro wondered aloud to his teenaged grandson as the Suiza motored past. "Won't need to if that be my car. What with my own black boy behind the wheel, I'd just sit back and enjoy. Course he can't dress better than me. There be no talking back, he takes my overalls and I get his fancy driving duds."

The old man's wistful dream was not shared by his grandson. "Don't be crazy. Where'd you take it? West Kinney? Spruce? Quitman? Ten minutes, maybe ten minutes the most and that car'd be cut up into pieces, the Nigger driver whipped and you'd be treated like a crazy man." The two were past understanding each other, the older still dreaming that life could be a Thanksgiving feast with all the trimmings, and the younger disbelieved there had ever been a fat bird in the first place.

It was a great football day played in the best minor league baseball stadium in the country. Rupert Stadium was owned by the New York Yankees, built for their top minor league team, the Newark Bears. The two elite military schools demanded the best, a neutral site where the ladies could preen and the men crow as they watched their pampered kids perform.

With a hand holding her right arm, Jason guided Regina Anne through the crowd to the stadium turn-styles. They spoke to no one. What was there to say? And to whom? They had just made an eighty-mile trip to see their cheating son perform for strangers. The cadets and marching bands from the two schools had already formed on cordoned-off Wilson Avenue and they weren't at all happy about it.

Jesus Christ, it's hot. I'm baking out here. Bordentown drum major Jeremy Britton's thoughts were vile and uncompromising. *No, no, they wouldn't listen when we said our summer parade dress was the ticket. That we had to twinkle and sparkle in these heavy fucking black and gold sacks just like West Point. Had to keep Mom and Pop happy.*

Britton glanced about and could see that other band members were melting just like him. Doubtless, Farragut's guys were creating sweat puddles in their heavy dark blue and silver Annapolis replicas a couple blocks away. There was not a black face among the two schools' wilting cadets, as they prepared for a colorful spectacle without color.

The Tumultys politely nudged their way through the reserved section of the stadium and were heading to their box seats when they ran into a protective phalanx of well-dressed men around a man with a locked-in-smile and an extended hand ready to pump any paw willing to grab it. There was no way the Tumultys could avoid him.

"Glad to see you. Should be a good game," he said as he pumped Jason Cullan Tumulty III's reluctant hand. "Mayor Vincent Murphy and like everyone here, proud to be hosting what should be a great game. Two evenly matched teams." He then turned to Regina Anne and the impossible happened, a smile that seemed set in stone widened even further without cracking. "I'm not going to ask you which institution. We're just proud to have them here. Is your son a player?"

"Yes, yes he is for Bordentown," she replied frostily, then turned to her husband for help.

"You won't miss him Mayor, he's number eight," Jason Cullan Tumulty, III said as he and his wife turned and headed to their seats. "He's a goddamned plumber's union boss, you know. A plumber in mayor's clothing. That's Newark for you."

A long drum roll followed by a trumpet fanfare ushered them into their box seats. "Yeah! Yeah!" Jason discarded his disdain for the place, and exalted in the moment. "Here they come. Damn it, but this is great. Yeah, yeah, Bordentown! Yeah, yeah, Bordentown!" Regina Anne tightened her hold on his right biceps with her left hand and entwined the fingers of her right hand with his. This was a side of her husband so seldom seen during the past few years. Was it the last Little Army-Navy Game? Could be.

All eyes turned to centerfield as the Bordentown marching band strode onto the stadium's outfield grass followed by the Academy's entire cadet corps. Admiral Farragut followed in short order.

Everybody in place, the respective drum majors silenced the crowd by pumping their batons into the air three times, puffing their cheeks and giving it their all with three shrill attention getters from their military-issue whistles. Then the mutually-agreed pre-game program began with *The Stars and Stripes Forever* followed by *El Capitan*. John Philip Sousa at his best.

Everything would have been perfect if not for the thin layer of smoke that blew in daily from the City dump three blocks away. At its worst, the smoke was a mildly noxious annoyance that reddened the eyes and coarsened the throat. Real fans learned to live with it. Today the windblown mist darkened, not for long, maybe forty-five seconds at the most, and with this darkened color there was a faint metallic smell of copper.

The smoke returned to its normal cirrus grey just as the two bands finished the National Anthem, and the crowd cheered the two cadet corps into their grandstand seats. Cheerleaders formed aisles leading from the two baseball dugouts, and exhorted the two teams out of the locker rooms and onto the field. Jason Cullan Tumulty III and Regina Anne Hodges Tumulty joined the more than 12,000 class-conscious voices in a welcoming roar. After all, this was the Little Army-Navy Game. Billy did them proud by scoring on a tackle-breaking thirty-five yard run.

CHAPTER SIX

Mike and Frank were a good twelve blocks from the stadium, out of earshot as their red Hudson Terraplane Coupe headed north on McCarter Highway. The two men had done as ordered. Today's was the worst. They were keeping the commitment made last year at Camp Kilmer. It was out of their control. Mister Rache was pulling all the strings.

Mike was about to drop Frank off at Bridge Street when shared anxiety and fear surfaced, "Jesus Christ, we left them behind!" Frank said. "The place is still closed for the weekend, so if we get right on it, shouldn't be any trouble."

"How the fuck did we miss them? Did everything else just right," Mike said. "Then we leave that bloody pile behind."

"You have the car so you draw the short straw," Frank said. "There's no need for two of us to go. Be seeing you later. I did my part." He slammed his door and headed to his car on Broad.

Mike, alone and pissed off, was uncertain why it was necessary to retrieve the smocks and coveralls, but he would go back and get them anyway. He turned the Hudson around toward Freilinghuysen, and crossed the county line into Elizabeth where he headed east to the small meat distributor owned by Frank's father. Frank learned the meat cutter's trade a stone's throw from the big Cudahy plant on Second Avenue that supplied Frank's dad with the sides of beef. The place was closed and dark when they had arrived shortly after midnight and was deserted now. Mike was not about to take any chances. He parked the Hudson a block away from the distributor, circled the building on foot and entered through the back door. The bloody garments were exactly where they left them, next to the door on the right.

Christ almighty, were we that fucked up and nervous that we couldn't see straight? Everything had been perfectly planned by Mister Rache. The body, protective clothing, large ball of hemp rope, scissors, utility knife, big supply of rubber gloves and two white sheets were on the floor wrapped in a canvas drop cloth when they arrived. The body was still slightly warm, strongly indicating that the big bloody hole in the back of the man's head was very recent. Despite having to contend with squirting blood and nausea, it was only a matter of minutes before Frank put the big saw through its paces taking off the head and right arm. It took a little longer to wrap and tie the bloody remains.

Mike gave everything a quick once over. He cursed their stupidity as he fingered what remained of the ball of heavy hemp rope that had also been left behind. He threw the garments into the least bloody smock, and tightly wrapped everything into a bundle that was secured with the remaining rope. He tucked the bundle under his left arm, and walked out to his Terraplane on Second Avenue.

He returned to downtown Newark, idled to a stop at the end of River Street and walked to the rock and rubble anchoring the garbage-strewn bank of the Passaic. The river grateful for every filthy morsel tossed its way, this time disappointed the ubiquitous bottom-feeders prowling its depths.

Careful no one was watching, he tossed the bundle over to be washed downstream to Newark Bay. He failed to notice that the bloody bundle had been trapped between two rip rap boulders where its discovery would provide the detectives with their first hard evidence.

All the way back from Elizabeth, Mike could think of little else than tomorrow night's meeting in Washington Park with Mister Rache. That had been their meeting place from the very start. *Who the hell knew it would reach this point? Mister Rache scares me shitless. He's so damn big and he's got those eyes. Jesus, they bore right through you. How the hell could you guess there was so much hate in him, and that he could so easily develop it in us. He sized us up at Dachau, then sucked us in completely at Kilmer.*

Tomorrow night it'd be the same, all three of them coming into the park from different directions, and ending up on benches at the bottom of the small hill where a big bronze George Washington and his horse kept vigil. Mister Rache as always would arrive fifteen minutes after he and Frank took their seats. They had little doubt he would be eyeballing them from a nearby vantage point.

Back at the dump, Tom Candless realized that his comfortable gig at the city dump, perhaps even his life, was about to change. It was hard for him to admit to himself that fear activated his combat connected limp, and that he had no intention to catch the two guys. His fear was well-placed. He should have known better, when he limped within thirty feet of the incinerator and spotted the crisscrossing trails of blood droplets on the ground. Their shape was irregular and already turning brown as they soaked into the dust, reminding Candless of Milk Duds, his favorite movie munchie along with Good & Plenty. *I'll be a son of a bitch*, Candless thought. *What the hell's all this?*

Candless arose from his stoop and for the first time scanned the entire area. The incinerator was still going full blast. The blood trails ended about five feet from the inferno's mouth, and the footprints in the dust were deeper.

Those guys were no fools, Candless surmised, *Dug in right here to get a toe hold with no danger of getting burned.* Then he spotted it. A blood-stained, oblong heap squashed against the front of the incinerator. It was a good eight feet from the flames. Candless figured that this was exactly where the two guys wanted it to be. Curiosity got the better of him, and he decided to overcome his revulsion to inspect whatever it was. *What the hell. Might as well handle it here. Not something for the police and probably my job anyway. A dog or a cat maybe.*

Candless was surprised to see that the bloody mess was wrapped in a white sheet held in place by heavy-duty hemp rope. He used his pocket knife to cut the rope and a stick to push back the sheet to expose the contents. First, there was a hand with imploring fingers extended to ward off the inevitable. A solid gold signet ring with a black stone in the middle was on the third finger. He could see that the ring was expensive. It had something engraved, not English, but some foreign crap or other. *Man oh man, no robbery here. Just wanted to do some slicing.* Blood-lacquered blonde hair encrusted the muscular right forearm and equally muscled biceps. A short-sleeved tan line ended just above the elbow. The muscles under the white skin above the tan line had already begun to constrict. Then he saw a two-inch black swastika. Beneath it was a two-line deck, "Camp Siegfried," and "Nuremberg 1938" centered under it. The arm had been separated from the right shoulder by someone who knew what he was doing. Candless backed off, lost his balance and plopped on his ass. *Man oh man, man oh man!*

Candless wobbled to his feet, brushed the dust from his rear end and eyed the entire scene. *This could be trouble. I had to stick my damn nose in and poke around*, self-indulgent blame grabbed hold and wouldn't let go. *Those ofay, dego cops are gonna wanna know who the hell I thought I was trying to be a big man doing police business. Better leave everything like it is. Could wrap it all up again, but no, better leave it.* Candless was about to limp toward the junkyard office and the phone, but not before a final compulsive eyeballing of the imploring butchered arm. A swarm of shining blue-green blow flies was closing in, and rats were probably on their way.

CHAPTER

SEVEN

Cisco sloshed down a third stale sugar-coated A&P dunker with his second cup of coffee, wiped his mouth, pushed away from the kitchen table and headed to the front door. He had already shoulder holstered his Colt .38 snubnose. This would be a bitch of a day. First he had made his call to Herman Gerhardt Peterson, and the early Sunday call pissed the Prosecutor off. Cisco quickly laid out what he knew about the unfolding mess, and Peterson's reaction was predictable.

"Everyone's on board, right," Peterson said. "A lot's at stake. Careers are on the line here. I'll see you and McClosky in my office at noon." The conversation ended with a hard hang-up.

Cisco knew where Peterson, a Republican, was coming from. He was a scion of one of Newark's oldest German Brahmin families, and nothing less than the governor's mansion in Trenton would make him happy. The first step would come in November when the Attorney General's job would be up for grabs, but only if Alfred Driscoll took over the governor's mansion as expected.

The word was out that populist reformer Driscoll had little use for Attorney General Walter Van Riper despite his success in closing down Jersey City's illegal horse parlors. When that word leaked out, the dance of the ass-kissers began, a minuet for which Peterson was ill-suited. He joined the pack of county prosecutors lusting for Van Riper's job anyway.

Family privacy, so cherished by the rich German-American elite, was sacrificed at the altar of ambition. It didn't help that Agnes Carla Heilmann Peterson considered the self-righteous Driscoll a condescending bore.

"Okay, I get it. I'm going to hate it, but I get it," she said when her husband explained how the family would join the battle. Two trips for dinner at Driscoll's Haddenfield home, and three to his Trenton office convinced him that brown-nosing was an art form he and his wife hadn't mastered. The Nazi Bund killings, if orchestrated for maximum pre-election headlines, would create the attention grabber needed to separate him from the other Driscoll supplicants.

After six years with the family practice in downtown Newark, mostly civil litigation, Peterson parlayed strong ties to Newark's powerful German-American community to land an Assistant Prosecutor's job at the Essex County Courthouse. Four years later at the age of thirty-four, he became the County's youngest prosecutor ever. And why wouldn't he? He was blonde, blue-eyed, pink skinned, stocky and strong at just under six feet, married to beautiful, blonde, blue-eyed, pink skinned Agnes Carla Heilmann, the high-profile brewery princess. A twelve year old son, Johan, and ten year old daughter, Sandra, were stashed away in private boarding schools.

"And that's where they're going to stay. There's no way, and I mean no way, you're going to use them!" Agnes warned when her husband suggested that the children be pulled from their classrooms for the two Haddenfield dinner trips.

From what he knew about the D.A., it would be hard for Cisco to imagine that a control freak like Peterson would be having trouble at home. He reconstructed this morning's brief talk with the condescending son of a bitch while driving to the morgue, and questioned for the hundredth time if the two silver captain's bars were worth it.

It took Cisco twenty minutes to drive his unmarked police car to the back entrance of the City Hospital Morgue on Fairmount where he parked it three spaces from McClosky's unmarked cruiser. Over the years he had grown to hate the place, its cold, impersonal stink and clammy dampness that encased you like a glove. He dreaded each forced visit. No matter how many times he had been there, it took days for him to blot out the memory of yet another cadaver being ripped apart. He walked through a basement door into a white-tiled anteroom that served as a parking lot for the morgue's gurneys. McClosky and a big Negro were seated on folding chairs near the entrance to the macabre icebox, with its steel-faced compartments stretching from floor to ceiling along two walls.

"Talked to the prosecutor, and he was at his sarcastic best," Cisco said. "He'll be waiting at his office."

"Been here about fifteen minutes," McClosky said as he and the other man arose. Cisco extended his hand to McClosky, then turned to Candless, but the Negro stood without gesture in front of his chair.

"Already talked to Tomokai. Sick son of a bitch. He thinks the whole thing's amusing. First time he's had only an arm to work on," McClosky said. "It's in number twenty-seven. He'll buzz us in when we're ready. This is Tom Candless. He knows that nothing gets out about this. He lives alone, no wife, kids or family so that closes one door we won't worry about."

"And I don't much care you talking about me as if I'm not right here listening," Candless pouted. He had his hands in the front pockets of his old army fatigues. Cisco couldn't help notice that the fabric rippled as Candless clinched and unclinched his fists inside his pockets. "Forced to be here. Nobody to talk to, just told to button-up. How long's this gonna go on?"

"Just a formality. We'll take you inside and you'll tell us if what you see here is what you found at the incinerator," Cisco said. "If anything comes to mind you haven't told the police already, now's the time. Then we'll see that you get home okay."

"More than just my time, it's my pocketbook too," Candless said accusably, his face the hard mask of a man who had always been forced to prove his worth. "This is a work day for me. Nobody's yet told me I'll be getting money for my time. What's the answer?"

"We'll talk to what's his name, your boss, Stigman, I think, isn't it?" McClosky said. "We don't see a problem here."

The three men walked to the large double door leading to the interior of the morgue. McClosky pushed a small steel button to the right and as though he had been waiting expectantly, Coroner Walter Tomokai greeted them with "Everything's ready. It shouldn't take long, only had to work with about a tenth of the product I'm used to."

Without a word the four men walked in tandem to a sheet draped gurney, Tomokai leading the way, with Cisco, a reluctant Candless and McClosky bringing up the rear. The sheet was pulled back exposing an arm with imploring curled fingers. A black jade signet ring had not been removed by Tomokai. A John Doe tag was tied to the thumb.

"Is this it, the arm you unwrapped yesterday at the dump?" Cisco asked. "Make sure now, before you say anything. We have what you said to Sergeant Gingold last night."

"Yeah, that's it, far as I can see. Been chewed up a bit, but it's the same, okay," Candless said. "And if you ask me now, I'll tell you it's the worst damn thing I ever did, cutting that bundle open. Wouldn't be here now, wouldn't be all this trouble. I don't even know if I got my pay coming, only got your word that you'd try."

"Look, look real close!" demanded McClosky, now past his breaking point after having endured the big Negro's petulant behavior all morning. "Take a close look at the tattoo and that ring. That's important. Do you recognize everything as the same as you saw yesterday?"

Candless peered down at the arm from his vantage point at least two feet from the side of the gurney. "Yeah, yeah it's the same. How the hell would you expect me to forget something like that."

There were some perfunctory questions, but it was obvious to Cisco and McClosky that they had gotten all that there was to get from Candless. "Wait for us outside. There's a bench against the wall by the telephone," Cisco said.

Tomokai hummed softly to himself as he pulled the sheet back over the arm and pushed it back into its compartment, he enjoyed his work.

"Always something to learn around here," he said, "first time I've ever had to fill out paperwork just for an arm. I'm curious, why is there a lid on this? Another swastika. Makes three of them. And we have three rings exactly the same. At least on this one, the arm's attached.

"The hands, had to split the jaws to pry them out of the mouths. Neat chop job by someone obviously at home with a meat cleaver. Handled mutilations before, but nothing like this. And with the ring, almost poetic. German wasn't my strong suit in med school, but I know a Nazi slogan when I see it. What does Peterson have up his sleeve?" Tomokai said, smiling sheepishly. "Forgive the pun, I couldn't help myself. This has spotlight all over it and you know how our prosecutor loves the spotlight.

"But now it's getting awkward. How long am I expected to keep the two stiffs and now an arm on ice? Until today I didn't think it could get any more bizarre, two bodies, hacked off hands, and you know the rest," Tomokai paused as he studied the two detectives, then shrugged. He didn't expect an answer. He realized that this could blow up in their faces. "Now I've got to quarantine three John Doe slabs until the prosecutor takes the lid off."

"He's got his reasons and the Chief is going along with him, at least for now," Cisco said. "We're just minions working in the field of American jurisprudence. We don't rotate the crops, we just pull the weeds."

"Nice, nice. I've missed you since you've moved up the promotion ladder," Tomokai admired. "You know, I can't ever remember any of your homicide buddies refer to themselves as minions, and then throw in jurisprudence. Very nice.

"You guys know the way out, come back and see me anytime," Tomokai said, flicking his left thumb at the three John Doe compartments behind him. "And the sooner the better."

"Weird son of a bitch," McClosky said as he reached for the door to the gurney crammed anteroom.

"Hell, he's a pathologist, what can you expect," Cisco said. "He doesn't have to shop around for customers. This is a great place for him."

Cisco and McClosky found Candless sitting amid the gurneys near the telephone, his expression sullen and accusing. "What the hell do I do now?" he demanded. "No way I can see you taking me back to the dump and I got no car."

"Why don't you go outside and get some fresh air. Find another seat for yourself and relax. We'll get you back to where you want to go. Just relax now, okay, and keep your mouth shut," McClosky said. He peered directly into the Negro's face and saw that peevishness could easily become defiance. There was no question that he had to scare this guy. "Not a word. Get it! You made a big mistake cutting open that bundle. We still haven't decided whether to charge you with tampering with evidence. You've got a good solid job and you'll want to keep it. Right?"

Candless got it alright. In an attempt to make his exit as casual as possible, he thrust his hands into his pants pockets as he turned and sauntered toward the door. It didn't work. As before, the detective could see that the big guy's hands were opening and closing into clenched fists of frustration.

With Candless out of the way, Cisco pushed through the gurneys to the telephone and called for a Fourth Precinct patrol to swing by and get rid of the troublesome Negro.

"What did you come up with on Camp Siegfried? We're going to need what you got when we meet with Peterson," Cisco said. "If there's any holes, you got a few hours to fill them before we get to his office."

"I think I have enough for the meeting, the more you look into it the more you come up with. The camp was near Yaphank, Long Island and was in operation from '36 to '41, so the '38 swastika tattoo fits. They drank a lot of beer, sang a lot of songs, and dished out Nazi-hate with a smile. Even paid for privileged Bund members to go to Germany. The boss was named Ernst Mueller. The Feds shut it down when Hitler declared war right after Pearl Harbor."

"Seems like we got enough to keep Peterson happy, at least for now," Cisco said. "Why don't you take off and I'll meet you downtown."

CHAPTER
EIGHT

Over the years the two detectives had developed more than a partnership. Their close working relationship began while still in uniform, then as partners working the robbery detail, and now with homicide. As cops they had been classified as draft-deferred essentials during the war. The two men were ambitious, but never to the point where mutual trust was violated. Off duty they socialized infrequently. McClosky was five years younger than Cisco and unmarried, played the horses, and worked his way to ringside seats at Laurel Gardens where he wagered heavily on the fights. He won much more than he lost. He had little doubt that his sergeant status motivated the tips whispered in his ear by shady insiders hoping some day for payback when they got caught crossing the line. The detective was on a first name basis with most of the local fighters and their mob-connected managers. He convinced himself that none of the sleaze would ever rub-off on him. He hit the slippery slope the night of October 26, 1942.

"Feels good, real good, don't it," Pussy Lieber croaked as he pushed three folded twenty dollar bills into the front pocket of McClosky's jacket with a deft touch that was hardly felt. The diminutive Lieber was turning from second-story cat burglary to bookmaking and was greasing his way with well-placed vigorish. McClosky had parlayed a muttered tip from Lieber into a 30-to-1 payoff on a two-dollar bet that Tippy Larkin would take out Abe Denner in the second round. The detective acknowledged nothing as though the payoff had never occurred. Lieber disappeared as silently as he had arrived, losing himself among the Laurel Garden crowd who couldn't get enough of the swarthy Larkin.

There was no reason for McClosky to rationalize any of this. He was betting real money from his meager police salary and taking his chances. So what if luck had become less and less a factor. Lieber and his cronies were crazy if they thought that someday there would be paybacks, he would squash them first.

He knew that Cisco was aware of his betting and the shadowy tips that put cash in his pocket, but his partner never said a word. Instead of confronting him, the older detective bullied him into night criminology courses at Rutgers that he had been taking for the past three years. Neither Victor McClosky, nor Rose McDougal McClosky had finished high school, and when their only kid pinned a badge on his police uniform, they were overjoyed that he had gotten a steady job. The McCloskys kept body and soul together during the Depression by working dawn-to-dusk to keep their small grocery store on upper Springfield alive. This would not be Kevin's life, and their pride exploded when he got his sergeant stripes.

Cisco and McClosky had developed that peculiar type of professional closeness that precluded intimacy, but inspired genuine fondness. McClosky wanted Connie and Nick back together again so he would no longer have to put up with his partner's increasingly shorter fuse and shitty remarks. The two swastika murders and now a third one hadn't made things easier.

Their visit to the morgue to view the severed arm added to their professional anxiety. They saw that the super-ambitious Tomokai was aware that correct procedures were being broken, and that it was only a matter of time before he would be shooting off his mouth.

Arising from Tomokai's morbid basement icebox, Cisco had taken only a few steps when he spotted a husky guy get out of a Dodge parked next to his unmarked police car. The man appeared to be no more than in his late twenties and was wearing a Fordham sweatshirt, baggy denim pants and brown scuffed loafers. He looked familiar, but Cisco couldn't quite place him. They were almost face-to-face and had been eyeing each other while enmeshed in the classical "who the hell is this guy? I know him but from where?" brain teaser. Then came the dawning.

"Lieutenant Cisco, good to see you again," the young man extended his hand with a smile. "Terry Nolan from Saint Mark's, about a year ago, you visited the rectory."

"Oh yes, I didn't place you at first," Cisco said. "I knew I was asking a lot, Father, but that Bancik kid and his family were more in need of a priest than a cop. It couldn't have been easy."

"I'll never forget Joey Bancik's mom and dad, the unbelieving horror on their faces when the sheet was pulled back and they saw their boy on that cold slab."

"The morgue is one hell of a place to renew acquaintances," Cisco said. "What's up?"

"They've asked me to come down, and possibly identify a body they swept up from the sidewalk near Saint Mark's," Nolan said. "An indigent who had apparently settled into the neighborhood over the past few months."

"Good luck on that one," Cisco said. "Have to get going. I have a busy day."

"Can you spare me just a minute or two? I know how you feel about kids who have been kicked around. There's no homicide here, but I'm afraid it could lead to one."

Cisco had pulled out his keys and was about to slide into his car, but the priest's words pulled him up short. "Okay, give it to me, Father, I have a few minutes."

"It's so damn complicated, so many strings attached. I think they might be tied right into the Archdiocese's inner circle, and I believe there's money talking. Quite frankly, I need help and I don't know where to turn."

"I'm really busy, will be for at least two or three weeks. Maybe after that if it can wait?"

"Guess it will have to. Hey, here's a thought. This coming Friday the *Clarion* is hosting a meeting to find ways to stuff Mayor Murphy's 'rampant street crime' genie back in its bottle. I'll be there as liaison for the Archdiocese. I know there'll be at least one street-smart cop sitting in. Any chance it could be you?"

"I don't know, it could be. I'll see how things are going in the next few days, see if I can clear two or three hours on Friday. If things fall into place, there's a chance. Take care of yourself, Father," Cisco said as the priest turned and headed toward the stairs to the morgue.

Do I really need something more on my plate, Cisco thought. *This is what I've got, three unsolved mob hits, newspapers who want my ass, a hacked-off arm, and a Hitler Bund camp nobody's heard of. Now Father Nolan says he needs my help because there's a homicide that might or might not happen.*

As if this wasn't enough, he faced another battle at Saint Anthony's with Connie on Wednesday. And that's what they were pure and simple, battles. With him and Connie, Father Sullivan was failing miserably as a mediator. He and Connie could hardly look each other in the eye so the first tentative steps toward reconciliation seemed absurd. Cisco doubted it would be any different this week. *Who knows, by Friday, a few hours with political hacks might be a welcome change.*

CHAPTER
NINE

The courthouse was almost deserted. The Sunday janitors were buffing the lobby's marble floor when Cisco and McClosky entered through the massive front door. Here he was strapped tightly into the straight jacket that this murder investigation had become, and all he could think about as he walked across the lobby was the first time he met Grace De Marco just down the hall in the Court Clerk's office.

Damn, he thought, *damn, damn, damn*. She had him by the balls ever since that first day three years ago. She knew it right from the start. Just some paperwork for a shitty little burglary case that he couldn't even remember. How did it start? Was it her dark eyes, the way she flipped her not quite auburn hair with just a slight turn of the neck, or her smiling lips that right away told him without forming a word that here they are buddy, but if you want them you have to earn them. And no nail polish, but her nails were shiny. The hands, maybe that's what got him. God, how those hands grabbed him! How he wanted them to dig into his back. He wanted to pull them away from those two crappy City forms. And God help him, how he wanted to put those fingers in his mouth and suck them right in front of everybody. God, first the fingers, and then the toes. Right from the first time she put her ankles on his shoulders. But never once with his wife Connie. Not even the thought of it.

"You got Gingold's report. I don't know how much it will add, but it's what we have up to this point," Cisco said as they headed up the stairs to Peterson's office. In response, McClosky silently flicked the file folder in his right hand. They reached the second floor landing and the Prosecutor's grilling would begin in a few minutes. That was work, what he was paid to do and could be handled. But handling the moral mess that was his life was another matter. His dad was right. He had flaunted it all, and couldn't imagine the hurt his wife was suffering. His guilty thoughts continued to cascade.

Connie enthusiastically followed his lead in bed no matter where he took her, but there was no way he would take her through the doors opened by Grace. Shamed him even to think of it. What was it with Grace? Love? Maybe, but what kind of love was it? Thought of little else. If he were a kid, the crotch ache would be a simple case of blue-balls. But he wasn't a kid anymore, so what the hell is it? One thing for certain is that when it comes to Grace his brains were in his crotch.

Cisco's guilt trip was brushed aside by the time the two detectives had reached the third floor. Knowing they were expected, they entered Peterson's outer office without knocking. Through the door to the inner office they could see the prosecutor sitting in shirt sleeves at his oversized mahogany desk. His back was to them as he sat peering through a large window looking out on Market Street. He swiveled around and motioned them to padded leather chairs in front of his desk.

"Okay let's get to it," Peterson said. "With what you gave me today, I filled in an inexcusable oversight on my part. Let's put it all together."

With his right knee, Cisco gave McClosky a "can you believe that" nudge. The impassive faces of the two detectives belied their sense of wonderment. Herman Gerhardt

Peterson was an imperious man seldom open to admitting oversights. For generations he and his family stumbled through very few of them. Law was their game and acknowledgement their quest. They needed a fiefdom. His father, Werner Hubert Peterson, staked out Furstenburg College in Pennsylvania's picturesque Lehigh Valley. The school's Lutheran roots, liberalism and strong pre-law curriculum were a perfect match. Furstenburg was small, and small schools could always use cash. Peterson family endowments came in bunches big enough to make the family one of the school's most important benefactors. Power accrued and very little happened at Furstenburg without Peterson family approval.

"Okay gentlemen, what do we have?" Peterson said leaning forward with his elbows on his desk. "Before I tell you what's been dropped in my lap, let's go through the background of each camp, the linkage between the three of them."

McClosky handed the file folder containing Gingold's report across the desk to Peterson. The prosecutor studied the three typewritten pages without saying a word. There were at least ten margin notations when he was finished.

"Tell me about Camp Siegfried. Until today I had never heard of it. Where is it?"

McClosky filled in the details, the camp's location near Yaphank, Long Island, its five years in operation, and how it had become an integral part of central Long Island about sixty miles from Manhattan.

"Plenty of oompah music, beer, songs, free German language lessons, master race bullshit, hunting and camping," McClosky said. "It got so popular they even ran a train out of Penn Station called the 'Camp Siegfried Special.'"

"Five years, is that right? When did it close?"

"The Feds moved in after Adolf joined the fun by declaring war a few days after Pearl Harbor," McClosky said.

"Okay, Lieutenant, closer to home, what do we have?"

"It's been seven days since we pulled the first floater out," Cisco said. "The second was fished out two days later, and yesterday there appears to have been a roasted body at the city dump, and a butchered right arm was left for us to admire. The connections jump out right away, the tattooed Nazi swastika, camp name, Nuremberg and date on each right arm, all the same, 1938. And the ring."

"Okay, so let's recap. We've got three Nazi Bund camps, two in Jersey and one way out on Long Island. In Jersey, we've got Camp Bergwald outside Bloomingdale in Passaic County, and the big one, Camp Nordland, out in Sussex County," said Peterson glancing through the piles of notes spread across his desk. "Okay, keep going."

"It's been years since Camp Bergwald was closed, but now some wackos calling themselves some sort of German vocational league say they were never spies," Cisco said. "They even have the balls to demand we give them back their old campgrounds."

"Krauts will be Krauts," Peterson said with a glacial grin. In public he displayed the acquired geniality of a man born to the politician's cloth, but once out of public eye humor was not a strong point. When a smile split his lips, his teeth were like the prow of a breaker crunching through an ice flow. "And if there's anyone who understands a Kraut, it's me. Hell, we're not people, we're a state of mind. Okay, so it's insane. We all get that. Let's tie it together."

"Well we have the obvious linkage," McClosky said, "big-time race insanity shared by bloodthirsty goons. You got it all there in front of you. Camp Nordland took center stage at the nut house. Even got the Klan to climb aboard with their sheets, hoods, and burning crosses. Camp Siegfried was a grab bag, a happy fascist hunting ground where Mussolini supporters joined up with the Bund."

With an officious smile, Peterson pulled two stapled sheets of paper from a pile of notes in front of him. "The U.S. Attorney's office, not Newark but Manhattan, came through for me," he said. "It seems that in 1938 the Nazi Bund financed trips for a select member in each camp to go to Nuremberg. Here's the list of the camps, Nordland and Bergwald are among them. They are listed alphabetically. After learning about Siegfried from you today, I glanced down to the end of the list and what do you know, there it was."

Cisco and McClosky shared a quick glance, and with it the pissed off agreement that this arrogant son of a bitch had been playing a game with them. He could have laid it all out at the very beginning. Peterson failed to notice their agitation even though their attempt to keep their facial features stoic had failed miserably. While they squirmed, the prosecutor reached for another sheet of paper.

"Here are the three names," Peterson said. "From Camp Bergwald, Boris Obermeyer. From Camp Nordland, Heinrich Bolz. From Camp Siegfried, Walter Weber. Every one of their moves was traced by the FBI. They traveled well, first-class on the Normandie from New York to Le Havre, where the French Sûreté kept them under surveillance until they got on the train, again first-class, to Nuremberg."

The two detectives scratched in little spiral notebooks as Peterson detailed this new information. The prosecutor was far from finished.

"These three men were chosen because they were good little American Nazis. As a reward, they got preferred seating at the Rally of Greater Germany in Nuremberg stadium. It celebrated the Austrian Anschluss when Hitler's thugs took over a country without firing a shot."

"I've got a question," Cisco said. "In fact, it's two questions. You said you didn't get your information from the U.S. Attorney here in Newark, but from the big boy in Manhattan. And in what, a day or two, or was it even less than that? Getting even the time of day from the Feds is tough enough, but you got all of this. Let us in on it, what's going on here?"

Peterson played with his pencil, arose slowly from his chair and walked the few feet to the window behind his desk. He leaned forward and put his hands on the windowsill, and peered out at the traffic below. The back of his blue shirt was dark with sweat. He knew he had to calculate his next words perfectly. He would be placing confidence with two men who had never been within his closely guarded circle of trust. He returned to his desk, sat down and faced them.

"What I'm about to tell you goes nowhere else, agreed," Peterson's gaze went from one face to another, pausing until he got an accepting nod. "We've got three murders on our hands. But there's much more to this case than that. As crazy as it might sound to you, this case could have a big bearing on Europe's future. I spent all of yesterday afternoon and most of the evening with the U.S. Attorney in New York, and this is what I've come home with." He then spread three sheets of paper in front of them.

"I'll take it point-by-point. First, there's concern that Germany's falling apart and the State Department fears that where Germany goes, so goes Europe. Germany has to be kept intact and on our side.

"Second, viable and experienced leadership is hard to find. Unfortunately, most of the capable leaders are former Nazis, either on trial or in prison. Some face the gallows. The United States needs them, but they just can't walk out free. Among them are members of the M.L. Kraus corporate hierarchy. The company has huge holdings here in New Jersey and other states. There's many millions involved.

"Third, those valuable Kraus properties have been confiscated by our government for the duration. Hearings will be held in U.S. District Court right here in Newark, they could start any day now. Do the properties go back to Kraus, or does our government sell them off?

"Fourth, the Feds don't want to offend either the Kraus people or Germany by waving the swastika in front of them. They want a fair settlement in District Court. That's where we and our three murders come in.

"Fifth, we're being asked to handle the three murders as discreetly as possible. If the Feds had their way, there'd be no investigation at all. In order to hold Germany together, the Feds feel that they need Kraus on board, along with other former Nazis they deem to be valuable.

"To sum it all up, if the Nazi Bund raises its ugly head again because of this case and anti-German hostility blows up in our faces, it's doubtful that Kraus is going to get a fair decision from the court. Nobody wants those buffoons in Washington to start screaming. If the Germans feel we've screwed them over, the Feds believe that even patchwork cooperation would be hard to get. We're not being asked to kill the case, just have a partial burial, if I can describe it that way."

"Tell me what I'm thinking is wrong-headed," Cisco said, "that we keep going, but only so far. Where might that be Mr. Peterson?"

"Normal police homicide procedure, take it all the way. Let me reduce how I feel to the bare essentials, 'fuck the Feds,' no matter what I might have assured them. Don't forget all three of us have a lot at stake here, so let's talk about crass ambition. If, as expected, Driscoll gets the governorship, the Attorney General job will be up for grabs. I want it. And you, Lieutenant Cisco, want the chief of homicide's job and the two bars that come with it. I'll have the muscle to get it for you. Sergeant McClosky, I see you got the top score in the lieutenant's exam earlier this month, but here in Newark brains don't mean a damn thing. It's ass-kissing that counts, and a lot of City Hall hacks will be asking the new Attorney General for favors."

CHAPTER

TEN

Peterson's game playing disgusted Cisco, but he disguised it well as he watched the self-satisfied prosecutor idly rearrange papers on his desk. Cisco glanced down to his right at McClosky's spiral notebook. In block letters his partner had printed "Fucking asshole," underlining the second word three times.

"I'm sure Sergeant McClosky shares my curiosity," Cisco said. "The U.S. Attorney gave you a shitload of information. How did he know about our case?" He bit his tongue and held back what he really wanted to say. *You bastard, you had us clamp a lid on everything, keep our mouths shut, sucked the police chief and coroner into it while you were working the federal side of the street without telling us.*

"When I saw the photos of what was left of the carcass from Camp Nordland," Peterson said, "I had a hunch the Feds might be interested. Nothing really to go on, just a swastika, the name of a Nazi Bund camp, and a date. So what the hell, why not give Jimmy Rathgate a call. The U.S. Attorney and I go back a long way. Less than two hours later the call came in from U.S. Attorney Justin Browning in Manhattan. Now you're up to date.

"Before we get on with this, let's be certain everything is buttoned up," Peterson said. "I've taken the chief off your back, at least for now. Wasn't easy. I had to assure him that it would be a mutual headline grab when we're ready. I have all the field reports and photos, and everything from Tomokai locked here in my desk drawer. Like your Chief, the coroner has never met a news reporter he didn't love just so long as he controlled the flow. This takes us to the police-beat scribblers."

"Jerry Saunders at the *Beacon* has sniffed around, but that's only with the Belleville Pike floater," Cisco said. "He doesn't know anything about Harrison Avenue. After the swastika connection with the Pike, we did as you asked and put the lid on. We got the downtown body over to Tomokai real fast, and made sure crime scene photos and initial reports stayed with us."

"How did Saunders stumble on this?" Peterson asked.

"He was tipped by a couple uniforms from the Second about the Pike body, nosed around for a report, and when he couldn't find it, wanted to know what was up. Jerry's a savvy guy and he smells something. I gave him the usual, that we're still working on it, and could lead to something bigger. The exclusive would be his when it all breaks."

"And, of course, Tomokai has them all tucked away and tagged as John Does, including the arm?" Peterson asked.

"Yeah, two big toes and a thumb," McClosky said.

"How long will Saunders sit on this," Peterson said, "and are you sure that Joe Luccio from the *Clarion* is out of the loop? He's been on the beat forever, and not much escapes him. How about the *Afro-American*? In the few years it's been here, the paper's put some good men on the street, been saying important things people are listening to. Has its guy been nosing around?"

"Not that we know. The same for Luccio," Cisco said. "But I think we're okay. It helps that in two months three other bodies have turned up. All mob hits, multiple shots to the head, favorite dumping grounds: two in the Meadows, and the third cut-up and stuffed into an oil drum that banged into a tug boat out on the bay. Reporters have been kept busy."

"Kevin, why don't you take it from here." Cisco took a deep breath, and welcomed the relaxed droop of his shoulders into the leather padded chair.

"Let's start with the first floater. We've got a name now, Boris Obermeyer, at least we think it's him. The evidence you just gave us is circumstantial, but strong. He was wired to two cinder blocks under the Belleville Pike Bridge. That was seven days ago. Two days later we find our second body, presumed to be Heinrich Bolz, floating under the Harrison Avenue Bridge. Just like the first floater, he's wired to two cinder blocks. Here's where it gets strange. Whoever dumped them wanted them found."

"Why do you say that?" Peterson said. "Wired to cinder blocks sure doesn't tell me they wanted the bodies floating ashore someplace or bobbing to the surface."

"That's what makes it strange. Whoever dumped them knew a lot about the river's tides. The wires were short enough to keep them always submerged, but long enough so that during low tide they'd be a foot to a foot-and-a-half below the surface, easy enough to be spotted from the bridge or a passing boat. Both were killed by a shot to the back of their heads. Big hole, big caliber gun, with the bullet in each case exiting through an eye socket. We think they were kneeling and bent over, that executions had been carried out."

"The chopped-off hands, how do the hands figure in all of this?" Peterson said. "A single shot to the head, quick and efficient. Then the work with the hands. That had to take time. You have any thoughts, Cisco?"

"The work with the hands was very exact, probably with a butcher's cleaver. I'd say whoever did it knew his job.

Jamming the bloody mess into the victims' mouths required a strong stomach. The wrists were shoved as far as they could go, leaving the fingers and that fancy ring dangling from the mouth."

Peterson leaned back in his chair, a beautifully crafted cherry wood and leather heirloom, and after a few deep breaths said, "Okay, we have the names, at least we think we do, of three Bund true believers. The FBI has them tracked all the way to Nuremberg and back again. I'll put in a call to New York, and ask Justin Browning to dig out three addresses from their dossiers. It's obvious the killers knew who they were after. Let's see if they left any footprints."

"The quicker we find out the better," McClosky said. "Tomokai already has the jitters, and how much longer can we expect the chief to sit on this?"

"You'll get everything Justin gives me by tomorrow," Peterson said. "Cut yourself loose from all other cases, and Cisco, as acting homicide chief, make sure everyone is kept busy. No idle minds, no idle hands, and no wagging tongues."

"I'll handle it," Cisco said, as he leafed through his notes. "It's obvious the killers wanted the floaters to be found, and so far no word, nothing out on the street at all. After all they've done to make the headlines, they've got to be pissed. With this arm, they feel it's going to happen. That we can't sit on it any longer."

Peterson drummed the polished, perfectly trimmed fingers of his right hand on the desk, barely able to hide his pique. His criminal brief was empty and he knew it. "We know there are at least two suspects. That they drove to the city dump in a red car. That the Nazi Bund is the connection. Agreed?"

"This has the stink of revenge," Cisco said. "The Bund's been gone for six years, so it's hatred, festering hatred."

“That’s a hell of a note, so we’ve got faceless hatred as a motive,” McClosky said. “There’s always been enough to go around in this town.”

“So let’s start with the obvious, the Minutemen,” Cisco said as he met Peterson’s inquiring gaze, and saw that all three men shared the same thought.

“Yeah, but right now what else do we have?” Peterson said. The three men displayed their impotence by silently fidgeting with their notebooks, pencils, and desk-tapping. It seemed only yesterday that the two cops and Peterson shared the futility of pursuing a quarry that, as war loomed, nobody wanted caught.

The roving gangs of Minutemen with their fists, sawed-off baseball bats, lead pipes and stink bombs were viewed as heroes by Newark’s Jewish storefront merchants and businessmen. The Bund had organized a boycott of their enterprises. It was hurting and had to be stopped. Young Jewish professional and amateur boxers from the Third Ward provided most of the muscle. The two detectives, still in uniform during the thirties, were assigned to the same squads placed on alert to keep Minutemen mayhem to a minimum. Peterson’s boss assigned him the thankless job of prosecuting patriots nobody wanted caught.

It was no secret that mobster Longy Zwillman provided most of the cash to keep the Minutemen going. Zwillman handpicked one of his Jewish pugs, cigar-smoking Nat Arno to handle the details. The attacks were simple and effective. By the time the cops arrived it was too late, Arno having been tipped off in advance by his police buddies.

In the autumn of 1946, the Bund was no more than a memory. The same could be said for the Minutemen. Or could it?

“They disbanded right after we entered the war. That’s about the time the Bund was outlawed. Most of the

Minutemen enlisted, and Arno joined up only days after Pearl Harbor," Cisco said.

"What do we know about the Minutemen now?" Peterson said. "The war's been over for more than a year. Certainly most should be home now. Have we been keeping track?"

"Not really, only a few of them have laced their gloves back on. There's never been any reason to nose around," McClosky said.

"We've got to get started with what we have now," Peterson said. He turned to McClosky, and with a tight smile and no apology said, "Am I to understand they're your kind of people?"

McClosky could hardly ignore Peterson's condescending tone. He carefully shaped each word and swallowed. "I always get a nod from the pinky-ringed at ringside, and haven't heard one word about Minutemen, but I can do some sniffing."

"Can we do it discreetly?" Peterson said. "Granted, it isn't much. McClosky, the job is yours, but only after we track down where the victims came from, then maybe we can connect the dots. Lieutenant Cisco, any thoughts?"

"Most of them are still around. Quite a few have jobs with Zwillman's legitimate fronts. The pugs he's hired go back to their days riding shotgun on Longy's beer and booze trucks. Zwillman might be a thug, but he's loyal. But no talk of the Minutemen. Seems that everyone's moved on."

CHAPTER ELEVEN

The two detectives were back on the sidewalk, and could sense Peterson's eyes peering down at them from his third floor office. "Wonder if he still's sweating," McClosky said.

"Don't like him much, do you," Cisco said. "I'm with you, but let's roll with it. We all want to get something out of this. Have any ideas on how you can pry something loose, if there is anything?"

"Yeah. There's a couple pretty good palookas going tomorrow night at Laurel and Saint Nick's," McClosky said. "I like LaRover, he should take Reguejo in the welterweight main at Laurel. And I can't see how Giosa, who can't hit worth shit but hardly ever takes a solid shot, is going to lose to Alvarez at Saint Nick's."

Cisco shot a glance at his partner. "You're amazing. How the hell do you keep all of that crap straight?"

"Simple, just got to sort out the stiffs. First up tomorrow, I'll be seeing Pussy Lieber, place a sawbuck each on LaRover and Giosa, and start scratching around."

"Don't waste too much time on the pugs, if it's going nowhere," Cisco said. "We've got the victims' names now. See what you can dig up, if any missing persons reports have come in. It's all yours. Pick the obvious, Sussex and Passaic Counties first. The old camps may have some magnetic appeal to old Nazi lovers. If you come up empty, hit Hudson, Bergen, Morris, and Union. Nothing leaks out, not even a whisper. We've both hooked into this thing for keeps."

"Discretion is my middle name. Hey, enough with that look!" McClosky said. "Even a gregarious, sociable, fun-loving guy like me can submerge his magnetism for the good of the team."

"What a heap of bullshit," Cisco said, his face darkened by the all-too-easy sarcasm that served him well in his battle in the department trenches.

"I'll get going on it," McClosky said. "Hate working this way. Don't mind flying solo, but a lone Newark homicide dick prowling North Jersey and asking questions, well, you know the drill."

"Figure it out as you go along," Cisco said. "Tell them that you're part of a survey team working for the governor. Hell, that's not half-bad. Trenton wants to know how many missing persons wind-up as homicides. It's just implausible enough for them to shake their heads and say, 'it's about time.'"

"We'll hook up in my office, late this afternoon to see where this mess is going. By that time, we should have the FBI stuff from New York. In the meantime, I'll find out what the hell is going on with the three mob hits. Got the names, and even the time and places, as usual, going nowhere. The news scribblers are getting hard-ass, and we've got to stroke them."

Six hours later, less than a mile from City Hall, the big bronze of George Washington and his horse receded into the twilight shadows of Washington Park. Mike tried unsuccessfully to pull off a casual stroll as he headed to the bench below the hillock crowned by the statue. Despite the autumn coolness, he was sweating. Frank was already there, sitting at one end of the slotted green bench.

Mike had parked his treasured Terraplane two blocks away on Broad Street. It had taken him more than an hour yesterday afternoon to clean all traces of blood from the sliding metal box in the car's trunk. He'd used a bucket of water drawn from a landscaper's hose, added some of his mom's detergent, and scrubbed like hell to accomplish the job under some trees in a secluded area of Branch Brook Park. The bloody rags were wrapped in newspaper and thrown into a trash can. He'd be back at work the next day at R&P Sundries, a subsidiary of Rogers, Peet & Company, which considered it a demeaning outrage when compared to Brooks Brothers. R&P's motto, "clothing accessories make the man." Mike was certain that after a few more good months on the road, he would find himself working the floor with his own client list at the parent company's five-story-citadel in Manhattan.

Mike tried hard, but failed to blot any memory of that dirty job from his mind as he approached the park bench. He still seethed as he took a seat by Frank. The two men silently waited.

Mister Rache witnessed their arrival from a doorway on the corner of Broad Street and Washington Place. He wanted them in place, waiting, and nervous. This would be their tenth meeting since those two days of mind control sessions at Camp Kilmer. There would be only a few more, and then it would be over and he could move on.

His journey was predestined. Something inside snapped on that warm April day last year when even the smallest hint of compassion was replaced by a hate that devoured his soul. Alone in his Jeep, he drove slowly along the cobbled streets of medieval Dachau. The ten-minute drive from the concentration camp propelled him into a world that seemed more like a mirage than reality. Everything was pristine, completely untouched by the horrors of a war that had destroyed much of western civilization.

Trees, shrubs and pink, white, and purple flowers were in full bloom. The almost empty streets were undamaged and free of debris. He felt nothing but contempt for what he saw, Teutonic tidiness at its best. He swallowed the bitter bile that had collected in his esophagus, but the sour taste remained when he glided his Jeep to a stop beside the railroad tracks that fed through the village to the death camp less than four miles away. He got out, walked to the tracks, stepped over the nearest rail and took firm footing on a wooden tie. He could feel cloistered eyes peering through cracks in curtained windows in homes up and down the track.

Were these good citizens just as curious about the freight cars with their doomed cargo as they are now about him? A smile, more a sneer, tightened his face as he abruptly turned to take in the three nearest homes. Sure enough, the discreetly opened curtains in four windows were quickly pulled together as his gaze moved from house-to-house.

He returned to his Jeep, shifted into gear, and slowly drove along several of the village streets before stopping at the corner of Augsburger and Karlsberg. He pulled a Lucky from his pack and lit up when something caught his eye about twenty yards away.

Two adults gently coaxed a little, smiling blond girl, no more than five years old, toward his Jeep with a small bouquet of red and white flowers. There was no sign of apprehension or fear when she reached him, handed him the bouquet and said, "*Für Sie mein lieber Herr.*" The adults, obviously her parents, were also smiling from a distance. Without a smile, he silently accepted the bouquet, placed it on the passenger seat and turned away. These three smiling faces that for years had lived with the death stench that permeated everything sealed his fate. He knew what he had to do.

For more than a year, bloodlust had fueled a quest now nearing completion. He crossed Washington Place, entered the park at an angle from the statue, and approached the bench from behind.

"Gentlemen, if I were to guess, I'd say you've all been thinking the same thing, when will it be over," Mister Rache said. He carefully positioned himself three feet in front of the bench, his hands thrust into the front pockets of his woolen Navy peacoat. It was too warm for the heavy garment, but he saw from the expression on the two faces that he had achieved the impression he wanted. At six feet one, broad shouldered, thick-necked, and heavily muscled, he knew that the thick coat reinforced an already formidable image. The sweat was worth it.

"One more time, that's it. It will be much different and much cleaner than before, and because it will close out our mission, much more important. The three Bund scum were gestures. This one will be a man who believed with all his heart that what we witnessed at Dachau was good and necessary. And he profited." He waited to see who would speak first. It was Frank.

"At Kilmer we were ready and willing. Five months, that's all it was since we had gone nuts with the hatred over what we saw at Dachau," Frank said. His steady voice belied the sour taste of fear in his mouth. "Both of us talked about it, and there've been no regrets. We agreed with you at Kilmer that our payback for Dachau had not been enough. More had to be done. That the Bund goons who supported the Dachau butchers also had to pay."

The big man saw that the three hypnotic reinforcing sessions at Kilmer with Frank and Mike had paid deadly dividends. But was his mastery of them as complete as he needed? The sessions at the Day Room had imbedded hatred and a thirst for revenge. Tonight, he wanted to be sure these two men were ready for the final step.

CHAPTER TWELVE

Warrant Officer Mordecai Munson's days as Special Affairs Officer at the Camp Kilmer Day Room came to an end the week that Mister Rache met with Frank and Mike for the first time since he had sized them up at Dachau. The operation had already been turned over to the Red Cross Doughnut Dollies. Among the shelves of paperback books, magazines, checkerboards, a dart board, and ping pong tables, Mister Rache found what he was looking for. The two eight-millimeter Bell & Howells provided returning GIs with their first look at the families they had left behind.

"It was amazing to see," Munson said. "It didn't make a damn bit of difference how battle-hardened they were, the tears just kept coming. No sobs, nothing like that and no embarrassment. I think some of these guys would have killed to get their hands on a projector overseas, but instead they had to wait until they got here to watch some of the most god-awful family footage ever. But to them it was Academy Award stuff."

"I see that the projectors and screens are just lying over there on a corner shelf," Mister Rache said. "No further use for them?"

"They got a lot of use early on, but there's been little call for them in recent weeks," Munson said. "Why do you ask?"

“I’d like to use one of them for what you could say will be a private screening of my own,” the big man said, “and if possible, could I use your office? I’m assuming you won’t be needing it. By the way, I like the little farewell you tacked on the door, ‘Pocatello and potatoes here I come.’”

The two men were sitting on stools in front of a make-believe small-town coffee shop counter. Munson eyed the imposing man in his freshly pressed officer’s uniform with insignia that carried unquestioned respect. The man’s eyes were, well how to describe it, both hard, cold, warm, and inviting all at the same time. He had little doubt that before he left that afternoon, he would be handing over his keys.

The next day Frank and Mike walked to the Day Room from the barracks where they had been billeted since arriving at Kilmer two weeks earlier. They were horny, bored and in need of a stiff drink, when a base orderly shouted their names along with a friendly “Get your asses over to Day Room Three, right now! And I mean right now!”

Frank and Mike pulled up short as soon as they spotted a familiar figure on the other side of the Day Room. “Jesus Christ, it’s him. I can’t believe it,” Mike said.

“I believe it,” Frank said. “He said he’d be seeing us again, and I don’t know why, but I never doubted it. It’s creepy as hell, but I never thought we’d seen the last of him.”

The big man greeted them from his chair at a card table, “I’ve been keeping track of you, and in a crazy place like Kilmer it wasn’t easy.”

They’re scared and puzzled. I like that. They don’t know what to expect. Apprehension, that’s what I’m looking for, and it looks like I’m getting it, he thought as he studied his approaching targets. He fingered the keys that Munson had given him, already put to use that morning when he moved a Bell & Howell, a projection screen, and two comfortable armchairs from the reading room into position in the darkened office. He knew the two men would be heading home in four days, so it had to start right now.

"A nice little Rainbow reunion," the big man said as he reached across the table and pumped their hands. "I've been looking forward to it. I hope it's the same all around." The two men nodded in silent agreement and pulled up two chairs.

The officer reached down and took a large manila envelope from a briefcase on the floor beside his chair. Opening the envelope, he pulled out three glossy photos, and a spool of eight-millimeter film. "Here's something I want you to see. First the photos, then we'll take a look at the film."

He spread the three photos across the table, and positioned them in front of Frank and Mike. "Take a close look. At first glance, nothing out of the ordinary."

He tapped one of the photos with his right index finger. "Her name's Ilse Koch. Take a close look. An ordinary, maybe even a pleasant looking woman, who right now is sitting in a prison cell in Germany. She's better known as the Red Witch of Buchenwald."

He studied their faces and noted the bewilderment. "Yes, I know you were never at Buchenwald, but I'm showing you these photos to enlighten you as to how universal evil can be, that the horrors you saw beyond Watchtower B didn't stop at Dachau. Watchtower B created a new reality for you. Watchtower B."

Again using his right forefinger, the officer focused their attention on the second photo. "Human skin, tattooed human skin, sliced from prisoners at Buchenwald on orders from Ilse Koch, a plain, red-haired woman with two children."

Frank pulled the photo closer, studied it intently, then slid it across the table to Mike. The two men leaned back in their chairs, their eyes filled with silent questions as they appraised the unsmiling face across from them.

"Remember what I said, the horrors you witnessed beyond Watchtower B weren't confined inside Dachau's fences." The big man drew attention to a third photo. "An ordinary lamp with an ordinary lampshade, something you might find in an ordinary home of an ordinary woman like Ilse Koch. Yes, very ordinary, if you consider lampshades made of human skin just the right adornments for your parlor. So you see, Watchtower B could be found in many places in Hitler's Germany." The officer's soothing voice belied the hatred that festered behind his words. "I know you share my resolve that what you saw beyond Watchtower B will never be forgotten."

He returned the three photos to the manila envelope, dropped it into his briefcase, and focused his attention on the spool of film. He got up from the table, and motioned the two men to follow him to Munson's office. "There's something else I want you to see."

The three men entered the office darkened by the tightly closed wooden blinds. It took the big man only a few minutes to thread the film into the projector, and cue it to an opening shot of a swastika being raised on a flagpole. "This, gentlemen, is Camp Bergwald where the German-American Bund celebrated Hitler at a time when Watchtower Bs were being built all over Germany. It's closed now. Wasn't far from here, near Pompton Lakes. It provided many happy hours for American Nazis, young, old, men and boys, grown women and girls, proudly wearing their swastikas."

The ten-minute film had been lovingly produced by the Bund to show the rapturous fun and games that defined Camp Bergwald, if not every Bund camp in America. "Get comfortable, take a deep breath, relax your arms, feet flat on the floor and watch. And while you're watching, try to picture Watchtower B in among the scenes you will see."

Frank and Mike were sucked into a dizzying stream of bare-chested men and boys, fresh-faced women and girls all cavorting in a wonderland of hiking trails, outdoor feasting, beer drinking, singing, dancing, communal swimming, speeches, flag waving marches, camp fire camaraderie, and hammering and sawing as new construction was erected with the promise of more to come.

Every two minutes their host said, “I’m still looking for Watchtower B, Watchtower B, and so are you.” He watched their reaction as the minutes slipped by. When the film ended, he was satisfied he had taken the initial step. Now for the first test to see if I picked the right men, he thought. He had been standing next to the projector with Frank and Mike seated in front of him. He turned it off, walked to the screen and turned slowly to assess the results.

“Frank. Mike. Now listen to me, listen to me. You are so relaxed. You are so ready to accept my words. You want to hear my words. As you listen to my words, you are feeling even more relaxed, more accepting. You will always remember what I am telling you now. I am telling you now that you will always remember Dachau. When you hear me say, Watchtower B, and only from me, you will remember what you saw at Dachau. You will remember everything you saw and did at Dachau. You are becoming even more relaxed now, more accepting of my words. You will always remember my words. From now on, I will no longer be the officer who shared the unthinkable with you at Dachau, but Mister Rache, your guide on your journey of revenge. Now listen to what I say. When you hear, and hear only from Mister Rache, Watchtower B, repeated again, Watchtower B, the words in close order you will no longer remember what happened at Dachau.

“But now that thought must be deep, the deepest thought you will ever have. You are relaxed, so relaxed you are amazed at what’s happening to you. Each of your left elbows, comfortable on the padded armrests, is doing something you can't control. Your elbow is pushing down, pushing down, pushing, pushing, pushing down. Your forearm is beginning to rise. Very slowly, very slowly, the sensation is wonderful. Relaxed motion you can't control. You remember Watchtower B. Your eyes are closed as your arm lifts ever upward, your hand turns toward your head. Your fingers are searching. Reaching for your forehead. Up, up and now they are ready to touch. Your head waits. Your eyes are closed. Now do it! All five fingers bunched over your eyes, the pressure increases. Your head is still. Through those fingers Watchtower B passes through your skull and into your brain. You know it's forever. Try now, try as hard as you can to pull your fingers away! You can't! Watchtower B, Watchtower B."

Mister Rache was convinced that the first step was a success. Their left forearms dropped to the armrests, they slowly opened their eyes, and reality returned.

"It was one hell of a movie," Mike said. "Right here in our backyard."

"And you, Frank, your reaction?"

"Hell, they might have been Nazi-lovers, but there were a lot of good-looking women there," Frank said. "We've been here for two weeks and, speaking for myself, I'm horny as hell."

For the next two days, Mister Rache's inductions were repeated, first in the morning then in the late afternoon. Gwen, the senior Red Cross Doughnut Dolly, never asked him what was going on, but it was obvious from her little chit-chats with the other Dollies, that sooner or later the curiosity would not be restrained. No matter, this phase of his plan was complete, and probably just in time before Gwen picked up a telephone and started asking questions.

That was a year ago. Mister Rache knew from the start that he was taking a big gamble with Mike and Frank.

Tonight he would find out if the subliminal reinforcement, so necessary to turn them into sacrificial killing machines, was deep enough for the final act.

CHAPTER THIRTEEN

Mister Rache decided that this was the night he would plumb the depths of Mike's and Frank's souls. Only the two magic words would be needed. He had to be sure that the ghastly acts they had witnessed and participated in at Dachau were indelible, the very essence of what they had become.

He walked to a bench, and sat down at a tangent so he could peer easily into the faces of the two men. He needed to know if they were ready.

Even though three Nazi-loving pieces of slime had been eliminated, his mission would only be complete if this final act was successful. He wanted to be sure their horrific memories of those first hours at Dachau had engulfed them with the hate necessary to proceed. This was the night to find out. He leaned forward, looked directly at them, and said, "Watchtower B will always be with us. You've kept it inside for so long."

Mike and Frank became restive, obviously agitated, exactly what he wanted. The big man, now a superfluous figure, sat back, waited and watched as the agonized men in front of him clenched and unclenched their fists, tightened their lips, and rolled their heads. Their subconscious had taken control.

He could only guess where Mike and Frank were now. Mike had dropped his hands to the outside of each thigh, and held tightly to the edge of the bench. His breathing was heavy and labored. Frank's arms no longer rested comfortably on the back of the bench. He dropped his hands into his lap, entwined his fingers, and began pushing and pulling them. His chin dropped to his chest.

Mister Rache had laid it all out for Mike, it was planned perfectly. At this point, he was unaware that Mike was living the fatal moment for which he was chosen. Flashbacks cascaded as a bloody kaleidoscope took over.

All he had to do was lock on the silencer to the Colt .45, point and pull the trigger. First there would be the begging, Boris Obermeyer on his knees on the front porch of Pamilco, the boyhood home of movie director Cecil B. De Mille.

It took only three weeks of Friday lunches for Mike to cultivate Obermeyer. Pompton Lakes was part of his R&P Sundries territory. Obermeyer floor-bossed the men's section of "only the best will do" Kluge's Apparel on Wanaque. It was all too easy for Mike to smooth his way into the luncheonette booth next door with movie talk of the Christian variety.

"I love what I'm doing, gives my life meaning," the blonde, blue-eyed Obermeyer said, washing down a bite of his egg salad sandwich with a gulp of coffee. "Pamilco must be preserved, a shrine to the great De Mille, a great Christian. His movies will live on forever, so must Pamilco. There's talk it will be torn down and I am leading the fight to save it."

"Boris, I'm really impressed with what you're trying to do with the old De Mille homestead," Mike said. "The memory of a man who could direct movies like *King of Kings* and *The Sign of the Cross* must be preserved."

"When you're a good Christian, and see what's happening around you, all those Jesus-killing Jews, then De Mille's name should never be dimmed," said Obermeyer, a thin, sallow man whose wary, probing eyes searched for affirmation. Satisfied, he continued, "I have little doubt from what you've said that you agree."

"Look, I've wrapped it up for the day. If I hang around until your quitting time, maybe you'd give me a tour of Pamilco." Obermeyer's wide smile said it all.

Late that afternoon, Mike, with Boris seated next to him, tooled his Hudson Terraplane along Wanaque Avenue to Terhune Drive. They were scarcely more than a stone's throw from where Obermeyer and other Nazi Bund thugs had planted the swastika atop Federal Hill in Bloomingdale, and declared their allegiance to Hitler by establishing Camp Bergwald.

"Looks like you've got your work cut out for you if you're going to save this place before it falls down on its own," Mike said. The two men climbed the stairs to the wrap-around covered porch of the three-story gabled wooden relic. It was getting dark, forcing them to walk in deepening shadows.

"If I'm right, that's to the south isn't it?" Mike asked.

"Yes, you're exactly right, that's Bloomingdale over there."

"It's more than just Bloomingdale, and you know that don't you," said Mike, his voice suddenly harsh.

Obermeyer, who had been leading the way, stopped abruptly. Uninvited fear took hold, and there was an involuntary twitching of his shoulders. "Who are you? What do you want of me?"

"First I want you on your knees. Get down on your fucking knees! I want you facing south toward your beloved Camp Bergwald." Mike pulled his .45 caliber pistol from an inside jacket pocket, and jabbed it into the nape of Obermeyer's neck. "On your knees goddamn it!" As the fear-stricken man fell to the porch, Mike quickly locked the silencer he had taken from another jacket pocket into place.

"Now I want you to beg. Beg for mercy. Just like those poor starving wretches at Dachau were forced to do."

"Dachau? What? Me and Dachau, no never, not me. Please, please, please. Yes, I'll obey, I'm begging. What did I have to do with Dachau?"

"Everything."

Mister Rache's programming snapped into place. The box cars. Tower B. The white flag. All of it. He pushed Obermeyer's head down, exactly where he wanted it. The pistol jumped in his hand, hardly a sound, then a thud as the bullet exploded through the skull, out the eye socket, and into the floor of the porch. Now the tarpaulin, roll up the son of a bitch. *Here, get the rags, wipe up the bone splinters, the pulverized eyeball, the blood and brains. Looks good.* Everything needed to do the job supplied by Mister Rache. The trunk of his Terraplane was open and waiting. *Goddamn, the skinny little shit is hard to handle* he thought as he dragged the body down the stairs, across the path and stuffed it away. There had been no passersby.

Mister Rache was waiting, this was the second test. He had parked on a gravel road off the Belleville Pike, east of the Passaic River Bridge. The wire and cinder blocks were waiting as was an open satchel exposing its contents, a meat cleaver and two pair of forearm-length rubber gloves. The meat cleaver was neat and efficient. One chop and it was over. Stuffing the wrist down Obermeyer's throat with his left hand was tough and very messy. A bone splinter punctured the thumb of Mike's rubber glove. It took only a few minutes to attach the cinder blocks to a trussed-up Boris Obermeyer, and sink his carcass under the bridge.

Now, it was a week and two bodies later as Mike and Frank sat transfixed on their park bench willingly trapped by Mister Rache's mastery.

"Let me remind you why I chose you. That's right, you were chosen. Let's remind ourselves why you were chosen.

"You, Frank, you're our youngest, only twenty-two. I sized you up then and I size you up now as a remorseless agent for retribution, and a true disciple of Nemesis, the eternal avenger." Mister Rache studied Frank, his face, nervous feet and hands. He knew he was still entrapped by a calling far beyond his control.

"Let's go back to the machine gun Frank, and the weeping boy firing it. Twelve of the SS scum were dead before the commanding officer pulled him off his weapon. You and I know there would have been more if he hadn't been dragged away. I saw it all, and admired the boy for what he had done. At the same time, I cursed the officer."

Mister Rache's words were crisp, concise and matter of fact. Just as he figured, his chilling denouement was triggering horrific memories. He began his reinforcement.

"With you Mike, there was weeping and then revenge. Bullet after bullet from your trusty carbine. I was fascinated by what you did when the Nazi guards spilled out of Watchtower B waving a little white flag. When you saw one of them had a pistol concealed behind his back, you pumped three bullets into him, and coldly watched as he died at your feet. How many were killed at the tower? Seventeen I believe, six of those bodies belonged to you. We all saw those forty open boxcars outside, the gate crammed with skin and bones that were once human. Some of you vomited, many like you, Mike, wept, and a few of you took action. All of us were diminished. Because of my job, I was free to go anywhere and see everything. I allowed myself to revel in hatred.

"Now to you, Frank. It was mid-afternoon when I ran into you and the other GIs holding back a hundred enraged Jews still strong enough to throw themselves at the guards rounded up in the center of the camp. From my Jeep, I saw how you and your squad opened fire on the Germans, not to kill them, but only to shoot them in the legs so they couldn't run, and the prisoners could get at them. When it was over, forty of the SS had been butchered, one of them decapitated with a bayonet supplied by one of your buddies. I watched you very closely. I sensed that with your Sergeant stripes you were in command. Like Mike, I saw only cold indifference. That's why I chose you, and that's why you're here. We are kindred spirits.

"All three of us walked through the shadow of Watchtower B. Walked together. Walked where? Through the shadow of Watchtower B!"

For Frank, the shadow of Watchtower B lengthened to the tiny Hudson County town of Guttenberg, where a murderous tapestry was woven. Heinrich Bolz was doomed from the moment he carried his exuberant hate onto the grounds of Camp Nordland during opening ceremonies on July 18, 1937. His fate was sealed when he earned a privileged trip to Nuremberg, and proudly displayed his swastika tattoo to admirers when he returned.

Mister Rache had laid it all out to perfection, Frank thought. He marveled how complete the plans were, how Bolz whose Jew-hating notoriety and guilt-ridden paranoia forced him into hiding in the German enclave of Guttenberg. Frank had trouble even finding the town, much less the tavern at 69th and Palisade.

"Bolz loves his beer, but money's been in short supply," Mister Rache informed him. At the same time handing over a cloth-wrapped package containing a pistol, silencer and ammunition, along with a rolled tarpaulin and some heavy rope. "Here's how you move in, not too fast now, start with the five cent beer. Get to know Bolz."

It was impossible for Frank to fathom how he had willingly surrendered everything to a man he feared, but couldn't resist. It all sounded crazy to Frank as he sat silently behind the wheel of his father's refrigerated meat truck, emblazoned on both sides with "Matt Beagan & Son, Wholesale Meats, Serving North Jersey for 10 Years, EL4-6000." He tried to absorb what Mister Rache was saying. Doubt and wonder creased his face, this didn't escape the big man.

"Bolz is in there almost every night, the place is German-American working class. No need to tell you the sentiments expressed, nor the regrets gurgled into the cheap beer. You understand don't you Karl, Karl Klinger," he smiled when he saw that his words had their intended impact.

"Karl Klinger, what the hell are you talking about?" said Frank, aware that this was the first he had ever raised his voice or questioned anything Mister Rache said.

"That's the name you'll be using. You and your family had been Bund sympathizers. Even attended a Bund rally at Camp Nordland. Be careful here, not too much detail, that you mostly remember the music, back-slapping, and how the good people of Andover welcomed everybody. You found this hole-in-the-wall bar strictly by chance, got lost on your way from Jersey City to Nungessers to pick up a friend coming in from New York. Bolz is a big guy and very suspicious, so be careful, don't be pushy. Also know he's lonely, not too many friends. Ten cent glasses of stout will open the door."

And they did. Frank marveled at Mister Rache's hard work. How many times had he been in this dive to put it all together. No matter, it all clicked. Bolz's one-bedroom apartment was a half-block away. Even down to the seldom-used alley next to the apartment building with its side door making it easy for him to park his pre-war Ford. Bolz would learn that the newly-minted Karl Klinger lived across the county line in Fort Lee, just far enough away to dispel any prying, but close enough to make twice-a-week beer drinking bouts plausible.

After three weeks bemoaning the ending of the Bund, Frank got his invite to Bolz's apartment to view photos taken at the 1938 Nuremberg Rally of Greater Germany. Frank assembled his pistol and silencer in the toilet down the hall, and returned to the apartment to find Bolz leaning over photos spread across a large table. There was a bloody burp as the bullet passed through the skull and table and spent itself on the floor. First the cleanup. He scooped up the snapshots, half of them sticky with blood, and tossed them into the large photo album on the table. Blood from Bolz's head wound dripped over the side of the table, and through the bullethole to create a spreading red puddle. Mister Rache had supplied him with plenty of clean-up rags, enough to do the job. It took all of his strength to wrap and tie Bolz's heavy carcass and drag it down to the trunk of the Ford. An hour later, Frank pulled to a stop in front of Mister Rache who had been waiting with wire, cinder blocks and satchel in a small river front lot only yards from the Harrison Avenue Bridge.

Now as they assembled on this Sunday evening beneath the gaze of George Washington, Mister Rache knew it was time to continue the conditioning he had so meticulously implanted. Mike and Frank had been thoughtless avengers at Dachau, mindless of consequences. This past week had been calculated revenge that carried with it a magnitude of risk that made the bloody retribution magnificent. It wasn't over yet, the closing chapter was at hand.

Mister Rache got up from his bench, and watched Mike and Frank squirm as he planted himself in front of them. He stretched, raising both arms straight above his head then sweeping them down to his sides. "Ah yes, it's always nice to reminisce even if it is about Watchtower B, Watchtower B." He was pleased with the reaction.

"We've come a long way from the Day Room at Kilmer, and we are so close to the final act," the big man intoned as Frank and Mike emerged from their subconscious. "Then we will all walk our separate ways, proud of what we have accomplished. I knew from the start that I had the two men perfectly suited to accompany me on my journey."

Doesn't he ever blink, Mike thought as he followed Mister Rache's eyes from him to Frank and then back again. *The expression never changed. No flex in the face. It was a mask.*

"Three bullets, one from each of us. Payback to the Bund lice who worshipped the gangsters responsible for Dachau. Three hate-mongers whose deaths were made even more delicious when they begged for their lives," Rache said. "We'll be closing out our mission. You'll hear from me very soon."

Frank and Mike stared mutely as the dark specter turned and disappeared as silently as he had arrived. Frank felt instant relief at the big man's departure, at the same time, he was overcome by guilt brought on by his betrayal of what Mister Rache had demanded of him. He had not forced Heinrich Bolz to beg before he put a bullet through his head. This meeting had taken less than fifteen minutes, but for the two men these minutes quantified what had become the pivotal points of their lives.

The butcher's son and haberdasher drummer allowed their seduction to be so total there was no way out. Unspoken, except for the nervous glances they shared in silence, the two men acknowledged their surrender as they headed to their cars a few blocks away. Their butchery and burning of a man whose name they didn't even know opened questions they would never pursue. Mister Rache had constructed a labyrinth of fun-house mirrors so complete that it distorted logic. It was not hard for Frank and Mike to imagine what happened when Mister Rache had exacted his revenge on the third victim. His searing hate reflected in his eyes, his contempt for mercy, and finally the satisfaction as brain, bone and flesh were blown away. For both of them, the image of Mister Rache reinforced what they knew was in store, that one last job.

Mister Rache basked in self-awareness as he recrossed Washington Place to his car parked around the corner on Broad Street. He was comfortable with the duality that encompassed self-loathing and justifiable revenge. For the demons that remained, the two simple men he had chosen as acolytes provided proof that his mission was predestined. In Mike and Frank, he had selected his exorcists wisely.

A big question remained. Frank and Mike were puzzled, how successful could their two acts of vengeance be if nobody knew they had happened? All that planning, including a study of Passaic River tide charts, Mister Rache supervised it all, even the length of the wire needed to keep the two bodies bobbing just below the river surface, but close enough to be seen at low tide. Everything was done to grab attention. The right hand chopped off just above the wrist and jammed into the victim's mouth as far as it could go. The five fingers dangled from between the lips. The ring finger was adorned with a round, gold signet ring with the inscription *Reichsparteitag Großdeutschland-1938* encircling a black stone. It was a story that reporters lived for.

How could anyone ignore the Nazi swastikas, and the names of two New Jersey Bund camps tattooed on the arms of the floaters? Yet there was not a word about the murders anywhere. Why not? Yesterday, Frank and Mike had shared their bewilderment while dismembering the corpse Mister Rache had left for them. They did not want to know how and where he had blown away this man's brains, knowing only that the victim would have begged for his life while pleading innocence which the big man would endure with contempt. It had been almost a week since the first murder, and they agreed that the big man also had to be puzzled. Something strange was going on, but what the hell could it be.

Would Mister Rache's final act also be ignored?

CHAPTER FOURTEEN

Nick Cisco looked up from a short stack of homicide updates on his desk, and with a wave of his right hand motioned Kevin McClosky into his office. McClosky parked himself in one of two wooden chairs in front of the desk, inhaled deeply and said, "Drew a blank so far, but there might still be a chance I can pick up something. Who knows."

"That's reassuring as hell," said Cisco, who leaned forward in a freshly laundered and starched white shirt, and Sunday best blue tie. "Anything at all that the Minutemen are still kicking around?"

"I may have hit it lucky in a way," McClosky said. "Nat Arno and his boss were at Laurel ringside Monday night. Zwillman had a couple of his boys on the card. They asked about you. Didn't know they cared."

"Why not? Arno and his Minutemen had to love us," Cisco said. "We were the Keystone cops who always left them laughing. I can still see Arno with that big, shit-eating grin on his face, barely able to hold it all in."

"And with a fat cigar stuck in his maw," McClosky said. "His thugs were all gone, leaving behind some cracked skulls, broken arms, smashed windows, and the stink of rotten eggs from the sulphur bombs. Nobody saw or heard anything.

“Nat was rubbing it in Monday night, wondered what we were doing for exercise nowadays,” McClosky said. “They’ve got one hell of a pipeline. He and Longy knew we’re up for promotion, and great guys that they are, wished us luck. I poked around as best I could, real casual like. I asked Pussy Lieber if he misses any of his old Minutemen buddies. It was like talking to a mummy. There’s a couple other books who owe me, and I’ll give them a try. I know these guys. I realize it’s early and that Peterson is on our asses, but right now, if you ask me, it’s all too obvious. I don’t think the Minutemen figure into this at all.”

“I’m getting there too,” Cisco said. “The link is too easy, Jews, Dachau, the Bund and revenge. What’s going on now isn’t simple head-busting. You know in a way I sort of admire the Minutemen.”

“How so?”

“Underneath it all they were patriots, not just a bunch of muscle-bound Jews with cauliflower ears. How many of them joined up after Pearl Harbor, just about all if I remember right.”

“Yeah, and some didn’t come home.”

“Keep working it. We’ll need to squeeze all your leads,” Cisco said. “I’ll be the police liaison this Friday at the mayor’s anti-crime meeting at the *Clarion*. Ain’t election year great? Peterson will be there, I’ll need something. Anything else? I’m leaving here early for another sit down with Connie and Father Sullivan at Saint Anthony’s.”

“Good luck,” McClosky’s voice softened as he pushed himself up from his chair. “Here’s something for you, no luck involved.”

Cisco paused as he tightened his tie in front of the small office mirror to the left of the office door, and watched his smiling partner approach from behind.

"One of Longy's boys, a kid named Don Petty, is going against Hopes, a real palooka, at the Laurel on the twenty-first," McClosky said. "He's got only one fight under his belt, a first-round KO. Smart money says Petty's a sure thing. Unh-uh it ain't so. That's where Longy wants it, get the odds his way. Word is he's hanging the kid out to dry, and real early, maybe even the first round."

Cisco had finished fumbling with his tie, and was pulling his suit coat on when he turned to his partner and said in feigned disbelief, "Do I sense a fix coming on, and that I should climb aboard?"

Their partnership went back a long way creating a conundrum for Cisco that entwined contempt and deep concern. Kevin lived well, and Nick knew it was only because of the dark chemistry he shared with gangsters. Despite Kevin's assurance that he had things under control, Nick knew better. Sooner or later there would be payback for his partner's tailored wardrobe, hefty stash, burlesque beauties, and De Soto convertible. When the demands came, they would face them together.

Nick knew that his long-time partner was offering camaraderie that had been in short supply since he and Connie busted up. Kevin's silent disapproval of his obsession with Grace De Marco was evident from the start. They were two flawed men uncertain how to reach out to each other.

"Well hell, if it's a sure thing, it'll be more like an exhibition than a real prize fight," Cisco joked. "Hit me up when it gets closer. I think I can pop for a century."

"So I made a believer out of you," McClosky said with a wide grin. "I saw it coming. No, no don't interrupt me. Got to get back to work now. Time to start nosing through missing persons' reports. I'll be heading out early tomorrow. And you, all duded-up, your best suit and all. Give my best to Connie. It's a nice day for a drive."

Cisco guided his unmarked sedan around a late afternoon traffic jam at Broad and Market, and headed uptown to South Orange Avenue. This would be his fourth attempt to reach something or other with Connie. There was no other way to put it. He was at a loss as to what to expect from these sessions at Saint Anthony's. The last one collapsed in less than fifteen minutes. Father Sullivan had thus far been a failure in his attempt to smooth the jagged edges of their widening fracture.

Cisco turned right off South Orange onto Littleton, and then left onto 13th Avenue and slowed to a stop in front of the Monastery of Saint Dominic's. *Maybe the cloistered nuns in their black veils and white habits had the right idea*, Cisco thought, *hiding themselves from inquisitors who would always be out there waiting. No man-woman anguish for them*. He started up and cruised to the corner of 10th, stopped and peered intently to his right at the Margotta house where Connie had fled when she walked out last spring. Saint Anthony's rectory loomed a few blocks away.

"Good, we're all here and right on time," a smiling Father Sullivan greeted Cisco when he walked through the door to the priest's office. He had passed through the outer vestibule with its lemon wax furniture smell, stain glass windows and an alcoved Saint Anthony, the patron of those seeking to recover what they had lost. *Very appropriate,* Cisco thought.

"Before we start, let's all take a deep breath," the priest said. "It didn't go well last time. Let's at least finish our coffee this time around. The pot, cream and sugar are over there on the tray."

"You're looking good. Eating well I hope," Connie said softly. She knew her words were the basic everyday stuff with which she was the most comfortable. *I'm always the first one to reach out,* Connie thought. *Why the hell is that, comes so natural at times I want to bite my tongue. Well that's it for today. It's his turn now, let's see if he'll pick up on it.* "I got your check, and like I said from the beginning, it's more than enough." *Damn it, here I go again*, Connie couldn't help herself and she knew it.

Nick listened and watched, it was all there, why he had willingly forfeited an artistic dream for a badge and a gun. The ankles and calves that beckoned from under a black wool dress were as inviting as ever. He doubted if she realized their affect. At forty-two, she was still pulling it off, that special kind of Latin beauty, trim but beguilingly soft. Her dark eyes were counterpoints to the thin gold necklace that he had given her. It adorned her neck and hung in a loop between her breasts. It was just like her to attach a small gold crucifix, not an empty cross, but a crucifix. There were no earrings to distract from lustrous black hair that graced her shoulders. No wrinkles, not even a hint of crow's-feet. *What the hell's wrong with me*, Cisco thought. *It's all there. Goddamn it. She's waiting, any move that I'd make would do it, but I can't and I know why.*

With this realization, he knew that this session would also be futile.

"Thanks for asking. Yeah, still doing my push-ups, some barbell work, but could use a lot more walking," his words snapped Nick from his self-deprecation. "Eating, well that's something else again. The kitchen and I are natural enemies, but I can manage. Still eat a lot on the run."

"Ready to get started?" the priest said leaning back in his swivel chair in what must be his best confessional pose, everything but the stole draping his shoulders to make the picture complete.

"Our last meeting came and went so fast I can hardly remember how it ended," Father Sullivan said. "Connie, can you pick it up?"

The incongruity was palpable. It folded all of them into an empty envelope that was already sealed, had been for the past six months. "I don't know where to begin," Connie said. "I've been thinking hard about it all. Trying to pull it apart piece-by-piece, trying to figure out how it happened, how I let it happen. That it was all my fault, but I can't figure what I did wrong. I need help, Father."

It was a plaintive, misdirected entreaty. Connie's eyes were fixated on the coffee cup she had been holding in her lap. She reached forward and placed it on the corner of the priest's desk. Leaning back, she patted her dress, turned toward Nick, and was about to continue, but flinched into silence when she saw his anger.

"Connie, you've done nothing wrong. Cut it out, just cut it out." *Here it goes again*, Cisco thought, *just like the last time. What right does she have to deny me my guilt.* "Look, if we're going to get any place, we've got to understand what it's all about, and let's be honest, we know what it's all about. Right, Father?"

"Keep going," the priest knew that reticence rather than advice was in order. *Yeah*, he thought, *I know what's going on*. His duties as a spiritual sparring partner in the confessional had made him a carnal expert. He probed Connie's face, and was surprised to find it expressionless in the wake of her husband's shattering words.

"Don't you know that I realize what I've done, what I'm still doing," Cisco's words failed to cleanse. "What can I say, pray for me, make novenas, stations of the cross, mix 'em up, shuffle them, then what?"

"Nick, we don't need any of that," Connie cast a fleeting glance at the priest, "sorry Father, but we don't." Connie's stoicism had disappeared, replaced by visible agitation fueled by anxiety that it was all slipping away. "We can make it work, Nick. You know we can. It's us, just us. To hell with what our families think. You're strong. You know you're strong. I needed your strength. But now I know that I'm strong, too. I know it's crazy for me to say it this way, but I proved my strength when I walked out on you. We can put it all together, make it work. But you're going to have to want it as much as I do. Together we can do it. But I'm not going to say please. I don't know if I'll ever say please again."

"That's the rub. That's what it's all about. Goddamn it to hell, I don't know where to go with all of this, what's happened to me," Cisco flushed the words out. "And Christ almighty, I've asked myself the same question a million times, and came up with the same answer. Connie, I don't even know if I want to stop."

Father Sullivan and Connie stared in silence. The small office had become unbearably claustrophobic. Connie's white knuckled grip on the wooden arms of her chair tightened even more. She twisted her hands and the highly waxed wood squeaked. The sound was deafening. Nick turned away from them, and stared at the portraits of Pope Pius XII and President Harry Truman on the wall behind Father Sullivan. The priest surveyed the human damage. He had made up his mind that he would do all in his power to thwart complete destruction.

"Let's wrap it up for today," Father Sullivan said. "But I'm not letting you out the door until I get a commitment from both of you that you're coming back next week. It will give you time, for what... I'm not exactly sure. Right here, same time."

Connie and Nick nodded affirmatively, their reluctance obvious. Neither said a word as they arose and turned toward the office door.

Just in time, the priest was fast approaching his boiling point. "Hey wait a damn minute. You're not going anywhere until I hear it from you." The priest quickly pulled his six-foot three frame away from his desk and sped to the door.

This was not going to be a getaway. "Say it right now, that you'll be here next week. Say it!"

"I'll be here, you've got my word," Nick said.

"The same for me," Connie said. She pushed her way past Nick into the vestibule. There was no way Nick would be the first one out, no way he would leave her behind, the way he did for that other woman.

CHAPTER

FIFTEEN

Cisco drove downtown to his office. He had some checking to do with the teams working the three mob hits from the homicide bullpen down the hall. He first touched base with Sergeant Milo Brunson at the front desk for messages, came up empty, then headed down the hall to be greeted a few steps outside his office door by McClosky.

"A couple of things," McClosky said. "One is in the evidence room tagged for our eyes only. We got the connection we needed for the butcher jobs."

"Let's get down there," Cisco said. McClosky's excitement was contagious. "Fill me in with the details as we go. And the second thing you mentioned, is it also connected?"

"Maybe, maybe not. It's a stretch, but my source is pretty damn good," McClosky said as they pushed their way into the basement evidence room. "What we've got here was handed over to a uniform patrol by some kids down at River Street. It was wedged in the rocks near the water's edge."

Sergeant Pat Halloran was waiting for them. The crusty, flush-faced thirty-year veteran was uneasy about the bundle from the moment it plopped onto the stainless steel evidence table. It had been cut open, and retied by the uniforms who brought it in. When Halloran saw the mosaic of dried blood that encrusted much of the bundle, it didn't take much to see it was something for homicide. McClosky answered his call. After Halloran described what he had, it took no more than forty-five seconds for McClosky to get downstairs, and another ten seconds to take a look and put the lid on.

"Tie it back up and stuff it in over there," McClosky pointed to an open spot on the shelf along the wall. "No list, I'll take care of the paperwork. The two uniforms, were they comfortable with turning it over and signing off?"

"Hell, who knows, they were at the end of their shift so I doubt they'll pump out a detailed report," Halloran said. "What's going on?"

"We've got three mob hits working right now," McClosky said, in an effort to mislead the sergeant. "Could fit in. Cisco will want to be in on this. Keep things buttoned up until I get him down here."

Halloran never liked it when his routine was disrupted. He had survived three decades of departmental turf battles with hardly a scratch. Kikes, dagos and micks had played a blood sport at the top. Halloran knew the game well. You survived by staying out of the way when the big boys were punching it out. He eyed Cisco and McClosky coming through the door, and wondered if they were on their way up, and if so, how serious his ass-kissing would have to be.

"Hi, Pat, been at least three months since I've been down here. Going okay?" Cisco said.

"Yeah, the usual," Halloran replied turning and reaching for the bundle on the shelf behind him. "Here it is, what you've come for, so you can take over. I'll be at my desk if you need anything."

The two detectives released the bowknots that secured the four strands of hemp rope around the bundle. They gently separated the blood-stiffened outer wrap to expose the contents. In less than a minute, the evidentiary scope widened.

"So we've got two guys in a red car at the city dump, and now we've got two bloody smocks. It looks like they were bathing partners," Cisco said. "Notice anything else?"

"The rope, you thinking the same thing?"

"Yeah, but let's make sure first," Cisco said turning toward Halloran seated at his desk across the room. "Pat, this hemp rope, did it come with the package?"

"That's what I got. They untied it, took a look, retied it and brought it in."

"Thanks," Cisco said. "We'll have Brunson run down their report later. Let's stash this bundle of joy out of sight. The paperwork is ours. Goes nowhere else." They headed upstairs to Cisco's office.

"The rope connection is clear, but where do we go with it," Cisco said from behind his desk. His excitement for the chase was palpable. "Til now, except for the barbecued body and the arm, we weren't even sure of a Newark connection. The ride to the roasting party could have started anywhere. But now we have the rope, not much but enough to drop this case into our laps."

"This should make Peterson jump with joy," McClosky said. "The Kraut didn't pull any punches that he wanted everything kept under his tent, made it clear our asses are on the line. A fucked-up way to work, but hell, this is Newark."

"Let's get back to that new lead. Fill me in."

"It's a long shot, but it might go somewhere," McClosky said. "It's that Minutemen link we kicked around in Peterson's office. Heard that Solly Castellane has some pretty good boys under his wing at the Newark Athletic

Club, so I stopped by the gym yesterday afternoon to do some sniffing."

Cisco leaned back in his chair and sighed, hopeful that McClosky would curb his ringside bullshit. He feigned annoyance, but with a smile.

"Hoped to find some old Third Ward Jewish pugs hanging out, and I might have hit it lucky. Found one of Nat Arno's bully boys, Sy Rossen, a damn good welterweight with a hammer for a right hand. There was even a time when Tippy avoided him."

"You're amazing. With your cauliflower ear and broken nose stuff," Cisco said. "There's got to be a Minutemen connection here, right?"

"Sy was never shy about his Minutemen head-knocking, and he knew that we knew. Now we have the KKK added to the mix."

"The Klan? I never heard anything about Zwillman and Arno going after the sheets. What's this all about?"

"As Sy tells it, he and six other Minutemen went out to Andover to see what was happening at Camp Nordland back in August 1940. They watched hiding as Klan members waved Stars and Stripes alongside swastikas. Sy and his buddies waited until the sheets came off, in his words, 'low and behold, who was it but Josh Levitz, a Jew in the Klan.'

"I did some homework at the library last night," McClosky shifted his shoulder holster and drew a small notebook from the left inside pocket of his jacket. "Here's the rub, and you talk about some crazy thinking, so I'll spare you most of the goofy details. It seems the Klan blamed the Bund for discrediting Arthur Bell as Grand Giant, which meant he lost control of 60,000 Klan members in Jersey. Josh Levitz was one of Bell's disciples. The Bund did this by orchestrating the Andover meeting, calling in reporters and newsreel cameramen to cover it. Whether high ranking

Klan insiders were in on this doesn't matter, they had gotten what they wanted, almost complete control of the Klan in Jersey. It was so easy, all they did was show the world that Bell had committed treason by sharing a stage with swastika-waving fascists. And it worked."

"Slick, very slick, they certainly knew how to cut each other's throats," Cisco said. "But how the hell does this murky stuff fit in with our case?"

McClosky leafed to another page. "Just last year Sy Rossen ran into Josh Levitz, the first time he'd seen him since the rally five years earlier at Andover. Their meeting started out real bad, almost a punch-out. After things calmed down, he said Levitz didn't back off being a Klansman, that he threw a sheet over his head because of his belief in Bell. Levitz made it clear that he was one of several sheets who had never forgotten what the Bund had done to their lord and master, and we can only speculate what else they had in mind.

"Sy told me it didn't take long for him to realize that Levitz was a crazy son of a bitch, a real nut with blood in his eyes."

"Jesus, this sounds like something straight out of the Spanish Inquisition. Jews, hoods and revenge."

"And we can't prove a damn thing," McClosky said. "But are we really sure that Levitz is a nut? Rossen obviously thinks so."

"Okay, so where do we go from here with what you've gotten out of Sy Rossen, or should we say with what Rossen got out of Levitz? The dots don't seem to connect to our case."

"Let's say we accept revenge. Sy was convinced that Levitz and his Klan cohorts wanted their pound of flesh, but he also felt they were loony."

“If we follow this absurd logic, you’re saying that because a bunch of betrayed Klan nuts can no longer get at the Bund big boys who arranged Bell’s downfall,” Cisco said, “they’re hacking up whatever small fry they can get their hands on? And all of this from a delusional creep mourning the good old days?”

“Look Nick, what do we have right now? We’ve got the most fucked-up case imaginable, and until today not even a hint of where we’re going. Now we have a bloody bundle in butcher wrap downstairs, and as weak as it is, one loon who hates the Bund for helping in the disposal of their Klan messiah.”

“Track down Levitz and find out what he’s been doing the past couple of weeks.” Cisco arose from behind his desk and reached for his jacket. “I need to relax. It’s been a very long day.”

“Heading out towards the park?” McClosky knew the answer but wished that he didn’t. His partner’s silence confirmed the obvious.

CHAPTER

SIXTEEN

It had begun to rain during Cisco's drive, not heavy but more than a drizzle. It was Mother Nature's scorn for Newark, a city that badly needed a cleansing. Sidewalk soot and gutter debris softened and moved alongside the crime, poverty, forced idleness, bored brutality, and post-war greed that flowed so easily from one Ward to another. Cisco had long recognized that this was a city of dark footprints.

He and Kevin, they'd been together for a long time, Cisco thought. He knew their rights of passage were relentlessly stripping them bare. For years they had been seeing too much, and feeling less and less about the empty chaos that sucked them in. When does moral indifference take control? It wasn't easy to keep his mouth shut. He saw it all then looked away. Kevin had also cultivated the same uncomfortable stoicism to what they saw around them. Cops with dirty hands poked into all the dark corners, and no shakedown was too small. The freelance hookers working the Tenderloin, and the penny-ante Third Ward policy runners were easy pickings, no different than Pigeon Pete who pumped out phony gas ration coupons from the back of his Avon Avenue pet shop.

It even got to be too much for the plumber sitting in the mayor's office. When Vincent Murphy decided to take a shot at the Governor's job, cleaning out dirty cops provided a nice ticket. Cisco and McClosky, just by keeping their mouths shut, packed their uniforms away, donned mufti and shoulder holsters, and joined the robbery detail. That was three years ago. Then last year Murphy lost, but the clean-up continued, and the two men found themselves in homicide.

Pick the place, pick the date when it all started, Cisco thought. It was becoming more and more surreal. Was it that night when they were still in uniform, part of the flying squad that had become a plaything of Nat Arno and his Minutemen? They had been called to the Piccadilly Club, when was that the spring of '41? When they arrived at the Tenderloin jazz joint on Peshine, the body of a black man had already been dragged out to the sidewalk. His throat had been cut from ear-to-ear. They checked him out. He was dead alright. They followed the trail of blood to the club's front door. That's where it ended.

"Jesus Christ, you believe this!" said McClosky as the two cops peered at the hastily wiped threshold. "Sliced him inside, then pulling crap like this. Who the hell they fooling? Look here, a splat they missed in the corner. Have to be half-blind to miss it."

"Think they give a damn?" said Cisco as he rose from a crouch and stepped over the body. "Why'd they even bother. This is one of Zwillman's. Got Georgie Haber and Roddy Rodberg running it."

"Just another Tenderloin mystery stiff," McClosky said. With his left foot he nudged a gray fedora with a wide purple ribbon from the middle of the sidewalk to the edge of the bloody pool surrounding the dead man's head. "Had his throat slit while just strolling by, never got inside at all. Now the homicide guys will work magic, and it'll all disappear."

"They're on their way. Let's get inside and hear the bullshit before they arrive."

The meat wagon from the morgue pulled to a stop at the curb. A crowd was forced to make room. Two other squad cars arrived, and blocked off the corner of Waverly and Peshine. Their flashers created a halo effect around the mostly black gaping faces.

Cisco and McClosky stepped inside the club, an eight-sided room with a big bar that enclosed a bandstand. Half of the twenty or so barstools were occupied by men and women, all Negroes except for two white men in full uniform seated at the far end. The dark suits, fancy white-on-white shirts, pearl-center gold cufflinks, black ties, expensive felt snap brim hats, star sapphire pinky rings, and heavy tonnage gold wristwatches failed to modulate the sneers of the young punks.

The two officers exchanged quick glances, surprised to see Richie the Boot Boiardo's boys this far from home. The Tenderloin wasn't Boiardo turf, it belonged to Zwillman. Maybe. Or maybe they were just jazz lovers. Maybe.

The practiced indifference of the patrons as well as the girl, no more than a kid seated at the piano behind the bar, would be grotesque if it were not such a perfect fit. At a time and a place like this, well-seasoned apathy was expected. A big lacquered black man in a dark suit, white shirt, red tie, and toothy smile was waiting.

"Surprise to all of us," he said. "Name's Luther, Luther McGinn. Don't know the man outside at all. Heard some yelling outside, but this little lady had some good piano riffs going, and was singing real sweet so couldn't make out much, none of us could. Ain't that right?"

The big man's words bounced off the back of the heads at the bar. The two punks remained silent, their sneers frozen in place. McGinn didn't expect a reply and didn't get one, only a murmur or two, and a few shoulder shrugs.

"What's your job?" McClosky asked.

"Sort of manage the place when Georgie and Roddy ain't around, like tonight," McGinn said. "They're over in the big city tonight, looking over some new talent."

"If the dead man never came in, how can you say you didn't know him?" Cisco said. "And of course, there's no chance at all he ever stepped inside."

"Nope, no chance at all," McGinn said. "Ain't that right little lady?" A pert, neatly-packed black girl swiveled around from the piano behind the bar to face the three men. She leaned back, rested her elbows on the hinged fall of the upright, and challenged them from beneath a tight white blouse with over-worked buttons.

"Everything in here was about me. See why can't ya," she said. Her broad smile was confident and sassy, devoid of any concern for the bloody stiff outside. The girl's straight hair fell to just above her shoulders, its pomaded brilliance accentuated by an overhead spot whose heat pushed sweat beads across her brow. "Hit me Johnny, can't you see I've got a goddamn nail waiting," the girl had popped a Kool from its pack and motioned the bartender over to give her a light. She inhaled deeply, turned to the cops, and exhaled long and slow, adolescent sophistication at its contemptuous best.

She was pretty, maybe too pretty, Cisco thought, and too goddamned young to be in this hole past midnight. "Okay little lady, need some answers before you start choking."

"Oh Christ, here it comes," she said before taking another deep pull. "I know where that shitty cop's brain of yours is going, so here it is. Name's Sarah, Sarah Singleton, and I know I should be home with my mom and pop. I'm seventeen, and been sitting in here a couple times a week. No pay, just practice."

Cisco and McClosky turned to McGinn, "That right, she's only seventeen?" McClosky said.

"Look fellas, none of this is up to me. You gotta talk to Georgie and Roddy, and like I said, they ain't here tonight. But one thing I can say, there's no money involved here. This sweet little thing just strolls in, plops down during the band's breaks, and gets us all mean and low. She's a good kid. Sings with her mama Ada in the choir at Ebenezer Baptist. Her daddy Jake's got some music in him too, plays a damn mean guitar."

"You go to school?" Cisco asked.

Before the girl could answer, the Piccadilly's door slammed open and two homicides stomped in. "We got it from here. Get your report to me, only to me, no fucking around with it," Sal Mussini said as he and sidekick Stash Shernoski swaggered across the room. Boiardo's boys rated no more than a brief flicker. Even with their Botany 500 duds, Florsheim wingtips and jaunty homburgs, the two detectives were unmistakably thugs. It was the first time Cisco and McClosky had run into them. The two sergeants were the homicide clean-up guys, you need a clean slate, you got the connections, you got it. This was Zwillman's place, enough said.

That corrupt circle jerk five years ago at the Piccadilly came back with a rush as Cisco muscled his unmarked cruiser through foot-deep waters that had backed up at debris-stuffed sewers along South Orange Avenue. Dirty cops, jewel encrusted mobsters, a sliced corpse, and Sarah Singleton, a beautiful young Negro girl who sang sweet and talked dirty. He and McClosky never even ID'd the dead guy, nor attempted to. Not a word anywhere, the system had worked perfectly. Everyone was complicit.

Damn, of all times for that night at the Piccadilly to crop up, Cisco thought, when he was escaping south to Grace and oblivion. But he knew why. It had been one hell of a Wednesday, and he was through with cop stuff for the evening. Switching from the police band, he picked up a medley, first *Body and Soul* followed by *Don't Blame Me*. The throaty contralto was smooth and seductive. Sarah Singleton, now Vaughn, had come a long way. Does she ever give the Piccadilly a passing thought? Cisco doubted it. That night at Peshine and Waverly it was all there, Newark at its worst, and with Sarah, what it could be if it gave itself a chance.

Mussini and Shernoski got theirs in '42 when they beat a Puerto Rican pimp to death while trying to force a false confession. The pimp's girls specialized in high-priced rough trade, and one of them ended up dead in a downtown hotel when a high flyer's chokehold went too far. A phone call here, followed by another over there, and there was no way that the rich trick would take the fall. The two police thugs were spotted as they stepped from an empty Greyhound bus behind the terminal on Market. A few minutes later, a clean-up crew found the pimp's body. Things were changing in the department, and the two goons had become expendable. After a short trial, they were doing life in Trenton, thankful they hadn't been parked in the prison's death row.

By the end of forty-one, the Minutemen were gone and so were the flying squads that performed more like inept boobs in their failed efforts to hang collars on Nat Arno and his Bund-busting Jewish pugs. In 1943, Vincent Murphy decided the mayor's office wasn't big enough and wanted the Governor's job. Police reform was a major plank in his campaign against Walter Edge. He lost, kept his Mayor's job, and was stuck with a police clean-up that had taken on a life of its own. McClosky and Cisco, now a sergeant, were out of uniform and new members of a robbery detail gutted by firings, resignations, early retirements, and grand jury indictments that went nowhere. Homicide and traffic, with its coin-spitting parking meters, were sliced and diced. Most of the big boys resigned, others were fired, and to everyone's surprise there were even a few small-fry convicted.

The early evening rain had picked up by the time Cisco crossed Bergen Street. Continuing on South Orange, he found it difficult to fight off a foreboding he couldn't quite fathom. Damn it, there was just too much to absorb in one day. And to top it off, Sarah's voice wasn't making things easy. Her *Everything I've Got is Yours*, down deep and dirty, and *I've Got A Crush on You* hit him where it hurt.

The rain provided the downbeat for the soft sounds purring from New York's powerful WOR. The station and Sarah shared refugee status. WOR had long ago abandoned Newark and its perch atop the roof of Bamberger's. For Sarah Vaughn, it didn't hurt to have rubbed shoulders with the likes of Billy Eckstein and Dizzy Gillespie along her path to the Billboard charts.

Sarah getting a rare WOR medley recognition like this meant an artist had arrived. Cisco increased the volume to mute the sound of a sudden cloudburst and was greeted by:

I would gladly give the sun to you
If the sun were only mine
I would gladly give this earth to you
And the stars that shine
Everything that I possess
I offer you

The squall ended as abruptly as it began. Cisco was at a loss as to what happened next. Without thinking, he had made an abrupt U-turn, and Ivy Hill Park, Grace De Marco, and that big house on Wilden Place were now behind him. He was on Littleton headed toward 13th Avenue, now a left and there it was again, the Monastery of Saint Dominic's. He couldn't chance a turn onto 10th and pulled to a stop at the corner.

The Margotta two-story, green clapboard house was barely a half-block away. Its big parlor window provided a prism which seemed to probe directly into the front seat of his car. Could Connie be standing there, only inches from the cold glass? He couldn't tell. He hoped for a glimpse of his wife, but the fogged windshield was her co-conspirator. What the hell was going on? His thoughts rattled to a conclusion that made him shiver. Goddamn if he hadn't become the stalker of the woman he loved and disgraced. With this realization he switched on the ignition, shifted into gear, and headed back toward Ivy Hill Park.

CHAPTER
SEVENTEEN

Grace tried unsuccessfully to adjust her sunglasses on that hot August afternoon in 1942 as she drove to her parents' house on Mount Prospect. If she pushed them up on the bridge of her nose, it felt as though her closed left eye was being stabbed by the frame. If she pushed them down her nose, her puffy cheek felt like it would explode under the weight of the frame. The glasses were a gift from her dad, handpicked from the latest shipment of Foster Grants at his optometry shop on Park Avenue. She knew he would be the one to contend with. Mom would cry a lot, pray a lot, but in the end would follow her father's lead. Augustos De Marco would require some work.

Grace loved and admired this man who had made what once seemed hopelessly unattainable possible, a middle-class life for his family. An only child, twelve years old when Augustos took her into his arms, sat her on his knee, something he hadn't done in at least two years, and explained that he would be gone for more than three months. He studied her face intently, searching for any reaction that would make it easier for him to stay in their cramped apartment on 13th Avenue. He mustn't allow even the slightest hint of fear to filter from his eyes and into her consciousness. He and Theresa had been planning this for a year, twelve months that he did without his daily pack of Chesterfields, and Theresa discreetly eliminating almost all "hootie-tootie" spending that included a cutback from three to one Sunday movie matinee a month.

"These are going to be my ticket out of here," Peter Shields said as he tapped a carousel that displayed men's sunglasses and single lens magnifiers fitted into fancy metal frames. They sat on top of a glass case that contained artistically arranged scarves, argyle and silk calf-length socks at one end, and ties and neatly rolled leather belts at the other. Augustos, the all around mister-fix-it at Hahne's Department Store, had just replaced one of the burnt out bulbs in the display case, and was caught up short by the salesman's self-congratulatory words. He didn't like Shields, but what the hell, he might as well listen.

"You're doing okay," he said. "A couple of years ago you were just a floorwalker on the prowl for shoplifters, and now you have a haberdasher's counter all to yourself. That triple-tipped handkerchief sticking out of your pocket looks great. I'd say you're doing just fine."

"I doubt you'll go anywhere with this Gus, but here's a couple of tips for you anyway," Shields said, ignoring the pique displayed by Shields' easy use of the diminutive. Only Augustos' closest friends ever referred to him as Gus, and Shields was definitely not one of them. "First, it's bad eyes, and boy, oh boy, there's plenty of them to go around. Second, it's Philadelphia Optical College, and the magic name is Dr. Christian Henry Brown. Get yourself a copy of *Black Mask*, ignore all the murder and mayhem, and go to the inside of the back cover, you'll see what I'm talking about. I just finished the course and am about to get going."

Like every other day at quitting time, Gus retrieved his time card from its assigned slot on the wall, joined a long line of hourly workers shuffling toward the time clock, punched his card, and then inserted it into another assigned slot on his way to the employee's exit. The following morning the routine would be reversed. Out on Broad Street, he crossed to Military Park to catch the northbound Public Service No. 29 electric trolley from the lower level terminal. The passenger platform was dominated by a newsstand that offered a haphazard array of magazines and newspapers. He poked around until he found *Black Mask* among the pulp fiction crime and mystery offerings. He was lucky to find a seat on the already crowded trolley, sat down, and immediately turned to the inside back cover.

There he was, Christian Henry Brown, M.D., the prophet of refractive optometry. By simply mailing in five cents to Dr. Brown's Philadelphia Optical College, 400 Perry Building, Philadelphia, Pennsylvania, Gus could learn all that the college offered, including "knowledge of anatomy and physiology of the eye" and how to "detect and correct its refractive and muscular anomalies." There were six month, three month, a one month crash course, and post-graduate residence programs, as well as enticing correspondence courses that put thousands of graduates on the road to middle-class comfort. Gus sent in his nickel, studied the school's prospectus, and opted for the three-month residency program that included a "dispensary for practical experience."

Gus shared a two-room tenement apartment with three other students, ate one meal a day, and shamelessly indulged himself with a rich, sugar laden espresso every evening. He was fascinated by everything in the school's dispensary, the polished lens-cutting and frame-shaping instruments, and the eye-testing equipment were never-ending sources of wonderment.

After three months and three days, and armed with a Philadelphia Optical College diploma, and volumes 1 and 2 of Dr. Brown's Optician's Manual, Gus presented himself at the Newark office of the New Jersey State Optical and Optimetrical Society. A skeptical Joseph Salov, the Society's Registrar, scanned Gus' limited credentials, and was surprised to find that instead of one of those laughable correspondence courses, this nervous supplicant had hands-on training as both oculist and optometrist, and acquitted himself very well when asked some tough questions. Salov liked what he saw, and uncharacteristically decided to take a chance.

"What is your age Mr. De Marco?"

"I am thirty-three, sir."

"Do you consider yourself to be a little old to get started in a new, very demanding profession?"

"No sir, I don't. I decidely don't," Gus said measuring every word because he knew that this would be his one and only shot. Fate was a quirky thing, and one wrong word today could doom him.

"Did you finish high school?"

This was the opportunity Gus was looking for, and he was going to give it everything he had. "Yes sir, I did. Barringer, class of '08, college preparatory. Two years of Latin and two years of German." He figured these had to be excellent selling points. Most of the instruments in Dr. Brown's dispensary were etched with German trademarks, and the textbooks contained many Latin phrases.

Salov smiled indulgently. "I believe we've covered what I wanted to know. If you'll bear with me and give me two days, until Wednesday, we can talk again, same time Wednesday, agreed?" Gus was sweating, and he hoped Salov would not offer to shake his hand. A soggy hand could be as deadly as a poorly-worded response. Salov remained seated as Gus got up.

"Yes sir, right here, same time Wednesday."

Two days later Gus found Salov where he had left him. Only this time he was joined by a short, pink-cheeked plump man in a blue pinstripe suit. He was standing to the left of Salov's desk with, surprisingly enough, his hand extended.

"So, Mr. De Marco, are you ready to get started? If so, then let me introduce myself, H.C. Aurnhammer. You have impressed Mr. Salov and he has asked me to, if I may say so, look you over. Sit down, sit down, get yourself comfortable."

It only lasted about twenty minutes, a polite inquisition during which Gus parried question after question, a great number of which he thought were rather personal. Aurnhammer wanted to know if he was married? Yes. If he had any children? Yes. How many? One. Very good, boy or girl? Girl. Her name? Grace. How old? Twelve. What was his wife's name? Theresa. Lovely name. And your neighborhood? North Ward, 13th Avenue. Your church? Our Lady of Good Counsel. Smoke? Yes. A drink every now and then? Mostly wine. You're Italian, read it, write it, and of course speak it? Yes, all of it.

As requested, Gus stepped out to the hall, and in a few minutes was called back in to be greeted by Aurnhammer and Salov standing with extended hands and smiles. "How does thirty-five dollars a week sound? There will be public contact, of course, but it should come easy for you," Aurnhammer said. "They will be your people, a comfortable fit, wouldn't you say?"

So there it was, Augustos De Marco was about to become the token wop for a plump little German, who with true Roaring Twenties rectitude, reached out for clients once held in contempt. Gus swallowed his pride, compiled a fat customer list that started with Sergio Antonioni, indexed through Scipio Broglio, Franco Manza, Victorio Trippi to Joseph Zippano. Families were constantly added, and after three years he had collected enough to walk away from H.C. Aurnhammer's without a backward glance.

The next day he walked into the recently opened Broad National Bank on Franklin Street, sat down with a loan officer, pulled out a velvet bag from his inside jacket pocket containing Theresa's family jewels along with an appraisal from Bessmer Jewelers, and in two weeks opened his business on Park Avenue. There was enough space for expansion and the green, white and red border that embellished the large front window left little doubt who the owner was even before your eyes caught:

Augustos De Marco
Optometrist and Optician
Refraction Specialist

Hours
Monday-Thursday 9:00 a.m. to 6:00 p.m.
Friday 9:00 a.m. to 8:00 p.m.
Saturday 9:00 a.m. to 1:00 p.m.

Appointments call MA-6391

Year after year Grace witnessed her father's ever-expanding miraculous world take shape. Since she was a toddler, she and her mom and dad would jump aboard Jimmy Falco's flatbed delivery truck to join Jimmy, his wife Mary, their son and three daughters, along with boxes of kitchen utensils and beach articles, for a two-hour bumpy ride to Keansburg. By pooling their meager vacation funds, the two families were able to afford one of the four-room bungalows that lined the shore of the tiny resort.

The summer before Grace's senior year at Our Lady of Good Counsel marked the fourth July in a row that Augustos De Marco, the refraction specialist, drove his family to Penn Station in his 1925 Oldsmobile Roadster. The car's $890 price was haggled down to $745 when Cosimo Lopinto, a kindred spirit at Bannion's Motors, waived his commission for six pairs of glasses for his family. He put Theresa and Grace aboard a New York and Long Branch Railroad commuter train for a cushioned ride to Asbury Park. Awaiting them was a four-room beach cottage, complete with kitchen, hot and cold running water, indoor bath, outdoor shower, and a wooden walkway to the surf. They stayed a month, with Gus joining them each Saturday afternoon and leaving on the first train out Monday morning.

How crazy is this, Grace thought as she drove to her parents' home for the confrontation she would have with her father. Instead of rehearsing, she found herself counting year-by-year all that had been made possible by the gentle man now awaiting her. He was also a man constricted by inherited values from the Old Country, that once in place were never questioned. A husband has his rights. A woman knows her place. A husband does not strike his wife without a reason. What would she say? She could offer no explanation, there wasn't one.

CHAPTER EIGHTEEN

The thirteen years since high school were an incoherent collection of the improbable. She almost had to browbeat Sister Ann Louise, her high school principal, into forwarding a transcript of her grades to New Jersey College for Women. A place the good sister considered a godless Babylon with sacrilegious feminist ideas. Grace collected skimpy scholarships from the NJC Associates Alumnae and Federation of Women's Club, but it was the cash from her father that made four years of college possible without a part-time job. Armed with a political science degree, she marched into Essex County Courthouse, and settled into a filing clerk's job that hardly paid her car fare. The files, now that was something else again, they were the beginning of her real education.

Grace pulled her car to the curb in front of her parents' home. Her father spotted her while she was still a half-block away, and was waiting for her on the front porch. She slid to the passenger side of the front seat, retrieved her purse from the floor, opened the door, and stepped out to the sidewalk. This was purposeful. She was not going to emerge on the street side, and expose herself any more than necessary. If seen by the neighbors, tongues would wag, and she did not want her parents to unwittingly share her shame and humiliation.

"Dad, don't look at me, not yet. Just back up, open the door, and let me inside, quick. Get my stuff from the car, casual like it's no big thing."

Grace climbed the steps, crossed the porch, and her father stepped aside as he silently held the door. She could feel her father's eyes boring through her tinted glasses to the carnage they had failed so miserably to conceal. For the first time, she realized she was about to begin a life she could not have imagined only hours before.

Grace was three steps inside the parlor when she decided it was as good a time as any to get it over with. She dropped her purse, removed her glasses, and faced her mother who was standing next to her beloved Queen Anne in the center of the room. Theresa De Marco's face had never been designed to handle the emotions that were about to erupt. She was a strong woman not given to tears. It was a mother's ruse that had established her as the family matriarch. The stabbing reality of this moment, fleeting yet eternal, pried open the floodgates.

"My God, oh my God, oh my dearest Jesus, what has happened to you?" Theresa sobbed, fought for air, failed, and as her knees weakened and dizziness set in, she grabbed for the back of the Queen Anne. She came away with only a fistful of doily, and with no support her knees began to buckle. By this time Grace had raced to within two feet of her mother, and was just in time to grab her under the arms and hold her upright. Theresa's head fell forward, and slammed into the left side of her daugher's face. The pain was excruciating. Grace stifled the urge to scream, instead words emerged from a deep recess, "Oh my God, mother, what has he done to both of us?"

Gus, who had been only a few steps behind Grace, was now beside his daughter. Each taking an arm, they lowered Theresa into the chair. Grace ignored her pain, and for the first time peered into her mother's eyes. The sadness and fear they conveyed was overwhelming. Grace turned from her mother in an effort to keep it all inside, she would not cry. That bastard wasn't worth her tears.

"Where did this accident happen?" Gus asked. "I checked the car, not a dent, not so much as a scratch. Have you seen a doctor?"

"Dad, it wasn't an accident." Grace felt her mother's hands tighten around each of her wrists, without a word Theresa conveyed quite clearly that she knew.

"Not an accident? Then what was it? What did this to you?" It was impossible for Gus to believe that anyone would hurt his precious daughter. Her auburn hair, misty dark eyes, delicately formed features and warm smile made her inviolable. She had inherited her mother's figure, firm, athletic and reaching to a height just above Gus's shoulders. John Fusina was a lucky man.

"It was John."

"John! Your husband John, your husband did this to you?"

"Yes, it was John. Don't ask me why, I don't know. And, no, I won't see a doctor."

"There had to be a reason. Johnny would never do this without a reason. Tell me he is not an animal. Damn it, he's a dentist, a successful dentist. The Fusinas are the biggest, most successful dentist family in the city. There had to be a reason, he's a good man. He has honor and he is truthful."

"Truth! Honor!" Grace's left cheek had swollen to where every word was painful. She was forced to spit each of them out the right side of her mouth past swollen, drooling lips. She had to get it all out now, while everything was right here in front of them. "Papa, let's talk about honor."

Papa? Where did that come from? Since her senior year in high school, Augustos had been dad, and not the papa of her childhood on Thirteenth Avenue. Grace's four years at NJC had permanently severed the old from the new. Perhaps now only a return to the old would make him understand. She glanced at her mother, and saw immediately that her mama understood that an entire family had been wounded and possibly scarred forever.

"Papa, my engagement ring, tell me where did it come from?"

"From Johnny, of course. It was the most beautiful to behold. Not because of its size, it was its beauty."

"Papa, try to understand. Tell me where did my honorable husband get the ring?"

"I know, and why do you ask a silly, stupid question like that? We all know. It was Johnny, his family and their contacts that put that ring on your finger. That thing of beauty."

"Papa, damn it, papa, please tell me where did my engagement ring come from!" It was the first time Grace had ever spoken to her father this way, but he had to understand the break she was making. Gus was stunned. He groped for an answer, but came up short, the abyss between young and old was too profound, too wide.

"It came from Vittorio's Castle. From the mafia. Straight out of the safe in Richie the Boot Boiardo's office. I was there papa. I saw it all. I was a kid, two years out of college, and I was staring at power. Real power. It might have been the mob, but it was real power. But was it honest, hell no it wasn't. When I saw that strongbox crammed with stolen jewelry, do you think I gave a damn? Hell no."

"Johnny told us how they treated you like a queen," a bewildered Gus said. "Ruggiero and his son Antonio had the best table in the restaurant waiting, and how after the meal they escorted you into the office to take your pick.

'Take the best, only the best for this beautiful lady who will soon be a member of the Fusina family,' is what Ruggiero said, and he said it directly to you."

"Do you want to know why? It took me awhile to sort it out, but here it is. I married into three generations of losers, whose integrity was measured in gamblers' chits. The Fusinas, grandfather, father and son owe their asses to the mob."

"What are you telling us, that Johnny, no not just Johnny, the whole family is owned by the mob? And your ring, don't ever be ashamed of it. Say what you want about Johnny, but he was in good company when he brought you to Vittorio's Castle. You know that Joe DiMaggio, the Yankee Clipper, selected the diamond for his wife's ring in that very same office."

It was Grace's turn to be stunned. This dear man, who at this moment she couldn't love more, found it incapable to accept betrayal of his daughter on any level. She turned to her mother, and was met by the silent stare of a confused woman clearly unable to speak. Grace realized this was her only chance to make it all clear to them regardless of the pain she would inflict.

"Truthfulness. You want truth? Now I want you to take a look at what truth is to John Fusina, my husband of seven years, the man who gave me what you see here today. And now you'll see some more."

Grace spun from where she had been standing in front of her shocked parents, her mother on the Queen Anne, her father scrunched uncomfortably on an ottoman. She retrieved her purse from the floor behind her. Grace turned, strode to a nearby sofa, pulled over the smallest of three nesting tables, and positioned it in front of her parents.

"The truth, you want to know John Fusina's brand of truth," she said, "here, I'll show it to you."

Kneeling in front of her parents, Grace placed her purse on the small mahogany table, loosened the clutch, reached inside and began searching the contents. She pulled out a purple velvet ring box, placed her purse on the floor, and with an angry flourish slammed the ring box onto the table.

"My ring, that object of beauty, that symbol of all the love that John Fusina had for me, well here papa, and here mama let me show it to you."

She snapped opened the ring box with her thumb, raised it to eye level and overturned its contents onto the table. The shiny dust and tiny particles spread like blowing sand across the inlaid leather top. "Paste, fucking paste. I'm sorry papa. I'm sorry mama. But here's that precious object of beauty, a fake, a goddamn fake." Grace had never been a profane woman, but for the second time today, the obscenities flowed beyond her control.

"But I saw the ring, and yes I'm not a diamond expert, but I know the real thing when I see it," said Gus at the same time reaching forward to squeeze two or three of the larger fragments between his right thumb and forefinger. "No, there is no way that this is what I saw when you and Johnny, so in love, so excited, raced from Vittorio's to show off the diamond."

"Stop it! Don't touch anything! I don't want you part of this!" Grace would not allow the contaminant that she had exposed infect her parents. "Yes, papa, the diamond you saw was real, real and worth a fortune, enough money to bring my husband to his knees and cry like a baby." Grace realized the cut would have to be deep. God forgive her, she wanted the hatred she had for her husband to be shared by her parents.

Theresa had never seen her daughter like this, nor could she have ever imagined that the horror unfolding before her could have been possible. She was transfixed by what she saw and heard, "*Mia carissima figlia, dove sei andato? Dimmi si tornerà di nuovo a noi.*"

"No mama, the daughter you knew will never be coming back to you again." Grace reached forward, and with her left index finger made a big circle in the debris on the table. "Today ends it all, my denial that my marriage was as big a fake as this circle in the dust. And you papa, you talk about truthfulness. I'll tell you how I found Fusina-style truth."

By this time Grace was coping with the pain that pulsated through the left side of her face and into her neck. What she was about to say would take some thought. She got up from her knees, and then settled on the floor with her legs crossed in front of her. No matter how hard she tried, Grace's memory of the day her love turned to contempt could never be erased. Today she was hiding nothing.

"It was an accident, an accident by me. We were invited to dinner, I forget who invited us, that's not important, but it was a big deal at Vittorio's Castle. So John naturally wanted me to wear something flashy, my engagement ring included. This was three years ago. I was doing serious spring cleaning, and had stored the ring in our bedroom safe. John and I were dressed for the evening, and the only thing left was to get the ring. I was about to put it on, but it slipped from my fingers and fell to the floor, that's when I accidentally stepped on it, and it shattered. John was downstairs ready to go. I called him upstairs to the bedroom and I let him have it.

"Am I going to believe this, should I believe this, the ring you gave me is a phony!" I didn't hold back. That night at Vittorio's Castle, it was like I was getting the crown jewels, mafia style of course, with Ruggiero and Antonio telling us that any queen would envy this diamond in her crown. What everyone said was the perfect stone somehow turned into paste. "Talk to me Johnny, how did it happen?"

"No, it's not possible. It was flawless, you heard them, you picked it out," John said. "They never screwed anybody. It was among friends. Big money was involved, my dad had to help me out. We knew them all. Can't say we were like family, but Jesus Christ, we were their dentists. Their wives, all of them in the family, got their crowns from us, and their kids got their braces. Now wait a minute, let me think. Maybe that's it, we were not family, just fixed their teeth."

"Are you saying they foisted off a phony diamond because you and your family weren't thugs like them? Is that what you're saying?"

"That's gotta be it. What else could it be?"

"Damn it, damn it! It can't end here like this. I won't let it. We'll be at Vittorio's tonight, and I'll get some answers," Grace said, her voice barely in control. "I'll run down Antonio, pin him to the wall if I have to, but I'll get an answer tonight. You can bet your ass on that."

"No, no, please don't do that," John pleaded. "Back off, you have to back off. You don't know what these guys are capable of."

"Back off, hell I will. What will Tony and Richie the Boot do to me? Probably laugh me off as an ignorant broad, but I'm going to get an answer tonight. I don't know what it'll be or what I'll do with it, but they won't ignore me."

"I beg you Grace, don't say a word. Back off, if you love me, you'll back off. It's me to blame, not them."

"What are you telling me, what the hell are you telling me?" Grace demanded. "What do you mean it's you and not the Boiardos?"

"I got in too deep. You know I gamble. I never told you how much. They figured me as a chip off the Fusina family block," John was crying now. "They wouldn't wait, and there was no way I could stiff them. Our mortgage was a no go. My parents co-signed on the note so there was no money there. Your ring was the only place I could find the cash."

"So you let your markers slide, is that what you're telling me?"

"Markers, you know about markers?" John's evident surprise raised Grace's anger to the boiling point.

"John, look at me, this is Newark, everyone knows some sap who swallowed his marker the hard way when he couldn't come up with the vigorish. Lift your goddamned eyes, and look at me and tell me that you couldn't even come up with the vigorish?"

"I was strapped, tied up so tight I was choking."

"So you became a sneak thief. Then what, don't tell me you took my ring to one of those sleazy pawn shops on Market, don't tell me that. I want to know everything, what you paid the Boiardos, how big a loser you are, and what you got for my ring."

"A couple phone calls and I got my contact, a heavy duty dealer in Bloomfield who could move just about anything."

She couldn't believe it, her husband was crying and bragging at the same time, and again she lost it. "I don't give a fuck about your contact! I want to know what you paid for my ring, how much your sorry ass was in hock for, and what you got for it."

"Twelve thousand dollars. A great price, a price only an insider gets."

"Johnny, Johnny, you're just not getting it. I don't want an act of contrition, or how many hidden angels you have in the closet, I just want to know the price tag of our marriage."

John gave up any pretense, and in a low voice unwrapped his package of guilt. "I've been hiding this from you for more than a year. They didn't say they'd break my legs or anything like that, but they wanted their seven thousand dollars. I got sixty-five hundred dollars, the best I could get anywhere, the other five hundred came from our savings."

Grace and John never left the bedroom that night, and would never again return to Vittorio's Castle. They sat for hours on the bed. Between sobs and sniffles, John begged for forgiveness. Grace could never fully understand what happened next, she forgave him. But she did know, didn't she, it was the sex. That night a weak man's sobs turned into commands she obeyed.

There, it was over, mama and papa had heard it all. They had been a silent study in disbelief. Grace had inflicted wounds from which she knew her parents would never fully recover. Augustos's face came to life. Grace had never seen it like this before. He arose from the ottoman, stretched his aching back, and peered deeply into Grace's one good eye. With it she saw hatred pulsating from the kind man standing over her. He reached down, gently stroked her right cheek, and walked to the parlor window where he stood silently rocking back and forth.

Without turning, and with a voice loud and distinct, he said, "*Lo ucciderò. Ucciderò il miserabile* son of a bitch. *Per questo cane di un uomo c'è solo una risposta!*"

Grace arose, walked to the window, and put her right arm around her father as they watched the late Sunday afternoon traffic on Mount Prospect, "No papa, no one is going to kill John, but believe me he is going to pay. Now let's get your Brownie Hawkeye and take some photos. It will be hard for you, but I'll want lots of them. I have plans. You and mama will not be part of them. Be convinced I will suck him dry."

CHAPTER NINETEEN

Her parents' home was Grace's hideout for three weeks, a busy time during which she took almost sole possession of the family telephone. She adroitly pulled the necessary strings at the Courthouse. She had a lot of sick leave coming, and for good measure added a week of long overdue vacation time. This gave her a month off. But early on she decided to cut the month short returning in three weeks. Her boss liked this kind of dedication, and Grace made sure he knew about it. Grace knew she needed another place to stay. She hinted from the beginning, she would be leaving when her face healed. There was opposition, of course, but Gus and Theresa eventually understood that their daughter had to rebuild her life. They knew they could not assuage her demons for her, this was best done alone.

Margot Schulman had been sharing weekly lunches with Grace for more than a year, and was looking forward to the special lunch they were planning for Labor Day Friday, when she got a surprise call from her former Jameson Hall roommate. If there was any truth to the bromide that opposites attract, then Grace and Margot supplied the punctuation mark. Margot was a discrete, unabashed lesbian, and Grace was an acknowledged virgin who in her senior year at NJC finally found her dream lover in John Fusina.

“Hi, Margot, here’s your roomie again. Have you got a few minutes?”

“Grace, is that you? You’re dribbling your words so bad I’ve checked my ear to see if it’s wet,” macabre humor was Margot’s stock-in-trade. “Booze or a shot of novocaine? Either way’s okay. Booze, I’m jealous. The big horse needle, I’m sympathetic.”

“It’s neither one. You think it’s bad now, you should have heard me Sunday night. I’ll explain all that later, but for now I’m calling off our lunch for this Friday.”

“Sunday night? It was either a kick-ass party or a bad idea. Do you want to talk about it?”

“Not right now, my jaw hurts like hell, so I’ll get right to it. Still have a spare bedroom at your place? If so, I want it. How about in three or four weeks? I think I’ll be staying awhile.”

“Sure, I’ve got a bedroom to spare, completely furnished. I’m sure you understand the ground rules, and who my friends are. Can you live with that?”

“Is that a trick question? We’ve always been comfortable with who we are, I wouldn’t have called otherwise if I thought I’d be moving into a Sapphic pleasure palace.”

“Nasty, nasty,” Margot jokingly chastised, in an attempt to mask her growing concern. Grace’s speech had become increasingly slurred. “Okay roomie, let’s call it quits for now. We’ll talk soon, and you’ll let me know when you’re ready.”

Margot replaced the phone on its stand and being nosy by nature marveled at her restraint. Was it a loss for words? She knew something was wrong, and most likely messy to boot. Theirs was a thirteen-year friendship that overrode sexual nuances and never pulled any punches. Margot would reluctantly wait for Grace’s next call knowing that her concern could turn to frenzy until she finally knew what the hell was going on.

One week later, with Margot on the back burner, Grace made another phone call.

"Law Office of Chester Bruno. Can I help you?" The woman's voice was youthful, soft and melodic, and Grace could picture an attractive, super-efficient woman at the other end.

"Yes, I would like to talk to Mr. Bruno, this is Grace De Marco Fusina. He knows who I am." It took less than a minute for the call to be put through.

"Grace, this is a surprise. What can I do for the one shining light in an otherwise drab Court Clerk's office?"

"I want to talk to you about a divorce, my divorce."

"Divorce? Are you telling me that you're thinking of dumping John Fusina, the youngest of the three drilling demons? Or is it the other way around?"

"I'm doing the dumping, and I want the hole to be as deep as you can make it. I want to get going on it right away."

"Have you taken a deep breath, maybe two or three, about this? You'll be tackling not only Johnny, but the entire family. Been married quite a while. I remember the two big Sunday spreads, big news. First your engagement, and then the wedding and honeymoon -- Rome, Naples and Capri, right?"

"I want a divorce, and I'm going to get it on my terms. And I want you to get it for me."

Bruno took the phone from his ear, placed it on his lap, leaned back in his padded desk chair for the five inches it would allow, took a deep breath and picked up the phone. "First, I'm a criminal attorney, not family law. Next, let's look at the lay of the land. You're an Italian woman married to an Italian man, who's a member of a well-known and powerful Italian family. A divorce from your end is *proibito da Dio e l'uomo,* it's just not done. Are you really sure about this?"

“I know who you are, and I know what I want, a cut-throat who goes for the jugular.”

“Very tactful, I like that. This is a departure that could be troublesome, but at the same time a lot of fun,” Bruno said. “I’ll need more before I take you on.”

“I’ll not only tell you, I’ll show you,” Grace said. “Let’s just say that right now I’m indisposed and you’ll have to come here to my parents’ house on Mount Prospect, the sooner the better, because if you want grounds for divorce, some of it is disappearing faster than I thought.”

Her parents home on Mount Prospect? So this is well on its way, Bruno thought, she’s made up her mind. He remembered the two parties he had attended at the pretentious Italian Renaissance mansion on Wilden Place. She’s moved out.

“It’s two o’clock. I’ll turn you over to my secretary, give her the address and your phone number, and I’ll clear up this mess on my desk. I’ll see you in about an hour.”

Grace greeted Bruno at the front door with a stiff smile, exposing only the right side of her face. He stepped over the threshold and extended his hand when she turned full face to expose everything. The swelling was just about gone, but the purple, yellow and black bruising remained. Bruno startled and speechless pulled back his hand, and left it dangling awkwardly between them. He recovered his voice and said, “Don’t say anything now, let’s get inside.”

Grace’s father was still at work, and she had alerted her mother that Bruno was on his way. Theresa decided to do some grocery shopping, and dutifully disappeared after leaving a pot of fresh brewed coffee. It required less than an hour for Bruno to absorb everything. This included the exhibits, six close-up photos of Grace’s battered face, and the ring box with its dusty particles. The timeline for the beating was set between the departure of the *Evening*

Clarion photography team that left John and Grace alone in their Wilden Place home, and Grace's arrival at her parents' place.

"Okay, I'll take the case. You know you'll be a pariah, the Fusinas will make sure of that. I can win, but how ugly do you want it?"

Grace's left eye was still partially closed, but wide enough to join her good one in what Bruno thought was the most hate-filled gaze he had ever encountered. "I know your reputation. I know who some of your clients are, and I know how you go for the throat. I mean this as a compliment, and that's why we're sitting here. Money? I have enough for a retainer and that's it. We are going to pick the Fusinas clean, court costs and most of all that Renaissance monstrosity on Wilden. I hate it now, but when I get it, loving it will come easy."

"That's it, that's the settlement you're looking for? I'll get it for you."

"No, not quite, the rest is in the details. To start with, I want my De Marco family name back," Grace dabbed at the spit that bubbled in the corner of her mouth, while silently cursing the embarrassment of Bruno's relentlessly probing eyes. "Let's cut to the chase. When it's over, I'm talking John Fusina's castration."

Bruno, whose combative sneer was legendary, smiled disarmingly. This could be fun. "Bragging? Of course I am. You and I both know I'm the only mouthpiece in town who'll get you what you want. Now I want something from you to close this part of the deal."

"I'm listening."

"Insider's information, discreet and legal, of course."

It was clear to Grace that her calculations were correct. This was the right guy to handle her case. There was no mistaking Bruno's ruthless ambition, it oozed from every pore. It would be up to her to decide the difference between discreet and illegal because she had little doubt that Bruno saw no difference between the two.

"From what I hear about the way you're moving onward and upward in the Clerk's office, you'll be in just the right spot to get what I need. Nothing illegal, you understand," Bruno's smile widened disingenuously. He didn't give a fiddler's fart whether the inside stuff was legal or not, he just wanted it.

"I'm taking these photos and this," the attorney said as he placed the photos in his inside jacket pocket. He lifted the ring box from the table, and with the thumb and forefinger of each hand, raised it to where it formed a pedestal over which his and Grace's eyes locked. Grace saw in Bruno's gaze the callous pursuit of power. She wondered what he saw, and was uncomfortable with the possibilities.

The attorney figured it would take no more than five phone calls to get the job done. The Bloomfield fence, the phony ring craftsman, and the jeweler who reset the stone were well known. With them in place, the fourth call would be a simple denouement describing how John Fusina's actions were a direct affront to mob pride. Retribution was clearly in order. The fifth phone call would be made to John Fusina, and it would not be made by Bruno.

The attorney got up, rekindled the creases in his expensive slacks with a few tugs, straightened the Windsor knot of his burgundy silk tie, buttoned his Harris tweed sports coat and smiled down at Grace, "Please, stay put, I'll find my way out. This should move along very fast. This is what you want, correct?"

During the past few years Grace had often traded wisecracks with the attorney when he was nosing around the Courthouse, and with her new-found confidence couldn't resist another one. "Chester, and I assume from now on

I can call you Chester, I'm surprised a smart guy like you would belabor the obvious at a time like this."

Bruno turned, and after a self-mocking grimace and shrug of his shoulders, headed to the front door. At the door, he turned back to the still seated Grace and said, "My law clerk will need some information from you for our filing. You can expect his call tomorrow."

Grace hadn't seen Nick since last Thursday, six long days ago and she missed him. His new duties as acting homicide chief were demanding more and more of his time. Today it didn't help that he had his dreaded counseling session with Connie. He needed his promotion to be permanent, strong affirmation that he was succeeding in a profession that he could barely endure.

She remembered the time she and Nick exchanged their first words. It was over some paperwork back in October of '43, a penny-ante burglary that Cisco and his sidekick, Kevin McClosky, were handling. Her divorce was not yet final and living with a precocious lesbian roommate didn't make things easier. She appreciated how Margot Schulman reached out to help, all the time working hard to mask a latent desire that each of them traced back to their first year as Jameson Hall roommates. Grace marveled at how many times they had come so close, when a push from either one of them would have done it.

John Fusina had been her only sexual partner. At first reluctantly, then with acquiescence, and finally with complete submission and abandon, she had accepted her husband's domination. Margot wanted to know it all, and after two months of gentle probing, she got it.

"And you enjoyed all that stuff, the slapping around, hair pulling and biting?" After a silent, nodding yes, Margot lost it, "How fucked up was that! You mean all along this was happening! The son of a bitch had that much control?"

Grace was amazed that a woman as strong as Margot could become so distraught. It was painful to watch and she was causing the pain. "I'm sorry, I'm sorry. Not for what I did with Johnny, because goddamn it, I enjoyed it. I'm sorry how learning about it has affected you. This is it, the only time we'll discuss it."

They were seated at opposite ends of a richly brocaded davenport. Grace reached across with both arms fully extended. Margot sat mute and motionless at the other end, clearly drained by her emotional outburst. Grace inched across the cushions and gently took hold of Margot's hands. She lifted them, pressed the palms together, and clasped them with all the strength she could summon. Their eyes bridged the gulf of silence, while clearly defining a love beyond resolution.

A month later, Margot was blithely recovering from a short-lived romance with a statuesque, dark haired woman introduced to Grace simply as Jennifer. "She was a bitch anyway, and you know when I took a close look, she wasn't that good looking. You met her a few times. You agree, don't you?"

"No, not really. As I recall, Jennifer had a lot going for her. You had to see something, discriminating bitch that you are."

"Weakness, just weakness on my part, how else can I explain it," Margot said. "It's over now, I have to move on. I've got an invite to a holiday party in Greenwich Village Monday night, it should be interesting, what do you say? And don't worry, I'll protect you."

CHAPTER TWENTY

Margot, a long-time denizen of Greenwich Village, parked her Nash at the west edge of Washington Square, got out, stretched her arms over her head, and inflated her red satin holiday dress with two deep breaths. “This will be fun, and for you, young lady, a journey of discovery.” She grabbed a matching shawl from the back seat, and slammed the door as Grace waited on the curb side of the car. She wore a green velvet, bow-necked sheath, black snake heels, and carried a small black clutch.

“It’s on West 10th, three blocks up and over,” Margot said as they strode north among holiday revelers searching for their party destinations.

The apartment fit in well among a row of buildings glued together with hard cash, lots of it. A doorman in full livery ushered them through a marbled lobby to the elevator where he pushed number five. The art deco doors slowly opened to reveal a tall and fashionably thin, dark haired man stepping forward to greet them like friends who had been strangers for too long. He withdrew his hand from the pocket of a well-tailored, dark blue pinstriped suit, “And, of course, you are....” With Margot taking the lead, they continued the game and threw out their names as if their last meeting with their obvious host had been aboard a yacht in Portofino. “Yes, yes, and you’re friends of....”

"Wally and Chrissy."

"The Steinmans were absolutely correct. You're both lovely." He gestured them toward the large double-door entrance that opened to a high ceiling room big enough to provide a family size badminton court.

"His voice, it's really familiar. I take it he's the host," Grace said as they entered the room, and began searching for Wally and Chrissy Steinman among the more than twenty guests already there.

"That's John Winthrop, the golden voice of radio news. Elegant son of a bitch isn't he," Margot hissed. "If his friend is here tonight, you'll see the closest thing to a matched set you'll find anywhere."

Wally and Chrissy, husband and wife celebrity decorators, were holding court in front of a large window angled toward Fifth Avenue. Four young men were getting free insiders advice, valuable enough to be minted. Margot met the Steinmans at a party a few years earlier just after taking over as designer and decorator for Bamberger's. A warm professional friendship had developed.

Three young, well-scrubbed guys in white shirts and black bow ties circulated with trays of champagne and canapés. Introductions were held to a minimum. This was not a gathering of strangers. Grace wasn't keeping count, but spotted at least four female headliners from Broadway and Hollywood circulating through friendly territory.

"I think it will start in about five minutes or so," Margot said. "Let's stake out a couple chairs, over there by the window should be pretty good."

Grace noticed that the two service tables had been removed from the center of the room clearing a rectangle bordered by French provincial chairs and sofas. The crystal chandelier had gone dark, and the only light was provided by sconces on three walls. Earlier John Winthrop was joined by a man who, as Margot had described, made them a matched set. While the guests silently selected their seats, he left Winthrop where they had been standing next to the fireplace, and motioned two of the bow-tied young men toward the center of the room. They brought over a dark blue, satin quilt and laid it over the terrazzo inlaid floor.

Entering on cue less than a minute later, two women emerged from a door hand-in-hand and walked to the center of the quilt. They wore loose kimono style robes. They were barefoot. The shorter one was blonde, and the younger of the two. The brunette was perhaps twenty-eight years old. Both were fair skinned and beautiful. The blonde affected haughty indifference as she looked past her partner toward the window, and directly at Grace and Margot. Her partner reached out with her right hand and stroked her cheek, gently grasped her chin then turned her head for an expected kiss. Grace knew it was rehearsed, but was still breathless in anticipation. The kiss was long and deep. The brunette was clearly taking control. She untied the silk belt of her partner's kimono which was then shrugged to the floor by the blonde. Her naked body was flawless, thin and softly muscular. With only a nod, the brunette commanded her partner to the floor. She removed her kimono, and with practiced insouciance gracefully dropped into a position where every inch of the blonde's body was available to her.

First there was another deep kiss, the brunette's lips and tongue were insatiable. Then came the neck. The blonde's breasts and nipples provided ravenous delight. The moans were at first discreet, but slowly became unrestrained as the performance progressed. They explored everything, their entire bodies were open for discovery. Watching their eyes and assenting smiles, Grace could see that every move, every probing gesture was done with sweet consent. For thirty minutes, two beautiful women gave a show that left no doubt that this was more than performance art, it was an outreach by lovers inviting privileged onlookers to share in their world.

The tenderness, damn, where did that come from, Grace thought. Seven years with John Fusina had created a sexual universe totally alien to what she was witnessing. The unblemished beauty of the two women as they sprawled, turned, twisted, kissed and incessantly probed everything, leaving nothing to chance had deeply embedded an image that Grace knew she would never forget. When the performance was over, the two women replaced their kimonos and silently walked through the door from which they had emerged. With their departure, Grace inexplicably felt both empty and exhilarated.

None of the guests lingered after the show. Margot and Grace were alone when they stepped from the elevator and walked to the street. They were well along 10th Street when they spoke for the first time. "Margot, tell me, what was that all about? Before you answer, I want to give you a big thank you. It was astonishing."

Their tight cheek-to-cheek embrace was fleeting. They pulled back and in the cold, yellow light of a filigreed streetlamp silently questioned each other with their eyes. "I wanted you to see that love didn't have to be John Fusina's way. You know how I feel about you, have always felt. We've had a special kind of love, and right now I realize that it's as far as it will ever go. I want you to know and really understand that I'm not just another tough-talking dyke, and that what you saw here tonight represents the heart, and if you believe in such things, maybe even the soul of who I am."

Grace couldn't help herself, she embraced Margot and planted a hard, closed-mouth kiss on her lips, pulling away before either of them were tempted to go any further. "Thank you. Now let's get the hell out of here before we start bawling."

CHAPTER

TWENTY-ONE

Despite assurances from Chester Bruno that the divorce would be smooth and swift, the initial papers were filed in November. This meant Grace would be homesteading at Margot's for thirteen months. The delay was worth it. She got everything she wanted and more. It seemed so easy. She knew where her muscle came from and didn't care. Everything was settled before they got into court. There was only one face-saving concession that Bruno allowed the Fusinas, and the rationale was *bisbigliare*, as he described to Grace, "Gossip about the divorce will hit the streets the day we file, and the snickering will bounce around town like a Verdi aria. The Fusinas couldn't take that. We're dealing with a tooth-pulling dynasty, Grace, let's give them a little something."

The filing was quietly moved down the Jersey shore to Toms River, the seat of Ocean County, where the Fusinas had beachfront homes in Seaside Park. No one was fooled, of course, but divorce notices in a rural weekly were hardly the same as what would be headline grabbers in the two Newark papers. Grace got the deed to the Italian Renaissance with all its furnishings, title to her Studebaker, generous alimony for ten years, monthly property maintenance, insurance payments, and weekly maid service.

Grace had only one question for Bruno during the negotiations, "Will a restraining order be needed?"

He replied, "No, there's no need for one. Don't worry it's been handled." And that was it. John Fusina was history.

That year of waiting for the final decree was a continual *non sequitur,* straight from a Marx Brothers' script. Grace invited several guys over but never slept with any of them, sending them away without a hint of remorse. Margot mockingly gloated after each rejection, "Hey gal, don't you know there's a war on, and you can bet pickings will get slimmer the longer it lasts. There are plenty of women around, not all bitches like me, and good looking, too."

Grace usually could find something handy to throw at the laughing Margot. Most of her dates were with attorneys having courthouse business. Maybe Margot was right, that only the losers were left. She could take flat feet, a punctured ear drum and acute myopia if they were wrapped in a real man.

It was on a morning a little more than a month before her final divorce decree when Sergeant Nick Cisco dropped some routine burglary paperwork in front of her. After a year of forced sexual abstinence, Grace was horny as hell and close to despair. Margot failed to make things better when, after ten months, she left two dildos, a jar of lubricant, and a note on her bed, "*The small one is for undergraduate work, the big one for a masters. Don't even think about a doctoral thesis. Be careful.*"

From the beginning, she and Nick held nothing back. Grace marveled at Nick's lack of pretense, and how during that first encounter she responded like a saloon pickup on the prowl. She saw how intently he studied her fingers, and actually licked his lips. It was quick and unconscious, prompting a deep red blush that started at his neck and glowed when it reached his ears. And what did she do? She flipped her hair from her shoulders, smiled, and without a word, gave him a look that would have had Rita Hayworth taking notes. She stamped the papers, in triplicate, of course, kept one for the clerk's files, and pushed the other two across the counter.

"That's it. That's all you'll need," she said as she turned to her left, and threw her copy into an overflowing basket. *My God, I can feel it, he's still there staring at me. What the hell, let's push it a little*. She turned to face him. "That's all you need. Have any questions?" she asked. She got the answer she was hoping for.

"No, nothing now. I'll be seeing you."

Five hours later there he was, leaning with feigned indifference against an unmarked police cruiser next to her Studebaker in the employee parking lot. She wasn't surprised. She decided to have some fun, to find out who this lug was. And on her terms.

"Hello again," Nick said.

"Again? I can't recall being introduced."

"Yeah, right. I'm Nick Cisco. Police Sergeant Nick Cisco, to be exact."

Grace was aware of how self-conscious the detective was. Damn, she thought, it's as though this was the first time he had come onto a woman. Keys in hand, she stood at the driver's side of her car, and saw that he was unsure whether to stay put or move into the unknown. He took the plunge, closing in one stride the three feet that separated their cars, put his elbows on the roof of her Studebaker, and made no attempt to hide his wedding ring. She liked what she saw. She was certain now that he was not a player, and this was his first time out on the prowl.

He eyed her suspiciously and said, "And you are?"

"You blind or something?"

"Huh?"

"You see this, it hasn't changed since eleven o'clock this morning. Maybe I should be asking whether you can read."

Nick's eyes dropped to the name tag pinned on a blue blouse and said, "Duh? Let me see now. G-r-a-c-e. That would be Grace, wouldn't it? And, let me catch my breath now, capital D, small e, capital M-a-r-c-o. That would be, now correct me if I'm wrong, Grace De Marco. Get it right, did I?"

Grace, by this time, had also placed her elbows on the roof. She and Nick were no more than three feet apart. The parking lot was emptying, and they were catching everyone's eye. "Hey Nick, naughty, naughty! This ain't the Tenderloin, let's move it out of here," a vice squad member warned in his best street cop *bravura*.

"I think we ought to go," Nick said.

"Where?"

"Oh hell, I don't know. Suggestions?"

"Nope." Grace still wasn't making it easy.

"Well, there's the Robert Treat just down the street. I hear it's a nice bar."

"You hear? You mean you don't know? You're inviting me to a place you don't know anything about?"

"You put it that way, I guess that's so. We'd be having a real blind date."

"Okay, buddy, I'm taking a chance with you. Close enough to walk. Ready to go?"

"Yeah, sure, let's do it." Cisco was flummoxed by how easy it had been, unaware of how tough it was going to be.

That was three years ago. Damn, Grace thought, hard to believe it's been that long. She peered through the rain-washed living room window hoping to spot Nick when he drove past to his favorite parking spot a block away. She reached for the Haig & Haig pinch bottle on the liquor table to her right, removed the cork and poured three fingers into a Scotch glass. She loved the shape of the three-sided bottle, and more often than not found herself toying with the wire mesh in which it was wrapped. This was class devoid of snobbery. For her, Scotch was an acquired taste that purged forever the hated memory of those horrible martinis she dutifully mixed for the Fusina clan. There would never be a bottle of Gordon's or Dolin Vermouth de Chambéry included in the liquor stockpile she always had on hand. It was a bonus that Scotch was also Nick's drink.

The rain was little more than a mist when Nick made a left off South Orange Avenue onto Ward Place. He reached Wilden, made a left and cruised slowly past Grace's home. Grace smiled as she watched the unmarked police cruiser go by. Nick continued for another block to Ivy Hill Park and eased into a parking space. He turned off the ignition, opened the driver's door, and stepped over an inch-deep stream of water coursing down the narrow, blacktopped street. The rain had stopped. He walked out to Wilden, waited for two cars to pass, and crossed over to where he had a clear view of the big Italian Renaissance that had become more his home than his and Connie's house on Delavan.

Grace sipped her Scotch and, with a smile, followed every cautious step Nick took as he crossed Eder Terrace. From the start, she marveled at the precautions he found necessary. Cop's intuition comes natural, he'd explained.

Grace savored another sip of Scotch as she thought back to her final month at Margot's, and her roommate's reaction when she sized-up Nick for the first time. "Where did you find this guy?" Margot said. She steered Grace to the kitchen, gently pushed her through the open door, then turned and formed a door block by turning her back, stretching her legs and grabbing each doorjamb with her hands. “Are you sure it’s safe for you to go back out there alone? Do you want me along?”

“Don’t be an ass. He’s okay, believe me, he might even be more than okay,” Grace said.

“Okay, okay, he’s a hunk, I can see that. Every one of the dozen or so wimps you brought here were poster boys for Hart, Schaffner and Marx. This guy looks like he’s wearing something off the bargain basement rack at Ohrbach’s.”

“He’s a cop,” Grace said, explaining in three words all that she felt was needed.

Grace poured another finger of Scotch into her glass, dropped in an ice cube and gave a connoisseur’s swirl or two to the rich brown liquid. She giggled as total recall kicked in. Grace had taken control from the start. She borrowed some of the rough business from her marriage, never denying she enjoyed a great deal of it, blended it with the gentleness displayed by two lesbian lovers in Greenwich Village, then added her own special brand of sexual humor, as bizarre as it might be. Could Nick live with it? She wanted to find out early on. The test came the final time they bedded down at Margot’s.

CHAPTER
TWENTY-TWO

"Not bad, not bad at all," Nick said between sips of Scotch, beads of sweat had trickled into his eyebrows, standard after each bout of their sexual warfare.

"The Scotch or my pussy? You've had more than a little of both," Grace teased. "Now if you give the right answer, you've got a nice treat coming. Well, which is it?"

"You can't be serious," he said as he reached over and placed his left hand between her legs.

"Correct, and for having the right answer, I have a surprise for you. Put your glass down on the nightstand. Fluff the pillows against the headboard so you can sit up straight and relax. Ahh, that's it, comfy? Now close your eyes and keep them closed. Put your left hand over your eyes, and no peeking now, promise?"

"Yeah, yeah, I promise."

Grace retrieved her glass from the opposite nightstand, dropped in five ice cubes, and poured in just enough Scotch to leave two of the cubes bobbing above the surface. Making sure Nick's eyes remained closed, she reached across the bed, gently took his semi-erect penis and plunged it into her glass. She got what she hoped for, thermal conductivity at its very best.

"Yeow! What the hell was that!" Nick uncovered his eyes, peered down at his crotch, and was horrified to see an ice cube firmly attached to the end of his penis.

Instinctively, he reached down only to have Grace grab his left wrist with a solicitous, "No, no big fella, I love that purple helmet of yours too much to have it skinned by an ice cube. There's only one way to get it off." She leaned over and took the ice cube and the tip of his penis into her mouth, and began to suck. Mission accomplished, she looked up, smiled, and said, "You now know the origin of the cocktail."

They looked at each other, and couldn't hold it in any longer, their laughter was loud enough to prompt a shout from the living room, "It better be legal! Your landlady demands it!"

Nick pulled Grace forward and after a long, deep kiss said, "Do it again." He had passed the test.

By this time Nick had crossed Eder Terrace, and was headed back across Wilden to Grace's front door. He was about to use his key when Grace opened the door and confronted him. "I'll never understand it. Here you've got keys to the front and back doors, a parking space in the back, and you're still pulling that undercover cop stuff parking more than a block away. Suppose it hadn't stopped raining, bet you don't even have a raincoat."

"I love it when you nag," Nick smiled. "I'll be your Petruchio and you be my Kate."

"Never mind that Shakespeare stuff, and by the way, who's taming who, big boy?"

She stifled a reply and simultaneously widened his eyes by placing her left index finger over his lips, and squeezed his crotch with her right hand as he kicked the door closed behind him.

Grace, as was the custom on days like this, had left work early to prepare dinner and set up the drinks. With their arms wrapped tightly around their waists, they walked toward the living room where they disentangled to allow Nick to shed his jacket and shoulder holster. He hung them on a clothes tree off to the left. Grace switched on the Philco record player, and the first of five seventy-eights dropped to the turntable. Dinah Shore's *You'd Be So Nice To Come Home To* bathed the high-ceilinged room. Nick never tired of the ritual, good Scotch, thirsty kisses, some pre-dinner groping, just so they never lost sight of things to come after the knives and forks were put away. Tonight it was chicken marsala, risotto, and antipasto to start it all off, with everything washed down with a bottle of Sangiovese.

By nine o'clock their sexual explorations had exhausted them. They were naked atop the covers of the rumpled bed when the telephone rang. Grace, who had been dozing off with her head on Nick's left shoulder, reached across his body to the nightstand on the right side of the bed, and picked up the phone. "Hello. Is it necessary? It's nine o'clock, he's already had a long day. Okay, okay, here he is." She handed the phone to Nick, who by this time knew who it was and was sitting up.

"When did it happen? I've been expecting it for a while. Who's handling it? Rizzo and Melnyk? Where are they now? Okay, give me drive time to get there."

"I wish you had never given your sidekick my number. I know, don't say it, that he hardly ever calls, only when life and death are involved. But then, you're the acting chief of homicide, what should I expect."

Nick fought for balance, cradling the phone on his shoulder while awkwardly pulling on his trousers. He hung up and finished dressing, put on his shoes and tied them, and wrapped his unknotted tie under the collar of his shirt. He leaned forward, kissed her softly on the lips, turned and walked quietly out of the bedroom.

Grace arose, pulled her robe from under the crumpled blanket at the foot of the bed, and slipped it on as she walked barefoot to the open door. She heard Nick pause in the foyer for his shoulder holster and jacket before heading out. She descended into the living room, and walked to the front window for a final glimpse of Nick, but he had already disappeared into the shadows of Ivy Hill Park.

Her anxiety troubled her. It didn't fit at all, an unwanted intrusion after a demanding bout of satisfying sex that should have left her warm and exhausted. She turned and peered across the dark room toward the far wall where a large, beautifully framed print was barely discernable. She walked over, switched on the picture light, and studied as she had done many times before Georges de La Tour's *Penitent Magdalene*. The print was a gift from Nick, chosen by her from a display rack at the New York Metropolitan Museum of Art.

The choice was easy after Nick told her that it was the prostitute Mary Magdalene. He lovingly explained every detail, the enlightening glare of the single candle on the table, Magdalene's imploring gaze as she leaned forward with her hand on her cheek, the other hand caressing a skull in her lap, her long hair hanging over her bare shoulder, a wooden cross on the table, and next to it the tightly knotted rope for self-flagellation. The museum visit came well into their second year together, and by that time de La Tour's masterpiece had already become prologue.

That day was the tipping point for Grace. As Nick traced every detail in the painting, she shed her guilt. His boyish enthusiasm was infectious. Using the eraser end of a pencil, he roamed from detail to detail, moving on only after he was certain that she understood. She realized she was watching a career that had died in gestation. No matter how far Nick advanced as a cop, she knew that the rewards could never match the gleam Georges de La Tour and other masters brought to his eyes.

CHAPTER

TWENTY-THREE

McClosky was draining a cup of coffee in the hall outside Cisco's office when his partner silently brushed past him, and took a seat at his desk.

"You said the suspect was Negro," Cisco said, "and that he was a veteran. All we need now is that he was a hero."

"Bingo!" McClosky said. "Wait til you see him. You'll see what Rizzo and Melnyk saw when they arrested him, a guy already dressed for the collar, just waiting to be cuffed."

"Dressed for the collar?" Cisco said.

"You'll see. We have him on ice in interrogation room one, a uniform's with him."

"First, I want to touch base with Rizzo and Melnyk," Cisco said as they walked into the homicide bullpen. He didn't like what he saw. The two detectives were collecting kudos and coffee refills from fellow officers for their collar. This isn't what he expected from his two greenest recruits, guys he had stolen from vice on the strength of their reputations as clean cops.

"Taking a break? You've got a possible homicide suspect down the hall, and you're standing around drinking coffee," a flushed Cisco said, his legendary temper barely in check. "Get your asses in my office. McClosky, I want you in there, too."

When Cisco's anger was at its explosive best, it spared no one. Rizzo and Melnyk parked their coffee cups on Rockford's desk, where they had been holding court, and sheepishly awaited the verbal sword thrust headed their way.

Cisco had taken only a few steps when he abruptly turned. "And you three, Rockford, Polski, Valentine, slipped your minds, has it, that we've got three unsolved mob hits that the press is jumping all over. And the wife in Vailsburg, who pancaked her husband in their driveway, leaving behind a squashed skull. Just drove away in the family Dodge. The *Beacon* is calling her the 'Artful Dodger.' And how about the shooting that dropped some poor sucker in the Tenderloin. Haven't come up with a single witness. Should I go on? Now get your lazy asses going."

Cisco turned to Rizzo and Melnyk, and with a jerk of his right thumb motioned them to his office. They shared uneasy glances as they followed in lockstep behind Cisco and McClosky.

McClosky took one of the two chairs in front of Cisco's desk. Rizzo grabbed the second chair, and Melnyk pulled in a metal folding chair from the hall. They watched as Cisco circled his desk and walked to the window that overlooked the parking lot, took four deep breaths to compose himself, then turned.

"Who is the suspect, and what do we know about him?" Cisco said.

"His name is Wilbert Robert Jeffries," Rizzo said, "and he's a talker. An Army vet who got wounded in Italy, earned a Bronze Star, and knows that his Army days were the best thing that ever happened to him."

"He wants to confess, but on his terms, and only if he is able to tell the world who he is," Melnyk said.

"We'll give him his chance," McClosky said.

“Now how about the victim, who is he and what do we know about him?” Cisco said. “I understand it’s a stabbing. Is he going to make it?”

“Name’s Brian B. Bristo, runs Three B Property Management for a long list of absentee owners. He’s over at County, still critical. Talked to the doc a few minutes ago. He said it’s touch-and-go whether he’ll pull through.”

“Give me some details.”

“Like I said, he’s a talker,” Rizzo said. “We can get it right from the horse’s mouth. Enough evidence to make the dumbest prosecutor salivate. We held off doing anything further until you got here. Wait til you see him, and I gotta tell ya, it makes you think.”

The four men were silent as they walked to the interrogation room. Once inside, Cisco acknowledged the uniform who had been standing watch for several hours. “Joe, you can barely keep your eyes open. Go home and get some sleep. And thanks.”

A skinny blonde court stenographer about forty, showed up and her body language let everyone know this was overtime. She set up her stenotype machine, took a seat at one end of the table, and pouted. Interrogation room one was barely big enough to accommodate the metal table in the center of the room, and the six wooden chairs grouped around it. Wilbert Robert Jeffries had the far side of the table all to himself.

“You realize, Mr. Jeffries, that you don’t have to say anything, and we can get you an attorney,” Cisco said.

“Where you get off, Mister Jeffries, don’t you see my sergeant stripes? It’s Sergeant Wilbert Robert Jeffries, if you please,” the slender black man said. He arose from his chair, and stood for full-dress inspection. A blue infantry service scarf was neatly overlapped and tucked inside a pressed Eisenhower jacket that displayed two rows of ribbons aligned above a Bronze Star, a Purple Heart, and even his Sharpshooter Medal. Pinned above the display was the Combat Infantryman Badge.

"See this patch here, on this shoulder, a Buffalo Soldier, that's what I am. We go all the way back to the Indian wars, us Buffalo Soldiers. And this patch here, on this shoulder, the 92nd Infantry Division, and damn proud of it." Jeffries was a man possessed. He wanted it all out now.

The four detectives and stenographer remained fixated, waiting for what would come next.

"The Arno and Serchio Rivers, bet you never heard of them. They're in Italy, tough country, but not too tough for us Buffalo Soldiers. A lot of black GIs shed a lot of red blood at those rivers. Here's something else I bet you didn't know, that the 92nd was all black. Yeah, we had white officers, but it was the black man who did the fighting and bleeding."

Jeffries was unaware that he was earning legendary status at police headquarters, a homicide suspect who had taken control of an interrogation, baring his soul to a silent audience until the stenographer timidly asked, "Sergeant Wilbert Robert Jeffries, I know how to spell Arno, but can you help me with Serchio?"

"You people know nothing. Here it is, S-E-R-C-H-I-O. The river Serchio, that's where I got these," Jeffries said, pointing first to the Purple Heart and then to the Bronze Star. "Real lucky, that's what I was, real lucky. That shrapnel got me in the arm and shoulders, could have been my head, but I kept on going, and my machine gun did the rest. Christ Almighty, you should have seen it!"

"We're sure it was something to see, Sergeant," Cisco said, "Now let's get to the action closer to home, to be specific, what happened between you and Brian B. Bristo at Three B Property Management? You can sit down now."

Jeffries searched their faces, hoping that his words to these four white men had sunk in. He slowly lowered himself into his chair, pulled it forward, placed his elbows and forearms on the table palms down. "I stabbed him, stabbed him with his own letter opener," he said. "He asked for it, and he got it. Am I sorry? Hell no, I'm not sorry."

"He asked for it," Cisco said, "how did he ask for it?"

"Don't tell me you don't know what's going on," Jeffries said. "I'm only a black guy from Central High, and I can see it clear and nasty what's going on out there."

"You need to explain what clear and nasty is all about, so enlighten us," Cisco said.

"You two over there," Jeffries said raising his right hand and pointing with his index finger at Rizzo and Melnyk, "picked me up, and with my wife and three kids crying and screaming, hauled me down here. And from where? A third floor, firetrap, walk-up at Sanford and Tremont."

"We've got all that," an impatient McClosky said. "We want to know what the hell happened at Three B Property Management."

"Then you want the whole story, not bits and pieces like the papers print," Jeffries said, sitting upright in his chair, with only his hands on the table, his military bearing intact. "I had the cash to pull it off. Could handle first and last months and security, but it made no fucking difference. First it was a two-story on Elmwood advertised for rent. Made an appointment. When the agent saw a black man and his wife come up the walkway, he probably came close to pissing his pants. The *For Rent* sign came out of the window real fast. The guy said he's sorry for wasting our time, that the place had rented a half-hour earlier. Just forgot about the sign. Lying son of a bitch!

"The same thing at Elliott, an empty first-floor apartment got suddenly rented when we showed up," Jeffries said.

"Told him I got good pay working the underground loading docks at Bamberger's, so no worry that I couldn't handle the rent. A big white guy, white shirt, black and red stripe tie, blue suit, turned his back on me, wasn't even facing me, when he said, 'You got here too late, nobody's fault, just too late.' Another lying white bastard!"

Cisco, McClosky, and the other two detectives made no effort to interrupt. Cisco could almost fill in the distasteful details that he knew were coming.

"I waited a couple of hours, and went back to the house on Elliott," Jeffries said. "The *For Rent* sign was back in the window. I wouldn't let my nose get rubbed in it again. So I decided to play the decorated veteran's card. As you can see, I went all the way.

"Three B had a five-room apartment on Kenwood. I walked to Kenwood to look it over. The sign in the window said it was still for rent, and to contact Brian B. Bristo at the rental office. When I walked in, they almost fainted. Bristo and his secretary, a white lady with steel-rim specs and gray hair, just gawked, their yaps wide open. Like I was a fancy-dressed monkey from the circus.

"Right off I told him I'd like to rent that apartment over on Kenwood," Jeffries said. "No messing around, right to the point. Bristo got up from behind his desk, and walked out to confront me with a dumb-as-hell look on his face. Then the fucking lies began.

"'Apartment on Kenwood? We have nothing on Kenwood,' the smiling bastard told me. Then he eyed my decorations with a 'who's he kidding' look, that my medals are up for grabs in any pawn shop on Market.

"So I told him, I was just at your Kenwood place. Your rental sign is in the front window. And oh yeah, I do know how to read.

"Without even looking at me, the bastard turned to his secretary." Then Jeffries acted out Bristo's part like he was on a grand stage. "Mrs. Watson, I told you the Kenwood property was no longer available should anybody call, that we signed it up on Monday. I asked you to stop by and take the sign from the window, you remember that, don't you?"

CHAPTER
TWENTY-FOUR

To this point, Jeffries had kept himself under control, although it was evident to the four detectives that each of his words was filled with venom. Then the wraps came off. He abruptly arose, and forcefully pushed his chair away. It crashed into a wastebasket. Paper coffee cups and assorted debris from past interrogations spilled across the floor. He leaned forward, and with two tightly clenched fists, pounded the heavy metal table until it vibrated. The stenographer barely fought off the urge to run out of the room. Cisco, McClosky, Rizzo, and Melnyk sat back and waited.

"There the motherfucker was, lying to me with a big shit-eating grin. That look on his face, some of our white officers in the 92nd had it before they sent us out to die, racism and white hate. Tried to ignore it, get it out of my mind, and most of the time it worked. Know why? Because I could take it out on those wop fascists with my machine gun. But I wasn't about to take Bristo's shit, not me, not anymore. And then it just happened. Can't explain it.

"I punched him, hit his chin and got his neck in one shot. He stumbled backward and grabbed a paperweight from his desk, but I was in close on him so he couldn't square-off and get me flush. He looked soft, but he wasn't, he was real strong. And here, take a look," Jeffries bent over and displayed two purple bruises on the back of his neck.

“It was wild! It was crazy! He was pounding me on the shoulders and neck. I had his other arm by the wrist, and all the time something was telling me, here’s my chance. Can’t let him get away with it, this racist son of a bitch. I had this white piece of shit in my hands, and I don’t know where it came from, this idea crammed my brain, that he was no more than an infected molar. Jesus Christ, can you get that! Here I am fighting like hell, and all I could think of was a tooth. But I knew that once this molar was cracked, and the poison came out, it would cure everything.

“It was like we were doing a rough dance in front of his desk. I knew I couldn’t take many more shots to the back of my head before I’d hit the floor. I spun him around, getting him where I’d have a good shot for a kick in the balls, that would do it, bring him to his knees.

“Then I saw it, a letter opener, sharp point and long, looked like a dagger. I grabbed it, and then I did it. I stabbed him in the chest, could feel the letter opener slide in until the hilt hit the ribcage. Bristo’s face was only a few inches from mine. I could hear the air hissing from his mouth. He never said a word. I let the letter opener stay where it was, and pushed him backwards onto the top of his desk. All the time that bitch, Watson, was screaming her brains out. Shit-scared she was, never even tried for the phone to call the cops.

“So that’s it. I straightened my jacket, saw there was no blood on it, made sure my medals were hanging straight, turned and walked out the door. Went home and waited until you two guys came to get me.”

Rizzo and Melnyk turned to each other, their facial expressions acknowledged that they had made probably the easiest homicide collar in the history of the department, but they also knew Bristo had to die for them to get the glory.

"You've gotten it all, everything, am I right?" Cisco said, turning to the stenographer. "By the way, what's your name? Detectives Rizzo and Melnyk will need it for their report."

"Amelia Griswald," the skinny blonde said, "that's Miss Amelia Griswald, if you please." The disdain, so evident when she entered the interrogation room, remained etched in place as she rolled up her stenotape and prepared to leave. "You'll have it all by tomorrow afternoon."

"He's all yours," Cisco said as he got up from the table and nodded toward Rizzo and Melnyk. "I'll want your report on my desk in the morning. I want you to check on Bristo's condition every half hour, got that? Every half hour, then get back to me."

McClosky got up to join his boss. The two men left the interrogation room without even a glance toward Jeffries, who for several minutes had held them silent captives as he spewed out his hatred and anger.

"You know that Jeffries is not the Lone Ranger," McClosky said as they entered Cisco's office. "They've redlined so much of this fucking city, a posse of black veterans has been mounting up for months now. Like the sorry son of a bitch we just listened to, firetrap tenements ain't cutting it."

"And who draws the lines?" Cisco said. "We both know where Jeffries called home, not quite a slum, but give it time. Here, take a look." Cisco motioned McClosky over to the city wall map. "Here are the three streets Jeffries mentioned, Elliott, Elmwood, and Kenwood. And here's Sanford and Tremont. The four streets are practically kissing each other."

"Christ, you're right," McClosky said as he studied the wall map. "An easy walk to all of them. Here, look at this, only two blocks from Jeffries' place to Elliott, four to Kenwood and five to Elmwood. Walk to any of them without a deep breath."

"Yeah, but somewhere in there a red line was drawn, and guys like Jeffries can't cross it, but their time is coming."

"I'll bet you every house on Jeffries' block is filled with pissed-off blacks looking for the Promised Land," McClosky said. "And hell, just like Jeffries, they can virtually reach out and touch it."

McClosky flopped into a chair, uneasily aware that they were experiencing the dry sweat of men trapped in a world where malevolent forces made all the rules. As uniforms, they had worked the Third Ward. He would always be haunted by the memory of Negro babies, not yet one, dying in their mothers' arms, their lungs destroyed by the toxic fumes of cheap kerosene and coal stoves that set the standard in every tenement walk-up. Crime was an easy way out, but from where to where? From a dump on Wallace, to a second-story over a butcher shop on South Orange, where you got higher rent and interior plumbing, a toilet seat and washtub not yet stained yellowish brown.

He remembered how Ronnie Hawkins, who ran a small policy parlor on Montgomery, had found heaven. "This is real living. The butcher boy downstairs got me real good pigs' knuckles, oxtails, and calves brains my lady could cook up just fine, just fine." Hawkins was sent to another heaven with three bullets in his head when a number paid off big, and he welched on the payoff to the wrong party.

By the time McClosky snapped out of it, put away his memories, Cisco had removed his jacket, hung it on the clothes tree in the corner, and took his seat at the desk, obviously troubled.

"Let's hope that Bristo doesn't die on us," Cisco said. "We don't need a dead, white racist on our hands right now."

"If the son of a bitch croaks, the prosecutor has a highly-decorated black veteran to deal with," McClosky said. "I can just see the blacks hitting the streets, with Father

Divine leading the way in his Cadillac. Jeffries is just their ticket, a guy who put his ass on the line for Uncle Sam, but can't find a decent place to live."

As if on cue, the two men ended eye contact, Cisco swiveling around to stare out the window, and McClosky tapping out an Old Gold and lighting up. Their ambition had trapped them into a rogue operation with Peterson, an arrogant son of a bitch, who had shackled them from the very beginning.

Turning from the window, Cisco reached across his desk for a folded copy of last night's *Clarion*. He spread it open and leafed through the pages until he found the article he was looking for.

"I don't suppose you had time for any reading the last few days," Cisco said. "Jeffries' blow-up ties into an AP article describing the red carpet laid out for that Kraut scientist Wernher Von Braun and his cronies. It quotes an Army Major Jim Hamill."

"Didn't read it. What's your point?" McClosky said.

"That we are going ga-ga over Wernher Von Braun, treating him and his gang like Hollywood celebrities. Hamill told the reporter they couldn't get it into their thick heads that they were the losers, not the winners. Von Braun and everyone else have been bitching and moaning about the weather, the food, and facilities in Texas, with the bastard going so far as to demand new flooring because they didn't want their dainty little feet walking on bare wood floors.

"Never bothered him that slave laborers by the thousands had been worked to death, and for what? So the Nazis would be the first to develop a new kind of killing machine, the V-2 rocket."

"So, the connection with Jeffries is what?" McClosky said.

"Only this. Here we have this little guy, maybe even a hero, who took shrapnel in his arm that could have taken his head off. A guy, who with his family, is living in a slum despite his Purple Heart and Bronze Star. And in Texas, we have a bunch of Krauts who had developed a weapon that Hitler hoped one day would destroy us."

"And this was all in the column, straight from the horse's mouth?" McClosky said. "Obviously, you believe it."

"Yeah, I do, and it makes me wonder why in hell we fought the god-damned war in the first place," Cisco said.

"Come on, Nick, let's get real, aren't we doing the same damn thing? Any way you cut it, we've been gagged from the start, never a word leaks out until the D.A. is good and ready. Can't get the industrial big-wigs in Germany mad at us now, can we?"

"And we don't need another war here in Newark. If the Jeffries' stabbing ever comes out, it's all there for another street circus that could get very bad," Cisco said. "Remember the Divine caravan last year, flatbed trucks packed with black vets showing off their medals and ribbons?"

"I was there, over on Market," McClosky said. "All the whooping and hollering, never ended. Black gals reaching out to touch their heroes, and the heroes reaching out to grab what they could. Divine handmaidens bombarded the crowd with handfuls of pennies."

"You know, if Bristo dies, they'll be out there again, wanting more than cheap feels from the back of a truck," Cisco said. "A lot of them are just hanging out now, waiting for something to happen. Our rap sheets are crammed with their names, generally petty stuff, but it tells us we're sitting on a time bomb."

"No jobs, shitholes to live in," McClosky said. "This redlining thing could be the fuse, and Jeffries the guy to light it."

"A pissed off clergy, black and white, has been making noises about the redlining," Cisco said. "One priest down in the Ironbound even said it was a government conspiracy, with the Federal Housing Authority calling the shots."

"No shit? The FHA?" McClosky said.

"I've also heard that the *Afro American* has had two of its best reporters working on it," Cisco said. "Can't wait for that story to come out."

"How about some coffee? Smells like a fresh pot is brewing in the bullpen," McClosky said. "Stay put, I'll get it." As he was walking out, he heard the telephone ring behind him. When he returned with two steaming cups, he was greeted with a smile.

"That was Rizzo. Bristo is going to make it," Cisco said. "The letter opener missed anything vital. No apparent complications. His condition has gone from critical to serious, and Rizzo said they should be able to question him maybe as early as tomorrow."

McClosky passed one cup across the desk to his partner, slumped into a chair, and took a long sip of his coffee. Their eyes met, as they savored a shared sense of relief.

"Let's get Rizzo and Melnyk in here," Cisco said. "I've decided how to handle it. Seems we have an unfortunate accident on our hands."

"Accident? This oughta be good," McClosky said.

Cisco waited for the two young detectives to settle into their chairs. He leaned forward, placed his forearms on the desk, and with a dismissive gesture of his hands said, "You've put a lot of effort into what has turned out to be an accidental stabbing case."

"Accidental?" Melnyk said. "I'm sorry, sir, but what the hell are you talking about?"

"Just that," Cisco said. "Your report will tell me that Bristo was demonstrating the heft and balance of his letter opener for a client named Jeffries, when he tripped on a loose carpet in his office, fell forward onto his desk and stabbed himself in the chest."

"Our report? We haven't written our report yet," Rizzo said.

"Oh, but you have, I just read it to you," Cisco said. "I don't care how much bullshit you put into it, embellish it, be creative if you want to, but when you both sign off, it will be another unfortunate inner city accident. Happens all the time, hardly newsworthy. Your report comes directly to me, won't be on the blotter. You got that?"

"What about Bristo?" Melnyk said. "What do we do about him? He'll scream his ass off when we tell him. We all know he won't go along with this."

"He will, and I'll tell you why," Cisco said. "You get to him as soon as he can talk, before he has a chance to lawyer-up. Let him know that if he opens his mouth, his career as a realtor and property manager in Newark is over. Every property he owns or manages will be targeted by inspectors he never knew existed. Let's start with plumbing, then electrical, structural, fire, did he get the right permits, are they on display, can we see them, are they all up to date. And then there's the taxes."

"We'll even call in animal control," McClosky joined in. "Rabies has become a big problem in Newark."

Rizzo and Melnyk left the office and returned to their desks with newfound knowledge of how things really work in the department.

“What about Sergeant Wilbert Robert Jeffries?” McClosky asked. “He’s one pissed-off son of a bitch expecting some big slammer time.”

“Let him cool off here tonight,” Cisco said. “Keep him in the interrogation room. Get someone to arrange for his wife and kids to visit him. Let’s have some food waiting when they arrive. Everything nice and gentle. I don’t want any of this to get out of here. The lid is clamped on starting now. There’ll be some asses in the grinder if there’s even a sniff.”

“He’ll have a lot of questions,” McClosky said. “From a near homicide to walking out a free man is one hell of a leap. He’s not dumb, far from it, in fact. His full-dress uniform tells us that.”

“There’ll be more like Jeffries,” Cisco said. “Redlining is cutting the city to pieces, the haves, like you and me, buddy, and the have-nots, like Jeffries. It’s a racial powder keg, and I don’t want someone like Jeffries lighting the fuse on my watch.”

It was all for the greater good. There would be no black martyr to stir things up, no protestors filling the streets, and hopefully, if all went well, no bloodshed.

CHAPTER TWENTY-FIVE

Cisco caught a few hours of sleep early Thursday morning in the Homicide Division's bunk room, borrowed Rockford's electric shaver, threw down a cup of coffee, and headed toward the interrogation room.

"Sergeant Jeffries, it looks like you're free to go," Cisco said. The black man stared at him, stiff and unblinking, his Eisenhower jacket draped over the back of his chair, and his shirt cuffs neatly rolled to his mid-forearm. The remains of a fried chicken dinner were on four paper plates, along with paper cups, and crumpled napkins.

"Free to go?" Jeffries said as he bent forward, his eyes following Cisco as he took a chair across the table. "A nasty little joke? If so, you can fuck off."

"It looks like Brian B. Bristo of Three B Property Management was a very clumsy man," Cisco said. "My detectives pieced together that Bristo was doing a little showing off with that stiletto letter opener, tripped on a loose carpet and fell, the blade making a nasty little hole in his chest. Nothing serious, he'll be out of the hospital in a day or two."

"You're not shitting me then?" an incredulous Jeffries said, not fully comprehending what he heard. "What about that old bag in the office, Mrs. Watson? What you say ain't what she saw."

"But it is what her boss will tell her to say. She's got a soft job, and wants to keep it, and Bristo will want to keep his license."

Jeffries' facial features were transformed. He was watching firsthand how the man played the game. Street-smart shrewdness took over. "I get it now. The way things are going in this city, to have a black war hero charged with stabbing a white racist son of a bitch, and a real estate tycoon to boot. Man-o-man, what troubles there would be, more than enough to spread around." Jeffries buttoned his collar, rolled down his sleeves, and reached for his jacket.

"Still gotta have a home, don't I? How about that apartment on Kenwood?"

"I think it can be arranged," Cisco said. "Give Bristo three or four days and he'll be ready with the rental papers."

"Damn, if I knew it was this easy, I'd of stabbed a honky a long time ago," Jeffries said as he stood up and took a tentative step toward the door. "Going now, if that's alright with you."

"Pick up your personal belongings on the way out."

Cisco left the interrogation room, and headed back to his office. Normally, he hated self-aggrandizement, but the way he handled Jeffries deserved a pat on the back. Now he had to get back to unfinished business. He wasn't looking forward to tomorrow's political circle-jerk at the *Clarion*.

The meeting was concocted by Mayor Murphy and Herbert Bix, who had inherited not only the publisher's chair at the *Clarion,* but an abiding love for blue-ribbon citizens panels. The fatal shooting last year of a top *Clarion* executive, who also happened to be Bix's closest friend, added to the publisher's righteous anger. At times like this, Cisco shared the belief that Murphy should have stayed a plumber, and the Bix family should never have let Herbert out of the *Clarion* mailroom. A cross-section of Newark's publicity mongers would be there, with Cisco the designated street-smart cop.

He also had to deal with Father Terry Nolan, and his vague suspicions concerning a homicide that hadn't yet happened. To add icing, the priest hinted the Archdiocese could be involved, along with big money and important people. Nolan had warned him during their chance encounter at the morgue that the meeting was coming, and urged him to attend.

By mid-afternoon, Cisco had gotten status reports on the homicide investigations still in progress. Nothing new on the three mob hits. No surprise there, real pros, nothing personal. But the Artful Dodger case, a crime of passion, was about to be wrapped up. Ethel Morgenstern, after crushing the life out of her husband, Fred, abandoned the family Dodge at the Trailways terminal downtown, and hopped the bus to Philadelphia. Her description was out, and he expected her to be in custody by the end of the day.

It was late afternoon when McClosky came into his office with news that a missing person report out of Pompton Lakes listed Boris Obermeyer, and another out of Bergenfield turned up Walter Weber. "By the way, clue me in, where's all that help Peterson promised we'd be getting from the Feds?"

"Don't hold your breath. How about Heinrich Bolz?" Cisco said. "Anything on him?"

"Nothing so far."

"Let's start with Obermeyer. Who reported him missing?"

"His wife, Cynthia Obermeyer, reported him missing more than a week ago. That was on a Tuesday. She hasn't seen him since he left for work the previous Friday. I didn't go in too deep, but did find out he had a couple of young kids, boy and girl, and had a good job at a local department store. Seemed to be a well-respected churchgoer."

"Put Pompton Lakes on your calendar, you'll be going there," Cisco said. "And Walter Weber?"

"His wife called it in yesterday," McClosky said. "Real anxious, called in on Monday, but he hadn't been missing long enough for a report to be filed. Her name's Louisa Weber. She and her husband were new to Bergenfield. Took over an established downtown hardware store, and from what I found out were doing real well. No kids. That's about it."

"Jot down Bergenfield next to Pompton Lakes," Cisco said. "You'll gumshoe as long as you can on your own. Keep the locals out of it as much as possible. I've been buttoned into the mayor's anti-crime meeting tomorrow afternoon. Peterson will be there, at least now I'll be able to throw him the few scraps we have."

Friday morning was press circus time at police headquarters. Thirty year old Ethel Morgenstern, the Artful Dodger, never made it to Philadelphia. She offered no resistance when taken off the Trailways bus by police at Camden. Mrs. Morgenstern, a demure woman just over five feet, surprised the arresting officers when she greeted them with a smile.

"Well, it was at least worth a try. Didn't plan it, just sort of happened, you know, and when it did, I felt happy about it," she said as a Camden police sergeant helped her up from her seat, slipped cuffs on her and led her down the aisle to the front of the bus.

"Easy does it, Mrs. Morgenstern," the sergeant said.

"No need to be formal, I'm Ethel," she said, and as if suddenly aware of where she was and what she was about to face, noticed that she was still wearing the kitchen apron she had put on yesterday morning before cooking a breakfast of fried eggs, sliced Taylor pork roll, toast and coffee for her husband, Fred. Her boys, Bobby and Georgie, had their milk.

Ethel Morgenstern wore no makeup, and two bobby pins held her frazzled, shoulder length, dirty blonde hair in place behind her ears. Brown freckles highlighted her cheeks. Two thin scars, each about one inch long, provided eye-catchers on the tip of her chin and along the jawbone below her left ear. Their appearance indicated they had healed without the benefit of professional medical attention. Her unpolished fingernails were clean and trimmed. Her apron protected a brown dress with buttons down the front. Nylons and polished dark brown shoes completed her morning ensemble. An engagement ring encrusted with diamond chips and a gold wedding band adorned her left hand.

Total awareness had not yet percolated to the surface when Ethel Morgenstern turned to the sergeant, and with the same disarming smile said, “And what’s your name?”

The uniformed cop, at least a foot taller, returned the smile and said, “Sergeant William Grogin. My friends call me Big Bill.”

“Then friends we are...Big Bill.”

At least a dozen reporters and as many uniform cops were waiting on the passenger platform. Big Bill pushed them aside and gently ushered his new friend to an unmarked Newark police cruiser, where a driver and two police matrons were waiting.

She was back in Newark a few hours later. Cisco, along with a gaggle of reporters, photographers, and even a newsreel camera crew from New York, were waiting. He got her through the mob and into the building, surrounded by a cordon of uniforms to keep the rabble at bay. Their loud, slobbered questions fought for recognition.

“Were you going to Philly to meet your lover, you got one don’t you?”

“Got any bruises? Show us what you’ve got, could be worth a nice little bonus.”

“Neighbors say you should have done it long ago, thinking self-defense?”

Ethel Morgenstern, silent and bemused, was whisked into an interrogation room by the matrons. Waiting for her were two very unhappy cops, Sergeants James Petri and Ryan McAdoo. The two detectives, first at the scene, had allowed this diminutive, over-wrought woman to slip past them without a backward glance. They knew they were a target for mocking headlines and biting wisecracks from their buddies.

Cisco didn’t make it easier for them when he said, “Here’s the dangerous quarry you’ve been looking for. Think you can handle her from here.”

CHAPTER TWENTY-SIX

Two hours later, Cisco found himself on the ninth floor of the *Clarion*, where he was expected to add his two cents worth on how to end the city's rampant street crime. Because of the Artful Dodger melee at police headquarters, he was a half-hour late. He was one of a mixed bag of twenty-two citizens who either chafed at the bit to be there, or were given a "get-your-ass-over-there-or-else" order by their superiors. The do-gooders were loud and enthusiastic, waved their arms a lot, careful not to spill their free coffee, and bore in almost nose-to-nose when making eye contact. Cisco, and the others compelled to be there, were easy to single out with their sullen features and mumbled responses. He was barely off the elevator when a firm tug of his left sleeve pulled him up short.

"You're late, I was beginning to worry whether you'd make it," Father Terry Nolan said withdrawing his hand. "I've already had my say, and it was short, pretty much word-for-word from the guidelines dealing with parish relevance."

"Sorry I missed it."

"Finished in the blink of an eye," said a smiling Nolan, surprised by what he detected under Cisco's sarcastic, tough-cop exterior. "I was just hanging around to see if you'd show up. I know you're a busy guy, and rubbing shoulders with this chattering bunch is probably the last thing you want to do."

Nolan's condescending glance around the room convinced Cisco that the priest was one of the mumblers who couldn't get out of there fast enough.

"It's not all a waste of time," Cisco said. "There is someone here I need to talk to. He's over there touching all his bases."

He and the priest turned and eyeballed County Prosecutor Herman Gerhardt Peterson, Mayor Vincent Murphy, Archbishop Thomas Joseph Walsh, and *Clarion* publisher Herbert Bix deliberating in the corner of the large conference room, Newark's power-elite in action.

"If you're not careful," Cisco said, "sooner or later you'll be playing their game, and paragraph one of their handbook is 'how to kiss each other's ass.'"

"You see it every day at the Chancery," Nolan said. "Shameless stuff in many cases, you wouldn't want to rattle around in the closets of some of our illustrious monsignors. More to the point of why I want to talk to you, take a look at that tall blonde guy over by the window."

"Never saw him before," Cisco said. "Well-tailored, sparkling blue eyes, with his nose in the air. He's too young for a monocle, but that would complete the picture. Who is he?"

"Hugo Manfred Franke," the priest said. "An important man with M.L. Kraus here in Jersey. Very important. As Kraus' Chief Counsel, he'll be negotiating how much of the company's holdings confiscated during the war they'll be getting back. Federal mediation will be here in Newark. Franke is here to drum up support and will pay for it if he has to."

"The Archdiocese included?" Cisco said.

"Franke's been working hard at it for years," the priest said, "made a big contribution to my boss's silver jubilee celebration three years ago. Made it clear it was M.L. Kraus beneficence, and that there could be more on its way if its New Jersey holdings returned to the corporate fold."

"Hypocrisy wrapped in greenbacks," Cisco said. "A church taking handouts from a company that made big bucks from its poison gas that killed millions."

The two men eyed the elevator, its door open and inviting, only fifteen feet away.

"Out of here?" Cisco said.

"You bet."

Cisco and Nolan edged their way through the contentious and increasingly noisy crowd that now included more than a dozen civic stalwarts, who had busted in and were demanding to be heard. The two men were crowded away from the elevator by other conference escapees when Cisco turned to the priest.

"How does Franke fit with what you said outside the morgue last Sunday? You said something about a homicide in the making. Sounded pretty sure of yourself, that the Archdiocese was involved. Anything to back it up?"

"A separated shoulder, a broken arm, bruised buttocks, ribs and thighs, and fear," the priest said. "The uncomprehending fear of a six year old girl. Will that do it for you?"

"Are you telling me Franke is responsible?" Cisco said. "And if he is, who is the victim and how does it all fit together? You're telling me the Church is a party to all this?"

"It's a complicated mess," the priest said, "I need help."

"Hold that thought, father," Cisco said. "I've got some business to attend to with Peterson, now that he's broken away from your boss and the others. Shouldn't take long, so why don't you get out of here. Grab a table at the Grand Bar and Grille a few doors away, we'll pick it up there."

Peterson spotted Cisco making his way toward him, smiled and nodded his way past a Negro clergyman, whose name he couldn't remember, and picked a spot near the now deserted conference table to wait.

"What've you got?" the prosecutor asked.

"McClosky's working the Weber and Obermeyer angles today and through the weekend," Cisco said. "No days off. He's pulled everything he could out of Louisa Weber in Bergenfield this morning, and is probably with Cynthia Obermeyer in Pompton Lakes right now."

"And Heinrich Bolz, where are we with him?" Peterson said.

"No where."

Cisco had been getting an increasingly uncomfortable itch for a couple of days now, that hooking up with Peterson, and dragging McClosky along with him, was a bad move. Ambition be damned. They had decided that morning to toss out the bullshit when going face-to-face with Peterson, that embellishing weak or non-existent leads only led to dead-ends and a pissed off prosecutor.

"What the hell does that mean?" Peterson demanded, his voice rising, his jugular popping to the surface. The prosecutor's fleshy face turned scarlet and his topaz blue eyes bulged. "No where! And why is that?"

"Weber and Obermeyer had families. There were missing persons reports, someone seemed to care, but with Bolz, well, until now, his whereabouts of the past two years are a total blank."

"A former Nazi Bund member fished out of the Passaic with his brains blown out is hardly a total blank," Peterson said. He was aware for the first time that several hangers-on were looking their way.

"The only thing we've got right now is that the Bund loved these three guys enough to send them first-class to Nuremberg in '38," the detective said. "When they got home, the FBI labeled Weber, Obermeyer and Bolz true believers, and never let them out of their sight. That's eight years ago, a long time. We don't even know if these guys knew each other, or even met over a bratwurst and beer in Nuremberg. The FBI had pre-war Bolz living in a series of rooming houses and apartments in Hudson County. Never married. He tried to enlist, but because of his Nazi-lover background, the military wouldn't touch him."

"The connection has to be the killers," Peterson said. "That's the only thing that makes sense."

"I'm leaning toward one person pulling the strings, a fucked-up mastermind if you will," Cisco said. "It took a hell of a lot of planning to figure out the ebb and flow of the Passaic's tide so that the stiffs would be bobbing just below the surface, but never above."

"Three camps, two here in Jersey, one on Long Island; three victims, two traced through their families, and a third from God knows where," Peterson said. "The FBI report indicated he loved those little shoe box towns along the river like North Bergen, West New York, Union City and Weehawken. Anything there?"

"Haven't gotten that far yet," Cisco said. He knew that if they talked much longer, his growing annoyance would surface, and this pompous ass now only a foot away would undoubtedly pick up on it.

Peterson laid in wait. Cisco's barely discernible irritation did not escape him, and he seized the opening to clear the air as to who was calling the shots. "Get on it," the prosecutor said. "A lot at stake here. For all of us. I expect a report no later than Sunday. Call anytime, I'll be home all weekend."

The conversation came to a merciful end when the Reverend Jonathon Haventhorpe assailed the two men with a friendly but inquisitive, "You've been huddling here for too long. Anything that we should all know about?"

"Good to see you again, Reverend. It's been a long time," Cisco said shaking the minister's hand. "I've got to run now, see what I can do to help rid the city of all the rampant crime we've been hearing about." With a parting nod to Peterson, he turned and headed to the elevator.

CHAPTER

TWENTY-SEVEN

Cisco spotted Terry Nolan seated in one of the small, naugahyde-upholstered booths that lined the wall to the right of the Grand Bar and Grille entrance. A plate with a half-eaten kosher dill pickle and crumpled napkin had been pushed to the center of the booth's small round table. In front of the priest was an ashtray containing three butts, a pack of Lucky Strikes, a zippo lighter, and an empty Pabst beer bottle. The priest was seated in the center of the circular booth nursing a glass of beer. He slid to his right when he saw the detective approach, pulling the ashtray, cigarettes and lighter along with him.

"Made it as fast as I could," Cisco said. "Sorry to keep you waiting, but it was unavoidable." He parked himself in the booth across from the priest, and motioned to the white-aproned bartender doing double-duty as a waiter. "Two more of the same, Joey. That okay with you, Father?"

"That's fine. Have one?" Nolan said tapping loose a cigarette from his pack of Luckies. Cisco accepted the offer. He inhaled deeply as the priest lit his cigarette and then his own. Peering through the smoke, Cisco saw a man not exactly nervous, but certainly anxious to get started with what he had to say.

"Okay, let's have the rest of it," Cisco said. "Who is the six-year-old girl, and how does this guy, Franke, and the

Archdiocese fit together? Those injuries you described, all to the same girl? If so, I'm surprised she's still alive. How do you figure into all of this, and why do you think I can help? This looks like something for juvenile court."

"If things continue, it'll never get there. And as to why I'm asking your help, it goes back to last year and the death of my Saint Mark's altar boy that should never have happened, if I'd only had balls enough to stop it."

"What you're describing now seems a long stretch from Saint Mark's," Cisco said. "From what you've told me, I'm not sure where I fit in, or if I fit in at all."

"I don't have an answer, only instinct. When you came to the rectory last year and asked for my help, I thought I recognized a kindred spirit, a cop with real compassion for the city's throw-away kids."

The priest stubbed out his cigarette, drained his Pabst, and motioned for another round. Cisco noted how the priest's gestures were easy and precise.

"On the surface, you're right," Nolan said. "From where you're sitting, it would be hard to compare the shootings last year with the helplessness of a six-year-old girl. Except for one thing."

"What would that be?"

"My involvement. If I had cared enough back then to do the right thing, the killings would not have happened. With Muriel, I'm trying my damndest to do the right thing."

"Muriel, finally there's a name to go with the bruises."

Cisco ignored the glass that came with his Pabst, reached for the bottle, gulped down half of it, placed the bottle on its Ballantine Ale coaster, and tapped his fingers on the table before reaching for his cigarette that balanced on the lip of the ashtray. He took a deep drag of his Lucky Strike, exhaled the smoke through his nostrils, and replaced the cigarette in the ashtray. He didn't know where to go with all of this. It wasn't like him. He was uncomfortable with the recognition that he was stalling for time. He knew the priest was studying his every move. He picked up his bottle and took a small swig to filter the nicotine taste from his mouth. Even the most trivial now drew his rapt attention. He zeroed in on the coaster and found Ballantine's trite *You get a smile every time with Ballantine* irresistible. Cisco raised his eyes from the brewery's feel-good, expertly-crafted bromide to find the priest draining his glass of beer.

"Muriel's last name couldn't be Franke, could it?" Cisco said.

"No, it isn't, but if Franke and his wife can pull it off, it will be," the priest said.

"Pull it off? What the hell does that mean?" demanded Cisco, now agitated by his own uncertainty.

The priest turned from the detective, caught Joey's eye, raised two fingers, and with a circular motion ordered two more beers.

"Okay with you?" he asked, and without waiting for a reply, "You hungry, Nick? It's one hell of a pastrami sandwich they make here."

Cisco noted the ease with which the priest had interjected his first name. Damn this guy's good, he thought. How old is he, barely remembering his notes from last year's meeting with the priest. Not yet thirty, he vaguely recalled, and already ticketed as one of the chancery's golden boys. The detective knew that it was his cue to respond with a nonchalant, Terry. Hell, why not.

"Let's make it clear, Terry, if you're looking for me to give your conscience a massage, you've got the wrong man," Cisco said. "You're the priest, not me. So the Franke family is buying an adoption, what else is new? Isn't that the way it's always done? And if they haven't adopted Muriel, how do they get their hands on the girl to the extent you've described? I'm just not getting it, where is the kid now?"

"Nick, let's get it straight," the priest said, "I don't need a surrogate, I need a cop with muscle, a weapon I guess you could say, to help me pry open the door to the Archbishop's office. It won't be easy, maybe impossible. After Muriel was pulled from school with a broken arm, ecstatic rumors circulated that M.L. Kraus was going to donate twenty thousand dollars toward work on the interior of the Sacred Heart Cathedral. Quite a coincidence, isn't it?"

"And Walsh doesn't want to look a gift horse in the mouth. Is that what you're saying?" Cisco said. "Just spell it out. Again, where is this little girl? If the Frankes haven't adopted her, how do they get their hands on her? If it's as bad as you say, and I have no reason to doubt you, is everyone else at the chancery wearing blinders? You talked about a possible homicide in the making, do you really believe this?"

"I try not to," the priest said. "I saw Muriel only twice. The last time was a little more than a week ago at the church welfare office downtown. She was with a social worker, Mary Fitzgerald, who has had her under tow from the start. They were on their way to Saint Joseph's Home for Boys in Englewood Cliffs, and what I got from Miss Fitzgerald, it was the second time they were hiding her from the Frankes. Her left arm was in a cast. Miss Fitzgerald tried to minimize it, said it was nothing serious, a hairline fracture."

"They were hiding Muriel? If the girl was taken from the Frankes and being cared for by Catholic Welfare, why the hell did they have to hide her?" Cisco said. "As for a homicide in waiting, it couldn't be paranoia could it?"

"Maybe, maybe not. That's why I'm talking to you. The first time I saw the girl and Miss Fitzgerald was two weeks earlier at the downtown Catholic Welfare office," Nolan said. "Miss Fitzgerald was dropping off a cash voucher for gas and lunch for her and Muriel that day. What I was looking at really didn't fit at all. So I got curious."

Cisco felt that he knew where the priest was going, and that he was capable of filling in the blanks himself. A poor little rich girl, probably pretty as a picture, seemingly well cared for, no hand-me-down clothes or shoes like most of the kids dumped at the welfare office, and correct and polite as hell. He decided to sit back and listen.

As if on cue, the two men drained their beer. The priest tapped out a cigarette for himself, lit it, and pushed the pack of Luckies and zippo lighter across the table to Cisco.

"On me," Joey said, picking up the two dead soldiers from the Ballantine coasters, and replacing them with two sweating bottles of Pabst.

Terry acknowledged the gesture with a nod and a smile, then absently scanned the room while he collected his thoughts. It was pitch time. And it had better be good. He would be asking a cop already under immense pressure to wade into an ugly morass that seemed hopeless.

"The first time I saw Muriel, she was seated next to a woman on a battered, high-backed wooden bench that was probably a salvaged pew from a church somewhere."

The tap was opened. Cisco weighed every word, amazed at the priest's recall, and wondered if he could fashion a coherent reason for getting involved. The priest began to ramble between sips of beer and puffs of smoke. He fashioned a sad bas-relief that depicted a small, healthy, blonde, blue-eyed girl, and a pretty thirtyish woman in classic bureaucratic uniform. Her brunette hair was bobbed. She wore sensible low-heeled black shoes, nylons, navy blue skirt and jacket worn over a wide collar white blouse. The only ornamentation was a gold necklace with a cross. The girl wore white patent leather shoes, pale blue anklets, a blue and white sailor dress, and to complete the picture, white cotton gloves. With one of her gloved hands, she fondled an obviously expensive teddy bear on her lap, and her other hand rested comfortably on the right hand of the woman beside her. To complete the picture, her left hand rested on a brown leather valise, stuffed to where it couldn't be closed.

"I walked over, patted the girl's teddy bear on the head, and asked if her Teddy had a name. She looked up and seemed to be surprised by my smiling interest. 'Rudy, his name is Rudy. Rudy is a strong man's name, and I want my teddy bear to be strong.'

"Why must Rudy be strong, is it to protect you?"

"'He tries, but sometimes he can't,' she told me. Bending closer, I spotted the yellow purple of a healing bruise on her neck that peaked out from under the starched collar of her dress."

"That was how long ago?" Cisco said. "I make it almost four weeks ago when you spotted a bruise on her neck. How long do you figure this has been going on?"

"I don't know and as I was about to find out, apparently neither does anyone else," the priest said. "The woman sitting next to Muriel seemed on edge, you know, the kind of edginess that comes from when you want to blurt out something, but unsure on how to do it. She said she was Muriel's case worker. Her eyes dug deep. She was searching for trust, and could I be that man. I pulled over a metal folding chair that had been propped against the wall at the same time Miss Fitzgerald was pulling a file folder from her bag.

"She handed me the folder and said, 'I'm sorry, Father, I don't even know your name, but I'm hoping that after seeing these photos you can do something, talk to the right people, anything to get Muriel out of harm's way.'"

It was all coming back to Cisco now, the feeling he had about Terry last year when he stopped by the rectory to ask the priest to intercede for him with the dead altar boy's parents. The priest came up just short of wearing sack cloth and ashes, when he was told his help meant a trip to the morgue to view the boy's remains. It appeared to the detective that the priest was following the same path again. He took another swig of beer and waited.

"There were about a dozen photos along with Miss Fitzgerald's notes," Nolan said. "You're a cop and have probably seen it all, so I'm not going to overwhelm you with detail. There were black and blue marks from her buttocks to her neck that included that bruise I described to you the first time I saw the girl. The largest bruise was to her right shoulder, the one that was separated. A hell of a lot of force had to be used to wrench Muriel's shoulder out of its socket, and now the broken arm. Miss Fitzgerald took this evidence to her superiors, warning that Muriel was not safe with the Frankes, that something had to be done before it was too late. The photos she showed me were copies that she made herself before handing over the originals and the negatives to Monsignor Garanti. I talked to him and was told it was under investigation, that the Frankes were important people, and each question had to be carefully worded so as not to offend them. He said the case had to be handled 'perfectly,' that's the Monsignor's word, not mine."

"How did the Frankes get their hands on Muriel in the first place?" Cisco said. "Catholic Adoptive Services are tough as hell on applicants. Has the girl been adopted or hasn't she?"

"No, not yet," Nolan said. "Apparently someone with real power, and I don't know who, is handling everything."

"What about Muriel's parents?"

"This is where it gets complicated. Her father was Flight Lieutenant William Sheffield, a fighter pilot with the Royal Canadian Air Force. He was killed in combat over North Africa. Before being shipped out, he married Kay Toner, an American student vacationing in Vancouver, his home town. The baby Muriel was born in Canada and has dual citizenship. Her mother was never accepted by the in-laws, so she returned to her home in Brooklyn, and tried to make a go of it as a war widow. Her own family didn't make things easy by turning their back on her. Kay Toner was only nineteen, hardly more than a kid. She discovered that in Connecticut there was a fancy home where unwed mothers with the right Catholic pedigree could have their babies, and then put them up for adoption, again to families with the right pedigree. Enter Hugo Manfred Franke and his wife, Honoria."

"Christ almighty! How many were involved in this international fuck-up? Canada, New York, Connecticut and now New Jersey," Cisco said. "Hugo and Honoria had to really pull some strings. Foundlings, even desirable ones like Muriel, who would be very much in demand, aren't easy to take across state lines."

"This is where it really gets interesting," the priest said. "I called the Maywood Home in Connecticut. It seems they received a phone call reference from one of the Frankes' DuPont friends in Delaware, and another from a Standard Oil executive in New York. Voilà! State lines and international borders disappeared."

"Any indication the same high-priced persuasion was used on Archbishop Walsh?" Cisco said. "Jesus Christ, if I may say so, Terry, Standard Oil, DuPont and M.L. Kraus can buy New Jersey, what they don't own already, so why not throw in an Archdiocese to sanctify the lot."

Nolan nodded in agreement. He warily eyed the remaining beer in his glass. It was almost empty, as was the bottle in front of him. Unlike Cisco, this was not his third Pabst, but his fourth, the first washed down the pastrami sandwich he devoured before Cisco arrived. He was getting sloshed, and he could feel the predictable urges coming on, the next stage would be growing combativeness. He emptied his glass and turned toward Cisco.

"Before you ask, the answer is no, I don't have the photos," the priest said. "In any event, they're a poor substitute for seeing Muriel yourself."

"Look, Terry, I hear you, but I still don't see where I fit in," Cisco said, "and for that matter, where do the courts come in? No charges have been filed, and it looks as though there never will be. Sure I want justice, maybe start by strangling the Frankes."

"I'm not expecting you to turn vigilante," Nolan said. "But I am hoping that anyone with a police badge, and I don't care who, is made aware of what's been happening, and how dangerous it would be if the Franke adoption goes through. The shootings last year gave us common ground, so I started with you. Now I'm asking for four, maybe five hours of your time. Can you spare them?"

"Right now, I'm up to my neck in real murders," Cisco said, "and the press has been kicking my ass calling for a real homicide chief instead of a fill-in like me. Did you see the *Clarion* editorial cartoon in yesterday's paper? It's got me sitting on a whoopee cushion to soothe my battered backside. Wheezing out is the warning, 'No arrests, No promotion.' And now I take it that you want me to jaunt off to Englewood Cliffs with you. Am I getting it right?"

"Exactly right," the priest said, "and I'm thinking Sunday morning. Out early, back early, then I'll be out of your hair."

If the priest only knew what he was asking. The detective couldn't help looking at all the disparate pieces of his screwed-up life. The *Clarion's* editorial cartoonist couldn't possibly know how uncomfortable the whoopee cushion was. He needed a break, and a quixotic gesture could fill the bill.

"Okay, Father, Sunday morning," Cisco said. "Six sharp. I'll pick you up outside Saint Mark's rectory. I saw that old Dodge you're driving, I think it's better we take my unmarked car. The gas is on the City."

CHAPTER
TWENTY-EIGHT

Father Nolan parked his car in his allotted space behind Saint Mark's rectory. The fresh, late morning air was invigorating, and he greedily sucked it in. He was returning from his weekly Saturday visit to hear the confession and administer communion to the widow Clementine Bates, a pastoral duty he inherited from his predecessor, Father Ludwig Koestler. It was after one such visit to the Bates' stifling, icon-stuffed apartment that Father Koestler suffered a massive stroke, and died on the sidewalk outside her parlor window. A few weeks later Terry was assigned by the Archdiocese to take his place.

As he walked along the path to the front porch of the rectory, he was thinking about the trip he and Nick Cisco would be taking the next morning to Saint Joseph's. He had cleared it with his pastor, Father James Schneider, and Jim had readily agreed to add Terry's early mass to his Sunday schedule. Turning to climb the four steps to the porch, Terry was surprised to find Jim waiting with a lopsided smile.

"You've got a visitor. Someone I'm certain will brighten things up after the redoubtable widow Bates." Terry reached the third step as Jim stepped aside to allow a full view of the man seated in the cushioned, wicker arm chair strategically placed in the rear shaded portion of the porch. "He showed up about twenty minutes ago, and has already filled me in about the seminary time you both endured."

"Well I'll be damned! Call out the militia, the enemy has arrived," Terry said as he quickly strode to greet his former spiritual advisor. "Father Peter Majeski! Father Ski, the only communist priest I've ever known." The older priest, not quite as tall as Terry, arose from the chair and the two men shared a long, back-slapping embrace. They backed off with their hands on each other's shoulders, each man searching for words.

"Would you believe, Jim, that Father Ski had once fallen in love with Ellen Dawson, the commie firebrand who organized the Passaic Garment Strike," Terry said.

"Would have followed that pretty lass anywhere, but alas, it was an unrequited love," the bulky, middle-aged priest said. "That whole Stalin-Trotsky thing did it for me. The accusations, lies, arrests, forced confessions and torture. So, I traded in my red scarf and beret for a starched collar."

Ski slumped back into the cushions of the wicker chair. He reached for a half-filled glass of Vat 69 that Jim had graciously offered when he arrived, swirled the two ice cubes around, and then took a healthy swig of the Scotch. Terry pulled over another chair, as Jim placed another glass of Scotch on the table between the two men. Then without another word, the pastor disappeared into the rectory.

"Okay, now tell me all about it," Terry said. "The last I heard you were blaspheming recruits at the Coast Guard boot camp at Cape May. That doesn't sound like you."

"It wasn't. I begged to get out of there," Ski said. "Chaplains were becoming a scarce commodity after the North African, Sicilian and Italian campaigns. Everyone knew that France was next, and they needed guys like me to say dead words over dying men. So, I found myself getting plastered at officers' clubs in London and South

Hampton to prepare myself. They posted me with the Third Army just before its big push across France into the Rhineland. And you?"

"Young buck that I was, I wanted action," Terry said, "and who better than the Marines. The Navy obliged my stupidity, and sent me ashore with the First Marines on Guadalcanal. Two years later I was shipped home from Saipan after a year of island-hopping with the Fourth. Now here we are back in Jersey, and what about you?"

"Once a Polack, always a Polack," Ski said. "They planted me across the river to help out at Saint Casimir's."

"Tell me more."

"Seventy-five percent speak only Polish. It's a crusty old place that's been handing out salvation for more than a hundred years. The pastor, Father Kaczinski, is a tired old man getting weaker by the day. Two Polish-speaking priests are on their way from a seminary in Massachusetts, and until they take over, I'm running things. For how long, I don't know."

"How did you find me?" Terry said.

"Wasn't hard. Stopped by the Chancery late yesterday morning, and heard your name mentioned," Ski said. "I asked about you, and two office minions waxed poetic. Said you were going to have some words for an anti-crime committee meeting that afternoon."

"Spellbinder that you are, you should have come over and given them a dose of law and order according to Trotsky," Terry said. "I did get that right, didn't I, that Trotsky was your guy?"

"You got it right," the older priest said, "and by the way, Saint Casimir's is right in the middle of where I spent some of my Bolshevik salad days."

Father Schneider returned to the porch with a small bucket of ice and empty glass in one hand, and a bottle of Vat 69 in the other. He placed them on the table, and with his fingers dropped four ice cubes into the empty glass, and two cubes into each of the other two glasses. He poured a good three fingers of Scotch into each of the glasses and lifted his own for a toast.

"I'm not an eavesdropper by nature, but I couldn't help overhearing," Jim said. "It's rare that I can host a real lefty at the rectory."

"Nazdaróvye!" Ski said.

"Nazdaróvye!" Terry and Jim echoed. The three men clicked glasses then swallowed deeply.

"I'm sorry it's not vodka," Jim said, "but what the hell."

He drained his glass, as did the other two priests. There was an awkward silence as the three men absently jiggled the ice cubes. At this point, Jim realized how serious an interloper he had become.

"You two have a lot of catching up to do," he said, at the same time turning to Ski and flicking his left thumb over his shoulder to the big black Buick parked at the curb. "I saw you pull up in that mechanized gorilla. Why don't you wind it up and take Terry on safari."

"Quite a beast," Ski said. "A big thank you from Saint Casimir's parishioners to Father Kaczinski for the twenty-five years he spent slapping band-aids on their souls. Like new, only three thousand miles."

"Why don't you two get lost for a couple of hours," Jim said.

"That's plenty of time," Ski said. "I'd like him to see my digs across the river, and meet a guy who really simplified things for me twenty years ago."

“Bring him back in one piece.” Father Schneider watched from the rectory porch as the Buick Super pulled from the curb and entered the traffic flow on High Street headed toward Market.

“Quite a car,” Terry said as he watched Ski expertly shift through the lower gears, the Buick picking up speed after turning off Market onto Broad. “I have an inkling that this guy I’ll be meeting has nothing to do with the church.”

“As far away from the church as you can get,” Ski said. “I was surprised as hell to find him still at his old battle station, tough as ever. Quite a religious guy in his own way.”

Ski turned off Broad Street heading east to the Clay Street Bridge, drove a block and a half where the Buick joined other cars backed up to allow the swing bridge to creak open, and let a tug and scrap-laden barge pass southward to Port Newark.

“After I heard your name mentioned at the Chancery,” Ski said, “I tried to run you down at that meeting yesterday. I was told I just missed you, that you left with a cop. What’s that all about? Serious enough for you to talk about?”

“Serious enough,” Terry said, “a lot of ugly things. Some big people involved. It could worsen into a tragedy. That’s why I called homicide.”

“Homicide, can’t get bigger than that. I take it you’re not going to elaborate?”

“Not right now, maybe never” Terry said. “I hope that things will shake out, and that will be the end of it.”

“Goddamned if you’re not being even more cryptic than you were at the seminary with all of your Jesuit platitudes. You were always pretty damn sure of yourself.”

“Not any more. Two years of Pacific island-hopping, one bloody beach after another, took care of that.”

Ski said nothing. His facial features hardened and then froze. His eyes, always alive and inquiring, turned gimlet hard and unblinking. His big hands strangled the steering wheel, an unconscious attempt to remove an inner frustration that had taken control. Terry was stunned by Ski's transformation. His jovial mentor had disappeared into a secret hiding place.

The swing bridge clanked back into place, and the barriers went up to allow traffic to flow east and west across the debris-strewn river. The two men remained silent as the Buick crossed the bridge, and turned south on Passaic Avenue. The traffic was bumper-to-bumper, the usual pretext for blather, so their silence was unduly awkward.

"Now where do we go from here?" Terry broke the silence.

"Bear with me, it'll be bumpy, but worth it," said Ski, his smile a clear indication that his inner demons had disappeared. He tooled the Buick along a railroad siding that led to a large, soot-encrusted, one-story concrete building. Six large windows on each side were spaced to run the length of the building just below the roof line.

"Here's as good a place as any to cross over," Ski said. Without slowing, he turned sharply to the left and the car went airborne as it cleared the tracks, and bounced to a stop about seventy-five feet from the north end of the factory.

"That's Samuel's office," Ski said. "Talked to him the other day, and said I might stop by. Said he'd be around 'til five. You'll like him."

There was no signage on the building. In this out of the way place, it would only be a grandiose and totally unnecessary corporate gesture. A twelve-foot wide, strongly reinforced wooden loading dock that ran the length of the building said it all. Six-foot rolls of heavy brown paper stood upright at the south end of the dock, waiting to be fork-lifted inside where huge machines would have their way. There were at least ten wooden skids loaded with bundled corrugated cardboard lined up for the next freight car. In the air was the unmistakable stench of rotten eggs, evidence that at least one skid had been left uncovered during last night's rain.

The two priests stepped from the car and stretched. Terry inhaled deeply and wished that he hadn't. He sensed Ski watching him, waiting for his reaction. As he had from the beginning of their short trip from Newark, Terry continued to wonder what this was all about. Ski didn't have to prove anything to him. He had done that during their rambling talks at the seminary, when this former tobacco-chewing, chain-smoking block of a man, a one-time Commie to boot, had taken him under his wing. Was Samuel a missing link? To connect what? Ski was hardly a game player, and Terry had no clue whether today was a charade or not.

"Scenic as hell," Terry said, "can't wait to get inside."

"I knew you'd like it. Come on, let's go."

They reached the last of the six steps leading to the platform outside Samuel's office when the door flung open, and a tall, gray haired man with the face of a prize fighter greeted them.

"Thought you were just bullshitting me on the phone the other day," Samuel said, "that you wanted to stop by and rehash the good old days, and there were some good ones."

Samuel and Ski laughed as they each shadow boxed a right jab and left hook before they clinched, pounded each other on the back, and separated. Terry watched, aware that he was witnessing the easy camaraderie of two old friends.

"Two stiff white collars at one time," said Samuel, for the first time taking the measure of Terry. His craggy features softened, as his brown eyes took in Terry's tall, angular and obviously well-muscled frame.

"So, you're the Fordham Whiz Kid Ski mentioned," said Samuel. He grabbed Terry's right hand, and pumped three times. "Said if you kept your nose clean, and kissed the right asses, you'd make it big time. Hell, if I knew what he was talking about, but I'll take his word for it. Come on in. Cramped and messy, but there are chairs. They're wooden, so watch out for the splinters."

CHAPTER TWENTY-NINE

Samuel ushered the two priests into his office. He eased himself into a cracked leather desk chair, and waited for Ski and Terry to take the two chairs facing him on the other side of the desk. There were three metal filing cabinets in the far-right corner of the office, a desk fan perched on one of them turned just enough to move the air in the windowless room. A wash basin was attached to the wall in the far-left corner, a towel rack to the right, and a small square mirror above it. A dirty soap dish adorned a corner of the sink. The floor of unpainted tongue-and-groove wooden planks was worn and cracked. The large door directly behind Samuel's desk gave direct access to the factory. The room was probably no more than twelve feet square, but more than adequate to allow for two additional wooden chairs to be placed on either side of the outside door.

Two overflowing IN and OUT boxes failed to give even a semblance of order to the jumbled mess of paper on top of Samuel's desk. Bills of lading, railroad timetables, invoices, payment vouchers, and ledgers crowded for space with employee timecards identified by shift, and bundled tightly with rubber bands. A modern, black telephone jutted from the heap. Terry noted that the phone had no dial, only three push buttons, prompting Samuel to say, "Yeah, it's an intercom connected to my three bosses, one of them with a direct line to the big man in New York."

"A hell of a change, wouldn't you say?" Ski said. "Here you are, an anarchist, now running a factory for capitalist swine. You damn well know they doesn't trust you. How many times a day does that thing ring?"

"Three, maybe four times," Samuel said. "They knew who I was, where I had been – Passaic, New Bedford, and Gastonia."

"The war's over, jobs are drying up," Ski said. "Hungry guys on the streets again, so here you are."

"Short and simple," Samuel said, "The company's spies have been working overtime. Found a lot of union sympathy among its rank and file. Even the thought of a strike scared the hell out of them, so they decided to sleep with the enemy, and here I am."

Samuel reached into the lower right drawer of his desk, pulled out a full bottle of Black & White Scotch, broke the seal, pushed aside some papers, and placed the bottle in the center of the clearing. He then retrieved three glasses from the same drawer, walked to the sink, rinsed them, and returned to his chair. He poured a healthy three fingers into each glass, recorked the bottle, leaned back in his chair, and with a conspirator's smile said, "Okay, it's bourgeois to be sure. What a pity the Kremlin bullshit we were fed never included Scotch for the masses. Enjoy."

The wall behind Samuel was dominated by a glass enclosed, twelve-by-sixteen photo in a black and gold lacquered frame. The scene was ugly. No words were necessary to describe what was happening at *Textile Strikers General Relief Store No. 3*, where a mob of half-starved kids pushed, shoved and kicked their way into a kitchen set up by working mothers.

Terry got up and walked to the wall for a closer look. He counted ten kids, four without shoes. He guessed that none were older than seven.

"Your bosses actually let you hang this?" an incredulous Terry asked. "Looks like something out of the *Daily Worker*."

"Doubt they even know about it. Never come here, do all their talking over that thing on my desk," Samuel said. "Hell, there's dozens more like it. Could wallpaper this place with them. The strike lasted for more than a year. This photo is tame."

Samuel reached for his whiskey glass, tipped it, and saw that it was empty. Holding the glass in his right hand, he turned it upside down. Not a drop. He closed his eyes and inhaled deeply, and after a few seconds, exhaled with a sigh that was more like a moan. Ski and Terry disappeared. Unbidden self-hypnosis took hold. The two priests silently watched as Samuel opened his eyes and studied the empty glass, oblivious of all around him.

Ski had been there himself, but because of the unquenchable hatred that engulfed him since Dachau, and fearing his rancor would become permanently embedded, he had put self-hypnosis on the backburner. For him and Samuel it began as a joke, Émile Coué's feel good anthem, *Every day in every way, I'm getting better and better.* Next, they discovered how the self-proclaimed *animal magnetism* of Charles Poyen mesmerized criminally overworked mill laborers into long, life-saving hours of sleep. That was their ticket. They devoured every hypnosis handbook they could lay their hands on, and practiced incessantly during their breaks from the strike lines at Passaic, New Bedford and Gastonia.

Samuel's subconscious jibberish became clearer the deeper he got.

"Just like babes at their mothers' teats, we took that first glorious suck of commie ambrosia. So sweet. We wanted to believe so much that Mother Russia had the answers. We were never meant to drain the glass…to find the poison at the bottom."

As quickly as he had left them, a smiling Samuel returned to the priests without a hint of embarrassment.

He reached for the bottle, refilled his glass, raised it in mock salute, and drained it with one gulp. "The truth, if there is truth in any of this, is that I joined the Reds because I wanted to get laid. Easy pickings." Samuel turned to Ski, "Wouldn't you say?"

"It was nymph heaven," Ski said. "Meat on the hook."

"Needed a tote board to keep track," Samuel said, "There'd be a gal from Gettysburg College one night, and a rich girl from Barnard the next.

"This guy, your revered mentor, grew up fast. He was a combination of a babe in the woods, and an arrogant son of a bitch. Waved his college degree like it was sacred script, but what he really needed was toilet paper. He didn't know shit from shinola. Got his first chaw of tobacco, puked all over himself."

"The press was everywhere," Ski said. "Everyone was ducking, dodging and running for cover. Reporters and newsreel crews armor-plated their cars, and covered their heads with anything they could find. So much for the dignity of the press."

Samuel chimed in, "I was ducking and dodging myself, but couldn't help laughing my butt off watching as this one pompous reporter balanced a frying pan on his head as he dived into a doorway."

Terry knew he was a privileged outsider who had been granted a rare opportunity to hear two old comrades relive their glory days. Anecdote-after-anecdote reinforced his perception that winning meant very little to them, it was the fight against insurmountable odds that burnished their memories so that each victory and every defeat glowed incandescently. Vivid memories of company goons and Passaic cops using billy clubs, night sticks, rifle butts, tear gas, and well-aimed kicks entranced Terry. Not even the kids were immune, the goons used high pressure water hoses on them during a peaceful parade, and knocked them off their feet. He glanced at the photo on the wall, and wondered how many of these shoeless kids had been washed into the gutter.

The bottle of Black & White was now the center of their attention. Terry offered his glass, and Samuel did the honors.

"It was ugly and brutal, and to tell you the truth, I wanted to murder those sons of bitches," Ski's voice was suddenly ominous and filled with venom. The same hard, gimlet-eyed stare that Terry witnessed in the car was back and frozen in place. "Top of my list was that crazed sadist, Police Chief Zober."

"I caught Ski making a deal with some slimy character for an old blunderbuss of a gun that would probably blow his hand off," Samuel said. "Talked him out of it. A bitch of an argument."

"With Zober it wouldn't have been murder, but an assassination," Ski said. "In the end, the bosses played it smart. They gave the strikers all they wanted, no pay cut, shorter work hours, overtime pay, and union recognition. It was all a mirage."

"Another one of our glorious failures," Samuel said. "Didn't take long for the lay-offs to start. Paychecks got smaller. No one wanted another strike. It took only two years for a twelve-thousand member union to dwindle to one hundred, and the United Textile Workers disappeared in Passaic."

Samuel took in Ski with a penetrating look, it was a private thing that excluded Terry. Ski dropped his eyes and scanned the desk. The younger priest had never seen his mentor, a man always in command, so obviously self-conscious. It just didn't fit, and Terry wondered what inner turmoil was causing it.

"Then it was on to New Bedford and Gastonia, and we got slapped around again," said Samuel, obviously feeling his Scotch, and never taking his eyes off Ski. "Then you packed it in, ran back to the mackerel snappers, and put that starched noose around your neck for good measure."

Ski sat motionless, never taking his eyes from the desk. Terry saw his face stiffen. It was the death mask at the swing bridge all over again. As with the Buick's steering wheel, it appeared to Terry that Ski had white knuckled his right hand around the whiskey bottle. He then tipped the bottle, splashed some Scotch into his glass and inhaled it.

"It was a good thing for you, getting out when you did," Samuel said. "Ellen Dawson, that beautiful wisp of a woman, did her best, but Christ almighty, we all knew that when the shooting began in Passaic, and they had all the guns, it was just a matter of time. Just another fucking failure." Rekindled frustration and hatred dripped from every syllable.

"So, what did you do?" Terry asked.

"Drifted for five or six years, or thereabouts. Joined the Wobblies out west for awhile, and when we got word that Stalin's purges were murdering millions, me, Jimmy Tinker and Pat Quinlan decided to find out if there was one son of a bitching thing good about the commies. Deckhanded on a freighter to London, a tramp steamer to Marseille, hoofed it into Spain and joined the Republicans in time for Ebro. It was a slaughter. Franco's fascists had Mussolini and Hitler behind them, and all we had were Commissars ready to shoot us in the head if we took one step backward."

"So, what came next? How'd you get out?" Terry said.

"I was one of the lucky ones who made it back into France. Won't bore you on how I got to the States, but here I am."

Ski got up and motioned for Terry to do likewise. It was obvious to Terry that the older priest had been diminished by Samuel's words, as matter of fact as they were and without a hint of superiority.

Throughout their meeting there was the constant noise generated by the three mammoth corrugators beyond the rear door of Samuel's office. "You wanna go back, take a look?" Samuel said.

"Nope, gotta get on our way," Ski said. "Got to deliver this guy back to Saint Mark's."

Samuel and Ski extended their right hands, but the handshake lacked the exuberance of their earlier greeting. The old Bolshevik pumped Terry's hand three times and said not unkindly, "Take care, kid. The bastards who run the Chancery simply wear a different uniform. Remember *accentuate the positive, eliminate the negative*, Johnny Mercer has it right."

Except for the radio, the drive home was made in silence. Ski scanned the Motorola dial several times with his right hand before settling on WOR and Dinah Shore's *Laughing on the Outside*. Several cloying songs by Frank Sinatra, Jo Stafford, Nat King Cole and Perry Como provided convenient white noise that masked the silence of the two priests. There would be no side trip to Saint Casimir's. Twenty-five minutes later, Terry was deposited at the rectory.

"Take care of yourself, Terry," said Ski extending his right hand along with a tight smile. "It was interesting, wouldn't you say?"

"That's one hell of an understatement," said Terry in an attempt to end the afternoon on a breezy note. "Samuel certainly wears it all out there on his sleeve. Quite a guy. Thanks for the invite."

Standing at the curb as Ski drove off, Terry found it hard to put a handle on what the past few hours were all about. Why had Ski brought him along? Certainly it wasn't to expose the internal, white-knuckled rage he exhibited in the ride across the river and then in Samuel's office. Or was it?

CHAPTER THIRTY

Muriel and five other girls silently climbed two flights of stairs from the first floor refectory where they shared their meals with fifteen novices. Their breakfast of a single pancake slathered with syrup and margarine, a generous portion of powdered eggs, and a glass of milk was a pleasant departure from the usual fare of oatmeal, two slices of dried toast with grape jelly and milk, all military surplus.

The good Sisters of Saint Joseph of Peace performed minor miracles to make the meals edible, and some meals were downright luscious. With Sister Bernadette at the helm, Spam provided the convent's answer to pheasant under glass. She enlisted the help of the orphan girls and novices to create a bountiful herb garden at the southeast end of the property. Rosemary, basil, thyme, chives, oregano and parsley were protected in a shallow wooden box covered with extra screening leftover from work at the boys' school. Rabbits were a constant threat. Always at the ready were two heavy pieces of oak shaped into clubs. Sister Bernadette's plan was to club the rabbits, skin them, and once they were dressed and ready for the spit, she used her herbal magic to transform them into a feast worthy of the finest tables in her native Tipperary. One club had six notches on it, and the other four.

Two large crab apple trees flanked the herb garden to the east and west. The small apples were tart and often pucker-inducing, but in the right hands made the best jelly. On Sundays they were sliced into wedges, sprinkled with sugar and baked for dessert.

Muriel's room was the fourth one on the left. The door was closed. Like all the others, it was never locked. Using her right hand, she turned the doorknob, and then freed her broken left arm from its sling, and nudged the door open with the cast that ran from her hand to just below her elbow. Although it was a room for two young girls, she'd had it all to herself ever since her roommate Winifred had left three days ago. This should have pleased her, Muriel loved her privacy, but instead she had a funny feeling in her stomach. It was an easy progression from youthful uncertainty to anxiety, and finally fear. Sister Immaculata had taken her aside after breakfast, and told her she would have two visitors that morning. It was Sunday, always a good day for strangers to poke around looking for an ideal child to fill their real or imagined emptiness.

Don't let it be them again. Two times it was nice when they first saw me and wanted me. Then it turned bad, and it wasn't so nice anymore. Please, don't let this be a third time. They hurt me, and last time Honoria hurt me real bad. The sisters here in New Jersey are nice and I will stay here if they let me. I don't really want to stay here, but I will ask to stay if Honoria and Hugo come to get me again.

It was the second time she had been taken to this strange place filled with all kinds of nuns. Some were old, others not too old, and there were others who were young, pretty and very kind. The older nuns wore long black dresses with stiff white things around their neck and on top of their head that looked like the wings of a bird. They didn't say too much and when they did, you knew that you had to listen. Those not so old wore long white dresses and the same bird wings. The ones she liked best were the youngest, they wore a simple dark dress and a scarf hiding their hair. Some of them weren't so good at it, and Muriel could see red, yellow and black hair peeking out. These were the nicest. They gave her big smiles the other night when they put a little birthday cake with six candles in the middle of the dinner table. Everyone sang "Happy Birthday" to her, including Winifred, whose empty bed next to hers made her feel sad. Winifred was chosen the day after Muriel's little birthday treat.

Sister Immaculata was the one who gave the good news and the bad news. She never said a girl was picked for adoption, she was chosen, a special calling by the Lord. The day after her birthday, Muriel was told to sit beside her bed in the room she shared with Winifred. Each girl had a bed, a chair, and a small chest of drawers with a mirror on top. She was told that Winifred would be getting a new father and mother that morning, and she should watch and learn so when her turn came, she would be ready.

The room was one of the few good ones with a window that looked out across a lawn, past the crab apple trees and the school for boys, and onto a big river with all kinds of boats, some with loud horns that made her wake up at night. The room was not at all like her room in the big, beautiful house from which she was taken. Her room in that house had everything she wanted, toys she had never seen before, including a big doll with five different dresses and matching shoes. That was Kristina. She was a friend, but not a protector. When things got bad, Muriel relied on her teddy bear, Rudy, to make her safe when the hitting began. She hugged Rudy to her chest, and moved him up and down, and side-to-side when she was about to be slapped. Rudy went everywhere with Muriel. She never knew when this soft and quiet guardian would be needed again. Rudy didn't seem to mind that he no longer had a big, soft bed, and that his rocking chair and Kristina were gone.

Everything in the room was green except for the cold, hard floor that was everywhere, even outside the door to the ends of the long hallway. There was one ceiling light in the room that went on at six o'clock in the morning, and off at eight o'clock in the evening. An eighteen-inch crucifix greeted visitors from its center position on the far wall. Under it was a wooden wardrobe with space for four pair of shoes on the bottom, a small shelf at the top, and room for six to eight hangers, there was no door. Privacy was never an option. There was a single towel rack on either side of the wardrobe holding one towel, one hand towel and a facecloth, all replaced and laundered along with the bed linen, every Saturday morning.

Sister Immaculata told her that she must be prim and proper, and not knowing what that meant, she sat stiff and quiet while she listened and watched seven year old Winifred do all those little things correctly that she must learn if she ever wanted a new mother and father. Anyone but Hugo and Honoria. She thought the young couple who chose Winifred was nice enough, but the woman fidgeted too much. The small suitcase they brought with them looked like it was made of cardboard. It was red and brown, and had two straps to tie it closed. It was not at all like the heavy leather bag with its brass locks that she had for her things. The couple did not say their names, and only nodded in her direction. The woman tugged and pulled at Winifred's blouse and skirt, but Muriel could not see why. Winifred, with her help and the help of the mirror, had fixed everything so it would be just right. The girls were satisfied, but the woman was not. The man said nothing, did nothing, not even a hug, everything was left to the woman. There was a, "Well, here we are Winifred, and you can rest assured that from now on it will be Winnie," the smiling woman said bending down to put her hand on the girl's shoulder. Muriel was puzzled that the woman did not try to pull Winifred close to her, but kept her arms out stiff.

She saw that Winifred had a sad look on her face, kind of like the looks she noticed on other girls who were expecting more, but weren't getting it. Winifred applied pressure with her shoulders, trying to get closer to the woman. The woman tightened her fingers on Winifred's shoulders, not enough to hurt, but clearly enough to control her. Muriel understood. All Winifred wanted was a hug.

"Now, Winnie, we have our whole life for hugs and kisses," the woman said, her tone admonishing and direct. "But here, your little friend Muriel, isn't it? She's ready with a big farewell hug and, of course, a little kiss on the cheek."

As though the two grown-up strangers had completely disappeared from the room, Muriel and Winifred threw their arms around each other and exchanged kisses on each cheek.

"I'd say that should do it," the man said as he opened the door.

"It's hard for friends to say goodbye," the woman said taking Winifred's right hand in hers. She lifted the cardboard suitcase from the floor, and they followed her husband out of the room.

CHAPTER THIRTY-ONE

This Sunday morning was the start of the third day Muriel had the room all to herself. Her left arm was really itching now. She gave up trying to find a way to scratch, because the cast was too tight. She hoped the two visitors today would be different than the man and woman who took Winifred away, and that her broken arm would not keep her from being chosen. Everything had to be perfect, just as she was taught at the Maywood Home.

She wished she was back at the home now, starting all over, and maybe things wouldn't be as bad as they are now. Her arm wouldn't be broken. Things like that would never happen at the home, Mrs. Thurgood would not allow it. She remembered that morning when she and her mother had gotten out of the taxi, and climbed to the top of the ten granite steps leading to the home's double-door glass entry. A thin, very pretty lady waited to greet them.

"Mrs. Sheffield? We were expecting you. I'm Mrs. Melissa Thurgood. I'm pleased you're dropping Muriel off in time for lunch. It's macaroni and cheese today, one of our favorites. Here, let me have that," she said taking the small overnight bag from Kay Sheffield's left hand, and replacing it with a small, white sealed envelope. The two women exchanged acknowledging glances to finalize the sale.

"Muriel, baby, I'll be leaving you here tonight with Mrs. Thurgood. This is a wonderful place, and I know you'll love it," Kay Sheffield refused to end this sad transaction with a lie that she would be back soon. She knew she would never see her daughter again.

A lot of planning had been necessary for Kay to make a job-hunting trip to Connecticut plausible to her precocious daughter. Day-after-day Muriel had watched as her mother circled help wanted ads in the *Brooklyn Eagle* and other newspapers. Each morning she watched her mother carefully apply her make-up, brush her hair, put on matching earrings and necklace, and put on one of two remaining "impress the boss" dresses, as her mom called them. Well cared for black patent leather shoes and matching handbag completed the ensemble. Kay then took Muriel by the hand, and walked the four blocks to Sheila Tollin's house, where Muriel would join three other girls being cared for by the middle-aged widow. She was down to her last few dollars when she heard about the Maywood Home from another job-hunting war widow.

There were three phone calls to the home. The third one sealing the deal when Mrs. Thurgood learned from Kay that her husband had not come from the great unwashed ranks of enlisted men, but had been an officer, and a gentleman, and a courageous fighter pilot killed in combat in the skies over North Africa.

Then the planning to deceive her daughter began. Despite the lure offered by Mrs. Thurgood's assurance that Muriel was a good fit for Maywood Home, Kay was aware that what she was about to do represented betrayal, but deceit was necessary.

"Baby, seems that Brooklyn's turned its back on us," Kay told her daughter while scrambling eggs for breakfast that morning that seemed so long, long ago. "We've got to look elsewhere, and I've come up with an idea."

"Mommy, you always have great ideas," Muriel said, "and I bet I know where your new idea came from...that newspaper you brought home last night. It's not the *Eagle,* but something new."

"You're right, I picked it up at that newsstand that sells out of town papers," Kay said. "It's from a town not too far away, and it offers some jobs I think I have a chance for. Tomorrow we'll take a look."

"So soon?" Muriel asked. "Does that mean I won't be staying at Mrs. Tollin's?"

"That's right, we'll be taking the early Greyhound bus so we can get there in the morning, got all these stops to make," Kay said as she spread a page of want ads from the paper's classified section on the table. She had no intention of job hunting in Maywood, but the pretense was necessary.

"Will I be coming along?"

"No, I found a wonderful place in town called the Maywood Home. They'll look after you while I'm out and about," Kay said. "They'll even have a taxi waiting for us when we get off the bus. Won't that be great! That's what I call job hunting in style! Put on your best dress for the trip. I think your yellow pinafore with the white shoes and socks will do the trick."

Muriel knew the next day would be special. Her mother never had her dress up to go to Mrs. Tollin's.

That was so long ago. Everything was different now. And her mommy, where could her mommy have gone?

Today, sitting on her bed awaiting the arrival of her two Sunday visitors, Sister Immaculata told her to look her best and have everything clean and tidy, and exactly in place for the visitors. Who were they? Would they be like the two who took Winifred away? She hoped not. One thing she could never forget, as hard as she tried, was the day she was given away for the first time without really even knowing it.

Her mother and Mrs. Thurgood had been talking, when her mother reached down, lifted Muriel and gave her a hug so strong and long that it took both their breaths away. Kay Sheffield knew she had to get off that porch before she started bawling. She gently put her daughter down, placed her hands on her cheeks, smiled, gave her a peck on the tip of her nose just as she had done since Muriel was an infant, and a tender farewell kiss on the lips. Kay arose from her crouch, nodded to Mrs. Thurgood, and without a glance at Muriel, turned and walked with her head erect to the taxi waiting at the bottom of the steps.

Mrs. Thurgood placed her left hand on Muriel's shoulder as they both turned and watched the taxi slowly drive away. For Muriel, the short taxi ride had been a first-time adventure. The home had arranged to have the cab meet them at the Greyhound station in Maywood, and for the driver to wait until the deal was completed. Mrs. Thurgood's fingers probed for any sign that the girl was aware of what had just occurred. She found none. Muriel's shoulder muscles were relaxed, evidence that she had been left alone many times while her mother searched for work, but had always come home to her.

It was so much easier for her and the Maywood staff to deal with mothers giving up their newborn babies than it was in cases like this. She dreaded that moment when five year old Muriel, like other girls before her, realized for the first time that her mother would never return. Abandonment of this kind was crude and raw. Mrs. Thurgood wondered how Muriel would cope with the realization that all hope of seeing her mother again was gone.

"I bet you're hungry," Mrs. Thurgood said as she retrieved the overnight bag that she had placed on a round marble table to the right of the door. "It's a long bus ride from Brooklyn. Any snacks along the way? An apple or maybe a candy bar? Baby Ruth is my favorite."

"Yes, my mother stopped at Gino's, and he put two apples and two bananas in a paper bag to take with us," Muriel said. "Gino has a fruit stand right outside our apartment. He likes my mother and me. Said he had some fresh pineapples coming and would save the very best for us when we got home. I love pineapple. I never had a Baby Ruth. Mother lets me have only one candy bar a week. Sugar Daddy is the one I like best, it lasts a long time."

Mrs. Thurgood was immediately aware of how easily Muriel's syntax and diction flowed together to form complete sentences, rare for a five year old. She visualized Mrs. Sheffield spending tedious hours on rote exercises to ensure that her fatherless daughter would grow up a well-spoken lady. With her shoulder length, wavy blonde hair, blue eyes, flawless complexion, and easily conveyed air of confidence, Mrs. Thurgood knew that Maywood Home had taken on an easy, and quite possibly big money, commodity.

Mrs. Thurgood steered Muriel through the front vestibule to a second double-door of filigreed ash, and pulled open both doors to reveal a large, high-ceilinged foyer. The room fell just short of pretentiousness with its dark paneling, tapestries, and overstuffed furniture scattered about. At the far end, thick arabesque carpeting provided an exotic touch to a double staircase. A crystal and gilt chandelier completed the picture.

"For now, you can put your bag right over there on that table," Mrs. Thurgood said, suddenly cognizant of a possible slip-up. Did Muriel catch it? She glanced down at the little girl and was met with a smile. They walked hand-in-hand into the dining room.

CHAPTER

THIRTY-TWO

Following his meeting with the young priest at the Grand Bar & Grille that Friday afternoon, Cisco had driven directly to Grace De Marco's home on Wilden Place, checking by radio to see if there were any new developments back at the bureau. Despite the usual sexual distractions and a pleasant surprise, Cisco had managed to get in a solid six hours of sleep at what he now considered his second home.

Nick and Grace enjoyed a simple meal of shrimp ravioli, smothered in a white sauce just right for dipping the fresh baked *cornettos* that Grace had delivered from her favorite bakery. The meal was washed down with a chilled bottle of Pigato. Biscotti and espresso topped things off.

"Now a surprise," Grace said as she arose from the kitchen table, and reached for his right hand. "Follow me."

Grace guided Nick through the short hall from the kitchen to the living room. "Close your eyes, I'll tell you when to open them." With Grace still holding his hand, they took four more steps. "Okay, open up."

She released Nick's hand and stepped back to watch a man transfixed by what he saw.

"*Las Meninas*! Maids of Honor!" Nick exclaimed. "And it's an oil, not a print. Where in the word did you find it?"

his eyes never leaving the reproduction, his words timid, almost childlike.

Grace put her right arm around his waist, and whispered in his left ear, "Find it, I did better than that, big boy, I commissioned it."

Nick turned from the painting and faced her. "Tell me, tell me everything."

"It's been in the works for a year. I contacted every museum big enough to have a telecopier, and found a print in the Philly gift shop, the only one they had in stock so I grabbed it. Completed a month ago, and framed only last week. I wanted everything to be perfect. Done right here in Newark. Everyone worked under the threat of painful death if word leaked out."

She marveled at the way Nick's eyes, at first wide and all-encompassing, began to squint as he took in every nuance of the four-foot-by-five-foot, framed art that silently swallowed him.

Grace stepped back a few feet, cognizant once again of a growing regret for what might have been. She had chosen music appreciation for one of her NJC humanities instead of art appreciation. How much deeper would her understanding of this man's unrequited love be if it was the other way around. She was an intruder, convinced she could never share in his visceral excitement. Grace stepped forward and replaced her arm around his waist.

"It's beautiful, the colors, the faces. The artist has reproduced it beautifully. Who did it?"

"Joseph Nigaro, operates that gallery downtown. The Fusinas commissioned him to do the family portrait. He did one hell of a job so I gave him a call. Because of the divorce, it took some coaxing. And here it is."

"Sucks you right in. You can feel it, can't you, Grace. I've been hunting for a print for years, never dreamed of an oil reproduction. I love it," Nick said, his voice tender and soft, almost a whisper.

He looked at the Velazquez masterpiece. "It's got everything. Even a self-portrait of the master himself standing there to the left. Damn, how he could use the brush, no artist did it better. And the dog, you can almost count the hairs, so delicate, so delicate. Nigaro captured it all."

Grace reached up and placed her index finger over Cisco's lips. She never tired of listening when Nick was unguarded. His insatiable search for artistic meaning was contagious. But tonight, enough was enough, she wanted to get laid.

They carried the half-filled bottle of Pigato up to the bedroom. A sip every now and then provided brief time-outs from their sexual rough and tumble. Eventually, they threw in the towel, and within minutes they were sound asleep.

Nick and Grace tried to ignore it, but the bedside telephone was an incessant monster ever ready for an early morning kill. It was six-forty-seven, and sunrise was still a half-hour away. They knew who the caller was. Cisco reached for the phone, "What's up?"

"A lot. I'm pretty goddamn sure I found where Boris Obermeyer was knocked off," McClosky said.

"Where are you now?"

"Back at homicide, putting my notes together."

"I'll be right down. Give me about thirty minutes," Nick said as he hung up the phone.

Nick ignored the sigh coming from the other side of the bed, and Grace's "oh shit, here we go again" mumbled into her pillow.

Grace tossed and turned a few times, and fluffed her two pillows in a futile attempt to get some more sleep. She pushed herself up, leaned back and again considered what was at one time imponderable, the end of their affair. Nick had never expressed any interest in meeting her parents, and he pulled her up short at even the slightest hint of her meeting his. But over the past few months, thoughts of Constance Sophia Margotta and her family crowded out any other assessment of where she and Nick were headed. The basics were easy. A few well-placed phone calls had told her all that she needed to know.

Dominic and Anna Margotta were married forty-five years ago, and Connie was the second of six children. Dominic owned a successful auto body and repair business on Central. He divided his time between his shop and his duties as Assembly Commander for the Knights of Columbus. Anna was very active in the Sodality of the Blessed Virgin Mary. Connie's older brother was a priest, and one younger sister a nun. There had never been a divorce in the family, and Grace realized there never would be.

She padded over to the framed print of the *Penitent Magdalene,* switched on the picture light, and studied as she had done hundreds of times before every detail of the masterpiece. Her gaze as always rested on the coil of flagellation rope, her unbidden talisman during her three years with Nick.

She turned and walked to the liquor cart, poured herself three-fingers of Haig & Haig Pinch, straight-up no ice, and sank onto the sofa over which she was sent head-over-heels by her husband John Fusina four years earlier. His punch changed her life forever.

Here it is again, another change. Damn it to hell, I've done it before with Johnny-boy, squeezed out everything I wanted. Now it's different with Nick, but I have to do it.

Nick and Connie had another counseling session with Father Sullivan on Wednesday. This gave her enough time to finalize everything. It would take some planning.

Connie's specter was Grace's constant companion from the very beginning. This left her with one last thing to accomplish before she cut the cord with Nick, it had to be clean, no lingering doubts. She knew what had to be done, and on Wednesday she would be taking the first steps.

For Nick, he knew it would be homicide business as usual when he entered his office and found an exhausted McClosky slumped in a chair in front of his desk. His partner was leafing through a spiral notebook making pencil notations on each page.

"I think we could both use a coffee," Cisco said. "Stay put, I'll handle it."

He returned with a coffee cup in each hand, placed one on the edge of the desk in front of McClosky, and then walked around to take his seat. The two men surveyed each other through bloodshot eyes, took a few sips, and Cisco said, "Okay, give."

"Would you believe they dusted him at Cecil B. De Mille's childhood home at Pompton Lakes. A relic they call Pamilco, only a few blocks from the Obermeyers."

"What's the connection with De Mille?"

"It seems that Pamilco was ready for the wrecking ball, and Obermeyer was a one-man crusade to save it. His wife said it was an obsession, dragged people out to see it all the time."

"What tells you that Obermeyer had his brains blown out there?" Cisco said.

"After talking to the wife, I got curious and decided to look the place over. Never got inside. Was about to call it quits when I spotted a badly repaired bullet-size hole in the floor of the porch. It looked like brain and bone residue in the splintered edges of the hole. The bullet went clean through the rotten floor board to the crawl space below. That's where I found it."

"A forty-five?"

"You got it. Ballistics is working on it. They also have the splinters I shaved off from around the hole."

"Any suspects?" Cisco said.

"I think we got our guy, in fact, I'm sure of it. It seems a salesman who supplied Obermeyer's store with men's clothing accessories got pretty close to Boris. They'd been having lunch together for several weeks. His name is Mike Hunter. One waitress called him 'class on wheels,' dressed great and a big tipper. Works for R&P Sundries, a subsidiary of Rogers Peet. I think it's more than a coincidence that nobody at the luncheonette or at Kluge's Apparel, where Boris worked, has seen 'class on wheels' for almost two weeks."

McClosky was like a hunter on the prowl as he relayed every Pompton Lakes detail to his partner. The coffee and cigarette added to his rush as he flipped from page-to-page of his notes.

"Nice job," Cisco said.

"Better than nice. Checked the phone book, and there he was, Michael J. Hunter, on Seventeenth just off Clinton. Wasn't planning to, but I was really pumped, so I detoured, and guess what...a red car parked at the curb. A real beauty, a Hudson Terraplane, hadn't seen one in years."

With his adrenaline pumping, McClosky had failed to notice a non-descript brown Dodge parked three-doors down from the Hunter home.

Cisco could sense the other man's excitement. He had been there many times himself. He waited while McClosky took a few more sips of his coffee, an attempt to slow things down to make sure the words would come out right.

"I parked around the corner on Clinton and nosed around a grocery store, you know the kind, where the owner and his wife know everything about everybody. Found out our boy is single, never married, and lives with his mother."

"Let's put him on ice for the time being, he's not going anywhere."

"Something else, I was handed a lead on Heinrich Bolz."

"Talk to me."

"I ran into Bill Fazio, brother of a gorgeous chick I dated a few years back. He works undercover for Hudson County police. He owes me a few favors, so I asked him if any high-quality types have come up missing recently. He said there were no headline grabbers, but there was a case called in almost two days ago he found interesting. He'll start working it on Monday. It was called in not by family, not by a friend or his boss, but by his landlord. Seems his apartment rent was due two weeks ago, and he was never late."

"Heinrich Bolz?"

"You got it."

"Did the landlord check out the apartment?" Cisco said. "Seems it would be the natural thing for him to do."

"Here's the rub, the landlord was shit-scared of this guy," McClosky said. "Told Fazio he was a big, mean son of a bitch who didn't say much, but made it clear he'd kick some ass if he found anyone nosing around his apartment."

"Let's start nosing. Where is Bolz's apartment?"

"Would you believe Guttenberg? Have to look hard to find it on the map, wedged in with West New York, North Bergen and those other bergs along the Hudson."

"What will your cover be this time?" Cisco said.

"Insurance, a chunk of money with Bolz's name on it, maybe three grand. And insurance adjuster James T. McBride won't rest easy until he can slap a three-thousand dollar check, courtesy of the Protective Life Insurance Company, into Bolz's beefy paw."

McClosky pulled a leather card case from an inside jacket pocket, removed an assortment of business cards, and spread them on the desk. He pointed out two identical cards for Cisco's inspection.

"Very nice, Mr. McBride."

"Can't go wrong when you're tossing money around."

"Finish your coffee, and see if you can fit in a few hours of shut-eye."

"Good idea, I'll grab an empty bunk. Then it's beautiful downtown Guttenberg. I've got an address, and the landlord's phone number from Fazio to start with."

With McClosky gone, Cisco turned his attention to the homicide reports, basically follow-ups going nowhere that chafed his raw nerves. The arrest of the Artful Dodger had removed his bureau from the cartoon pages, but the three mob hits might just as well have occurred in some gangster never-never land for all the progress that had been made.

Cisco spent the rest of the day questioning detectives Rockford, Polski and Valentine to see if their teams had come up with any new leads, anything at all. He was hoping for even the smallest morsel that could justify bringing in Richie the Boot Boiardo or Longy Zwillman for questioning. Once again...nothing.

CHAPTER
THIRTY-THREE

It required only a few minutes of gloomy banter for him to realize that his pessimism was shared by guys who had been spinning their wheels for weeks.

"For the mob, killings like these are rote exercises," Rockford said, "just do it right the first time, it all comes easy after that."

"We know that the Boot or Longy had to give the nod for jobs like these," Cisco said. "Damn it, there's got to be a connection."

"Longy and the Boot never get dirty," Polski said. "Always come out clean and fresh as a baby's butt."

"For me, I lean toward the Boot," Valentine said. "We've ID'd the stiff in the oil drum as Bobby Boyarski. Word on the street is that he pocketed a big chunk of the loot from the Richardson jewelry heist."

"Diamonds have always been Boiardo's best friends," Cisco said. "I'd bust a ball to see what he has in his office strongbox at Vittorio's. Let's get burglary in on this. I don't give a shit what it is, just anything that gets us a search warrant into the castle."

It was five o'clock and Cisco was about to call it a day, heading out not to Grace's place, but to his empty nest on Delavan when Police Chief Patrick Riley appeared in the doorway. Cisco made no attempt to mask his surprise. He and the Chief had never been pals, and the reason was obvious. Riley was a survivor, who to everyone's surprise, kept his job during the mayor's police purge a few years back. While other heads rolled, resignations reluctantly handed in, and even some minor criminal charges filed, he remained untouched.

Riley knew there were still deep suspicions about him being a whistle-blower, who readily sacrificed a few fellow drunks in order to keep his job. He was never comfortable with those who had moved up the promotion ladder as a result of Murphy's housecleaning. Cisco was at the top of that list.

Cisco leaned back and waited for the Chief to get it off his chest. He knew what was coming. He studied the compact, ruddy-faced man, who without a word, took a seat in front of his desk. The chief was a functional boozer, a crafty tactician who for thirty years displayed an uncanny ability to identify whose ass had to be kissed to get ahead. He was equally adept at playing a charmer or bully. No one had ever seen him drunk, but his face bore the tattoos of a long time lush...broken purple veins webbed his nose and there were dark saddlebags under his eyes.

"Thought I'd touch base, see how it's going," the Chief said noting the quizzical raised eyebrows of his supercilious subordinate. "Got your boys working around the clock. Reports on my desk first thing every morning. Now, about that other thing."

"That other thing?"

"Don't be cute," the Chief said. "We've all got a stake in it. A lot of asses on the line, including the anointed one, the exalted Herman Gerhardt Peterson. How close are you?"

"Very close," Cisco said, "but no promises."

"Very close! I don't know what the fuck 'very close' means to you," the Chief said. "For me, it means no more than the next couple of days. At the most, I'll give you till the end of next week to make me happy." He pushed himself up from the chair, and left the room without another word.

Cisco knew the lush was right, time was running out. It didn't make it any easier that he was heading up a multiple murder investigation that ignored police procedures while dancing around more than a few laws. At the same time, there was other homicide business that needed attention. Teams were needed to handle two fatal barroom stabbings in the Ironbound, a sliced throat and a bathtub drowning in the Third Ward. Cisco walked to his office door and peered into the bullpen.

"Melnyk. Rizzo. Get in here!" Cisco shouted. He turned and perched himself on the corner of his desk, folded his arms and waited.

"Couple of things here to keep you busy," Cisco said reaching behind him with this left hand for the initial barroom stabbings reports. "These are right up your alley. Close together, too. Only a few blocks apart."

Rizzo took the reports, handed one to Melnyk while he studied the other. He looked up and gave Cisco a questioning glance.

"This is it?" Rizzo said.

"That's it. They're all yours," Cisco said. He knew that his two latest recruits were still stewing in their juices since he yanked the Jeffries' stabbing away from them. It was time to put them to work now that they knew just how things got done in homicide.

He turned his attention to the other reports on his desk. Damn it all, his night was just beginning.

Still at his desk, it was exactly five forty-five Sunday morning when Cisco called Saint Mark's to give the bad news to Father Nolan.

"Sorry, Father, but I can't make it until later today. Maybe we can still squeeze in our little trip this afternoon. That be okay on your end?"

"I'm almost sure I can free up the time," the priest said, "and since I'll be taking the six-thirty mass off my boss's hands, I can't see any reason why he would object."

"I'll call you no later than eleven," said Cisco, his words slow and labored. It was obvious to the priest that he was talking to a very tired man. "Been at it all night, and have to admit I'm not as young as I used to be."

It was six-thirty when Cisco fumbled through his key ring to find the front door lock and deadbolt key to his Delavan Avenue home. He opened the door, and with his left foot pushed aside six days of postal rubbish that had collected. He had cancelled his subscriptions to the *Beacon* and *Clarion* five months ago. He switched on the hall light, walked into the parlor, then in turn switched on one of the two floor lamps near the mantle and a table lamp near the sofa. He shed his jacket and tie, removed his shoulder holster and tossed them onto the sofa under the front window. He pulled open the drapes to allow the soft early morning sun to penetrate the emptiness of the room, and the hollow feeling that engulfed him every time he returned to the home he and Connie had shared for seven years.

To fill the void, he walked to a small table nestled in the southeast corner of the room, reached for the bottle of Haig & Haig Pinch, uncorked it and poured himself a stiff shot. He stepped to the fireplace, studied Velazquez's *Waterseller of Seville,* turned, took two deep breaths, collapsed into the soft cushions of his favorite wingback chair, and kicked off his shoes. After a few gulps the Scotch was gone, and minutes later Cisco was snoring.

It was ten-thirty when he stretched out the kinks in his neck and shoulders after almost four hours of sleeping on the diagonal. The left wing of the chair was holding his head in place and the only thing keeping him from rolling to the floor. The Scotch had lubricated a dreamless and fitful sleep that upon wakening left Cisco wondering where he was. The *Waterseller* came to his rescue. *Well, old boy, thanks for putting everything in perspective.*

Cisco got up and padded his way through the dining room and into the kitchen. His destination was the Frigidaire. He knew what he would find there, courtesy of Connie. For the past five months his wife had been replenishing basic foods that even he could make use of. Today in the large compartment there was a bottle of milk, a dozen eggs, bacon, cream cheese, a jar of chunky peanut butter, strawberry preserves, two packages of Thomas English muffins, and butter. All with the A&P stamp. In the two lower fresh food bins were three apples, two pears, two oranges, three small tomatoes and a cucumber.

He closed the refrigerator door and turned his attention to the Kent vacuum coffeemaker waiting on a sideboard next to the stove. He removed the upper glass bowl and filter, filled the bottom bowl with cold tap water, replaced the filter and top bowl, and opened the fresh bag of Eight O'Clock coffee that he knew Connie had left as much a symbol as to meet his caffeine needs. As Nick watched the water in the bottom globe of the coffeemaker come to a boil, the implicit irony of the moment didn't escape him.

He and Connie loved their early morning and evening coffee together. The A&P's three brands of coffee were their whimsical rights-of-passage. During Nick's early years on the force it was Eight O'Clock, the cheapest. His sergeant stripes called for something a little stronger so Red Circle was the ticket at a few cents more a pound. They broke out a black bag of Bokar, the most expensive, when the lieutenant bar was pinned on.

When Connie began her food bank five months ago, it had always been Bokar, and now for the first time it was back to Eight O'Clock. Nick guessed it had been placed in the kitchen after their meeting with Father Sullivan last Wednesday. He knew all of this was an entreaty from Connie that she wasn't giving up and neither should he.

Nick poured himself a cup of coffee and carried it over to the kitchen window. While sipping the hot liquid, his eyes roamed from the garden outside across the kitchen to the bag of coffee. He realized Connie was telling him this was how it was at the beginning. It was simple and direct, we can have it again if we want it. His wife was using the only weapons she had. If successful, would she even recognize that the man she'd be getting back carried baggage she could never comprehend.

He emptied his first cup of coffee, filled another and carried it to the breakfast nook. He pulled a folded scrap of paper from his shirt pocket, flattened it on the table, reached for the telephone and hesitated. Instead of the telephone, he picked up his cup, took two deep swallows, and decided what to do next. A call to Saint Mark's would carry commitment. How much would be up to him. Father Nolan was a very persuasive and passionate guy. He emptied his cup and made the call.

It took Nick less than a half-hour to slather peanut butter and jelly on two English muffins, wash them down with a third cup of coffee, shave, shower, throw on fresh clothes, strap his shoulder holster in place, and leave word at homicide that he would be out-of-pocket for at least three hours, but would check-in periodically. Fifteen minutes later he pulled his black, unmarked car to a stop at the curb in front of Saint Mark's rectory, still uncertain what he was letting himself in for. A smiling Terry Nolan moved down from the rectory porch to meet him at the curb.

CHAPTER THIRTY-FOUR

About a hundred miles southwest of Newark, a pajama-clad Jason Cullan Tumulty III pushed open the burnished chestnut pocket door to his office, and walked to his desk. It was eight o'clock. Eighteen hours earlier a telegram from the Treasury Department had arrived at the Tumulty Mainline mansion west of Philadelphia. He had been expecting it, but not this soon. He had rousted James Cuthbert, Travis Williamson and Richard Markham, associates at Dilberry, Tumulty & Benson, and told them to pack their bags. They were going to Newark. Theirs would be the grunt work of going through thousands of pages of legal documents, and taking additional depositions that would help the judge decide how to divvy up M.L. Kraus' enormous holdings and huge bank accounts in the United States. The Philadelphia firm, as it had in 1942, would represent the Treasury Department.

Tumulty was uncomfortable with the insider whispers coming out of Washington in recent weeks. Unlike 1942 when the government came down hard on Kraus, it appeared now that Dilberry, Tumulty & Benson, renowned courtroom cut-throat, would have to put its scalpel away. Fairness would be the goal. Fifty top and middle echelon Kraus executives, many of them American citizens, had gotten the boot four years ago. Several of them had been allowed to drift back during the past nine months, and although there were figurehead American executives at the top of the heap, these returning neo-Nazis had taken charge of the shop. They joined Hugo Manfred Franke, who had been left in place as legal buffer during the transition.

A call from the U.S. Attorney's office in Washington provided substance to what Tumulty had been hearing. Germany is the key to Europe's post-war stability. It had to be kept together. It needed leaders, but most of the capable leaders are former Nazis, either on trial or in prison. Among them are former high-echelon members of the M.L. Kraus corporate hierarchy. The State Department wants a fair deposition of the Kraus holdings in the United States. This would be the news throughout Germany, that Uncle Sam was bending over backwards to be fair. The M.L. Kraus settlement will provide a shining example. Tumulty was certain that the Truman administration's fairness policy stuck in the craw of Tom C. Clark, the good old boy Attorney General who had earned his job by going after war fraud bandits.

Franke wasted no time getting in touch with him. His call came in at three o'clock, barely an hour after Tumulty had received Treasury's telegram. Smug, as usual, Franke made no effort to inhibit his enthusiasm. The whispers flowing from Foggy Bottom had doubtless come ashore at the Kraus corporate offices on the banks of the Rahway River in Jersey.

"Hugo here," Franke said, laughingly adding, "Am I speaking to Jason, or should I say Jace? The big day has arrived, this Friday before Judge Harold Hockmeier, at ten sharp."

Tumulty, stifling the urge to spit out one or two profanities, lied, "Jason will do. I'm looking forward to it."

"Remember, you're our guest. I will not take no for an answer," Franke said. "Your suite is ready and waiting. Good times ahead, Jason, don't you agree?"

"Remains to be seen. I'm taking you up on your offer, but if even the slightest conflict crops up, I'll be joining my team at their hotel. Agreed?"

"Conflict? What kind of conflict could there possibly be? You will have your privacy and even solitude of the best kind. There is a beautiful little stream nearby, perfect for you to stroll and hatch your courtroom schemes."

"You can expect me Monday evening." Tumulty had had enough of Franke's supercilious bullshit. "Exact time, I don't know."

"Honoria and I, and if you're lucky, little Muriel, soon to be our adopted daughter, will be waiting."

Across the Passaic, a big dark-visioned man was about to put into play the end of a plan that began more than a year ago.

This was the week Mister Rache had targeted to end it all. Two phone calls and the inexorable pull of Watchtower B had sucked Frank Beagan and Mike Hunter back to their bench in Washington Park. Mister Rache studied them closely, looking for any sign that their murderous intent had diminished. It was nine o'clock Sunday evening, and except for an indifferent passerby, the little park was deserted, and he had his two acolytes all to himself. Stepping from the shadow cast by the statue of George Washington and his horse, he approached them from behind and intoned, "Watchtower B."

In response, both men stiffened and waited. Mister Rache circled the bench, and halted four feet in front of them. As in all of the inductions at the park during the past year, the sublimating power of Watchtower B had taken control. The outside world disappeared, and only the glory of their deadly mission remained. The pattern never varied. Mike's breathing was heavy and labored. He dropped his hands and tightly gripped the front edge of the bench.

Frank's hands were now in his lap, the fingers entwined. His chin rested on his chest. Mister Rache was satisfied they were ready.

"We three have been united in a noble cause. What we saw at Watchtower B cried out for revenge. We have done our small part. Three Nazi-loving scum are dead. Remembering the dark shadow cast by Watchtower B, we know our calling is not yet complete. There is one more debt to be paid...and can only be paid in blood. Agreed?"

The big man now faced Frank and Mike from his seat on the bench six feet in front of them. His inductions during the months since Camp Kilmer convinced him that this was the ideal distance for him to take control. Not too close, and yet far enough away to allow his words to be safely ethereal. He was gratified to find what he was looking for. The two men nodded in agreement, their movement barely perceptible.

"Watchtower B will be making its final demand this Thursday evening. We agree that Thursday must be kept free. Excuses must be made and lies, if necessary, to make sure we are free to complete our mission. We will proceed as proud members of the 42nd Rainbow Division. Fatigue battle dress with fully-loaded pistols in hand, don't forget your silencers. Then the pleading of the subhuman who will be paying the price demanded by Watchtower B."

He got up and approached the two men. Standing in the short space that separated them, he reached out with both arms, and with his index and middle fingers gently rubbed the center of their foreheads. The circular motion was repeated, the reinforcement ending with "Watchtower B." He retraced his steps and sat down.

"Both of you will be waiting Tuesday at your assigned public phone booths for my instructions. There will be two phone calls. The first will give you all you need to know about our final rendezvous. You will drive separately to the rendezvous point, Mike in the morning and Frank in the afternoon, to make certain every square foot of enemy terrain is deeply embedded in your mind. Returning home, you will sleep the sleep of the anointed, chosen to avenge all that you saw at Watchtower B.

"Frank, I will call you Thursday afternoon at exactly two-fifty. And Mike, my call to you on Thursday will come at five minutes after three o'clock. It will be then that you learn who the Nazi-malignancy is, and how we will exterminate it. If you remember nothing else, remember the times I have given you when all will be revealed.

"Watchtower B, Watchtower B."

The three men stood and faced each other in a tight circle between the benches. The big man buttoned his peacoat, and with his arms around their shoulders, pulled the two men in close. "Damn I'm hungry," he smiled. "How about you two guys?"

"I could eat a horse," Mike said, feeling the hunger spasm that followed each induction.

"I'm with you," Frank said.

It was the first time the two men had ever shared a moment of intimacy with Mister Rache. It would be the last. They failed to notice the man hidden in the shadow of George Washington and his horse, and the brown Dodge parked a block away.

CHAPTER THIRTY-FIVE

McClosky was pumping enough adrenaline to stampede an elephant when he pulled off his jacket and shoulder holster, removed his shirt and tie, and collapsed onto a bunk at headquarters Saturday morning. After four hours of restless sleep, he gave up. They had names now and places. Things were beginning to move. He could feel it in his gut. He got up and grabbed one of the two abused electric shavers that hung from outlets on both sides of a wall mirror in the detectives' bunk room. *Goddamn it, has to be Valentine, the lazy son of a bitch*, he thought as he cleaned black whiskers from one of the Remingtons. He finished his shave, washed his hands and face, ran a pocket comb through his mop of brown hair, and put on his shirt, tie, holster and jacket. He looked in the mirror and tried unsuccessfully to flatten the bags under his eyes with his thumb and forefinger. He thought *it ain't good, but it ain't that bad either.*

He walked into the bullpen and over to the coffeepot on the table under the window, drained the dregs into a clean paper cup, and surveyed the room. He had it all to himself. Cisco, as good as his word, was cracking the whip. On his way out, he stopped only for a second at the open door of Cisco's office, and was waved on with neither man saying a word.

Downstairs he held open the door to the police parking lot, and stepped aside as two uniformed cops used their nightsticks to prod a handcuffed young Negro, his left ear swollen and bloody, into the hall on his way to a holding cell. He figured the kid was at most nineteen.

"Hey guys, what gives?" McClosky said.

"Sidewalk fight, outside the Savoy," the taller cop said. "Got a little rough. The matinee crowd had just emptied out. A young buck and some dame had just gotten into it, some serious punching, kicking and screaming. That's when Tim and me moved in."

"Don't know how old the girl was, but she was young, real young, and a real screamer," Tim said. "When she saw us coming, she ran back into the movie, and this stupid son of a bitch, what did he do? He ran at us and took a wild swing at Dan."

"Everyone's egging this guy on and cheering, so goddamn if he doesn't turn and take a swing at Tim," Dan said. "So that's when our sticks came out."

Recalling for a moment his years on the street, McClosky said, "It could have been a hell of a lot worse." He turned and watched the two white cops escort the young Negro down the hall, and then used their sticks to push him into a cell.

Outside in the parking lot, McClosky's first order of business was to find the fastest way to Guttenberg. He parked himself in the driver's seat and spread open a Hudson County street map, courtesy of Sinclair Oil. Using the locater keys, numbers running down the side of the map and letters across the top and bottom, he traced a route that would take him over the swamps on the Pulaski Skyway to Hoboken Avenue, then it was Bergenline Avenue, which he was amazed to see ran through almost every piss-ant town in the county.

As he drove north on Bergenline Avenue, McClosky had already passed though Jersey City, Hoboken and Weehawken, when he stopped at a Union City deli and ordered a corn beef on rye, kosher dill, and large black coffee to go. Back in his car, he wolfed down the sandwich and pickle, and slowly sipped his coffee while going through the notes that almost filled his spiral notebook. For a couple of days now, he had basked in the knowledge that he and Nick were going to pull this thing together despite that son of a bitch Peterson.

Bill Fazio had supplied a gem when he gave him Heinrich Bolz's name. Now it was up to James T. McBride to polish it. That meant getting to the Bolz apartment and snooping around the neighborhood before Fazio. He had a little more than a day to get it done. Fazio was no fool and doubtless had been giving some thought as to why a Newark homicide dick had wandered so far off his turf.

A phone call to Friedlander assured the landlord that he would be right beside him when he unlocked Bolz's apartment and poked his nose inside. The two of them together would be more than a match for Bolz should they run into him. He convinced Friedlander that it's done all the time. After all he was more than just an insurance adjuster, he was an investigator as well. The insurance sting was a natural. He and Nick had used it with success during jewelry theft investigations. He finished his coffee, stuffed the sandwich and pickle wrappings into the empty cup and dropped it onto the floor in front of the passenger seat.

Continuing north on Bergenline, he turned onto 69th and following the directions he had been given by Friedlander, parked in front of a three-story red brick apartment building that had seen better days. A tall, gaunt, gray-haired man, who looked as though he hadn't eaten in weeks, stood in the open double-door to the building. He wore a white shirt buttoned to the neck, its sleeves rolled half-way up arms so thin they made his large hands appear mallet-like. Black suspenders supported the man's neatly pressed brown trousers decorated by a cheap wristwatch that hung from one of its belt loops. His wing-tip brogues had been worn past the point of redemption. It was easy to see why the skinny, old man was afraid of Bolz.

"Hans Friedlander?" McClosky said, as he studied the tall man's anxious face.

"Yes, and you are..." Friedlander paused to pull a folded piece of paper from his shirt pocket, looked it over and replaced it. He studied the man at the bottom of the three-step stoop. "You are James T. McBride. You are from Protective Life Insurance Company, all the way from Newark?"

By this time, McClosky had started up the steps and was handing him his business card. "You got it right, Mr. Friedlander. It's not that far, and every now and then a change in scenery can be a good thing. I have some questions, but before we get going, I want to thank you for your time and your help."

"Maybe we help each other," the landlord said. "It would be a good thing, yes."

The man's German accent was pronounced, and McClosky figured his parents were first generation Germans who spoke little English when he was a child, and he was still catching up.

"This is all new for me, so maybe we go inside now, and you can tell me what you want to see, and for me to tell you what I know."

"First, we go into Heinrich Bolz's apartment. After we've seen everything, then we can talk. I think you will have much to tell me about your tenant."

"Yes, yes, of course. Like you, I must learn what has happened. Is Herr Bolz gone for good? Will he come back?

I am not a rich man, and I have two empty apartments upstairs. I live by my rents."

The two men walked down the dark first floor hall to apartment number three, the last one on the right. "This is it," the landlord said as he unlocked the door with his master key. "After this, after we talk, then I can come and go inside when I want?"

"Yeah, sure," the detective lied. He knew that if any forensic evidence indicated that Bolz had been knocked off here, it would have to be turned over to Bill Fazio, and the hapless landlord would be sucked into the investigation.

Before entering the apartment, the detective took a moment to look up and down the hall, and found what he expected, genteel poverty holding back the inevitable. The black and white floor linoleum was highly polished, and its cracked edges had been carefully tacked in place. The gray baseboard had been recently painted and was dust free, an easy and cheap cosmetic touch. The walls were off-white and free of disfiguring scuff marks. There were four apartments on each of the three floors, a nice living for Friedlander.

"What's behind that door at the end of the hall?" McClosky asked.

"The toilet."

"For all four apartments?"

"Yes, for all four. I want to make better, but the war you know," Friedlander shrugged. "So maybe now, with no more rationing and things easier to get, I will be able to do my best for my tenants."

It was obvious that the landlord was uncertain what his next move should be. Instead of entering the apartment in lock-step with the detective, he hesitated at the door. McClosky made it easy.

"It looks like nobody's here, so please Mr. Friedlander, come on in and look around. But be careful, do not touch anything. Who knows, this could become a police matter if something has happened to Mr. Bolz."

The apartment's musty smell was an immediate tip-off that they were the first ones to cut through the heavy stale air since Bolz came up missing.

"Mr. McBride, you have not told me why you look for Mr. Bolz," the landlord said. "It must be so big that you come all the way from Newark."

"Your tenant has come into some money," McClosky said. "An uncle who lived in Rhode Island has died, and left him three thousand dollars from his life insurance policy with my company. But first we must find Mr. Bolz."

Friedlander's reaction was immediate. He had been walking slowly about the apartment, scanning everything but touching nothing. He stopped abruptly at the bedroom door, turned and leveled the detective with an acquisitive stare.

"If you find him, or don't find him, where does the money go? I do not know about life insurance. Does your company pay me the rent he owes me? It will be two months very soon. And the gas? And the electric?"

"Easy now, Mr. Friedlander, first we must find out everything about Mr. Bolz. Let me look around, and maybe I will see something that helps us."

Displayed on two of the walls in the main room were several framed prints depicting lush mountain scenes and snowcapped peaks. Engraved brass plates identified one as Saint Sebastian's church in Ramsau, and another the Crucifixion scene from the *Passion Play* at Oberammergau. Centered on the biggest wall were two large, expensively framed family photos, mother, father, two daughters and a son. The kids aged somewhere between ten and fourteen.

All were blonde. The father and son wore lederhosen, white linen shirts, knee-high socks and sensible walking shoes. The mother and daughters wore the traditional dirndl outfits. The boy's stocky frame gave promise of big things to come.

So Bolz was Bavarian, McClosky thought as he scanned the pastoral scenes before focusing on the two family portraits. Jesus Christ, he had all of that only to end up in this rabbit hole. *Sieg Heil, you stupid son of a bitch, der Fűhrer really did right by you, didn't he. Is this where your love affair ended, Herr Bolz, let's find out.*

After a quick survey of the two and a half rooms, that included a kitchenette, small bedroom and a living-dining room, he focused his attention on an expensive looking mahogany table with a large leather-bound photo album as its centerpiece. Scuff marks on the floor indicated the table had been pushed about three feet from its original position in the middle of the room.

While the landlord carefully studied the pictures on the wall, McClosky opened the album's front cover and counted several four-by-five inch snapshots that had been removed from the inside pages. Four of them were stuck together in a bloody clump. So, this is where it ended for Heinrich Bolz. A long, long way from beautiful, snowcapped Bavaria. McClosky guessed the snapshots had been pulled from the album to create a collage on the table. If so, the photo display was a convincing study that age was no barrier when it came to racial hatred and hysterical hero worship. Men, women and children, some barely more than toddlers, raised their right arms in joyous stiff-arm salute to the man who was about to address them, and then drag them down the road to national disaster. On the back of each photo was the inscription "Nuremberg-1938, Rally of Greater Germany."

He replaced the photos where he found them, closed the album, and with his right hand pushed it off to the side then found all he needed, a splintered bullet hole. He knew that Bill Fazio hated surprises, and this one would be a real kick in the ass. He'd have to call Bill after finishing up with Friedlander.

McClosky returned the album to its original position in the center of the table. The entire apartment was now forensic evidence. He wanted everything to appear untouched. Fazio had gone out of his way by providing an innocuous missing person tip, but would now have to deal with a nervous Friedlander and the homicide boys in Jersey City. A bitch of a job at best. He'd be pissed, cursing a good deed gone bad. *Sorry Bill, I'll make it up to you sometime*.

"I think we've both seen enough. It's time to lock up," McClosky said.

The two men stepped from the apartment, and McClosky waited while the landlord locked the door.

"It appears that your tenant hasn't been home for a long time," McClosky said, "and perhaps it's a good idea to call the police. You should keep the apartment locked until they get here. Will he return, who knows?" He measured every word knowing that everything he said would be repeated to Fazio and the homicide dicks. He couldn't afford even a hint that he was a cop, and not an insurance adjuster.

"Who knows? I do not understand 'who knows.' Explain to me."

"That's why I'm here, to see if you can help me find our missing Mr. Bolz, and of course, your missing rent money," McClosky said. "That way we both get what we want."

"Help you how?"

The detective figured a change in scenery might help, and he motioned Friedlander to accompany him to the front door. "Any little thing, any habit that you can remember about Mr. Bolz?" McClosky studied the landlord's face to see if his words were registering. “Perhaps friends, did he have any friends that you know of? If so, where did he go to meet them? Any ideas, any ideas at all?”

McClosky had decided to clam up and allow Friedlander to absorb what he had said. When they reached the stoop, Friedlander extended his left arm and pointed to a two-story wooden building on the opposite corner. Curtains in the top floor windows indicated living quarters above a bar that opened directly onto an old-fashion slab slate sidewalk that extended to the curb. To either side of the front door were windows painted green to eye level, and over the entrance a painted sign that read “Rolf's.”

CHAPTER THIRTY-SIX

"Over there, that tavern. This I know about Herr Bolz, he went there. I think maybe it was his favorite place."

"And you, do you go there, too?"

"Oh yes, not like Herr Bolz, of course, but I like the owner, Herr Fischer," and with a smile, Friedlander added, "I like he still charges a nickel for a beer, a small one, and only a dime for his best, a good, strong Porter."

"So. Porter it is. Please, be my guest."

McClosky took hold of the landlord's spindle-thin arm and guided him across the street. Once inside, it took a few seconds for McClosky to adjust to the dimly lit pocket bar. Long and narrow with ten stools and two small tables at the rear. Nothing fancy, a room clearly meant for drinking and gossip. Dark wainscoting and white walls to the ceiling ringed the room. Three mirrors, obvious promotional tools supplied free by breweries, were the only wall-adornments. Two hat racks were strategically placed near the front door. Seven bar stools were taken by middle-age men speaking a patois liberally sprinkled with German phrases.

"Hans, always good to see my old friend," the white-aproned bartender said as he reached for two of the smaller glasses stacked in front of three Schmidt's taps. "A little early for you, is it not? And this young man, who do we have here?"

"No Schmidt's for me today, Herr Rolf," the landlord said with a big grin, at the same time pointing to two tall Ballentine taps.

"No doubt courtesy of your young friend," the owner said as he filled two of the larger glasses with dark brown porter, then ceremoniously cleared the overflow with a stainless steel foam scrapper. He placed the drinks on Ballentine coasters in front of the two men before addressing McClosky, "And you are…."

"James T. McBride. But you can call me Jim, if I can call you Rolf."

"Just like old friends," Rolf said as he watched McClosky and Friedlander finish their first deep swigs of beer. "Jim, what do you do that brings you here with my good friend Hans?"

"I work for an insurance company, and Hans has agreed to help me find one of his tenants. You know him, one of your regular customers, Heinrich Bolz. For his help today, all of Mr. Friedlander's drinks are on me."

"What do you do for this insurance company, and why do you have to find Herr Bolz?"

Peering over the rim of his beer glass, McClosky noted that Rolf's eyes were now wary and probing, also that his voice had lost its friendly tone. The detective could see that this was alien territory, and things would have to lighten up.

"I give away money for Protective Life Insurance Company. In this case, three thousand dollars that Heinrich Bolz has waiting for him. That is if we can find him."

As if they were controlled by a master puppeteer, the seven men seated at the bar turned in unison and stared in his direction.

"Three thousand dollars! Does Bolz know this?" Rolf had taken the bait, and his voice had softened. "If you know even a little bit about Bolz, you know he is one cheap son of a bitch. My God, even if it was only three thousand pennies, he would be parked at your doorstep."

"Where does the money come from?" a voice from the end of the bar chimed in.

"It was left to him by an uncle who died last month in Rhode Island. We just have to find him."

McClosky attempted to parse through a cacophony of shouted suggestions as to where Bolz might be. Several useful bits of information emerged. No one had seen him for two weeks. His absence was the longest anyone could remember. Before he disappeared, he had been coming in regularly every Tuesday and Friday evening at six o'clock. Bolz was probably the least friendly guy in the world. He never talked to strangers, until those men but not on those two nights. McClosky detected a rehearsed scenario in which two men seemingly went out of their way to befriend Bolz.

"We never saw these guys before," Rolf said. "This is a friendly place and as long as they paid, and caused no trouble, they were welcome."

"Especially by Bolz," a bar patron joked. "We could all see that with these guys, he didn't spend a nickel of his own money."

"Yeah, that's true, but not at first," a swarthy, muscular man of about forty said. "I remember the big guy, you know, a man that you notice right away when he walks into a room. He sat down right next to me. It was a hot day, his shirt was wet with sweat. He put down two beers real fast. He saw my glass was empty, nodded with a smile in my direction, and tipped his empty glass toward mine. 'How about it?' That's all he said. I tipped my glass and nodded back. I joined him for two free rounds."

"Where does Bolz come in?" McClosky said.

"I remember that first day, too, just like Paul here told you," Rolf said. "Then he got up, asked for the toilet which is in the rear, and the next thing I know he's sitting down with Bolz at one of my back tables."

"Just like that, walked in and made himself right at home from the start," McClosky said.

"No, not just like that, it was just Bolz," another bar-fly said. "We all saw who was buying the drinks, and hell yes, when they stepped up to porter, we all wanted a piece of the action. But no way."

"It's like they adopted each other," said Rolf. "It was easy for Bolz, the big guy was putting up all the dimes, and then it ended."

"You mean the big guy stopped coming or just stopped spending?" the detective said. "By the way did he tell anyone his name?"

"He stopped coming. That's one crazy thing about it, I don't think anyone knew his name or even asked," Rolf said. "To be honest, his size and sometimes when he got that look on his face, it told you he didn't like questions."

"How long did it go on, and does anyone know what he was driving or how he got here?" McClosky asked, hoping his questions hadn't crossed the line.

"Late this summer, don't know for sure, maybe two months. His car? Never saw one. Anybody here know anything?" Rolf said. In response, he got negative nods up and down the bar.

These guys are not the bashful sort, McClosky thought, and beer-primed questions would be normal. The big guy had to be one intimidating bastard for them to keep their mouths shut. Hell, they never even asked his name or where he came from, just popped in out of the blue and befriended a pariah who might be the most unfriendly man in town. But it wasn't the same with the second adopting angel, a much friendlier sort. He had a name, Karl Klinger. A chronology was falling into place. Unlike the big man who volunteered nothing, Klinger strolled into Rolf's explaining that he had lost his way to Nungessers to pick up a friend, got frustrated and decided he needed a beer to sort things out. That was three weeks before Bolz disappeared, during which Klinger was a sociable facsimile of the big man in almost every way. First, the five cent Schmidt's, then ten cent Ballentine porters, and to everyone's surprise, Klinger even got Bolz to laugh a few times during his visits.

All this seemed to be getting McClosky nowhere, and he was about to throw in the sponge when he finally got what he was looking for.

"By any chance, do any of you know what kind of car Klinger was driving?"

"Yeah, I do," a voice from the end of the bar cut through the chatter. "A Ford. Pre-war. Blue and in real good shape. Good rubber on all four. I notice things like that. That's how he always got here."

"Unh-uh, you're wrong there, I know that for a fact," another voice said. "Once he came in a truck, parked around the corner, and I got the idea he didn't want anyone to see it."

"Can you describe it?" McClosky knew he was pushing the envelope, sounding more and more like a cop rather than an insurance man.

"It was all white, a small refrigerated truck."

"Anything else, anything at all you can remember?" McClosky could feel the collective curiosity that had initially filled the tavern was turning to suspicion. What the hell, he thought, let's give it a last shot. "Any name on the truck?"

He held his breath and waited. The silence was palpable.

"Let's see now, the name was in red, in real big letters. Matt Beagan & Sons Wholesale Meats. There was more, but I don't remember."

Bingo! Two shooters down and one more to go. Yeah, we've only got Weber's arm, but I'll bet that he took one in the back of the head, too. Now it's time for me to get my ass out of here. First let's take care of Hans. He noticed the landlord never said a word during the give-and-take bull session, but had made a big dent in the two bucks he had thrown on the bar for beer.

"Thank you, Hans, you've been a big help." For emphasis, he placed his right hand on Friedlander's bony shoulder, peered into his bloodshot eyes and added, "Who knows, I might be back someday, and we can hoist a few more."

McClosky wasted no time getting to his car, throwing it in gear and heading back to Bergenline Avenue. He pulled over when he spotted a pay phone mounted outside a diner. He had a gut feeling that things were beginning to perk. He leafed through his notebook, flipped to the page he wanted, and got out of the car. A waitress in the diner was more than happy to trade in her tips for the three bucks that he offered in exchange. He laid out the coins according to value on the telephone's narrow ledge, and dialed his first number.

"I would like to speak with Mrs. Louisa Weber, please," he said.

"She's at the back of the store with a customer," a young woman's voice answered. "Can I tell her who's calling?"

"Police Sergeant Kevin McClosky, and it's about her husband, Walter." In less than a minute, Louisa Weber's anxious voice was on the line.

"Sergeant McClosky? Should I know you? Trudy said you have some news."

"Not exactly. I'm hoping you can help me out."

"I want to know who I'm talking to. There's no Sergeant McClosky with our local police, are you with the Sheriff's office?" The initial anxiety McClosky had detected when Mrs. Weber came to the phone was no longer apparent. Her voice was now hard and probing.

"No, I'm with a special governor's task force hoping to profile why a growing number of our state's citizens have gone missing since the end of the war," the detective lied. This is where he was at his best, smooth, reassuring, and capable of easy embellishment whenever needed.

It took about five seconds for Louisa Weber to absorb what she had heard. "My husband Walter, he's part of your profile? I don't want him profiled, I want him back. Can you or can't you find him? Why else should I talk to you?"

"Because I can help you..., but only if you help me," McClosky said. "Our task force is exploring every angle, talking to investigators all over the state. Just a few questions, that's all I have."

"Okay, I guess, go ahead, ask your questions."

"First, can you recall the sequence of events those last two days before your husband disappeared? Customers perhaps, unusual customers. Not neighborhood regulars who live in Bergenfield, maybe your store was supplying a new out of town contractor?"

"We're not a big store, not a big supplier to contractors. Walter is trying hard to expand, so one thing does come to mind," she said.

“What’s that?” He hoped that the adrenaline rush he was experiencing was not coming across over the phone.

“This man, I was never introduced to him, met with Walter, I believe, two times here at the store. They were short visits. He said he needed a large amount of plumbing fixtures, windows, new doors, and other things for a triplex he was remodeling in Wycliff.”

“You said you never spoke to him, but did you see him? Would you recognize him if he you saw him again?”

“Well, I was back with a customer at the cash register the second time he talked with my husband. They were toward the front of the store when the man looked in my direction, nodded and smiled. I got a very good look at him.”

McClosky took a deep breath, fed two more dimes into the phone, took another deep breath and asked, “Can you describe him?”

“He was a handsome man, dark hair, and well-dressed. He looked like he was about forty years old.”

“Anything distinctive?”

“Oh yes, he was big. I don’t mean just tall, but wide and muscular from what I saw. My husband is not a small man, I’d say average height, but this man was at least a head taller.”

“Do you remember his name?”

“Yes, in fact I wrote it down. Here it is, Rache, Edward Rache.”

“So that was the last time you saw this Rache? How about your husband?”

“I think so. Walter did say that they would be meeting again at the store the next week. That would give my husband a chance to drive out alone to see the Wycliff triplex.

Mister Rache had given him the keys to inspect the place to see if he wanted the job or not."

McClosky got what he wanted, a third man which he had suspected all along. And a name, phony as hell to be sure, but a name. He had one more question for Mrs. Weber, he knew what the answer would be, but he asked anyway. "Did Rache show up for his meeting with your husband?"

"No, to be honest I haven't given Mister Rache much thought, but no, he didn't."

"Thank you, Mrs. Weber. You may not think so, but you've been a big help," McClosky said.

Detective Slick had pulled it off again. His lies, all for the greater good, of course, had gotten him what he wanted. It mattered little to him that all that remained of Walter Weber was a sawed-off arm hidden away in the Coroner's chamber of horrors.

CHAPTER
THIRTY-SEVEN

It was almost noon on Sunday when Nick Cisco reached over and opened the passenger door for a smiling Father Nolan, obviously eager to get started on their mission. The priest was in full uniform, his stiff, white Roman collar in sharp contrast to his black shirt, jacket and trousers. His black tassel loafers, a youthful conceit, and black socks completed the ensemble of a priest ready for canonical action.

"Good morning, Terry," Nick said. The need for formality had disappeared Friday afternoon along with the beers they shared at the Grand Bar and Grille. Nick turned on the ignition, and pulled away from the curb as the priest angled his tall, muscled body into place beside him.

"Great day for a ride," Terry said. "Seems the stars are all aligned for our meeting with Muriel."

"You can fill me in along the way," Nick said. "I've decided to take the Bergen County scenic route, such as it is. A little longer, but a lot nicer ride to get to the Palisades."

"Sounds like you know the way. Sure hope so, because I don't."

"If Saint Joe's is where you say it is, perched on the Palisades not far from the George Washington Bridge, we won't have a problem. They're expecting us, right?"

"I talked to the boss lady, Sister Immaculata, and she agreed to lower the drawbridge and let us spend a few minutes with Muriel. She's a piece of work. Even checked with the rectory to see if I was legit."

"Sounds like they're really protecting the kid."

"When you meet her, you'll see why."

Sunday afternoon traffic was surprisingly light, given the good weather. The two men eased into comfortable silence as they crossed the Passaic into East Newark, followed the river through Kearny, turned east onto the Belleville Pike, and then crossed the Bergen County line on Ridge Road into North Arlington.

"It's as good a time as any to bring me up to date," Nick said as they passed through tiny Lyndhurst and into Rutherford. "We should be there in about twenty-five minutes."

"Except for Mary Fitzgerald, nobody's been forthcoming about Muriel," Terry said. "She's been blindsided by Monsignor Garanti. A real throw-back to the days when church intrigue was a blood sport."

"Mary Fitzgerald?"

"Remember what I told you at the Grand, she's Muriel's caseworker. She gave me some useful phone numbers, contacts she was afraid to call herself. Didn't want to lose her job. I also did more nosing around, it was all disturbing as hell."

The priest took out a pack of Lucky Strikes from his inside jacket pocket, tapped one out, lit it with his Zippo, and exhaled two plumes of smoke. He worked another cigarette half-way out of the pack, and offered it to Nick. By the time they reached Teaneck, the two men were forced to open the side vent windows to release the nicotine cloud.

“So, without Garanti, they wouldn’t stand a chance of adopting Muriel,” Nick said. “Have I got that right? Who does he answer to? It’s hard for me to believe that a monsignor is pulling all the strings in a top-loaded bureaucracy like the archdiocese.”

“I don’t know. My guess is that money is involved, Kraus money, and that Hugo is the man with the Midas touch,” Terry said.

By this time, they had reached Fort Lee, and Nick was busy maneuvering the car across and around the traffic lanes that fed the George Washington Bridge. “If my guess is right, we head north from here. Palisades Avenue, let’s give it a try.”

“There it is, on the right, Saint Michael’s Novitiate,” Terry said. “Damn, look at the size of it.”

“Saint Michael’s Novitiate? I thought we were going to Saint Joe’s Home for Boys.”

“One and the same. The nuns are a tough lot. They handle the boys in a separate building, and recently began hiding out abused girls like Muriel in the novitiate.”

Nick parked the car behind a utility van on the front circular driveway. The two men headed toward the five steps leading to the entrance, then paused to take it all in. They exchanged appreciative glances. With its classic Romanesque design, the yellow brick, four-story building, complete with a red tile roof and square central tower dominated the Palisades skyline.

“I’m impressed,” Nick said. “Who did you say put all this together?”

“The Sisters of Saint Joseph of Peace. Don’t know much about them. Only that they have an endless supply of young lassies from the Emerald Isle. All of them from poor families, not yet recovered from the potato famine.”

"And that was a hundred years ago?"

They climbed the steps, and Terry gave three raps with the brass knocker mounted on the massive oak double-doors. In less than a minute, the right door swung slowly open, and a diminutive young woman, no more than nineteen, greeted them.

"Good afternoon," her voice a charming Irish brogue.

"Let us introduce ourselves. I'm Father Terrance Nolan, and this is Police Lieutenant Nick Cisco. I believe we are expected."

"Yes. I'm Postulant Mary Theresa, and I was given instructions to bring you directly to Sister Immaculata." Her dark hair was cut short, and her pretty face free of make-up was without a blemish. She wore a long-sleeve, white blouse under a loose black jumper that reached her ankles. She stepped aside to allow the two men to enter into the foyer.

"Please follow me," Mary Theresa said.

The two men followed her down the terrazzo-tiled hallway. They nodded politely at the bareheaded postulants, white veiled novices, and black veiled sisters who glided silently in and out of various rooms along the way.

Sister Immaculata was waiting for them in a small, windowless office on the first floor of the south wing. The room looked as if it had been hastily furnished with leftovers. There was the mandatory crucifix centered on the back wall. To its left was a framed photo of Pope Pius XII, and to its right a romantic rendering of a sword-wielding, winged Saint Michael the Archangel, guardian of the Church. A small wooden desk was topped with a goose-necked desk lamp and blotter. There were four wooden straight back chairs, one behind the desk and three forming a semi-circle in front of it. There were no rugs on the gray tiled floor.

Father Nolan and Lieutenant Cisco recognized an authority figure when they saw one. She arose from her chair, but remained behind her desk.

"Come in Father and Lieutenant," she said reaching across the desk to shake their hands. "Please sit down. You both know the sad details of Muriel's circumstances, and why she is here. You are aware that she is a ward of the Archdiocese, and is here at its behest. She can be taken from Saint Michael's at any time. We have no control over where the poor girl goes. The decision to allow you to see her is entirely mine. Monsignor Garanti has not been told, nor will he be. Father, I consented to allow you and Lieutenant Cisco to speak with Muriel on the condition that your visit is informal, and not an official interrogation. You will have ten minutes alone with Muriel in her room, that's all. Any questions?"

"Who controls her movements, is responsible for her welfare?" Nick said. "I'm here only because Father Nolan feels strongly that Muriel's life might be in danger. I'm still not convinced."

"The Archdiocese has the final say as to Muriel's future," Sister Immaculata said. "But while she is here at Saint Michael's, her welfare is in our hands. You will see for yourself whether Father Nolan's fears are justified. Muriel has not been told who you are, only that she will have two visitors today."

"Thank you, Sister. I know I'm asking a lot, and that it required soul searching on your part to bend the rules this way," the priest said. "Shall we get started?"

As she had done so many times before, Muriel made everything in her room prim and proper. Her teddy bear, Rudy, was perched on her pillow at the top of the bed. The bed was neatly made with the blanket tucked under the mattress. Her black patent leather shoes at the bottom of her open wardrobe were bright and shiny. Above the shoes, three dresses and a sweater were hanging neatly spaced as she had been taught. The oval mirror on top of her small bureau formed the centerpiece for her comb and brush. She hoped that her visitors today would not bother to open the bureau drawers, because she wasn't sure her undergarments, socks, handkerchiefs and nightgown were neatly folded.

No matter how hard she tried, she couldn't stop thinking of the day her mother left her. She inspected herself in the mirror. She wore the same yellow pinafore, white socks, and white patent leather shoes, as on the day her mother hugged her so hard it took her breath away, and gave her that last light kiss on the tip of her nose. She knew in her heart that the yellow pinafore was magic, that if it was beautiful enough on the day her mother rode away, then it would be even more beautiful on the day she would come back to her. The magic hadn't worked the two times she wore the pinafore and waited for her mother at the bottom of the steps. She had even jumped up and waved her arms to be seen from the street. But nobody stopped, or even slowed down to look at her. She could not remember how many nights she sat down by the sidewalk until it got so dark nobody would be able to see her. Then Miss Mona came and got her, and took her to her room. The last time she cried all night, and she knew she would not go back to the bottom of the stairs again.

She kept a promise to herself until that day Mrs. Thurgood came for her after breakfast, and told her to pick out her nicest dress and get ready for a surprise. Miss Mona was waiting in her room to help her look her prettiest. Then they packed everything else she had into her small overnight bag, went downstairs, shared a big stuffed seat, and waited for her surprise.

It didn't take long before a smiling Mrs. Thurgood came from her office, crossed the foyer, picked up Muriel's bag, and with a nod motioned Miss Mona to leave.

“Are you ready for your surprise? It’s waiting outside.” She didn’t expect an answer from a perplexed Muriel who obediently followed her to the street. A tall, blonde man in dark clothes was waiting for them beside a big, black car. He opened the rear door and ushered Muriel into the back seat. Mrs. Thurgood bent down and kissed Muriel on the cheek, “Muriel, you don’t know how lucky you are. Your new life starts right now.”

Muriel didn’t know exactly what a new life meant. Three hours later she would find out, as the world of Hugo and Honoria Franke engulfed her.

And today she would be meeting two more people. She hoped they would not be like Hugo and Honoria.

“I can’t imagine what’s been going through Muriel’s mind since you told her two mystery guests would be coming to see her today,” Father Nolan said.

“Anxiety and fear are not strangers to the girls they send us,” Sister Immaculata said. “Muriel’s a strong little girl, very resilient.”

With Sister Immaculata leading the way, they took the stairs to the second floor. “I’ll introduce you, and wait in the hall. I will return in ten minutes.”

CHAPTER
THIRTY-EIGHT

Muriel flinched at the sound of footsteps getting ever closer to her open door. She knew that she needed Rudy to be with her. She reached across the bed and quickly snatched the teddy bear from its perch, returned to her chair at the foot of the bed, smoothed her dress, placed Rudy in her lap and turned towards the door.

"So, we meet again, Muriel, you and Rudy. You remember me, when I met you with your friend Miss Fitzgerald." Nolan was all smiles as he stepped through the door in front of Sister Immaculata, and effectively set the tone for the meeting. "Sister, we can take it from here. Muriel, Rudy and I are old friends. And for you little lady, I have a new friend, his name is Nick Cisco."

"I'm very pleased to meet you Muriel, and you too, Rudy. You can call me Nick," Cisco said. He reached forward to shake her hand, scratched the stuffed animal behind its well-worn ears, and pointed to the cast on her left arm. "You know when a friend is hurt so bad she needs one of these, your real friends put their names on it so you know they want you to get well as fast as you can. Do you think maybe you could let me and Father Nolan be your real friends?"

The priest was surprised how easily Cisco put Muriel at ease, while at the same time getting to the heart of the matter. He could picture Cisco smoothly working over a homicide suspect in the interrogation room. Muriel loosened her tight, two-fisted hold on Rudy, as her arms and shoulders relaxed.

"Nick. I like that name," Muriel said as she studied his eyes, a broad dimpled smile enlivening her face. "It reminds me of a Christmas song my mother taught me. We'd sing it together. Did you ever come down the chimney like old Saint Nick?"

"No, I leave that to Santa Claus. Maybe your old friend, Father Nolan, dropped down a chimney or two."

"No, I was always too big for that," the priest said. "But today you have me, an old friend, and Nick, a new friend, but no Saint Nick. We're here to let you know how much we care for you, that we want you to feel better. Can you tell us how your arm is doing?"

"It itches a lot. I try to scratch it, but I can't get my fingers under here." Muriel for the first time let go of Rudy, and with her right hand indicated that she couldn't get more than fingernail deep under the cast. "Sister Immaculata told me not to scratch, but at night I can't help it. It wakes me up."

They made certain they did not crowd Muriel. After the introduction, the priest settled down on the empty bed, and the detective took the unused chair. They understood how this beautiful little blonde, blue-eyed girl had captivated Hugo and Honoria Franke.

"Do you want to tell us about the arm, how it got hurt?" Father Nolan said. "You can if you want to, but you don't have to."

Muriel's features tightened, and her hands moved back to Rudy. She clasped her furry protector close to her chest as she moved her lips in an effort to find the right words to tell her friends.

"You can take your time, Muriel," Cisco said. "You don't have to say anything you don't want to."

"I want to, but..."

"Did you fall on it? Maybe from your bike, or down the stairs? Anything like that?" Cisco said. "Maybe it's easier for you to tell your old friend Father Nolan."

Muriel's eyes shifted from the detective to the priest. She hunched her shoulders, and pulled Rudy tighter to her chest.

"The day you were with Miss Fitzgerald, and we became friends," Father Nolan said, "that's when you told me that Rudy was your protector. Did Rudy try to protect you when you hurt your arm?"

"Rudy was in my bedroom when it happened."

"So, he couldn't help you. Is that right Muriel?" the priest said.

"He would not let Honoria shake me so hard. I told her I was sorry that I dropped the tray, and made a big mess at the party. Their friends laughed and said it was okay, but I knew Honoria and Hugo were mad at me."

"So, what did they do?" Cisco asked. "Did Honoria shake you in front of all their friends at the party?"

"No. It was just like the party when I called them father and mother instead of what they taught me, *vater* and *mutter*. They waited until all their friends left. That was when Hugo grabbed my shoulders real hard, and hurt this one real bad," she said as she raised her left arm to her right shoulder.

"Did this happen whenever you made a mistake?" Cisco said.

"No, but I knew when they were going to hurt me."

"How did you know?" a shaken Nolan asked.

"They talked loud and mean, and very fast. When they talked like that, it was hard for me to know what I did wrong."

The two men exchanged knowing glances, and silently watched Muriel scratch Rudy behind the ears.

"Was there anything else that told you they were going to punish you?" Cisco said.

"They smelled bad when they got close and shouted at me. And sometimes Honoria walked funny."

"I know it's hard for you to talk to us about this," Cisco said, "but can you tell us how many times they did this to you?"

"After parties, if I did something wrong. Other times when I was not doing as I was told, forgot to speak German and not English."

"You must be very smart to learn German. Who taught you?" Cisco said.

"They taught me. And Ingrid, the cook. And Frieda, the maid. They told me what to say to their friends, but I would get nervous and forget."

Cisco could sense he and the priest were pushing her to the brink. He looked to the priest for help.

"We're here to help you," Nolan said. "Telling us all about it means you have two more protectors just like Rudy."

The girl instinctively tightened her grip. They still had a long way to go in order to reach her.

"Rudy would like that. He tries so hard. But when they knock Rudy out of my hands, he can't help me, and that's when they hurt me. Not all the time, mostly at night after I made a big mistake at the party and everybody's gone."

"Do they tell you why they hurt you?" Cisco tried hard to hide his anger.

"They said they wanted their friends to see that I was a perfect little German girl. My friends were different, they didn't care if I spoke German."

"Your friends, they sound very nice" the priest said.

"Yes, they are. When Hans and Winifred and Freida and Klaus and Josef come over to play with me, they speak German and English. When I don't understand, they don't care. But mostly we speak English."

"You must miss them when you're here with the good sisters," Nolan said. "Where did you play?"

"We played a little game. Every day we went to a different house. That way we shared each other's toys, and we always had special treats waiting for us."

"How did you get from house-to-house?" Cisco said.

"We just walked. All our houses are close together around a big circle where our little street comes to an end."

"Would you like to see your friends again, let's see, Hans, Winifred, Klaus, Freida and Josef?" the priest asked.

The two men watched in awkward silence as Muriel frowned and fidgeted first with Rudy's ears, and then with the ruffles on her pinafore. Her anguish as she searched for the right answer was painful to witness. Sister Immaculata came to her rescue.

"Muriel, the visit is over," the nun said as she pushed open the door, and stepped into the room. The two men turned from Muriel and got up to greet her. "Father Nolan and Lieutenant Cisco have work to do."

"Thank you, sister," the priest said. "We appreciate the time you've given us."

"Will I see you again? You're my new best friends. Rudy and I would be very happy if we could see you again." Muriel positioned herself between Sister Immaculata and the door, her broken left arm clasping Rudy to her chest. "Sister Immaculata, you will tell them it's okay to see me again, won't you?"

"We'll see. Everybody knows how important new friends are."

The two men paused on their way out to scratch Rudy behind the ears, and were almost through the door when the priest tugged Cisco's arm and turned toward Muriel. "Golly, we almost forgot," he said taking a ballpoint pen from his jacket pocket. "Hold out your arm. That's it, just like that. Now Nick and I will make sure you won't forget your new friends. It's okay, isn't it, sister?"

After getting an approving nod from Sister Immaculata, first Nolan and then Cisco, each with a flourish, declared their friendship by signing their names.

"Father Nolan and I will never forget you, you can be sure of that, Muriel," Cisco said.

With Sister Immaculata leading the way, they silently retraced their steps to the front entrance of the novitiate where they were handed off to the Postulant Mary Theresa.

She held open the door, obviously surprised by the brevity of their visit, "Going so soon? Please come back to see us, you'll always be welcome."

Nick drove his car to the end of the driveway, turned off the ignition, and pulled a cigarette from the pack of Luckies offered by the priest. They both lit up, and rolled down the windows.

"Well, did you hear and see enough?" the priest said.

"More than enough to see what that kid is going through."

"And so?"

"I hate to say it, but I don't see where homicide comes in," the detective said. "My heart goes out for her, but as the boss lady made very plain, she's a ward of the Diocese. Nobody in that hallowed hall has filed a police complaint, nor are they about to."

"So, you're washing your hands, is that what you're saying?"

The helplessness that had gripped Nick in Muriel's room now surfaced as putrid bile in his throat. He had to spit it out. "You'd be wrong if you think this hasn't affected me."

Nick's words were a shared catharsis. Terry watched as Nick restarted the car, threw it in gear and slowly drove away from Saint Michael's Novitiate.

A half-hour, later a black limousine pulled to a stop in front of the novitiate's massive entrance. A tall, blonde man in dark livery slid from behind the wheel, and opened the rear passenger doors. Hugo Franke stepped out onto the pavement on one side, and a short, dark man wearing a red skull cap stepped from the other side, tugged his red-trimmed cape and purple sash in place before ascending the steps with Hugo.

CHAPTER
THIRTY-NINE

By mid-morning Sunday, the mist that usually shrouded New Jersey in the early fall had already burnt off, and it promised to be a warm, cloudless day.

Regina Anne Hodges Tumulty had just finished packing the second of two suitcases her husband was taking to Newark. It was a hurry-up job. The packing was not as neat as it could be, but all the essentials were there. She smiled as she pictured Jason Cullan Tumulty III's dismay when he discovers that his socks are in with his pajamas, slippers, toiletries, and extra shirts, and his underwear is jumbled together with handkerchiefs, two extra belts, and two pairs of shoes. She zipped two suits, extra trousers, a sweater and overcoat into a garment bag to complete the job.

She walked across the bedroom to the home intercom panel next to the bathroom door, lifted the handset from its hook, and waited for the click on the other end. "Everything's ready here. You can send Peter up to get your bags," Regina said. "How's things going in your office, all your legal ammunition loaded and ready for the Huns?"

"Just about," Jason said, "come on down. Martha just poked her head in and said breakfast is ready and waiting. I'm starved."

Regina loosened the sash of her robe, and let it fall to the floor. She studied her naked image in the wardrobe's full-length mirror. *Still got it*, she thought. *I know it, Jason knows it, and last night we proved it.* It was just as it had been from the very beginning. She had always known how to put that brain of his to sleep, while getting his hormones pumping.

She realized early on how much sex controlled their lives. She led him to believe he was a sexual beast beyond compare, but never let on that all the hot buttons were hers. Jason needed a jump start before every important case, and last night was no different.

Taking their seats in the dining room, the Tumultys basked in the warmth of the anticipated financial windfall that would fatten the coffers of Dilberry, Tumulty & Benson as a result of Jason's trip. Their stoic acceptance of entitlement blended well with their Sunday brunch ritual. Damask linen napkins and tablecloths were mandatory. Sterling silver place settings complimented Wedgewood china, and crystal glassware. Three silver chafing dishes offered sausage, bacon, herring, French toast, scrambled eggs for Regina, and sunny-side up for Jason.

"I'll be taking the Packard," Jason said. "Make sure Peter gasses up the station wagon for you. It's close to empty."

"Thanks," Regina said. "Do you have any idea how long it will take you to get there? It's Sunday, and God only knows what the traffic will be."

"I'm giving it no more than five hours," Jason said. "I'm thinking of making a stop at Bordentown to see Billy, offer kudos for his two touchdowns against Pingry yesterday."

"He'd like that. I still don't believe you'll be breaking bread and bedding down with your favorite Nazi."

"Easy now, Hugo Manfred Franke may be an unctuous ass, but he's sharp, and we have to deal with him. There's no getting around it. I'm hoping to palm off Herr Franke to one of my legal team. I'll see them briefly tonight for a light meal, and to put our battle plan together. Our two top legal assistants, Joyce Budding and Brenda Holden, will also sit in. They know this case inside-out, been on it from the beginning. They've been in town for a week converting a suite at the hotel into our war room."

"What comes next?"

"We'll be getting our ducks in line tomorrow, and have a couple of sit-downs with Treasury scheduled for Tuesday and Wednesday."

"And Herr Franke...."

"He's expecting me tomorrow night. No doubt he'll be pulling out all the stops."

"It's crazy, he's an adversary, and then again he's not an adversary. And to boot, you'll be breaking bread with him, a guy you can't stand."

"You've got it right, in spades. Walk me out, I'm ready to go."

Eight-five miles northeast of Philadelphia, an adrenaline-drenched McClosky was back at his desk at Newark homicide. His amygdala had been fox-trotting since leaving Guttenberg two hours earlier, and a pleasant lightheadedness had set in. First, he'd left a message at Hudson County police headquarters for what undoubtedly would be a pissed-off Bill Fazio. Then he turned to the matter at hand.

As always, everything came into play whenever he was closing in on the prey. Ever since the gabfest at Rolf's bar, he could taste it, smell it, feel it. A creature of habit, he took his spiral notebook from his inside jacket pocket, placed it on the desk, removed his jacket, and draped it over the back of his chair. He poured himself a mug of stale Joe from the still warm coffeepot, sat down, and leafed through the telephone directory's yellow pages. There was no Matt Beagan & Son listed in Essex County, so he walked to a corner of the bull pen, and pulled a Union County phone book from a stack of state directories.

There it was, listed alphabetically under *Wholesale Meat Suppliers,* taking up the top right corner of the page: *Matt Beagan & Son, Wholesale Meats, Serving North Jersey for 10 Years EL4-6000,* with an address on Second Avenue in Elizabeth.

Elizabeth was hardly alien turf for the detective. Along with Laurel Gardens, its Armory was one of the two top boxing arenas in north Jersey. Like the Laurel, ringside at the Armory provided a comfort zone for French-cuffed and pinky-ringed thugs and their peroxide blonde women. Some actually married to each other. One local bookmaker had pointed out to him no less than four plainclothes cops in the ringside mix. At the Laurel, it might be Longy or Richie the Boot holding center stage, but at the Armory, Stefano Badami was the boss.

Badami's boxing stable, just like his mob, included only Sicilians. So, it surprised no one when Charley Fucco, a good looking, stylistic kid from Alcama, became a main event fixture at the Armory.

Smart money had a distinctive smell, and McClosky followed the odor to Elizabeth, where he took in Fucco's two main event decisions over Joey Peralta the previous December and March. The fights were no-brainers with tidy pay-offs.

The vigorish he pocketed from the March fight was big enough for him to waltz into the fur salon at Hahne's to join a dozen others for the unveiling of the store's spring line. Sized-up as an outsider, he was reluctantly seated by the salon manager, and handed a small plate with tiny cucumber and watercress sandwiches. Three statuesque models paraded about in a wide variety of stoles, shawls and full-length coats.

This was not the Empire Burlesque. This was class with a capital C, the only thing acceptable for his mother's sixtieth birthday. He plopped down two hundred dollars cash, plus tax, for his selection after having a model swish and turn three times before making his decision. For an hour the inexorable corrosion from the shootings, stabbings, fatal beatings, and fixed-fight payoffs had disappeared.

Rose McClosky was braising short ribs on the kitchen stove when she heard the front door open and close, followed by a muffled exchange between Victor and their son. She had no way of knowing that Kevin had shushed his father with his right index finger over his lips before dropping his gaze to the ribboned gift box under his left arm.

"Wait where you are, Mom, we're coming in," Kevin said, then turned to his father and whispered, "Here, Dad, you give it to her. I'll just stand back and watch."

Rose had just wiped her hands on her apron and turned as her husband handed her a large, flat box emblazoned with *Hahne's – The Store With the Friendly Spirit.*

"Oh my God, Hahne's!"

"Happy birthday, Mom," said Kevin, not moving from the kitchen door where he could take-in everything. He watched his father, never a demonstrative man, cup his wife's face in his hands and kiss her on the lips.

"Happy birthday," he said, his words barely audible as Rose fought back tears.

Father and son watched as Rose nervously removed the ribbon that secured the box, open it, and pull back white tissue paper to expose a mink stole.

"Oh my God, oh my God, mink! This can't be!"

"It is, and it's taken too long to get here," Kevin said as he crossed the kitchen to join his parents. He bent over the table, removed the stole from the box and draped it over his mother's shoulders. At least for now, in his mind, he had turned dirty money into something good.

He cupped his mother's hands as she secured the stole on her shoulders. Except for her blunt, hard-callused left index finger, sliced while trimming a head of cabbage and never properly healed, her slender hands were beautiful. Victor gladly shared her self-indulgence when he ponied-up fifteen dollars, including tip, for a monthly manicure at Irene's, the top of the line beauty parlor on upper Springfield.

"Go on, Mom, take a look," Kevin said steering her gently into the dining room with its large, gilt-framed mirror. He and his dad watched his mom, now giddy and childlike, as she sashayed in front of the mirror, turned and with a coquettish wink said, "How am I doing, boys? Come up and see me sometime."

"My God," Victor said, "I've had Mae West under my roof all these years and didn't know it!"

"I don't want this to be a solo act," said Rose, suddenly serious as she walked around the dining room table, stopped in front of Kevin and gave him a hard, no-nonsense look. "Down to brass tacks, now. When will you have a lady here to share the spotlight? I had high hopes for Mary, and then poof, she's gone."

Kevin didn't have the heart to tell his mother that the Mary she had such high hopes for was a burlesque headliner. As "The Naughty Girl Next Door," Mary Mack's act filled skin-houses from the east coast to Chicago. He caught her opening night at the Empire in January. It was class with a capital "C," and unlike the case with other headliners, he kept coming back for more.

Mary was young, tall, brunette and beautiful, with a body that wouldn't quit, legs that reached her armpits, and a not bad singing voice. She brought in big bucks for the burlesque circuit and was back in Newark every two months or so. It was the second time around and only after some expensive wining and dining that he got up the nerve to suggest they share some heavy bedtime breathing. He had fallen hard, and he liked the feeling.

"Thought you'd never ask," Mary said. "You're kind of old for me, but you've got all your teeth and I never dated a cop, so why the hell not." They discovered they got along quite well both in and out of bed.

In May, after another boffo week at the Empire and with an open night before two weeks at the Trocadero in Philly, he drove her uptown for the first time.

"Where you taking me, big boy?" Mary said as they drove along a treelined street of one-family homes. "Didn't know Newark had this many trees and green grass. Are we having a picnic?"

"To see my mom and dad. You'll like them. Mom's a great cook and I told Pop a Manhattan's your drink, but only with the best bourbon, no cheap rye, the bitters, and a maraschino cherry, of course."

"Your mom and dad! Given it some real thought?" Mary sat back and with the top of Kevin's convertible down, her hair swirled in the warm spring breeze. She took a final pull on her Lucky, tossed it away and smiled. "This is a first for me, sucking up drinks and breaking bread with a stage-door Johnny's mom and pop. Can't wait to hear how you introduce me."

"Dad's no problem, he'll wink and nod in his harmless, lascivious way, and mom's heart will skip a beat when I walk in with a woman on my arm. He's Victor, she's Rose, and only their first names are acceptable."

"And you pass me off as what, a traveling sales lady?"

"Great minds think alike. I've mapped it all out. You're a traveling sales rep for Elizabeth Arden. Checked out the jars on mom's dressing table, she uses Lizzie's moisturizer and rouge. It gives you something to talk about."

He reached into the glove compartment, pulled out a gift-wrapped box and dropped it in Mary's lap. "Here's your gift for mom."

The evening went well. Rose went ga-ga when she unwrapped the oversize jar of moisturizer and the rouge. Dinner was southern fried chicken, collard greens, okra, mashed potatoes and gravy. This led to an intense exchange of southern recipes after Mary described her family roots in Kentucky, and her dream of someday opening her own restaurant. It ended with hugs and kisses at the door.

There were repeat performances at the McClosky home in early July and September. From the outset, Mary never pulled her punches. She liked him, liked him a lot. Their lovemaking was great and they had each learned a few new tricks, but at thirty-eight, he was sixteen years older, and for her that was a lifetime. There was never a face-to-face split. Mary was good enough to grab the attention of Harold Minsky, and a featured spot on his national circuit with his big rococo houses, twenty-four hour publicity mill, and fat paychecks. For the McCloskys, the Elizabeth Arden traveling saleslady was history.

CHAPTER
FORTY

During the month of September, McClosky repeatedly kicked himself in the ass when forced to avow that he had sucker-punched himself into a relationship that was doomed from the outset. Self-recrimination was never his game, but there was no denying that he had jumped head first into the bottomless pool of pussy-whipped losers.

Could it happen again? He had learned the hard way to never say never. But now he was a player in a totally new game. *I'll be god damned if I wasn't played a cuckold by Mary who jumped when a greasy burlesque boss waved big bucks. I had to bounce back, and boy, did I find a real ass kicker...a circle-jerk with just about everyone but the meter maids in a rogue operation with more holes in it than my dad's swiss cheese. Gotta admit it's pushed Mary onto the back burner and for a while, there was no way in hell that would've happened.*

This Sunday morning, McClosky thought only of the business at hand, a trip onto gangster turf that had to be quick and hopefully, invisible. Over the years, he had had little contact with Elizabeth police, now he would be nosing around in a city where a killer like Badami called the shots.

This wasn't Bergenfield and Pompton Lakes where a Newark homicide dick nosing around solo might raise a few questions, just enough to keep the record straight.

This was Elizabeth, and with the cops in Badami's pocket, an uninvited Newark cop cruising their streets was sure to piss-off all the wrong people. He had to get the lay of the land, so he grabbed his notebook and jacket, and headed downstairs to his unmarked cruiser.

Forty minutes later, he had completed a swing around Beagan & Son, and as expected on a Sunday, the building was closed. He parked at a rear loading dock, walked around to the front office door, and found what he was looking for. Neatly stenciled under the company name were *Matt Beagan, Owner,* and *Frank Beagan, Manager.* So, he had three names now, two of them legit, and the third, Ed Rache, probably phony. They could roundup Frank and Mike at any time, but Rache, who and where the hell was he.

A troubled Cisco was sitting in his office when McClosky arrived back at headquarters.

"Nick, we're getting close, in fact we're just about there," McClosky said. "Two names, Frank Beagan and Mike Hunter, and one more to go. Like you, I'm convinced that Ed Rache is a phony name, and there's no way that either Hunter or Beagan is the mastermind."

After taking out his notebook from an inside pocket, McClosky tossed his jacket on one of the two chairs in front of Cisco's desk. It took him about ten minutes to give a full account of his day. His raucous encounter with the patrons at Rolf's confirmed what he was told by Louisa Weber, that Ed Rache was a big, likeable guy who easily caught your attention. At Rolf's, he had set up everything to perfection for Frank Beagan, including giving him a new name, Karl Klinger, which was sure to go over big with that crowd.

"And where did Bolz get it?" Cisco said.

"In his apartment, across the street and down the block from Rolf's. It looked like Bolz was showing off snaps taken at that Nuremberg rally when he got it in the back of the head. The building had a side door into an alley, and it's my guess that's where Beagan stuffed the body into the trunk of a car."

"And nobody saw or heard anything, or wondered what happened to Bolz?"

"Nick, nobody gave a damn. This guy was a big, mean son of a bitch, and a cheap bastard to boot. So, when first Rache, and then Beagan, popped in and began buying him drinks, and only him, it grabbed everyone's attention."

"Even after two weeks, there were no questions, right?" Cisco said.

"Not until I showed up with his landlord, Hans Friedlander, and started buying rounds."

"And this guy Rache, or whoever he is, is still out there, and I have no doubt he has another target lined up," Cisco said.

"We could collar Beagan and Hunter right now, and start sweating them about Rache, but you know damn well we'll have Peterson to deal with."

Cisco studied his desk calendar, drew a circle around the date, October 27, then turned the page to November and circled November 5. "Time's running out, only nine days till the election, and everybody's getting jumpy."

"Everybody?"

"Got a note from Tomokai. He wants to talk, and pronto. At best, he's a nervous guy, and with two stiffs, and the arm of a third on ice, he's no doubt twitching. And the chief paid me a surprise visit."

"What the hell did the old drunk want?"

"He wants out. Not in so many words, but he wants the case buttoned-up by the end of the week. I've already called Peterson, I'll be in his office first thing tomorrow morning."

"Talking to that Kraut at any time is a ball-buster," McClosky said.

"If it were only that simple," Cisco said. "Remember Father Nolan don't you, got him involved in the shootings at The Breakers last year?"

"Christ, who can forget. Frank Gazzi, the dumbest cop on the force accidentally shoots and kills a newsboy, and another kid shoots and kills his circulation boss."

"I asked Nolan to do my job for me, to break the news to the kid's parents that their son was on a slab at the morgue. I didn't have the heart for it. He came through for me, and last week he asked for payback. I'll tell you, Kevin, I'm having trouble with this. It involves an abused six-year old girl, a lot of power, and a lot of money. Right now, it's not a case for homicide, but Nolan fears it might end up in our laps."

"Did he explain why?"

"Yeah, but he wanted me to see for myself. This afternoon we drove out to a convent on the Palisades, that's where they have the girl sequestered. The prettiest, brightest, little blue-eyed, blonde girl you ever saw. Her left arm was in a cast, and her dislocated right shoulder had just healed. She said she was banged around for making mistakes and dropping things at parties."

"Jesus Christ, what kind of mistake could be big enough to break her arm?"

"Try this on for size," Cisco said. "Speaking English instead of German."

"Well, at least we know now that she's in safe hands with the good sisters, or do we?"

"And like most little girls, she had her own personal protector, no doubt the only one she trusts," Cisco said.

"And who is that?" McClosky asked.

“Her teddy bear, Rudy, that she was pressing to her chest when talking to me and Nolan today.”

McClosky could see that his partner was having a hard time getting the words out. It was good a time to move on.

“I’ll have my report, two copies, on your desk in the morning,” McClosky said. “We both know that with Peterson, if it’s not in writing, it doesn’t exist.”

“I know you’re dragging, but make it meaty,” Cisco said. “Let’s give him a lot to chew on. Do we have anything new on Josh Levitz, and a possible Klan and Minutemen revenge connection?”

“I asked around, and it looks like Levitz’s clean. He’s a journeyman carpenter, been working on those army barracks being converted into cheap housing in Weequahic Park. In fact, can’t find a sheet anywhere.”

“Good. At least I’ll have that for Peterson. I want to stay a jump ahead. After you get some shut-eye, give Louisa Weber a call. Then pick-up the police artist and take him out to Bergenfield. We’ll see if she recalls enough for him to put together a reasonable resemblance. Smooth talking bastard that you are, you can convince them this is all for the governor’s task force.”

CHAPTER

FORTY-ONE

District Attorney Peterson was a conflicted man when he arrived at his office early Monday morning. He set his brief-case next to his desk, and pulled out the final edition of the *Beacon*. With only eight days until the election, things were looking good on the gubernatorial front. He could have written the paper's editorial himself.

Point-by-point it ripped Democrat Lewis G. Hansen apart, stating he would be no more than a stooge for Jersey City Mayor Frank Hague if elected. It noted that Hague was wounded politically and economically when the current Republican administration padlocked illegal gambling operations throughout Hudson County. With his puppet in office, Hague would be pulling the strings, and there would be no racket-busting attorney general for him to worry about.

The editorial also noted the clear contrast Republican Alfred E. Driscoll offered voters. Riding the crest of the GOP's Clean Government movement, Driscoll had a squeaky-clean record as he rose through the party's ranks, making him the paper's clear choice for governor.

Peterson folded the paper and pushed it aside, reached into his briefcase and removed a fat file folder. He and his wife, Agnes, had endured two excruciatingly boring dinners with the Driscolls at their Haddenfield home. Three brief meetings with Driscoll at his Trenton office weren't any better. As the D.A. of Essex County, the state's richest and most important, it was hard for him not to be condescending when face-to-face with a man who had come out of nowhere.

His five sessions with Driscoll convinced him he was one of three finalists for Attorney General, but at no time did the bland, holier-than-thou, son of a bitch give the slightest hint who the forerunner was. He knew solving the Bund murders would be the clincher, and to pull it off he was relying on two detectives he never fully trusted.

Peterson had just finished the *Beacon,* and was placing a yellow legal pad and three neatly arranged pencils in front of him, when Cisco walked through his open door with McClosky's four-page report and notes of his own. It was not quite eight, and except for two police security guards, they had the courthouse to themselves.

"Take a seat Lieutenant, and let's get right to it."

"Getting close, real close, but still no cigar," Cisco said as he sat down and pushed McClosky's report across the desk. "I've got a copy too, and some additional stuff, but I'll give you time to digest my partner's report. Talk you through it, if you want."

"I'll let you know as I go along."

Cisco sat back, watched and silently waited. Peterson never glanced up as his attention shifted from McClosky's report to the legal pad, which after twenty minutes, contained two-and-a-half pages of penciled notes.

"Good work. Three names, and let me see here," Peterson said, as he checked his scribbled notes, "two of them, Mike Hunter and Frank Beagan, we can pick up at any time. And the third suspect, the obvious mastermind Ed Rache, where the hell is he?"

"We're between a rock and a hard place. If we round-up Hunter and Beagan, and begin sweating them about Rache, it will blow our cover. Even the dumbest cop will sniff out that we've been running a rogue operation. And how much longer can we expect the *Beacon's* Jerry Saunders to wait for his scoop?"

"Anything more? We're running out of time."

"Everybody's getting uptight. Chief Riley is chafing at the bit to play hero at a big news conference. Told me on Friday he wanted this case put away by today, then backed off and said no later than the end of this week. And there's a note on my desk from Tomokai to give him a call. I haven't gotten back to him yet, but you can bet he's nervous as hell."

"There's no chance they'll back away from this. They're in too deep, and that's exactly where I wanted them. You said you had some more stuff. What is it?"

"A couple of things. I'm certain we've eliminated any Bund and Klan revenge connection. Josh Levitz has thrown away his sheet, and been a good boy. He's a carpenter working on those converted Army barracks over at Weequahic. Kept his nose clean. In fact, the entire Klan seems to have disappeared."

"What else?"

"Police procedure, a real long shot, but I think we ought to make a stab. Sergeant McClosky and a police artist will be out at the Weber home this afternoon to see if she can give us a worthwhile sketch."

"It's only natural there'll be some questions."

"We've covered that," Cisco said. "To explain why a Newark homicide dick is gumshoeing around north Jersey, we created a governor's task force investigating why so many missing persons end up dead."

"And you actually got people to buy that?"

"It turns out that McClosky only had to convince Louisa Weber and Cynthia Obermeyer. He got what he needed from them, and never had to approach local cops. And to rundown Heinrich Bolz, he was James McBride, an insurance adjuster with three thousand bucks for Bolz if he could only find him. It's amazing how big bucks can jog people's memories."

Listening to Cisco, the D.A. realized that he and the two detectives existed in parallel worlds. Nowhere in the four-page report was there any mention of a phony governor's commission, or an insurance adjuster named McBride. What else didn't he know? Had he been underestimating them all along? He was not expecting surprises like this so close to the end game. Until now, he had been sure he was in command of their operation. From the start, blind ambition was the glue that held them together. Was it enough?

"Any other lines you've crossed that I should know about?" Peterson asked, tapping a pencil on his notes for effect.

"It got you what you wanted, didn't it?" Never before had Cisco seen Peterson so uncertain. It was as good a time as ever to fuel the D.A.'s anxiety. "It crossed my mind that we can pull out right now with only two scalps instead of three. Still be a big headline grab that only gets bigger as we launch a search for Ed Rache."

"We made a deal, spelled out what we wanted. So, let's take a deep breath, and explore our options and obstacles. We can pull the plug at any time. Tomokai's no problem, and I know you'll handle Jerry Saunders. If we take Chief Riley at his word, we've got the rest of the week. It wasn't just drunken blather on his part, was it?"

"He was sober. He was scared. And he was serious."

At that moment, Peterson knew he was about to accept a notion so personally alien and distasteful, the mere thought of it made his stomach churn. Compromise. His life had been devoid of trade-offs. First it was pre-law at Furstenberg College, the family fiefdom in Pennsylvania; Law Review at Penn; the pick of the crop when he married Agnes Carla Heilman; calling in family chips to become Essex County's youngest ever prosecutor; and now the county's district attorney, thirsting for more.

"Let's give it until Friday morning," he said.

"For what?" Cisco said

"One way or the other, we'll have a parade for the press vultures. At worst it will be Beagan and Hunter alone, or at best they'll be shackled to the mystery man, Ed Rache. I want a twenty-four hour tail on those two. I don't care if we have to flush their toilets, but they don't piss or shit without us knowing it. I'll expect reports from you or McClosky around the clock."

It was noon when McClosky returned from Bergenfield, and found Cisco seated at his desk going over a short stack of that weekend's police reports.

"Anything more from Mrs. Weber?" Cisco said.

"Just as we expected, nothing. How did it go with the Kraut?"

It took less than ten minutes for Cisco to give his partner the details, and that the district attorney was no longer the rock-solid schemer who had sucked them into a rogue operation.

"He's got the jitters, no doubt about it," Cisco said.

"Well, well, well. So that pompous asshole has joined the crowd. We've been lugging his water all along, so it's about time he picked up a bucket himself. Like us, he ain't going nowhere till Friday morning, Rache or no Rache."

“I’ve already had Rizzo, Melnyk, Petri and McAdoo in my office this morning. I’ve pulled them off the regular duty roster. I had each team in separately. Rizzo and Melnyk are from dawn-to-dusk on Beagan, and Petri and McAdoo have Hunter. I called ahead and lined up two cars from the impound lot. Told them I wanted middle of the line sedans, dependable, no rust buckets, or gangster Caddies. I don’t want the marks getting suspicious.”

“From dawn-to-dusk? That’s a big chance isn’t it? Our two marks could be night owls.”

“That’s unlikely. I don’t want to push it any further. Besides, Hunter’s a mama’s boy, used to that home-cooking, and Beagan is up at first light to load his meat truck.”

“They had to have questions. How the hell did you explain it?” McClosky said.

“As little as possible. Didn’t connect any dots. They don’t know they’re working in tandem. They’re out-of-pocket for the rest of the week, and there’s little chance they’ll be running into each other. I made it clear the marks are never out of their sight. Any breaks in their routines, we want to know.”

“Routines? What routines?”

“Deliveries. Hunter and Beagan are essentially delivery boys. As long as they’re going from stop-to-stop, it’s okay, but any side-trips, we want to know right away.”

“Got it. And with all that overtime, they’ve gotta be happy campers.”

A little more than a mile away, two young men were nervously pacing a platform at Penn Station. Fathers Theodore Monski and Phillip Snell wondered where their contact was. They were waiting for Father Peter Majeski as instructed for more than half an hour, each with one large suitcase and a small leather grip containing their newly-consecrated chalices. Father Majeski, the priest they would be replacing at Saint Casimir, had been described to them as a big man, hard to miss even in a crowded railroad station.

They hadn't eaten since leaving Saint Hyacinth Seminary outside Boston eight hours earlier, and the candy and cigarette stand at the end of the platform was very enticing. Their temptation was snuffed when from behind them came a booming, "Father Monski! Father Snell! Sorry to be so damn late."

He extended his right hand, and with the perfunctory handshakes out of the way, he studied the two stunned faces.

"Father Peter Majeski, but for my pals, I'm Father Ski. Here, let me get those," the big priest said, as he bent to pick up the two large suitcases. "Follow me, boys, the car's just outside." After only a few steps, he pulled up short and spun around, the two young priests stumbling in near collision.

"Have you eaten anything at all since the Franciscans sent you packing? Come on, there's a Nedick's inside. A couple of hot dogs and some orange pop will set you up just fine."

Father Ski made good use of the twenty-minute drive from Penn Station to Saint Casimir's rectory to explain to the two cherubs in the back seat the fading physical health of the pastor, Father Kaczinski, and the ethnic make-up of the parish.

"You have your work cut out for you," Father Ski tossed over his shoulder as he tooled the pastor's Buick Super over the Clay Street Bridge into Harrison. *Czy twój polski jest na bieżąco, nie podręcznik, ale amerykański.*"

"Tak," the two young priests replied in unison. Father Monski added with a smile, "We even know a lot of cuss words."

"Great, because you'll be hearing a lot of them in and out of the confessional."

The housekeeper was waiting for them on the front porch of the rectory. Since her husband's death ten years ago, the portly, no-nonsense widow had devoted her life to Father Kaczinski. She watched silently and without facial expression as Father Ski helped the two young priests pull their suitcases from the trunk of the car.

"She's all yours," Father Ski said. "Her name's Agata Cernak, and in her case, appearances are not deceiving. She's as mean as she looks. I've got a few errands to run, but I'll be back in time for supper."

He recalled his first uncertain steps when fresh from the seminary he'd climbed down from a Greyhound, and hoofed it more than half a mile to Saint Anne's, a tiny parish in the midst of Burlington County's cranberry bogs. By the time he slid behind the wheel of the big Buick, the two young priests had marched in lock step behind the housekeeper into the dark parlor.

He waited until they had disappeared, then pulled away and headed back across the Passaic into Newark, and the destination he had chosen to end his quest. This would be his sixth and final time to reconnoiter the cul-de-sac which circled around a grassy knoll that provided access to three Gothic mansions, Hugo Manfred Franke's being the sprawling centerpiece. There were no fences. All were the property of M.L Kraus, and the occupants, like Franke, were crypto-Nazis. Each had a circular driveway leading to an ornate portico entrance, and shared a stream that meandered along the rear of each estate. A small wooden footbridge crossed the stream into a heavily-wooded public park.

A poorly maintained gravel service road ran along the stream before it took a sharp turn into the thick bushes directly opposite the Franke mansion. He couldn't have asked for anything better to complete his mission, the thick woods would hide their cars, there were no fences or barriers to hinder them, and the only streetlights were far off at the cul-de-sac entrance. Tomorrow during their pre-arranged phone calls, he would lay it all out for Frank and Mike. They would study the terrain on Wednesday, and the following day, two Rainbow Division warriors would carry-out his final bidding.

It was three-thirty by the time Father Ski slowly guided the Buick around the cul-de-sac. The generosity of Saint Casimir's parishioners was paying off this afternoon. The big, black car had cost them a bundle, and fit in well with the expensive chariots parked along the curb and in the driveways of the three mansions. His hate was at its zenith as he drove past the Franke mansion in this self-contained bastion of wealth and privilege.

Symbols of upper-class American gentility were spread across the lawns: a badminton net, croquet wickets and stacked mallets, randomly placed white-cushioned Adirondack chairs, and in what appeared to be shared space, a clay tennis court. And from what he was reading, and what the radio newscasters were saying, it was only the beginning. M.L. Kraus was about to get back all of its American holdings confiscated by the government in 1942. Never mind their poison gas chambers and bloody hands, we are now being told that Nazis and their ilk must be wooed if Germany was to be saved.

The big priest tightened his grip on the steering wheel as he slowed the car and scanned the upper windows of the Franke mansion. He decided to make a second pass. This time around, he came to a near stop at the cul-de-sac entrance to allow a Packard touring sedan with Pennsylvania plates to pass, then followed the big, tan car until it turned into the Franke driveway. He circled the knoll and watched as a man in a white shirt and tie step from the touring car who was immediately greeted by Franke and a blonde, rather plain woman, who was obviously his wife.

A polite distance behind them was a pretty, little, blonde girl with a cast on her left arm. Was she the Frankes' daughter? If so, she created a problem he hadn't considered. He had no qualms about eradicating the wife should she get in the way, and even the hired help, if necessary. But an innocent little girl was out of the question. He and his acolytes were vindicators, not butchers.

This would complicate tonight's final vigil. He had to be certain where the little girl slept.

He slowly drove out of the cul de sac, and turned left until he reached a thickly-wooded boundary of a park, which like the three mansions on the other side, shared frontage along a meandering stream. The other side of the forest was defined by a well-tended gravel service road easily accessible from the street and from a smaller service road that reached through the woods to a small footbridge across the stream. The bridge led directly into the backyard of the Franke mansion. This was a bonus Rache never expected.

CHAPTER FORTY-TWO

Tumulty still hadn't figured out why he had accepted Franke's invitation when he phoned ahead to tell him he was on his way. He had just completed six intense hours with his legal team at the hotel. The German's instructions were precise, right down to the exact moment he could expect to be pulling into their driveway. The enthusiastic greeting by Franke and his wife was more like a thinly disguised warm-up for an ambush than the precursor for a legal pow-wow. And the little girl with the broken arm, that must be Muriel.

"Well, Jason, you've made it up the hill safe and sound." Franke extended his right hand, and then turned to the woman beside him. "This is my wife, Honoria."

"Ich freue mich sehr, Frau Franke zu treffen," Tumulty stumbled through one of the few German phrases he had memorized.

"Likewise, I am very pleased to meet you, at long last," Honoria said. "And your German is delightful."

"You just heard most of it, I'm afraid," Tumulty said, then turned to the little girl, her troubled face a clear indication she was uncertain what to do. He noted that her cast was inscribed in two places.

"And who do we have here," he said, as he bent to shake her right hand.

"Don't be shy. Mr. Tumulty doesn't bite," Franke said with a tight smile, as Honoria drew the little girl in close to her left side, her hand firmly in place on the girl's shoulder.

"I'm Muriel. It's an easy name to remember. I've always been told that when you hear it, you never forget it."

"They are right, you know. But tell me, who said that to you?" Tumulty asked, quickly realizing that he had just stepped over a line of some sort.

The girl glanced up to Franke, and then to Honoria, the woman's left hand all the while firm and tight on Muriel's right shoulder. She turned back to Tumulty and replied, "My mother."

Talk about a pregnant pause, Tumulty thought, *this is a beauty. Just look at them, two grown-ups and a little girl, apparently frightened out of her skin, all not knowing what to say next, hoping someone else will break the ice.*

"It's a wonderful story, Jason," Franke said as he moved behind his wife and Muriel, placing his hands on both their shoulders. "And Honoria and I are overjoyed to be part of it. With help from the Archdiocese, we are well on our way to adopting Muriel, calling her our own. But that's enough for now. You will see during your stay with us what a wonderful girl she is, and how blessed we are."

Franke removed his hands from their shoulders, a clear signal that it was time to move on.

"Come, Jason, I think it's about time for a drink," Franke said, and not waiting for a reply, turned and ushered his wife and Muriel toward the front door. On cue, a tall, blonde Teuton in black livery appeared out of nowhere, gestured for the car keys, popped the Packard's trunk, removed

Tumulty's suitcases and garment bag, and then returned the keys.

A well-oiled machine, if I ever saw one, Tumulty thought as he followed the Frankes, never taking his eyes off Muriel. *But a family? I'm no shrink, but this kid is scared. And that cast, how'd that happen?*

"And now for that drink," Franke said. "But first, of course, you'll want to freshen up. Sebastian will show you to your room. We've put a telephone at your disposal."

A stocky, middle-age man, with gray hair, emerged from a parlor to the left. He wore razor-creased dark pants, black shoes, white shirt, and black bow tie. A black vest completed the ensemble.

The front door behind Tumulty closed with a click, and when he turned, his suitcases and garment bag were on the sideboard. The Teuton had disappeared as quickly and as silently as he had appeared.

"Or perhaps you would like to browse about before going up," Franke said. "Should we say fifteen minutes down here in the parlor?" Without waiting for a reply, he and Honoria with Muriel in tow, headed to the stairs.

Tumulty decided to take Franke's suggestion. When he'd stepped into the high-domed foyer, everything was overwhelmingly heavy, including the air. Directly ahead was a wide marble staircase with an ornate wrought iron railing. Tall archways with elaborately carved oak doors opened into four spacious rooms, each the handiwork of an over-zealous interior designer. Terrazzo floors were smothered by too many thick rugs, while tapestries and expensively framed oils of every description competed for wall space. All four doors were open -- parlor, dining room, library and study. It took five minutes to complete his museum tour, and with the baggage toting Sebastian showing the way, he was ushered into a second-floor suite.

Sebastian placed his suitcases on a padded cedar chest that ran the width of a four poster, then carried his garment bag to a silent butler, and opened the door to a walk-in closet. Without so much as a gesture toward Tumulty, he unzipped the bag, removed two suits, two extra pairs of slacks, a sweater and overcoat, and placed them in the closet along with the empty garment bag. He walked to the foot of the bed, opened the suitcases, left the contents untouched, then cracked open the bathroom door to complete his silent mission.

Tumulty watched the rote exercise from his vantage point at a French door that opened onto a granite balcony that spanned across the entire back of the house, each end flowing gracefully down a spiral, wrought iron staircase to a marble terrace below. Hugo and Honoria's voices staccatoed rapidly back and forth in German from the open bedroom suite to his left. He turned to his right to find a silently imploring Muriel staring at him from across the fifteen feet or so that separated their French doors.

"Hi there, Muriel. I see we're neighbors." He waved prompting her to turn abruptly without a word and step back inside. *Damn, if she isn't one scared kid. What the hell is going on here?*

With growing concern for the kid, he turned and peered over the balcony balustrade, pulled an engraved silver cigarette case from an inside jacket pocket, a silver lighter from an outside pocket and lit up.

Cloistered less than twenty feet away behind the French doors of her bedroom, Muriel threw herself on her bed, reached for Rudy and whispered, "I wish Miss Mona was here. You do the best you can to protect me, but you're just a little fellow. My two new best friends, I don't know if they'll ever visit me again. And the man next door, who's he? If we only had Miss Mona with us now. Maybe she's forgotten me."

She had no way of knowing that Miss Mona did not forget, and from the very beginning had tried unsuccessfully to suppress instincts that told her that more than a big cash payout to Maywood Home was involved. Her four phone calls to New Jersey, the last one only three days earlier, got her little more than abrupt hang-ups. It was as though Muriel had been engulfed in...what? Perhaps she was only a pawn to be used by the Frankes. But that's crazy, she's just an innocent little kid. Miss Mona was aware that Hugo Franke would try to restore an M.L. Kraus empire compensated by the U.S. government during the war. The press couldn't get enough of the story. Was Muriel part of it?

Muriel hugged Rudy to her chest, scratched his loopy teddy bear ears and remembered how fast her first day at Maywood had come and gone. She couldn't remember the name of the three, or was it four girls and two boys about her age that shared lunch, and showed her around. They pointed out one place they never went. It was a long hallway behind glass doors where Muriel saw ladies dressed in white standing around a large desk. One of them was holding a baby in her arms. They were all giggling. With them was a nice, older lady everyone called Miss Mona. It was Miss Mona who told her this was the nursery.

The sun was going down, and the hands on the big clock in the hallway were getting close to the time her mother would be returning from job hunting. Muriel had forgotten all about her overnight bag. Now she would need it when her mother came to get her, but when she went to the table where she had left it, it was gone.

"Miss Mona, I don't know where my bag is," said Muriel, who for the first time was feeling something in her stomach like the times when she was afraid. "Mommy put my clothes in it. I have to have it when she comes to get me."

"Oh, I'm so sorry, Muriel," Miss Mona said. "It's been a very busy day. It must have slipped Mrs. Thurgood's mind to tell you that your mother called. She will be late, too late to pick you up, so she asked if we would be good enough to put you up for the night."

"She didn't want to talk to me?"

"I'm sure she did, but from what Mrs. Thurgood told me, she had just enough time to catch a bus to her next job interview," Miss Mona lied, knowing that this would be the first of many.

Muriel tried to think when was the last time a day ended without her mother's little kiss on the nose and the big kiss goodnight. She tried hard, very hard, and her answer came with tears that puddled her eyes and dampened her cheeks.

"Now, now Muriel, no need for tears," Miss Mona said, stepping easily down the road of further deceit. "We've put your bag upstairs on a bed in a room that will be all your own for the night."

After dinner, she climbed the fancy stairs to the second floor, found which room was hers, only because the door was open and she saw her bag on the bed. Next to the bag was a white nightgown trimmed with blue ribbon, and a pair of cloth slippers. She opened the bag and couldn't believe what she saw. There were no play clothes, the kind she wore at Mrs. Tollin's. No scuffed shoes. Instead, there were three of her four best dresses neatly pressed and folded, four new pairs of panties she had never seen before, four pair of anklets with lace trim, and her very best black patent leather shoes. A comb and brush set with a small mirror were in a paper bag secured with a rubberband.

"So, this is where you disappeared to," said Mrs. Thurgood, who had silently studied Muriel from the bedroom door. "We all missed you downstairs."

"What beautiful dresses!" she said. "Your yellow pinafore is just right for you, I bet these other three dresses will make you look just as good, just as beautiful."

“But I have nothing real to wear, you know real clothes that you wear every day to play in. Mommy forgot to pack them,” Muriel said.

“You’ll have some very nice jumpers, blouses and play shoes to choose from in the morning when Miss Mona wakes you up.”

CHAPTER

FORTY-THREE

The next morning was just like Mrs. Thurgood said. All the clothes were on the table waiting for Muriel to choose. She decided she liked the dark brown corduroy jumper and blue blouse the best. She put on white socks and was happy when the brown and white saddle shoes fit her just right.

Thinking back to that first day at the home, she could still feel how strange it was to wear another girl's clothes, and not to be with her mother for breakfast. That first day was also when she learned all about perfection from Mrs. Thurgood. She was told over-and-over again, "To be as perfect as you can. It's sort of like a game with a lot of little tricks you can play to make it fun. When you get older, it's called putting your best foot forward."

"That's what I'll do this afternoon," Muriel said, "when my mother comes to pick me up, I'll put my best foot forward. I will be perfect as I can, and I know mommy will kiss and hug me when she sees me in the fancy blue dress."

Downstairs, Mrs. Thurgood and Miss Mona and the other children had gathered in the parlor for the daily talk about perfection, and other important things. Muriel's blind faith, the certainty that her mother would return for her that very day, had taken the two women by surprise.

"I have to leave early today," Mrs. Thurgood said, "so I'm trusting you won't lose sight of Muriel this afternoon. Tell Luke to park the station wagon across the street and keep his eye out just in case. We don't need another runaway with police knocking at our door."

"I'll wait until dark before I go down and get her," Miss Mona said. "I hate it when things like this happen. Don't really like myself very much."

"None of us do."

Muriel kept a careful eye on the big clock in the hall, and when she saw it was the right time, she raced up the stairs to her room. She took off her borrowed clothes and put on the blue dress, white lace anklets and black patent leather shoes. She combed and brushed her hair, just like mommy had taught her, then used the little mirror to make sure that everything was just right. She put the comb, brush and mirror back in the paper bag, and placed them in her overnight case. She picked up the case and walked into the hallway leading to the stairs.

She raced down the steps to the foyer, through the double-doors and the vestibule, out the glass doors to the porch, and finally down the ten steps to the sidewalk. She placed her bag on the bottom step, took a deep breath and walked to the curb, and looked both ways to see if a taxicab or maybe a bus was coming. Except for one parked car, the street was empty. She reluctantly returned to the stairs, and sat down beside her bag, but she couldn't sit still. Every time she heard a car, she jumped up and ran to the curb.

Miss Mona had been watching from the porch. She counted eight times that Muriel had hopefully leaped to her feet, only to be disappointed. It was really getting dark now, and there were no street lights. Miss Mona feared for Muriel's safety, how easy it would be for her to trip and fall. It was time for her to go down and bring the girl back.

Muriel had been putting her best foot forward, being as perfect as she could, and mommy would somehow find out and come back to her.

For three afternoons, the entire staff witnessed innocence being sapped from a child, to be replaced by reluctant recognition that things you were told, promises that were made, weren't always true. But she had to be sure for herself.

Each day Muriel waited for the bewitching hour to arrive before racing to her room, and putting on in turn first her white dress, then the pink dress, and finally the yellow pinafore. Her hair was combed just right, and she switched between the black and white patent leather shoes. She no longer floated in joyous rapture as she did that first afternoon. Car after car drove by each evening. None stopped. No doors opened, and no mommy came walking toward her with that big smile and welcoming arms.

Each night she and Miss Mona climbed the stairs in the darkness. They weren't alone. For the first time, Muriel would feel an intruder walking beside her, doubt. The first two nights she said nothing, made no sound at all. On the third night, Miss Mona could hear the sobbing coming from her room. Deceit, so unfathomable to a five-year-old girl, had laid down beside her.

"Why did you let it go on so long?" head nurse Rachel Fischer inquired, making no attempt to hide her scorn as she confronted Mrs. Thurgood. "My God, four evenings. Thought I saw it all in my ten years here, but I was wrong."

"Arrangements had been made," Mrs. Thurgood said. "Important people involved. They were expected to visit with Muriel the second day she was here. We should be hearing from them very soon. I saw no harm in letting Muriel play her little game."

"Game, what I saw wasn't a game," the nurse said. "I only hope that little girl's spirit hasn't been broken."

"We're not in the business of breaking spirits, but we do play one game with a very simple goal, to find a perfect match for our children."

As the days went by, Muriel tried not to cry, but sometimes she couldn't help herself when she began to think that her mommy might be gone forever.

"Is my mommy hurt, is that why she hasn't come back to take me home?" She searched Mrs. Thurgood's face for an answer. She didn't like what she saw. It was the same annoyed reaction she got whenever she asked her mother a foolish question.

"No, Muriel, nothing has happened to your mother," Mrs. Thurgood said. "We would be the first to know."

She wished her mother had put a picture of herself in with the dresses so she could see every day how pretty her mommy is. She was all alone, so the only thing left for her was to play Mrs. Thurgood's game.

For Mrs. Thurgood and her staff, it wasn't enough to perceive perfection, there had to be visible evidence as well. "One thing you can't trick them about is your writing," she intoned. "Palmer penmanship will be a big part of the game, and you will work at it."

She quickly learned that the game included smiling at strangers, even when you didn't want to. Keeping yourself neat and clean with everything in place, and this was everything from your hair to your shoes. She got away with picking her nose twice while visitors were there. Small victories to be sure, but worth it. She endured searching eyes, what she thought were stupid questions, and too many smiles.

With Hugo Manfred Franke and his wife Honoria, it was different. There were no stupid questions, or glued-on smiles. It was Mrs. Thurgood who made the introductions, something she never did with the others. This couple said very little, inquired politely about Muriel's health, and saw that everything in the small room was in its proper place. Honoria thumbed through Muriel's notebook, stopping several times to glance appreciatively at the girl, and closed the book with a smile. "And you are five years old?" Mrs. Franke said. "Very nice work I see here."

"I'm almost six."

"You are a big surprise, more than my wife and I had expected," Franke said. He bent forward and smiled at the obviously puzzled girl. "Don't you worry, it is all good, or as we say in German, *alles wird gut, Leben wird gut zu dir sein.*"

Mrs. Thurgood had stayed in the room throughout the short visit making herself as unobtrusive as possible. Nothing escaped her.

Muriel liked this man and woman. She could not remember their names, Mrs. Thurgood's introduction came so fast, and she had never heard names like that before. It had been three weeks since her mother left her at the home, and two weeks since she stopped crying. Her mother was gone. She remembered her mother getting into that taxicab with a folded newspaper under her arm. Was it all part of a trick played on her? A kind of game like hide-and-go-seek at Mrs. Tollin's? Was she "It" and her mother hiding from her? Had she been tricked by her mother?

Two days after the visit by the man who spoke German and his wife, Mrs. Thurgood told her to pack all her things into her overnight bag because she was leaving. The couple had a car waiting to drive her away to a new place where she would wait for everything to be settled, and she could move into a big, wonderful new home. Muriel didn't know what "being settled" meant, but if those nice people were doing it, she was sure it would be alright. She packed her bag, knelt beside her bed, and prayed that Mrs. Thurgood was not part of a new trick to be played on her.

Mrs. Thurgood walked her down to the bottom of the ten granite steps of the Maywood Home where a tall blonde man held open the rear door of a very big, black car. He nodded to the woman, turned to Muriel, and with a big smile helped her into the backseat. *Guten morgen, es ist ein schöner Tag für einen antrieb*. A box lunch and a thermos of hot cocoa were sitting on a tray extending from the rear of the front passenger seat. Three hours later they crossed the George Washington Bridge, so big it took her breath away. First through the passenger window, and then on her knees through the rear window, Muriel's eyes traced every contour of the huge steel structure. *Es ist der berühmte George Washington Brücke. Er ehrt Ihre erste Präsident*. These were the only words he spoke during the entire trip. Twenty minutes later, the car pulled up to the convent run by the Sisters of Saint Joseph of Peace.

Hugo Manfred Franke and Honoria visited Muriel two times in the next week. Sister Immaculata silently performed her sentry duty from Winifred's bed. On their second visit, the Frankes were shepherded by a Monsignor Garanti. Muriel had never seen a priest like him before. He wasn't very tall, and the dark skin around his black eyes made him look spooky, like she had seen in comic books. He wore a small red beanie on the back of his head, had a short black cape with red around the edges, a silver cross hung from his neck on a long chain, and there was a shiny purple cloth around his middle. He didn't look comfortable at all, and Muriel felt sorry for him.

After a polite greeting, Hugo, Honoria and the Monsignor, basically ignored Muriel who remained seated in the chair between her bed and dresser at the far end of the room. She couldn't take her eyes off of them as they huddled near the door, and rarely allowed their voices to raise above a whisper. Three times they turned toward her, switched on their smiles, and retreated back to their huddle. Finally, the whispering ended, and the three of them turned to Muriel.

"Come here little one, I have great news for you," the strange little priest said. "It isn't final yet, some important matters have to be seen to first, but I can tell you now that Mr. and Mrs. Franke want you for their daughter."

"Even before everything is settled, you will come to our home and see what a happy life is in store for you. It's all been arranged," Hugo said. "We must go now to start preparing for that wonderful day when you will be one of us."

First Honoria, and then Hugo stepped forward and gave Muriel a kiss on the forehead. Neither reached out to embrace her.

CHAPTER
FORTY-FOUR

Never an eavesdropper, Tumulty nonetheless found himself waiting at the balcony balustrade for even the smallest sound to escape from Muriel's room. His unwitting concern was met with silence. He was well into his second cigarette after taking in a lawn that swept down to a stream, and a small bridge. There was also a clay tennis court, and two large groupings of lawn furniture.

A well-oiled machine, no doubt about it, Tumulty thought. *Christ, just look at it, right down to the furniture. Everything perfect, good enough for a "Town & Country" cover. It's going to be interesting.*

He checked his watch. It was four-thirty, and he knew his wife would be waiting for his call. He walked to the phone conveniently placed on the nightstand next to the bed, and dialed home.

"Regina, I'm here. Just got unpacked at the Frankes," he said. "Everything's smooth so far. How about your end?"

Before his wife replied, Tumulty heard a barely discernable click on the line. *I can't believe it!* he thought, *a wiretap, and a crude one at that. Certainly, they could have done better.* He realized that it had been a mistake to accept Franke's offer, and that as long as he remained in this

Gothic horror of a house, he would be under surveillance. He decided to let the phone call playout.

"Tell me everything. Any swastikas laying around?" Regina said. "Does the help click their heels? They're too upper class for oom-pah-pah, so there has to be some muted Wagner. Don't leave anything out."

From experience, Jason knew that Regina was just warming up, that it would be wise to head her off before she reached her acerbic best. He decided to start with a recount of his brief stop at Bordentown Military to congratulate Billy for his two touchdowns that weekend. His ploy slowed her down a bit, but she still managed to get in a couple of anti-fascist remarks during their five minutes on the phone.

"I'll be eager to hear how they feed you tonight."

"Let's make it the same time tomorrow," Tumulty said. "Love you."

"Love you, too."

Before he hung up, his wiretap suspicion was confirmed with another click on the line. This would be his only night at the Franke mansion. He checked his watch, and saw that he was five minutes late for drinks downstairs. He would make sure his first was a stiff one.

Downstairs, Hugo and Honoria had not bothered to wait. Drinks in hand, they greeted him at the parlor door, and together they walked to a curved mahogany bar where Sebastian, now in a red vest, awaited. Tumulty noted that there were three other couples in cocktail attire standing around with drinks in their hands.

"First a drink, and then the introductions." Franke waited until Tumulty had his first sip of Johnny Walker Black, then turned to the nearest couple.

“Otto, Harriett, come meet Jason Tumulty the third. Like me, you will discover that Jason is proof that a legal adversary need not be your enemy, and indeed, can be a friend.”

Franke turned back to Tumulty and said, “You could not find better neighbors than Otto and Harriett Sternberg, except when you meet them on the tennis court. They are absolutely ruthless. Otto is our treasurer, and you will get to know him very well in the days ahead.” There were smiles and handshakes all around.

Franke was no less florid when he introduced the next couple. His attempts at humor were met with obligatory smiles and raised glasses. Franke’s other neighbors, Loretta and Bernhardt Gerber, ruled supreme when it came to croquet. Franke gushed that Bernhardt, as chief chemist, supervised an operation that supplied fifty percent of the khaki and camouflage dyes needed by the U.S. military.

“We took good care of your boys in uniform,” Franke failed in his attempt to hide his condescension. “Wouldn’t you say so, Jason?”

“Your work during the war speaks for itself,” Tumulty said, backing off from his immediate reaction to punch this arrogant son of a bitch in the face.

The third couple, Delmira and Eduard Siemens, interested him the most. They had flown over from Germany only the week before, giving Tumulty’s legal team little time to research how this guy fit into the picture.

“He’s hardcore Prussian,” Brenda informed him earlier that afternoon at the hotel, adding that she and Joyce had put aside their other paralegal work to concentrate on exchanging cable messages with Europe since last Thursday. “He was a judge during the Weimar years, gave up his robe and white tie, and jumped in bed with Hitler in thirty-three. Became the Nazi’s legal hitman whenever they wanted to confiscate assets to which they weren't legally entitled."

"What else?" Tumulty said.

"He's one of a bunch of former Nazis and high-borne sympathizers, whitewashed for Germany's greater good, if you can believe that."

"Yeah, that's the line from the White House," Tumulty said. "As goes Germany, so goes Europe. Gotta keep Uncle Joe and the commies out, so we put the Nazis back in. It worked before the war, just ask DuPont, Standard Oil, and General Electric."

"And they're all on the Kraus list of friendly witnesses," Brenda said. "They made a bundle then, and now they're looking for more."

"Brenda, you're too young to be so cynical." He knew how hollow his quip must sound, coming as it did from the head of a legal team that would be collecting a high, six-figure fee.

Tumulty figured that Siemens was older than the others, about fifty-five. His wife was considerably younger, and he could see that she fit in well with the other three couples while her husband made little effort to do so. After the introductions and some pointless banter, Tumulty joined Siemens at the bar.

"As if I didn't have enough legal fire power already aimed my way, a judge has joined the Kraus team," Tumulty said as he tipped his glass for a refill. He then turned to see what affect, if any, his comment had made. He came up empty.

"So, Herr Tumulty, you have done your homework," said Siemens, his face expressionless and his eyes probing. 'But that was a long time ago."

"You're here now to...."

"To contribute whatever I can to Herr Franke and his legal team," Siemens said, a tight smile barely creased his features. "But only if I am asked. You undoubtedly know where my expertise lies."

Tumulty, who considered himself a quick retort wizard, was still searching for the perfect rejoinder when Franke came to his rescue.

"Dinner is served," the host said, leading his guests into the dining room. "I trust you'll find your assigned place at the table. We are all in for a special treat tonight, pheasant under glass. Our cook, Ingrid, is renowned for what she accomplishes with this dish. A true epicurean delight awaits you."

For the first time, children's voices and laughter were heard coming from an adjoining dining alcove. Their joking was a mixture of high-pitched German and English. He counted six of them, three boys and three girls, who ranged in age from five to perhaps ten. Tumulty noticed that a transformed Muriel was the center of attention as he took his seat. The somber, sad-faced girl he had encountered was now giggling without restraint.

As promised, the meal was a delight, the vintage wines, a rich onion soup, fresh baked rolls, elaborate garnishes, and the proud birds themselves. There were exuberant oohs and aahs when the glass domes were removed from three silver platters. A rich aroma filled the room. Tumulty, no slouch as a cook himself, was impressed by what he saw. Steaming mushrooms and shallots ringed each bird which he knew would be stuffed with heavily seasoned wild rice. Each platter shared table space with a silver gravy boat of creamy cognac sauce.

"You will no doubt savor the cognac in the sauce," Honoria said. "Hugo and I must confess that we've been hoarding it for the duration, waiting for that special moment. Tonight is such a moment."

The dinner conversation could not have been more tedious. Tumulty knew he was there to be sized up, not so much by Franke who already had a complete dossier, but by Siemens. Several times during the two-hour meal, he instinctively felt the Nazi prosecutor studying him, and when he looked over, his gaze was met with a disinterested nod. The others concentrated on the mundane, never indicating they were aware of the role he played in M.L. Kraus' future. A little after eight, he decided to call it quits.

"Excuse me, I've been sitting around a lot today, and I'd like to stretch my legs before retiring," Tumulty said. "A stroll along that little stream I saw from my window will do me a world of good. So, goodnight everyone. And my special thanks to you, Hugo and Honoria, for the wonderful feast."

"I see through the window we have a nice moon tonight," Franke said. "Your walk should be delightful. Sebastian will show you the easiest way to the path."

He pushed from the table just as the kids were being ushered from the dining alcove into the foyer, jabbering and laughing all the way. He was astounded by Muriel's transformation as she giggled her way up the stairs behind a maid.

Across the stream, partially obscured in the stand of trees and waist-high bushes, a large dark figure stood with his back to a Mulberry. It was the second time that day that he had driven across the Passaic to make sure every square foot of ground and every room in Franke's mansion was accounted for. He got the assurance he needed when the light from the far-left bedroom silhouetted the little girl with the cast as she stepped onto the balcony. Tomorrow he would relay this information by phone to Frank and Mike to prepare them for their rehearsal on Wednesday. Today there was only one surprise, the little girl. She would be added to their hypnotic inductions tomorrow, commands he would reinforce just before he sends them on their deadly journey Thursday night. The girl must not be harmed. Everything must be precisely understood.

A bright crescent moon provided Tumulty with all the light he needed. He avoided the croquet wickets, ducked under the badminton net, and was about to cross the bridge when he was startled by movement in the wooded thicket on the other side of the stream.

"Who's there? Whoever you are, come on out!"

A passing cloud obscured the moon, and Tumulty found himself in pitch dark. He could hear rustling in the under-brush, and crackling of tree branches as whoever it was blindly pushed their way out of the woods. After a few strides, he quickly abandoned his first instinct to give chase, and stopped where a narrow service road curved away from the stream. Pursuit would be foolhardy, and he was no fool.

Tumulty waited and listened. There was total silence on this side of the stream, while behind him well lubricated laughter and voices poured from the open windows of the parlor. The bacchanal had moved from the dining room, and he had no doubt that Sebastian was earning his keep at the bar. At that moment, the covering cloud blew away, and the moonlight exposed what he thought was a large sedan kicking up gravel as it sped away on the service road.

He returned to the house, entered through a rear service door, and carefully avoided the parlor before climbing the stairs to his room. After brushing his teeth, he collected his toiletries, repacked his suitcases and garment bag, rewound his alarm clock and set it for six o'clock.

He sat down on the bed, picked up the phone and dialed his wife. Regina picked up after four rings and before she spoke, he heard two clicks on the line.

"Honey, I hope it's not too late," he said, noting on the alarm that it was nine-fifteen. "I don't know how I missed it, but I just reviewed one of the briefs, and an important issue I somehow overlooked has to be dealt with immediately. So, I'm pulling out of here tomorrow and heading back to the hotel, but only after a good night's sleep, maybe ten or ten-thirty."

"Must be really important," Regina said. "But you'll be raring to go after getting some solid shut-eye."

"Just wanted to let you know that's where you can reach me from now on. Goodnight, hon, we'll talk tomorrow."

"Love and kisses, big boy."

He didn't replace the phone until he once again heard the click. *I think I've given them an earful and something more to worry about*, he thought. *Pulling out early in order to deal with an important issue, that'll keep them guessing. They'll have even more to think about when I tip-toe out of here four hours early.*

CHAPTER

FORTY-FIVE

Detective Melnyk was still wondering Tuesday morning what the hell was going on when he pulled up behind a gray, Chevy two-door sedan parked a half-block from the Beagan & Son meat packing plant in Elizabeth. He got out from behind the wheel of his unmarked cruiser and walked over to the driver's side of the Chevy and asked, "Anything?"

"Nope," his partner, Rizzo, said. "Looks like they're about done loading the truck. It's all yours, have fun." They switched places, Rizzo taking over the police cruiser while Melnyk slid into the Chevy. There was a quick check to confirm their radios were connected.

By eighty-fifty, with Melnyk tailing him a good half-block behind, Frank Beagan had already made two quick deliveries, one to a neighborhood butcher shop in Union, and a restaurant drop-off in Springfield. It was all routine.

About the same time in Newark, Petri and McAdoo were completing the same surveillance ritual, with McAdoo taking over a green Plymouth parked a block away from the house Mike Hunter shared with his mother. A brown Dodge drove past, and at the end of the block made a U-turn and glided into a parking space near the corner.

By nine-ten, McAdoo was already bored. *Damn, this guy has one hell of a job. Great hours, great car, and probably a paycheck that puts mine to shame.* He tapped out his second cigarette and was lighting-up when Hunter emerged and strolled casually to his car. *Look at that will ya, not a fucking care in the world, and me without a clue why I'm tailing him.*

He waited until Hunter tooled the Terraplane from his house and was half-a-block away before he pulled from the curb, and began his mystery surveillance. He failed to notice the brown Dodge following him at a discrete distance. There was no telling where Hunter was off to, only that he was headed north towards East Orange and probably beyond.

"Believe it or not, it's fresh, someone even cleaned the pot. Brave son of a bitch, whoever he is," McClosky said as he walked into Cisco's office with two cups of coffee.

Cisco reached for the cup McClosky pushed across his desk. He could see from the expression on his partner's face that they shared the same growing edginess, a sort of "what the hell do we do now" look that surfaced when options were running out. Cisco shook out a Chesterfield and tossed the pack over to McClosky. They took a few deep drags and gargled down some coffee.

"So, what do we have?" Cisco said. "The only thing we know for sure is that Hunter and Beagan were the hit men, and maybe, just maybe, a guy by the name of Ed Rache is the crazy mastermind."

"There is something we can both bet on," McClosky said. "That Friday afternoon, Rache or no Rache, there will be a big headline grab by the D.A. and the Chief, maybe even call in the mayor."

"And you can bet your sweet ass that as soon as the floodgates are open, Tomokai will jump on board," Cisco didn't try to hide his anxiety. "He called yesterday and he's looking to bail out any way he can."

"We know Rache is a big guy. He's personable, could even make friends with a morbid bastard like Bolz. People pay attention when he enters a room. Louisa Weber only saw him twice, for a few seconds each time, but had no trouble recalling he was big, well-dressed, and had a nice smile."

"Sounds like Father Sullivan," Cisco said.

"Father Sullivan?"

"Yeah, at Saint Anthony's. He's been mediating the sessions with Connie, the next one tomorrow afternoon. Got to give him credit, he has the patience of Job, and he's needed it."

"So, you can't be reached starting at what time?" McClosky said.

"From four until I don't know when. The crews will be all yours on the two-ways around three o'clock. I'll sign back in after my session with Connie."

"I know this is one hell of a time for second-guessing, but tell me Nick, has all this been worth it?" McClosky drained his coffee cup, took a final drag and stubbed out his cigarette and eased back in his chair. "I'm not Roy Rogers ready to go down with my six-gun blazing, how about you?"

"The same. We all sized each other up from the get-go. Nobody was suckered in. One way or the other, it's only three more days."

"I needed a shower after every meeting with Peterson. Pompous, well-dressed dirt is still dirt," McClosky said. "And let's face it, Nick, as hard as it is to face up to it, we've been kissing his ass from the get-go."

"Second thoughts will kill you." Cisco searched his partner's face. "It's too late now to circle-jerk yourself with questions you can't answer."

"I can answer them okay. I'll never forget the smiles, the almost unbelieving joy of my mom and dad when I walked into our kitchen wearing my sergeant stripes. A shiny silver lieutenant's bar, Jesus Christ, Nick, I can't even imagine what this will mean to them. So what's troubling you?"

"Everything. I wish it was as simple for me. I had hoped that homicide chief and the twin bars that go with it, was worth the game we've been playing. But now, I don't know, I just don't know."

McClosky watched his partner as he swiveled around and peered at the large city wall map with six stickpins marking the most recent homicides. He was about to add a seventh stickpin, this one at the intersection of West Kinney and Broome, when his telephone rang.

"Grab that will you," Cisco said as he finished up at the map and swiveled back to his desk.

"Yeah, this is McClosky. What've you got, McAdoo?"

Cisco studied his partner's face looking for the slightest hint that McAdoo had something worthwhile to report.

"Uh-huh, Uh-huh. So that's it, just a phone call? And where was that?" A pause. "A pay phone on South Orange. Did Hunter make the call, or did he pull up and wait for the ring?" Another pause. "So, it looks like it was prearranged, is that what you're saying?" A final pause. Then McClosky ended the call with, "I don't care how you do it, but you know where he is every fucking minute from now on. Pass it along to Petri."

"Was there enough for McAdoo to tell us that things are busting loose?" Cisco said.

"I think that's a reach, but who knows. Let's wait for what Melnyk's got."

Less than an hour later they had their answer. Melnyk called in from his surveillance spot, a few store fronts from the butcher shop where Beagan was making one of his regular deliveries. His call was little different than McAdoo's, a prearranged call to a public telephone just outside a business that Beagan obviously serviced on the same day and at the same time every week.

"So, what do you think?" Cisco asked.

"I think if it's gonna happen, it better be pretty goddamned fast, we're running out of time for the big showdown on Friday."

Not far from headquarters, time constraints of a different sort were imposing themselves on a sweaty group of legal hounds and their assistants at the Robert Treat Hotel. Tumulty and his three associates were down to their shirtsleeves, ties loose, and cuffs rolled as they tackled stacks of legal briefs neatly arranged on two folding tables by paralegals Joyce and Brenda. In three days, they would be facing off with the Germans before Judge Harold Hockmeier. Tumulty had yet to explain why he wasn't bedding-down with the Frankes and everyone was itching to hear the details.

Brenda, ever the pushy one, couldn't hold it back any longer. "Come on, boss, let's have it. You walked away from a big, soft, feather bed, a bribery bag filled with gourmet food, vintage wines, great booze and neo-Nazi babble. Leave anything out, perhaps some cloak and dagger shenanigans?"

"Okay, okay," Tumulty said. "It's about time for lunch, so let's order up some sandwiches. I see you got your priorities straight, that fridge in the corner, got any beer left?"

"You betcha," Travis chimed in with a glance toward a wastebasket crammed with empty beer bottles. "Plenty still alive and kicking in the fridge."

Munching their BLT's and ham and cheese on rye, all washed down with healthy gulps of Schlitz, the quintet hung on every word as Tumulty painted a gothic picture, complete with phony gaiety, pheasant under glass, a hoarded bottle of cognac, and dark portraits passing judgment from their perches on every wall. Into his second beer, he decided to leave nothing out.

"Jesus Christ, I can't believe they wiretapped you!" Richard couldn't hide his incredulity. "And you actually heard the clicks on the line, how crude can you get."

Tumulty had them laughing when he recounted his phone call with Regina claiming that he would be leaving the next morning about ten o'clock for the hotel to study a brief that had surfaced earlier that week. He'd already had his bags packed when he made the call, and at six that morning, he tip-toed out to his car without a word to anyone.

"So, I left them something to chew on. A mysterious brief, important enough to justify my escape."

"Very un-German," James wisecracked. "How ungrateful can you get. And after pheasant under glass and vintage cognac."

"Enough. Let's get serious. There are two things I hadn't expected that have me wondering. There was a beautiful, little, blonde girl, probably about six, who the Frankes want to adopt. She was scared witless when around them, but all smiles and laughter while dining with other kids at a separate table. She had a cast on one arm. When I tried to make nice with her later in the evening, she would have none of it and ran away to her bedroom. That broken arm tells me something bad happened, and there was nothing I could do."

His rapt listeners shifted uneasily and averted eye contact, unaccustomed as they were to seeing their boss reveal even one iota of helplessness.

"And now we have former Nazi Judge Eduard Siemens and his wife, Delmira. You did a hell of a job filling me in, Brenda. Thanks. Even with your information, I can't figure this guy out, why he's here, and what role he'll play when we go before Hockmeier. Quite frankly, he gives me the creeps. Everyone showed him deference, no groveling, but it was obvious that Franke and his entourage were eating humble pie."

"Did you talk to him at all?" Travis said.

"Briefly. All I got was he's here to contribute if it becomes necessary, but only if he's asked."

"We got more stuff coming in over cable," Brenda said, "you'll have a complete dossier by Friday."

"How about the outing you had on your agenda," Tumulty said, "fill me in."

"Brenda and I took in the plant at Linden. You could fool me the war was over. It was going full steam ahead," Travis said. "Chemicals were spilling out in a big way. Tanker cars were lined up end-to-end to catch it, and barges were tied up all along Arthur Kill. It stank to high heaven."

"And guess who the next-door neighbors are?" Brenda said. "Standard Oil's Bayway Refinery holding hands on one side, and DuPont on the other."

"No surprise there," Tumulty said. "They both filed *amicus curiae* back in forty-two stating that M.L. Kraus wasn't so bad, and could be a big help during the war."

"Well, they were right about that," Joyce said, "the plant got the Army-Navy E Production Award for making all those camouflage dyes."

"And at the same time big brother in Germany was working overtime producing Zyklon B for the Nazi gas chambers," Tumulty clamped his jaw and tightened his facial muscles, a failed effort to hide his disgust.

Somewhat composed, he turned to face his young cohorts. In short order, he would find out who had the goods to earn an engraved brass nameplate in the entrance lobby of Dilberry, Tumulty & Benson. His three ivy-draped associates reeked with ambition, but did they share his courtroom killer instincts? The shop-worn adage that money has no conscience came to mind. And there would be a lot of buried conscience when it came time to count the legal fees.

For Tumulty, having Brenda on the team only added to his sense of superiority over his adversaries. Her curiosity was insatiable, and her research showed it.

"You should take a look at these," Brenda said earlier that day, as she pushed across a stack of file folders. "After reading these, you begin to wonder who's the real enemy."

He riffled the folders and slowly scanned the names on the tabs: Chase Bank, Dow Chemical, IBM, Standard Oil, Ford, General Motors, Alcoa, ITT, Hearst Publications, DuPont, and to his surprise, Ambassador William Dodd.

He pulled the Dodd file, reached for the coffee Brenda had placed next to the folders, and read what the U.S. Ambassador to Germany had to say in 1937. "A clique of U.S. industrialists is hell-bent to bring a fascist state to supplant our democratic government and is working closely with the fascist regime in Germany and Italy. I have had plenty of opportunity in my post in Berlin to witness how close some of our American ruling families are to the Nazi regime."

Brenda, who had been watching him intently, said, "They made a pile of loot before the war, and stacked it into a mountain during the war."

"Calling it loot is pretty damn harsh, wouldn't you say. There had to be contracts," Tumulty said.

"Oh yeah, there were contracts," Brenda said pulling the Hearst file from the stack of folders. "Here's what

Ambassador Dodd discovered in a 1934 contract between Adolf and William Randolph, simply stated, Hearst would get four hundred thousand bucks a year to project a goody-two-shoes image of the Nazis in America, and always be friendly in print.

"And how about old, loveable Henry Ford," Brenda said opening another folder. "Hitler loved the guy, awarded him the Grand Cross of the German Eagle in 1938 after reading Ford's four volume, *The International Jew.*"

"That's enough!" Tumulty snapped, his anger prompted instant silence throughout the room. "You want to talk about big bucks, damn it, then let's talk about tetraethyl lead, developed, manufactured and then supplied, along with the formula, to the Nazi Luftwaffe by DuPont, GM and Standard Oil. It supercharged the Messerschmitt 109, turning it into a high-altitude killer that slaughtered our bombers over Europe."

The silence was deafening as he scanned their faces. "Here's a name you'll never find in your research. Captain James Hamilton Wickham, Jimmy to his family and many friends. He'd be twenty-two next month. My wife was his godmother. Killed when his B-17 went down over Cologne. It was his twenty-fourth mission, one more and he would be home. Witnesses said his bomber formation was attacked by swarms of 109s, compliments of DuPont, GM and Standard Oil."

Joyce, a Sarah Lawrence literature major, leaned back in her folding chair, readily accepted a Schlitz offered by Travis and took a swig. She had never completely bought into the Dilberry, Tumulty & Benson creed that ethics is fine, but money is better.

There's nothing tawdry the way we're raking it in, Joyce thought. *We do it with delusionary upper-crust class. No overt money-grubbing here.*

She might be a little tipsy, and it took some effort on her part to recall what Tolstoy had said about hypocrisy, “The least wide-awake of children recognizes it, and is revolted by it, however ingenuous it may be disguised.”

CHAPTER FORTY-SIX

Grace De Marco arose very early Wednesday morning. She had slept alone last night, the second in a row without Nick beside her. On Monday morning, Nick told her that with his schedule the next two days would be easier if he bedded down at his home on Delavan. She was pleased that he found time to poke his head into the County Clerk's office before and after his meeting with Peterson. Today it required almost an hour to tidy up what had to be done. The pre-dawn darkness did not help matters. When she finished, the results of her work were placed in the hall closet next to the front door. She bathed and completed her toilette with dabs of Shalimar behind her ears.

She chose a blue merino wool, jacket and skirt by Pierre Balmain, a white, silk blouse, a single strand of pearls, and a silver Gotham lapel watch, silver drop earrings, sheer nylons, black patent leather heels and purse completed the ensemble. Her brunette hair was pulled back into a chignon, and makeup was held to a minimum. It didn't matter that no one else was aware how big this day was, she knew and made damn sure she was dressed for the occasion.

Twenty minutes later she pulled into her assigned parking space at the courthouse, got out, locked the car and headed upstairs to confirm earlier arrangements made with Flo Nassini, her chief file clerk.

Her Studebaker would remain in the garage. Nick, good cop that he is, would spot it a mile away.

Flo was busy as usual at the mundane task of sorting and dating legal affidavits and documents that define a subculture that had forever lost its anonymity.

"Good morning, Flo," Grace said. "Hard at it as always. Remember what we said yesterday, still willing?"

"Sure, no problem," Flo said. "But I can't understand why you want to switch out. Your nifty Studebaker is one hell of a lot better than my putt-putt Plymouth."

"I'll only have it for at most three hours. I'll have it back before quitting time, and with a full tank of gas."

Flo, the office wisecracker, said with a smile, "Why not patch the spare tire as well?"

"Still might happen, who knows. I'll grab the keys on my way out to lunch."

Uptown on Tenth Street, Connie had just pulled the Ciscos' 1940 Pontiac Torpedo out of the garage in the rear of the Margotta home. She turned down the narrow service road, rounded the corner and parked in front of the family's two-story frame and shingle house. Today would be the eighth counseling session for her and Nick, with Father Sullivan, the impatient but increasingly hopeful referee.

Each drive to Saint Anthony's brought back memories to the day Nick introduced her to the top of the line, 1940 Pontiac Torpedo. That was in 1943, one week after Nick shed his uniform for mufti and joined the robbery squad along with Kevin. It was their reward for being clean cops and surviving Mayor Murphy's sweeping purge of the department.

"It's beautiful," she said after opening the passenger front door and running her hand over the leather upholstery. "Look at that, how streamlined everything is. A radio, a heater, and look where the shift is, under the steering wheel. And a clock, too! Nick, can we afford it?"

"Easy there, it's used, four years old," Nick said. "Thank your dad, he ran it down for me, checked it out from front to back and gave it his thumbs-up. He's a wizard."

"Again, are you sure we can afford it?"

"Yeah, we can. Worked out a deal with the owner and being on the robbery squad didn't hurt one little bit. I think you get what I mean."

At first, Connie really didn't understand, but as time went along, other "neat little deals" kept popping up. The results of these deals could be seen in their kitchen, dining room and the parlor of their Delavan home.

Connie parked the car and slid out on the passenger side. She knew exactly where she was headed. The large front living room window offered an unrestricted view up and down the block, including a clear shot at the Monastery of Saint Dominic's at the corner of Thirteenth.

At least five times during the past two months, an unmarked police cruiser glided to the corner, stopped momentarily, and then pulled away. When the little stop-and-go maneuver occurred three times in the past two weeks, she was certain that it was Nick. *Like me he's getting anxious. And dare I think it, hopeful as well.*

Anna Margotta watched her statuesque daughter from a discrete dining room vantage point. *Cosa c'è che non va con quell'idiota. We all know Nick's not an idiot, and we know he's not blind. Just look at Constance Sophia, a true beauty. So, my husband says stai fuori dai suoi capelli. So, for months we stay out of her hair.*

She knew that her daughter was meticulous in preparing for these meeting with Father Sullivan. The result, even if Nick was half-blind, had to be captivating. Connie, as usual, had on just enough make-up to highlight her cheekbones and eyes. The only splash was her lipstick dubbed *Victory Red* by Besame. Her deep purple dress was complimented with a black leather belt and heels. The gold crucifix necklace from Nick was her only jewelry.

When the ten minutes were up, Connie turned from the window, nodded in the direction of her mother, reached for her purse and walked out to the parked Torpedo. If she'd waited three more minutes, Nick would be at the corner waving her on.

Connie wasn't the only one headed toward Saint Anthony's. Grace tooled Flo's car out of the courthouse parking lot onto Market Street. A week earlier she had driven to Saint Anthony's to get the lay of the land. Parking space was no problem, so she could easily pick a spot across from the church and wait.

Knowing Nick, she figured that he and Connie would arrive and leave separately. She was reassured when Connie parked in front of the rectory and was greeted at the front door by a big, smiling priest. He extended his hand as she climbed the entrance steps, then followed her into the vestibule and closed the door behind him.

Five minutes later, Nick parked his car at the end of the block, a good one hundred yards away.

Damn, he just can't shake it, Grace thought. *Ever the cop, ever the detective. Can't be too careful, never know who's watching, maybe some nosy nuns with dirty minds. We've been at it three years, hardly a secret, and he's still playing cloak and dagger.*

She knew her man. Nick got out of his car, carefully opened the rear door on the street side, retrieved his jacket and a small, brown paper-wrapped package, closed the door and locked up.

She marveled at Nick's insouciance as he strolled to the rectory. She was curious about the package that somehow didn't fit, or did it? After another warm greeting by the priest, Nick disappeared inside. Grace waited five minutes, drove to the corner, made a U-turn, and parked a safe car-length behind Connie to begin her surveillance.

Forty-five minutes later, Nick, still with the package, and Connie emerged from the rectory, stopped at the bottom of the steps, and turned to acknowledge a smiling Father Sullivan. Out on the sidewalk, several passersby nodded appreciatively as Nick lifted Connie's chin and kissed her lightly on the lips. He handed her the package and said something that brought a smile to her face. Whatever they were, his words were certain to make Grace's job a lot easier. Everyone was on the same page.

Father Sullivan tapped out a Camel, lit up, and watched Nick saunter back to his car, and after clearing up things at homicide to another night alone on Delavan. Father turned to the sidewalk, gave Connie a thumbs-up, and went back inside.

Connie went to her Pontiac, paused to watch Nick walk to his car, and slid into the driver's seat. She was happily unaware that every one of their moves had been closely scrutinized.

Connie took a pack of Lucky's from her purse, lit up and attempted to hold the cigarette in her mouth, but her trembling lips betrayed her. She tossed the fag out the window and unwrapped the package to find two one-pound bags of Eight O'Clock coffee. Tears welled in her eyes. Her attention was momentarily diverted when a beat-up Plymouth chugged past, trailing a gray exhaust cloud. She failed to notice the woman behind the wheel.

Battling with the Plymouth's reluctant gears, Grace cursed under her breath as Connie's parked car slowly disappeared from the rearview mirror.

Well, it's what I expected. No more Nick, and I don't know how to take it, she thought. *With a sense of guilt? Sure. Am I sad? I guess I am. He was my guy when I needed him. The sex we had, damn how it took our breaths away. How about love, let me see now, did we every really discuss it? Three years was a long time, a very long time, and I have to say no. There's a closet full of memories waiting for him to pick-up, but not tonight. He'll need some time, and God knows so will I.*

Grace pulled into the courthouse parking lot with a surprising sense of freedom, at the same time thinking the next few weeks would be very, very interesting. Once in her office, she picked up the phone and made a necessary call.

Connie was also trying to piece together what had happened today. Father Sullivan had made no attempt to hide his unabashed confidence that today's session would be a turning point. The open hostility of the last two months had given way to conciliatory gestures.

"Nick, Connie, it's been three meetings without lacing-up the gloves. So how goes it today?" the priest said pushing an ashtray to within easy reach at the front of his desk. Impossible to imagine two months earlier, Nick tapped out two Chesterfields, and without asking, Connie reached over, took one, placed it between her lips and waited with a smile. Nick Zippoed both of them, then reached across the desk and fired-up Father Sullivan's Camel.

Father Sullivan sensed that he was witnessing something extraordinary. Nick and Connie had shed their rancor and were taking hesitant, sometimes awkward, steps back to becoming Mr. and Mrs. Cisco.

"I've always been amused how even filthy habits like this can have a coalescing effect on once hopeless cases," he said before taking another deep drag and exhaling with a smile. His grin was infectious, filling the room with enthusiasm that was palpable. He led them in harmless banter that led into meaningful questions and answers. Replying to Connie, Nick broke the ice.

"We've got a long way to go, and hell, I still can't see where we're going and what it will be when we get there," he said turning to Connie. "Help me on this one. You never wanted any of this. It was me from the start."

"Don't, please don't go there again. I've choked enough on our recriminations. I know and you know it will never be the same for us and our families. I prayed, that's right Nick, I prayed that there was still a world out there for us to share."

The priest was on his third cigarette, watching, listening and saying nothing. To define heartbreak, you need not look any further than the two decent people in front of him. Nick had taken Connie's hands during her painful discourse. He raised her right arm and brushed his lips across the back of her hand.

"Connie, I'm a cop, with cop instincts. After what we've been going through, can I ever trust our thinking about each other? Can we get back to where we were? We both know I've been a son of a bitch, admitted it over and over in this very room."

"Nick, look at me!" Connie's stern admonition bounced around the small office like a loose grenade. "We're going to leave all your 'son of a bitch' crap here in the office right now, today. Get it!"

The two men looked at each other. Their initial surprise was contagious starting first with grins, then a low chuckle and finally outright laughter.

"Well, I'll be goddamned, please pardon my expression," the priest said. "But I think, Nick, that you and I have just glimpsed Connie's new world. You ready to take her, on mutual terms, of course?"

Nick, his paws still enfolding Connie's right hand, loosened his grip and once again slowly brushed his lips from knuckle to knuckle. He looked up to be met with a penetrating gaze that said 'I'm here, I've always been here.'

With Father Sullivan joining in, they talked about their families. Nick knew that Connie had been seeing his folks regularly, though it was never mentioned during their sessions. There were no secrets in Newark's close-knit Italian community. Not one, but two, family reconciliations would be needed. Nick had his work cut out for him.

"Let me know if you need me. I'm serious, just pick up a phone," the priest said taking them in with that loopy grin that made him a parish favorite. "Okay, you two, get out of here and by God, you'll be walking out together!"

Half-way to the front door, the priest called a halt. "Stop and take a look. You think this fellow had anything to do with what happened today?" he said pointing to a statue nestled in a wall niche. "St Anthony, looks depressed doesn't he, but don't be fooled. He's the patron saint of hopeless people seeking hope."

Nick reacted with a shrug, and Connie, after a fast glance at the statue, smiled knowingly. They turned and headed out the door together.

It might have only been a whiff of happiness that Connie experienced in Father Sullivan's office, but, for now, it was more than she had hoped for. *Nick is right,* she thought, *there's a lot of work to be done. Suspicions, what do we do with them? Can they be erased forever or simply kicked under the rug? We've got the time, and it's up to us from now on.*

Stopped at a traffic light, Connie touched the package on the passenger seat, it wasn't coffee, it was hope.

CHAPTER
FORTY-SEVEN

Valentine's call wasn't the one McClosky expected, but it had to be attended to. He put on his jacket, headed downstairs and stopped at the front desk to stir Sergeant Bronson.

"Lieutenant Cisco is out-of-pocket for the next hour or so, all homicide calls are to be funneled to my two-way. No exceptions," he said.

Ten minutes later, he pulled up to the front of a small, rusting warehouse that edged down to the bank of the Passaic. Windy Valentine was waiting with his usual shit-eating grin, a tip-off he was bursting with good news.

"What do we have?" McClosky said, scanning the area. The metal warehouse barely held together. A small office door with flaked paint, cardboard over the broken window, and two large metal doors hung from corroded hinges. A small panel truck was parked inside. The building fit in well with three rickety neighbors, all still in operation.

I can only guess what the building inspector's been pocketing for signing off on these derelicts, he thought. *Enough vigorish here for at least a beach bungalow, maybe not Spring Lake, but Ocean Grove ain't bad either. City hall at it's finest.*

“He’s inside, name’s Gino Brazzi,” Valentine said. “The welding shop is his, or so he says. Come inside and you’ll see what else goes on.”

The two detectives walked past piles of steel rods, stacks of metal sheeting, acetylene tanks, welding masks hanging from hooks, and two dollies on heavy caster metal wheels. A handcuffed Brazzi was seated on a stool at the rear of the building with two uniforms standing watch.

“I don’t do nothin’ but weld, that’s all, weld,” blurted Brazzi, a swarthy, thick-bodied man who looked to be just short of six feet. “You find nothin’ here that says different, just try to prove something.”

“Shut the fuck up! I’ll tell you when to talk. Maybe you don’t hear too good,” Valentine said, then stepped forward to give Brazzi a stiff back-hand to his right ear. “That should clear some wax out. Open up again, and we’ll try the other side.”

McClosky had just watched a veteran of homicide’s old guard in action. Valentine got his homicide badge four years before he and Cisco came aboard, a no bullshit, no apology cop, who had managed, by some miracle, to survive the mayor’s cleanup. One rule was simple, never punch a suspect in the face, a hard back-hand to the temple or a shot to the kidneys, did just as well without a bruise or a broken nose. Valentine watched the two expressionless cops pull the slumping Brazzi upright to keep him from sliding off the stool, and turned to McClosky.

“Come on, take a look, it’s not much, but it could lead to a break in the Boyarski case. Part of this dumb son of a bitch’s dodge is collecting surplus oil drums, power spraying them clean for resale with Brazzi and Company stenciled across the middle. Here, take a look.”

Stacked in a corner were eight drums, four of them intact, the others with their tops cutoff with an acetylene torch. The tops of the drums could easily be rewelded for further use.

“Look at this place, not much to see is there. The drums have to be a big part of his business. No doubt in my mind that he’s been a hands-on casket-maker for the mob. It’s his dumb luck one popped up with his name on it.”

“Not the brightest guy in the world is he, painting his name on his steel coffins,” McClosky said. “Any sheet on him?

“Two B and E’s, both dismissed, an attempted liquor store robbery, also dismissed when the owner backed off,” Valentine said. “You could’ve guessed, his only conviction was ninety days for wife-beating, put her in the hospital for almost a week.”

At that point, a third uniform who had remained outside, called in, “Sergeant McClosky, you’ve got a call on your two-way. Seems urgent.”

“Okay, Windy, good work. Really squeeze this guy. He’s already pissing his pants. Let’s see what his squealing gets us. Gotta run.”

McClosky took off his jacket, threw it in the backseat, loosened his tie, settled behind the wheel of his cruiser and idled out of earshot. McAdoo got right to the point.

“Craziest, goddamned thing, can’t figure it out” he said. “Our mark decided to call it quits after lunch. What does he do, he drives out to the park for a stroll, then wanders into the woods down by the stream. Took maybe twenty minutes, then got back in his car and drove home. He’s there now.”

“And where are you?”

“Back at his house. Tucked him in with his mama, then made a roundtrip back to the park, his car hasn’t moved.”

“From the beginning, let’s have it all.”

"Like I said, he just finished a call at a men's shop in Bloomfield, that was shortly after noon. A blue-plate special for lunch at Newberry's, he stayed on his stool at the counter, never went near the payphone. Then it was off to the park. He pulled onto a service road while I parked at the curb. Had a good view of everything. He idled along those woods down by the stream, you know the place, real thick with a lot of bushes, great spot to get laid, if you can stand the bugs."

"Forget the nostalgia, get to the point."

"Our mark is taking in Mother Nature until he gets to another service road cutting through the woods, he took it. When he disappeared, I scampered to the edge of the woods, but couldn't see a thing, it was too damn thick. Twenty minutes later he was back in his car and headed home. That was about one-fifteen. I followed and waited until he parked and mama came out and gave him a big welcome."

"Let's get back to your roundtrip, find anything?"

"Yes and no. Just a beat-up gravel road that lead to another service road that ran along the stream. Straight ahead was a little, wood footbridge to, how else can I say it, another world. Nobody around, so I walked across to a big lawn area with fancy outdoor furniture, a tennis court, and from what I've seen in the movies, croquet wickets. At the top of a rise overlooking it all was a house more like a castle."

"Find out who lives there?"

"I'm way ahead of you. The house was one of three on a cul-de-sac, all mansions. Hit it lucky, caught the postman as he was finishing up and got the names."

"I'm waiting." McClosky's patience was exhausted, but he knew where McAdoo was coming from. He had been there himself on jobs that seemed to be going nowhere. This was the first meat on the bone and McAdoo was savoring it.

"They're all Krauts, Hugo Franke, Otto Sternberg, and Bernhardt Gerber. The mailman hates Krauts, no Christmas tips, and never even a hello. He was a talkative guy. According to the mail they've been getting, they all work for M.L. Kraus. Cute set-up, don't you think?"

"How long did the roundtrip take?"

"It's two-o-five now, so give or take forty-five minutes."

"And the car didn't move, that's good. Be sure to fill Petri in when he relieves you. I'm heading downtown."

As was the case during his previous two days of surveillance, McAdoo failed to notice the brown Dodge parked a half-block behind him at the park. The driver witnessed everything.

Twenty minutes later, McClosky found Cisco in his office, his phone cocked to his ear while he jotted notes on a pad. He went to the bullpen, grabbed a cup of coffee and returned to the office just as his partner hung up.

"That was Melnyk, finally with something to say after playing grab-ass with Beagan for two days and coming up empty," Cisco said as he reached for his notes.

"Let's hear it, and then I'll fill you in with what I got from McAdoo," McClosky said.

Cisco sat back and began scanning his notes, he underlined some of them, looked across his desk with a smile, something rare with him over the past two weeks. "Melnyk said that right in the middle of his deliveries, Beagan decides to take a stroll in the park. This guy runs a tight schedule, one meat drop-off after another all day long, so this hardly made any sense to him."

"A stroll in the park?" McClosky came close to choking on his coffee, cleared his throat and asked, "Where in the park did this return to Mother Nature occur?"

"In and around that heavily wooded area at the edge of the park down near the stream."

"Have I got this right, that Beagan simply drove his truck into the park and then what?" McClosky said.

"That's it, parked and took a nice leisurely walk in and around the woods, for about fifteen, maybe twenty minutes."

"How long ago was this?"

"Melnyk said it was about one-forty-five."

"I'll be a son of a bitch if McAdoo's call wasn't a dress rehearsal. Same place, same routine, right down to the amount of time Hunter took for his birdwatching." Going step-by-step through his notes, McClosky recounted everything.

It didn't escape McClosky that his partner's lips had tightened and his face took on that mean, hard look that surfaced whenever he was forced to suppress an inner rage.

"The mansion directly above the footbridge, Franke's?" Cisco said.

"Yeah, according to McAdoo, Franke's."

The two detectives spent the next ten minutes wondering what the hell all this meant. If it were a break, then where did it lead? With everything so close together, they agreed that someone with a keen sense of timing had planned it all, and Beagan and Hunter were apparent pawns.

"What do you think, Rache?" McClosky asked.

"That's my guess," his partner answered. "Grab your jacket, and come on. Let's take a look at that cul-de-sac. First, give me a minute to call Peterson."

After getting his jacket, McClosky found his partner seated on the corner of his desk, his face once again an angry scowl.

"Yeah, we've got that covered as well," Cisco said. "Everything's set, Rache or no Rache. We can collar our two marks at any time."

Cisco's body language told McClosky all he needed to know. He was getting a bucket of crap from the D.A. After about a minute of nods, raised eyebrows and rolled eyes, Cisco reluctantly accepted Peterson's edict.

"You're the boss. You want it that way, that's the way we'll handle it." he said, then paused for another earful. "I agree Rache has them on leashes, and their nature walks were his idea. It's no coincidence the homes of three neo-Nazis were right there, too."

After choking on a few more words of wisdom from the D.A., Cisco slammed the phone down.

"Take a few deep breaths, Nick. It looks like you need them," Kevin said. "What the hell was that all about?"

"Today's developments have Peterson wetting his pants, thinks it's the best thing since sliced bread. Friday's news circus will be another suck-up to his meal-ticket Al Driscoll. First, he'll parade out German-haters Beagan and Hunter with all the gory details, and then comes today's bonus."

"Bonus? What the hell are you talking about?"

"His word for it, not mine. You have to admit he's fast on his feet even when he's punching over his weight. Got it worked out how just in the nick of time he uncovered a plot to kill M.L. Kraus executives asleep in their beds."

"He can say whatever the hell he wants, and who says it ain't so?" McClosky said. "It's a sure thing, like shaved dice at a back-alley crap game."

"And we'll be up on stage with him to acknowledge everything he says proving there's no substitute for honest, nose-to-the-grindstone police work," Cisco said. "Tomokai will describe the gruesome details, the stiffs he's had on ice. The Chief will purple-nose himself up to the mic and brag about how he followed the investigation every step of the way.

"I wanted to pick them up tonight, but Peterson nixed it. So, we wait thirty-six hours. They're not going anywhere. Rizzo and Melnyk will pick-up Beagan at the family plant, and Petri and McAdoo will grab Hunter at his house. Now let's go take a look at that cul-de-sac."

They were stopped on their way out by the desk sergeant who held up his telephone, one hand cupped over the mouthpiece. "Call here for you, lieutenant. Want it here or in your office?"

"I'll take it here." He listened for less than a minute and said, "I'll be there. A big day tomorrow, so let's say nine o'clock."

CHAPTER FORTY-EIGHT

Cisco, for the first time ever, parked his car in front of Grace's house Thursday morning, strode to the front door and using his own key, let himself in. He found Grace standing near the fireplace.

"Nick, hold it right there for a moment," she said. "It's the last time, and I want to devour it all. This won't be happening again. We knew this was coming, so there's no need for histrionics. Agreed?"

Nick stepped into the living room and approached the fireplace. "I know it's kind of early, but if a farewell toast was ever in order, this is it. What do you say?"

"Sure, why not," she said. "But I still feel like a passenger on the Titanic."

"Only they never saw the iceberg until it was too late," Nick said. "We've always had that iceberg in sight, drawing closer and closer, and here we are today."

Grace went to the liquor cart and tossed over her shoulder, "I'll do the honors, three fingers as usual. Remember, big fellow, you have a meeting this afternoon, don't want you glassy-eyed."

Nick moved from the fireplace and walked to the framed print of the *Penitent Magdalene.* "She's yours, also I want you to have *Las Meninas.*"

"I had every intention, but still I'm glad you said that," she said. "Taking them with you would be like a slap in the face for Connie. We may have been oversexed creeps, but we're not monsters."

Nick joined Grace at the front window where she handed him his scotch on the rocks. They silently tipped their glasses, and avoiding eye contact, turned to watch the outside traffic.

They finished their drinks, and as if on cue, turned to face each other. "I think this is what pulp fiction hacks call 'an awkward moment.' Awkward or not...."

"Let's just call it inevitable, we both knew it, lived with it, and now here we are," he said, taking her glass and placing it with his on the liquor cart. They closed the small gap between them, and like two bashful teenagers, they embraced and tenderly brushed their lips.

"Now get out of here. Grab your stuff from the closet on your way out," she said, as her first defiant tears trickled down her cheeks. He had never seen her cry and he never would, "And damn it, don't look back."

She watched as Nick popped open the trunk of his car, placed his two suitcases inside, slammed it closed and took the driver's seat. Without looking her way, he drove off leaving behind the three best years of her life. *We had it all, and didn't give a damn what anyone thought. The tongue-wagging, the worst from our families. Their love, it was always there, but we shoved it aside because... because why. Simple enough, we had our brains between our legs. But God almighty, was it great.*

She picked up her glass, dropped in three fresh cubes, and poured herself a stiff one. After three sips, her tears began their freefall, turning to deep sobs as she sank into Nick's favorite overstuffed chair.

Downtown, two legal teams were hard at work preparing for their appearance before Federal Judge Harold Hockmeier the next day. Hugo Manfred Franke had taken over half of the executive offices at M.L. Kraus' huge chemical plant on Arthur Kill. Jason Cullen Tumulty III and his much smaller team were putting the finishing touches on their briefs at the Robert Treat. The verbal punching and counterpunching had been going on between them since late Tuesday morning.

"I was surprised, you might even say shocked, when I learned upon awakening this morning, that you were no longer with us," an unctuous Franke intoned that morning. "We had many good things waiting for you to enjoy, but now you'll miss them. And as we say in Germany, *So ist das Leben."*

"I'm sure you heard an important issue had surfaced that I can only deal with here at the hotel with my team," Tumulty restated the lie he'd concocted during the wiretapped-call.

"Jason, I had no idea such an important issue has arisen," Franke, a master sycophant, was back on a first-name basis. "I'm certain we will all learn about it when we go before the good Judge Hockmeier."

"You'll have your chance on center stage, doubtless with a long list of Teutonic witticisms to keep the daggers sheathed," Tumulty said. "But, Hugo, I have to admit, I can't for the life of me, recall the name of any German humorist."

"Ah, Jason, you poke fun so easily, but it's useful when important matters are being considered," Hugo said. "The future of my beloved Germany, and yes, even that of Europe cannot be trifled with, but some levity is welcome."

"If things get too frivolous, you can always throw in Schopenhauer and Nietzsche."

Their jousting during the past few days barely concealed what both men knew, that their dislike and distrust of each other was just beneath the surface, and would have to remain there during the hearing. For Dilberry, Tumulty & Benson, big bucks and added prestige were involved, for Franke and M.L. Kraus, it was power in all its forms on both sides of the Atlantic, and for the Truman White House, it was locking up the Commies east of the Elbe.

Many things had been troubling Tumulty since his overnight stop at the Franke mansion. The wiretapping and surveillance was crude enough to be laughable, but little Muriel, she was something else. He was certain that this beautiful girl, frightened enough to hide in her room when he offered his hand, was living a tormented life in that dark and cold mansion.

"Tell me, Hugo, how is little Muriel doing?" Jason asked. "She's a sweet and bright little thing, and that cast on her arm, will it be coming off any day soon?"

"Muriel is becoming more and more a little German princess. Honoria and I could not be more pleased with her progress," Hugo said. "Thank you very much for asking. *Auf Wiedersehen* until tomorrow."

Muriel's progress, so closely monitored by Honoria, had taken another step that morning when she went through her mandatory drills. First, two hours tackling German pronunciation with Frieda, the housekeeper, followed with two hours of grammar with Ingrid, the cook. When it was over, Muriel was exhausted in body and spirit. The all-seeing Ingrid recognized for some time that Honoria's drinking, and Hugo's callous unconcern were misshaping a bright girl who, at the beginning, was so happy and gay.

"I have your favorite apple streusel straight from the oven *kleines Mädchen,*" said Ingrid, who believed that the best way to learn German was through the stomach. "And we have another of your favorites, *split erbsensuppe mit schinken."*

"What a treat, streusel and pea soup with ham," Muriel said as she raised herself onto a kitchen chair propped with two cushions. "I am a little tired right now. So, when I finish, a little nap will be okay with Honoria, won't it?"

"Of course, *kleines Mädchen,* and if Frau Franke comes from the library and asks about you, I will tell her what wonderful lessons you had today, and that you and Rudy are taking a nice rest."

The kitchen clock said one-fifteen, and if her daily routine was in place, the mistress of the house should be well into her schnapps. Ubiquitous Sebastian would be ready with a refill, and if needed to uncork a new bottle, or to steady Frau Franke on her way to her room. The tall, muscular chauffeur, Herman, was always within earshot.

After Muriel had washed down the streusel with a tall glass of milk, Ingrid pulled her chair from the table, lifted her from the cushions and whispered, "Go upstairs and join Rudy, you know he is waiting."

Freida walked Muriel upstairs to her room. She drew open the drapes and the double French doors to allow the early afternoon sun to come in.

Muriel wore a dark blue jumper, a white, soft collar blouse, white lace-top anklets, and black strapped shoes, the perfect German schoolgirl uniform. She waited for Freida to leave, retrieved Rudy from his perch on her bed, her doll Kristina from her rocking chair, and walked out to the balcony. This was their favorite place. Nobody bothered them when they talked. She placed them on the balustrade and whispered, "Look how nice it is, and from up here it is all for us. We don't have to share with anybody. Down there with my friends it is very nice, and I really, really like Klaus, he makes me giggle, but I don't love them the way I love you."

Across the stream, concealed by the thick bushes of the woods, Mister Rache was closely watching everything in and around the Franke mansion. For the last time, he confirmed that everything was in place for tonight. He was about to turn away and return to his car when the little girl with the cast on her arm appeared on the balcony with a doll and teddy bear. A surprisingly easy smile softened his features as he watched her happily jabber back-and-forth with her companions. This pleasant respite from his hate-driven mission was quickly pushed aside by the indelible vision of another beautiful child and her obsequious parents at Dachau. It would always be with him.

He watched for a few more seconds, then turned abruptly and retraced his steps through the woods. Back behind the wheel of Father Kaczinski's Buick, he drove downtown to his final rendezvous with Mike and Frank. It will be early evening and foot traffic at Washington Park would be sparse. Infrequent passersby would give no more than a glance to the three men seated on benches below the big bronze of George and his horse.

His first stop was at a drugstore payphone on Market Street. The call to Frank was at precisely two-fifty, followed by the call to Mike at exactly five minutes after three. Three hours later, they would receive their final orders at Washington Park.

Up until early afternoon, it was an easy day for the police surveillance teams. Rizzo and Melnyk were puzzled when Beagan failed to show-up for work and his father closed shop to take over his son's delivery schedule. They switched their surveillance to the family's Clinton Hill home.

"What time did he come out?" McClosky said, jotting notes while he continued to listen. "Rizzo, you're absolutely sure it was the same payphone as before... outside the same butcher shop." Another pause. "Took only a couple minutes, then straight back home. Okay, got it. Where are you now?"

"Parked about a half-block from the family digs," Rizzo said. "If you ask me, he's in for the night. I'm no expert, but it was like he was sleepwalking. Didn't look up, down or sideways when he got into his Ford. Same thing at the payphone."

Five minutes earlier, Cisco had finished his phone call with Petri and was waiting impatiently for his partner to get off the phone. "Don't tell me. I can connect the dots."

Until about one-thirty, Petri and McAdoo took turns twiddling their thumbs in their surveillance car when Hunter finally came out.

They went over their notes comparing each nuance, and came away with the same conclusion. The two marks had behaved like robots programmed by the mysterious, still missing, Rache.

"Kevin, let's give our teams until five o'clock, it should be getting dark by then. Beagan and Hunter aren't going any place tonight. We'll want collars first thing in the morning. They'll stash Beagan in the Third's lock-up, and Hunter goes to the Sixth's. I've already made the calls. Everyone keeps their mouths shut."

CHAPTER FORTY-NINE

If the two surveillance teams were puzzled by the unforeseen behavior of Beagan and Hunter, it was not the case with police Sergeant Josh Gingold. It began the morning McClosky picked up his report that described in gruesome detail the severed-arm at the incinerator. This was not a routine case, and both cops knew it.

He saw how throwing around D.A. Peterson's name could cow into silence even a tough, no bullshit cop like Murdock. Two cellophane wrapped packets with the logo of an upscale haberdasher prompted his phone call to the company's New York headquarters, and the name and address of Mike Hunter.

It required less than a week of sick leave to discover that homicide also had its eye on Hunter. First it was McClosky tracing Hunter's route all the way to Pompton Lakes, and starting last Monday, dawn-to-dusk surveillance of every Hunter move.

Yesterday required a little more work on his part. After watching Hunter and Petri's maneuvers, he left his car at the curb for a closer look-see at the woods and the three mansions across the stream. Less than an hour later, he had scanned the public directory at a nearby library, and found what he suspected, the names of three top men at

M.L. Kraus, the supplier of poison gas to the Nazi death camps. Were they the next target?

If his latest hunch was right, this would be no ordinary Thursday. Gingold pulled to the curb and parked his Dodge in its accustomed spot at the corner of Seventeenth and Clinton. It wasn't long before Petri took up surveillance a half-block in front of him. Everything in place except for Hunter who didn't appear until one-thirty when he listlessly walked to his car, and drove off at the head of a three-car convoy.

When Hunter turned onto South Orange Avenue, the familiar payphone and men's store only a few blocks away, Gingold headed back to Seventeenth. His latest hunch was holding up well. There would be another phone call and Hunter would return home. Gingold would be waiting.

Once Hunter was again sequestered in his house, Petri took his normal spot a half-block away. The maxim that police surveillance could bore you to death, rang true. Gingold, fighting off drowsiness, wondered why Petri had not been relieved by McAdoo as usual at four o'clock. An hour later, he got his answer when Petri drove away, the day's surveillance had ended for them, but not for him.

He tried unsuccessfully to control the thoughts that drifted across his years before and after joining the force. Boxing was his ticket, but he had been too goddamned dumb to figure it out. He was a clean 175, a natural light heavy, in a division filled with palookas. *And hell, I wasn't half-bad while still learning, twenty-five amateur bouts, only four losses and never off my feet, a draw and fourteen knockouts says something.*

Gingold polished off the coffee and pastrami on rye he'd picked up on his way back from South Orange Avenue, fired up a Camel and allowed a self-deprecating smile to crinkle his face as he recalled what it was like back then.

Even Meyer Ellenstein, our mayor for two terms when things were really tough in town, laced-on gloves for more than a decade. Fought as Kid Meyer, not very original, but he was a sweetheart Flyweight. 115 pounds with a stiff jab, solid right hand, and never lost as an amateur. A banty rooster who got real respect from all the East Ward Jewish pugs, and that was really saying something. His timing was great, got out just before the Jews walked away from City Hall and the courthouse to find other ways to rake it in without getting their fingernails dirty.

I was just one, maybe two years too late, that's all it was for me. Sure, Zwillman was still calling shots downtown and half the cops were on his payroll, but the wops and micks were moving in big time.

Ten days earlier, a puzzled McClosky had asked him why he had thrown his gloves away, but there was no explaining to a *goy*. Emil Sitkoff, a dirty brawler from Elizabeth, decided for him. It was his final fight and the only time he wanted to really hurt an opponent, not just hurt, but to punish.

During a fourth-round clinch, Sitkoff sneered in his ear, "You fuckin' kikes. Can't fight for shit." He knew every dirty trick, using each clinch to dig his elbows into Gingold's upper arms, making them too heavy and weak for a good defense. The racist brawler was too slow to realize that his words set in motion his worst beating ever.

A blind, mindless fury took control of Gingold. During the next four and a half minutes, he opened up cuts over both of Sitkoff's eyes, sliced open his nose, then leaned forward in a clinch and said, "Not bad for a yid, is it you mother fucker."

Next round he caught Sitkoff dangling in the ropes with four quick combinations. A hard right flattened the cartilage of his nose and blood spurted from both nostrils. The ref stopped it with fifteen seconds to go in the fifth of a scheduled six-rounder.

His wife Emma was overjoyed when he donned his police uniform for the first time. It meant a steady paycheck and with two growing young boys to feed, he understood. Of course, the kids saw it differently. Their old man was a prize fighter, and a good one. When he turned pro, he would go after Slapsie Maxie's light heavy title. Their buddies were told that a cream puff hitter like Rosenblum never stood a chance against their dad.

Josh was using up his sick leave, and his wife Emma didn't like it one bit. She was convinced he was pursuing a dangerous pipe dream, and that morning she let it all hang out.

"After you've wasted your sick leave that's the end of it," Emma said as Josh reached for the front door. "You're not taking a day of your vacation away from the family, not for a crazy scheme with no payoff in sight."

"Do I have to say it again. Yeah, it's only a hunch, but if I'm right it could mean a big move up," he said. "I've had sergeant stripes for too long, passed the lieutenant's test with flying colors, but with a Jew-hater like Jim Murdock my boss, I could wait until hell freezes over."

Emma reached up, and with her hands on his shoulders, pulled him down for a kiss. "Now get going, just don't get yourself shot. Promise?"

"Promise."

It was thirty minutes since Petri had pulled out and he was about to call it quits himself when Hunter emerged, not in civilian garb, but wearing Army battle fatigues, complete with shoulder patch and sergeant stripes. *Goddamn if it's not just the way Tom Candless described the two guys who unloaded the meat at the city dump. Both in fatigues and even wearing combat boots. Something's in the works tonight, and there's no way in hell I'm not there when it happens.*

He waited until Hunter pulled away, and if his hunch was right, Gingold knew exactly where he was headed. By six o'clock, the downtown rush hour traffic had thinned considerably and Hunter had little trouble weaving his way to a parking spot on Broad. Washignton Park was less than a block away. Gingold knew what would happen next, a reprise of the previous Sunday. He parked his car on Washington Place and casually disappeared into the deep shadow of George Washington and his horse.

Hunter had already joined another fatigue-clad guy on the bench. They sat trance-like three feet apart, a silent nod their only acknowledgement. As before, the big man strolled from across the street to park himself on a bench within arm's-length of the two men. Gingold was too far away to hear him, but saw that his words had an immediate effect. All he could do was wait and see, increasingly aware that his pounding heart was playing hell with his ribcage. This was going to be the night for something to happen. He just knew it, could feel it. Should he have heard the big man's words, there would be no doubt.

CHAPTER

FIFTY

After taking his seat, Mister Rache leaned forward, studied the two faces and said, "One thought has crowded my mind. Watchtower B. We all know that the horror of Watchtower B will be with us always. Tonight, we will take the final step to avenge what we saw at Watchtower B.

"First I must explain why I am not now clad in the battle dress of our beloved Rainbow Division." Mister Rache was not by nature a deceitful man, but sometimes mendacity was called for. "There were necessary duties to perform before our mission tonight, but I will be in full uniform with you as we move shoulder-to-shoulder to erase the Nazi swine."

Mister Rache never considered walking shoulder-to-shoulder with Mike and Frank. He would be there, but only as an observer from a distance. If they were sacrificed, there could not be a worthier cause. He was pleased by the results of his induction. They were attentive, but still relaxed. Their body language convinced him that his phone calls and their reconnaissance of the target area had worked to perfection. Just a few more suggestions and they would be ready.

"Tonight, hated Watchtower B will be eradicated forever. I see you have your satchels with all that is needed to complete your mission. Frank, please show me your weapons of revenge."

Mister Rache waited while Frank undid the satchel's hasp, reached inside and withdrew a .45 caliber, Army-issue automatic pistol. He took it, released the magazine to see that it was fully loaded, and handed it back. Frank next withdrew a Maxim silencer specially made for a .45 colt automatic, and handed it over. Again, a silent nod of approval from Mister Rache. Frank then produced two fully loaded magazines for inspection. The rote exercise was repeated with Mike, and the drill was over.

Gingold was transfixed by what he was witnessing, a master puppeteer at work, but the big guy was no Geppetto and you would never mistake Hunter or his fatigue-clad cohort for Pinocchio.

He drove back to the park, made sure it was empty, then glided his car into a nook in the woods he had discovered the day before. Camouflaged by the thick bushes around it, the small clearing was just big enough for one car. It provided excellent vantage to observe almost everything in and around the woods.

Gingold removed his Smith and Wesson from his shoulder holster, and for the fourth time today, cracked open and spun the cylinder to count the cartridges. He snapped off its safety and placed it on the seat beside him. One thing was for certain, they would be coming to him and he'd be waiting. He checked his watch, it was almost seven, and it dawned on him that he should've saved half that pastrami on rye.

His wait ticked-tocked toward nine o'clock, and he wondered if, for the first time, his hunch was wrong. He was about to get out and stretch his legs when two cars turned into the park and drove slowly past his lookout. Sure enough, the lead car was Hunter's Hudson Terraplane followed by a Ford sedan. They stopped where the road reached the smaller service road leading through the woods to the footbridge across the stream.

Gingold picked up his revolver, made sure the safety was off and reholstered it. He slid out of the driver's seat, and carefully inched his way along a line of bushes to the edge of the road. Neither Hunter nor the other driver had left their cars.

Fifteen minutes later, he heard a third car slowly idle down a service road that ran along another thicket one hundred yards across a well-manicured lawn. The half-moon afforded just enough light to make out the silhouettes of a long, dark car and the big man who emerged. The metallic click of the closing door could be heard across the open space. As if on cue, the two men got out with their weapon-laden satchels.

Was that the puppeteer at work again, or what? Could barely hear that little click, but they sure as shit could. Gingold thought. *Just about jumped from their cars. Christ almighty, these two guys are ready for action.*

Crouched, with his revolver drawn, he slowly inched his way toward the two parked cars. Both men placed their satchels on the car hoods, opened them and withdrew the pistols. He was now within fifteen feet, but still hidden in the shadow of the bushes. *What the hell are those? Are they what I think they are?*

He got his answer when the two men next removed long metal cylinders that he immediately recognized... silencers. He knew that once they were attached to the pistols, these guys would be ready for action, and he had to stop them right now.

"Police! Hold it right there, not another move. Don't make me shoot!" Gingold shouted stepping from the shadows to assume his stance at the right rear fender of the Ford. "Drop the guns! I want you face down on the ground...do it now!"

What happened next propelled Gingold into a netherworld he could not have imagined. Without speaking, Hunter and his accomplice turned first toward each other, and then across the open space to the looming silhouette. The dark specter stepped out of the shadows and let loose an agonized howl, "Watchtower B!"

With their pistols now at the ready, the two men focused their attention on Gingold. "You don't understand," Hunter said moving from behind the front end of his beloved Terraplane.

"Don't understand? What's to understand? Drop the guns and we can talk," Gingold said, hoping to head off another O.K. Corral.

"Our mission," the other gunman said from his position at the front end of his Ford, and close enough for Gingold to hear his breathing.

"Mission, what mission!"

"To kill the Nazi-loving swine still among us. To kill, not surrender," the gunman said.

Just in time, Gingold caught the glint of Hunter's pistol as he raised it and took aim. He dropped to the ground with two loud BAMs exploding in his ears, the bullets whizzing past his head and into the fender of the Ford. In rapid succession, Gingold rolled over and, propped on his elbows, got off two shots.

"Oh my God, oh my..." Hunter's words turning into a bloody gurgle.

Gingold's first shot hit him in the left chest, angled upward and exited through his shoulder. The second shot fractured his sternum. Hunter hit the ground, a few more breaths, and for him the mission was over.

The other gunman crouched down behind the Ford.

Still on his belly, Gingold used his elbows to drag himself to the rear of the car and waited for the gunman to appear. "Mike! Mike, are you still there? Say something!" his entreaty was met with ominent silence.

"He's gone! Don't be next. Throw down your gun and come on out."

Still crouching, the gunman emerged from the far side of the car, spotted Gingold on the ground and without taking careful aim, squeezed off two wild shots. BAM, BAM. The bullets kicked loose gravel into Gingold's face as they rocketed into the road. Gingold, barely able to see, fired three times hitting the gunman in the right knee, belly and chest.

He arose, walked over and stooped to the dying man, "Your name, at least your name."

"My name's not important, only the mission, our mission. And Mister Rache, he will understand. He will...." His body convulsed, and with bloody spit drooling from his mouth, he died.

Mister Rache? Who the hell is Mister Rache? Well fuck, it's gotta be the big guy. Realizing this, he raced to the edge of the road and peered across the open space to the other thicket. The big car threw up gravel as it sped out of the park. Police sirens were getting closer and the flashing dome lights of two cruisers were already in sight.

The gunfire broke out fifteen minutes after Franke's dinner guests left for their neighboring mansions. An hour earlier, Muriel gave her playmates a reluctant good night, followed by hugs all around. The first four shots, two heavy reports from the .45s, and two crisper replies from Gingold's Smith and Wesson, propelled Hugo and Honoria to their bedroom balcony. Leaning over the balustrade, they peered across the footbridge and down the road through the woods. Nothing, only dark silence. They failed to notice the three furtive figures approaching from behind.

Then five more shots, again a blending, that told the Frankes at least two gunmen were involved in a deadly fight only a short distance from their privileged sanctuary. Honoria was jolted back into the here and now when two heavy hands were laid on her shoulders, "Come, get back. You must get back inside, Frau Franke." It was Herman, a man who rarely spoke and who was now giving her orders. Hugo turned from the balustrade as his angry wife laid down the law to Herman.

"You, a servant, no, less than that, a *nur ein Chauffeur,* giving me orders? You are lucky to have a job," she shrieked. "And we will see about that!"

Hugo stood and watched, saying nothing, and for the first time saw that Herman was not alone. Eduard Siemens and Frieda were advancing from their vantage at the foot of the bed.

"I must advise you, Frau Franke, that circumstances have changed," Siemens said. "Herman, Frieda here, and Sebastian were chosen, after much deliberation, to spend the war years, not in our Fatherland, but serving the Fuhrer here in America."

"Spies? Are you saying they've been spying on us all these years?" Hugo said.

"Spy, such a harsh word," Siemens said, as he turned and smiled down at Frieda. "Fraulein Frieda Gottlieb has been a trusted and valuable counter-agent for more than a decade. To say spy is very counterproductive."

"And you have valuable work awaiting you in the morning when you and the enemy go before Judge Hockmeier," Frieda said. "Your head must be clear if we are to get back what has been taken from us by the American war mongers."

"Of course, we understand, they will exact a big price, a price we will gladly pay to ensure the future of our Reich."

"Words like 'we' and 'ours,' who is this mysterious 'our' and 'we?'" Hugo said. "Am I not a part of M.L. Kraus' plan for the future? If not, why have we been here for the past five years?"

Siemens made no attempt to hide his exasperation when he sighed, "Because you are so pliable, so ready to accept without question our orders. And Honoria, let's just say that with her problem, she could serve us much better here."

"You had everything we were looking for," Frieda said, laying out in a few words their Faustian plan. "Both the same age, blonde, blue-eyed, with elite families and schooling, and with Honoria's permanent infertility, you would be the ideal couple to adopt a young, blonde, blue-eyed American child. The end result, a German couple has blended perfectly into American society."

"Now your mission is about to end," Siemens said. He studied their faces and feigning a lapse in memory added, "Oh yes, get rid of Muriel, she's no longer needed, and the sooner the better."

"Why!" Honoria, not quite tipsy but close, sprang to life. "We are quite happy with her progress, she is molding well. You do agree Frieda, Herman?"

"Yes, she is a *kleines Mädchen,"* Frieda said, "but she no longer serves any purpose."

"Back to your question why," Siemens said with a glance down at the service road and the pulsating red dome lights of at least three police cruisers. "Herman never misses anything, and during the past week he observed what must be called warning signals. Herman, perhaps you should explain."

"My curiosity was aroused Monday night when Sebastian showed your guest, Herr Tumulty, the best way to tour the grounds. He crossed the bridge and encountered someone in the dark, shouted for him to come out and show himself, but got no answer. Next I heard a car drive away."

"The next day, I saw a big man in dark clothing walking about on the other side of the stream. He was taking in everything, but his main focus was over here. Then earlier today the same man in the same clothes repeated everything. Yesterday, two men, at different times, came and went but not until they repeated every move the big man had made, it was as though they were all tied together by some invisible string," Herman concluded with a wane smile.

"What does that mean? A coincidence perhaps?" Hugo said.

"Herman is trained to observe and interpret," Siemens said. "He knows when someone is a target, and Hugo, you and Honoria have undoubtedly been targeted."

"For what?" Honoria said.

"To be killed. Those shots we all heard could have been your reprieve. If true, it is good for all of us. Judge Hockmeier is waiting."

"And it doesn't matter whether Muriel is still with us or not?" said Hugo, clearly frustrated and bewildered, knowing a final decision had been made.

"Who will notice or even care once the huge holdings of M.L. Kraus are made public," Siemens said. "The public will be screaming for its pound of flesh."

CHAPTER

FIFTY-ONE

Dr. Walter Tomokai was aroused by the persistent ring of his bedside telephone, and after listening to the report on the other end, he glanced at the luminous dials of the alarm clock and smiled. It was ten past ten o'clock, and with the two local newspapers already put to bed, he had ample time to prepare for the press in the morning. He had an uncanny instinct when there was a headline in the making. A shoot-out that left two men dead at a park in one of the city's safest neighborhoods deserves at least a 40-point Boldface above the frontpage centerfold.

Close behind his two car police escort, he sped to the park, and after putting on rubber gloves, joined his forensic team already busy at work. A muscular man, obviously a cop in plainclothes but one he didn't recognize, was standing watch. The coroner surveyed the scene and immediately realized he would not be tonight's headline-maker. Two bodies in blood-soaked Army combat fatigues, and on the ground nearby two .45 caliber blunderbusses and two silencers gave him a queasy feeling.

Where the hell are Cisco and McClosky? And who is this cop? No doubt he's in charge, probably the trigger-man. What does he know about our rogue cover-up, if anything? Been along for the ride, but right now it looks like everything's coming apart.

He walked over to Gingold who was directing two uniforms where to stretch the yellow crime scene tape. "Didn't get your name. What the hell happened here?" he said in a lame attempt to impose his authority.

"Gingold. Sergeant Josh Gingold. Had been following one of these guys, the one over there, name's Mike Hunter. When he left his house in combat fatigues, I had a feeling something was up and decided to follow him. It seems this was a prearranged meeting place. Then things got real crazy, still don't understand it all...."

It required only a few minutes for Gingold to lay it all out, including the presence of a third man across the clearing and his eerie command that spurred the two shooters into action.

"You'll have a report pronto, right?" the coroner said. "I have some calls to make. Handle everything here according to procedure, but I really don't have to tell you that, do I."

Tomokai's first call was to Chief Patrick Riley, and it only added to his growing anxiety.

"Gingold, who the hell is Gingold?" the Chief demanded. "And how the fuck did he get involved? I don't like it, don't like it at all."

"He's one of your sergeants, works plainclothes in the Third," Tomokai said. "Like you, never heard of him before. Don't have a goddamned idea how he stumbled on us."

"Who else you call? Cisco, McClosky, Peterson?" the Chief knew his blood pressure was skyrocketing, his throbbing temples and buzzing ears were early tip-offs. "I'll call Gingold's boss, you handle the others. Forget our big showcase at the D.A.'s in the afternoon, I'm setting a meeting on my turf for ten, and Peterson can shove it up his arrogant ass if he don't like it. I want everybody in my office no later than eight o'clock."

“But Chief, he’s a damn good cop, even if he is a Jew,” Lieutenant Jim Murdock said after enduring the Chief’s opening harangue. “He had two years sick leave piled up and decided to take it. Nothing I could do about it, he earned it. Why the hell are you asking me how he spent his time off, ask him, you’re the police chief.” He and the Chief went back a long way, and they didn’t pull their punches.

A half-hour later, Tomokai confirmed with the Chief that he had contacted everyone, and the D.A.’s reaction was classic paranoia. “Peterson really pumped me about Gingold, and of course, I told him I knew nothing, but that wasn’t good enough. He asked me if I knew whether Gingold was a lone rogue, or was working secretly with Cisco and McClosky. I’m telling you, Chief, we’ve got to put together one hell of a story for the news vultures. Has to ring true.”

“Don’t worry about that, been at it for a long time,” the Chief said. “I’ll get Gingold in here early, straighten him out real fast. After we put our heads together, it’ll be straight from our good Lord’s bible, just like turning water into wine.”

After getting the warning shot across the bough from Tomokai, Cisco and McClosky touched based immediately. Cisco got hold of Rizzo, told him to pass the word on to Melnyk, that their gumshoe days were over, and to return their impound car after pulling out the two-way. McClosky gave the same instructions to McAdoo and Petrie. Both surveillance teams were to be in Cisco’s office at six-thirty to get final instructions before joining the crowd in Chief Riley’s office..

At seven-thirty, Gingold was the first to arrive, surprised to find that he was alone with the Chief who’s welcome was a red face growl, “Set your ass down and give it to me, all of it. And it better be one fucking hell of a story!”

Gingold was unabashed, the Chief’s outburst confirming that he was in the driver’s seat and the Chief knew it. It took no more than seven minutes to repeat essentially what he told Tomokai the evening before. He embellished it by detailing how he willing gave up sick leave time, making it possible for him to gumshoe Hunter, taking notes on each move he made. "It wasn't easy, and Emma was really pissed about me giving up sick leave time for, I guess you could say, the greater good."

"The greater good, what a bucket of bullshit! And your notes, where are they? Hand them over!"

"There up here," Gingold tapped his right temple and smiled. "But it's easy enough to write it all out if I think it's worth it."

The Chief sat back and closely scrutinized the arrogant Jew across his desk. He had survived the years when the Yids had ruled the roost because of his infallible instinct to assess greed and ambition.

"What the fuck do you want Gingold?"

"A silver bar on each shoulder, I earned them. And you can't play dumb, Chief. How many times have you gone over my folder since last night, twice maybe three times, to find out everything about me. You saw I was first in the lieutenant's test three years ago, and I'm still waiting. I want it now. What I've got up here," Gingold tapped his temple, smiled and met the Chief's scornful glare, "can easily be put in writing for the right people."

"What do you have that's worth anything? I don't think you have a goddamned thing."

"How about a rogue operation that involves the D.A., the coroner, the police chief, the acting head of homicide, and his sidekick. That's just for openers. There's no telling what enterprising news scribblers will come up with when they start digging. And you can bet your ass they'll do a lot of digging."

"It won't be that easy," the Chief said. "McClosky also finished first."

"That was last year, I've been waiting three years. Talk it over with Peterson, I know he's been running things from the start. With your two brains working together, everything will come up roses."

Cisco and McClosky sauntered in from the homicide bullpen at eight, and found a relaxed Gingold seated in a chair against the wall, his legs splayed in front of him.

Next, Petri and McAdoo, his senior officers, came in and took seats. Rizzo and Melnyk followed taking seats on the opposite side of the office.

Then it was Tomokai and Murdock, the only outsider to read Gingold's report. The Chief was touching all bases.

There was some awkward small talk until Peterson showed up at eight-thirty. He scanned the entire room and realized he was adrift among the great unwashed, and in danger of falling overboard. He still had high hopes for the Attorney General's job, just have to button a few things up to stay afloat. It was time to take charge.

"This will be old news for those who have been with me from the beginning, and an eye-opener for the late arrivals. When we go out on the stage to meet with the news ghouls, and you know they'll be thirsting for blood, I'll tell them we have just completed the most intense and successful criminal investigation like none before. We all have to be on the same page. This was not a rogue operation. That Sergeant Josh Gingold...Josh, show yourself, let me see who you are...big and strapping, very good. Photographers will have a field day."

Gingold sat down after showing himself as ordered by the D.A., and the chattering began. The first real news was brought to light by Detective McAdoo when he jabbed angrily, "Josh, we go back a long way, what the hell is this shit about instinct. For Christ's sake, let's have the straight skinny!"

"Credit Rogers Peet. That's right, Rogers Peet, who sells posh clothes we can't afford. Two of their fancy cellophane-wrapped garter belts fell out of the get-away car at the city dump. I picked them up, put two-and-two together, and made a phone call to the Peet headquarters in New York. Posed as a haberdasher who wanted Rogers Peet stuff in my store. They gave me the name of a salesman, you guessed it, Mike Hunter. And the rest is history."

"Why you son of a bitch, you kept all of this to yourself!" McClosky shouted. "That's withholding evidence!"

"Like the D.A. says, all for the greater good," Gingold smiled, and having stood up for his revelation, sat back and relaxed as the explosion erupted.

Profane epithets bounced off the walls and accusing fingers crissed-crossed like dueling sabers. Everything was going so good, how the hell did the lid come off. Tomokai reminded them that two stiffs and an arm had been held on ice, and added uncharacteristically, "Without a fucking peep from anyone. Don't talk to me about not putting the lid on!"

Murdock was the next to bleat. He had been left out of the loop by one of his underlings, killing any chance to share in the glory. "Gingold, you sly son of a bitch, almost got on your knees and begged for your sick time. Then you kicked me in the ass when you turned vigilante without telling me."

For Rizzo and Melnyk, it was like a Saturday matinee. They got a taste of how the department really worked when the Jeffries stabbing was pulled out from under them, and they lost an attempted murder collar. Now the big boys were in action. "Christ, this is fun," Rizzo said, "it's the Keystone Cops."

“Yeah, and directed by Count Dracula,” Melnyk whispered in reply after watching the D.A. gesticulate angrily while making a point with Cisco.

“You know you were breaking the law when you had your sidekick pose as the point man for a governor’s task force that doesn’t exist,” he said. “And then as a phony insurance agent to squeeze information out of a witness. All of this behind my back.”

“We got results didn’t we?” Cisco replied.

The names of people and places were thrown about like Civil War grapeshot: Obermeyer, Friedlander, Weber, Nuremberg, Pompton Lakes, Fazio, Cecil B. DeMille, Bolz, Guttenberg.

“Where the hell is Guttenberg, never heard of it?” McAdoo demanded. “Clue me in, Bavaria, Germany, Austria?”

“Try Hudson County,” McClosky said.

“I’ll be damned, live and learn,” McAdoo said.

By nine o’clock, the Chief had enough. “We’ve got an hour before the news conference, enough time for everyone to cool down. D.A. Peterson spelled it out, Sergeant Gingold is the star of the show, but we’ll all be up there with him. We’ll all have a chance at the mic. Be a good idea to start putting your thoughts together, no stumbling and mumbling. The conference will be packed so we’ll be walking across to the city council chamber. I cleared it with Mayor Murphy, and you better believe he’ll be there.”

By the time they arrived at the council chambers and took their seats, the gallery was filled with reporters, photographers, and City Hall hangers-on. Radio station crews, four from New York City, and four representing the national networks had already set-up their microphones. This was international news, and the AP, UP, INS and Reuters scribblers had front row seats.

McClosky, ever the silver-tongued oracle, decided to lay it on thick during a two-minute spiel that ended with, "Only a wide manhunt made it possible for us to track down Heinrich Bolz in Guttenberg." A young reporter from the *Asbury Park Press* fell for it hook, line and sinker.

"So, this was an international effort. To what extent was Interpol involved?" the cub reporter said. "Geography is not my strong suit. Is that in Austria or Germany?"

"Try Hudson County, New Jersey, United States of America," a voice, well cured in tobacco and booze, growled from the press gallery. "Ever try using an Atlas?"

Even Mayor Murphy, who was relegated to fifth dibs at the mic, agreed that it was a rip-roaring success.

CHAPTER FIFTY-TWO

Unnoticed during the near chaos at City Hall, another event with much broader international implications had gotten underway at the federal building. Hugo Manfred Franke, along with Eduard Siemens and their large legal team in lock step, arrived at eight o'clock. An M.L. Kraus office grunt loaded six boxes of legal documents onto a dolly and headed toward the service elevator. Franke and Siemens were surprised to find the Dilberry, Tumulty & Benson crew already sorting their briefs on two tables.

The combatants exchanged perfunctory handshakes and Jason Cullen Tumulty III couldn't help noticing that Franke made no effort to exude his usual oily charm. He was anxious to see who would be running the German show, he'd have to wait until Judge Hockmeier banged his gavel at ten o'clock, but his bet was on Herr Siemens.

Hugo wasn't the only Franke pressed into service this morning. Against her wishes, Honoria found herself in the rear seat of a black Daimler limousine on its way once again to Saint Michael's Novitiate in Englewood Cliffs. To her left, Muriel sat hugging Rudy and Kristina, and to her right was Frieda Gottlieb. Herman was driving and Sebastian had the other front seat. It was clear to Honoria they would never let her out of their sight.

When they arrived, Mother Superior Immaculata and Muriel's caseworker, Mary Fitzgerald, were waiting outside. Herman held their door open, and seeing that Muriel was having trouble getting out with Rudy and Kristina, extended his hand to help her. Honoria followed and they both headed up the stairs. By the time they reached the entrance, Frieda had joined Herman outside the car, both taking rigid positions on the driver's side while absorbing every perfunctory nuance.

Sebastian removed Muriel's luggage from the trunk, and silently climbed the steps to deposit the bags inside the lobby. His task accomplished, Sebastian stepped back outside and with his arms crossed, struck a pose, watched and listened only a few feet from where the group was exchanging empty words before saying goodbye. Honoria barely acknowledged the child for whom she had once professed undying love, but was now abandoning.

It took no more than ten minutes for it all to end, an episode straight from the classroom, Nazi classic surveillance 101, and they made no effort to disguise it. The Daimler disappeared leaving behind an injured little girl who was never any more than a propaganda experiment.

"Your room is waiting for you," Mother Superior said. "Just like you left it and wanted it to be."

"That makes me happy. I'm always happy here, and now I know more of the kids, I will be even happier."

"Were you ever happy with Honoria and Hugo," the caseworker asked. Since getting word that the Frankes were giving up Muriel, she carefully studied every page of the final report on her case. It was filed by Monsignor Garanti, but it didn't take long for her to see it had been written by Hugo and merely notarized by the cleric.

"Sometimes yes, but other times not so happy. I was not very happy when I was hurt, when things like this happened." She rubbed her right hand over the cast on her left arm, and looked up to see if the two women understood. Assured by what she saw she said, "But there were also good times that made me happy, especially with Herman."

"How did Herman make you happy?" the nun asked.

"Well, he was teaching me his favorite German song, one that he whistled all the time when he was not singing. Do you want to know something funny, Herman only whistled and sang when he was with me. Isn't that funny."

"What was the song?" the caseworker asked.

"Lili Marlene. I've already learned the first lines, do you want to hear them?"

"In German?" the caseworker asked.

"In German and in English," Muriel said, and without waiting, began to sing in a thin melodic voice:

Vor den Kasernen am Ecklicht
Ich werde immer stehen und nachts auf dich warten
Wir werden eine Welt für zwei schaffen
Ich werde die ganze Nacht auf dich warten
Für dich, Lili Marlene

Muriel's recital in the lobby drew looks of amazement not only from the Mother Superior and caseworker, but from the growing number of sisters, novices and postulants who had gathered around. Muriel, ever the ham, shared her smile and said, "And now in English."

Outside the barracks, by the corner light
I'll always stand and wait for you at night
We will create a world for two
I'll wait for you the whole night through
For you, Lili Marlene

The weekend began on a happy note for Muriel, but with growing apprehension for others. One of them was District Attorney Herman Gerhardt Peterson who was yet to hear conclusively that the surefire Governor-Elect, Alfred Driscoll, would be putting current Attorney General Walter Van Riper out to pasture. The D.A. had done all that he could to get to the front of the line, turning rogue for a headline grab and bribing others to join him. He had taken liberties with the law, put his trust in men well below his social station, and convinced his vainglorious wife Agnes, that sometimes you had to kiss-ass to get what you wanted. All he could do now was wait.

Late Monday morning, Police Chief Riley had recovered enough from long hours of boozing with other roustabouts, to schedule an afternoon news conference. He wasn't taking the action by choice, it was the result of out-and-out blackmail on one hand, and a quid pro quo agreement with the D.A. on the other. At two o'clock, Sergeants Josh Gingold and Kevin McClosky would be newly anointed lieutenants.

It didn't end there, Mayor Murphy watched the ceremony and stepped forward to announce what he had long believed, that the police department lacked a sense of direction, which could be tied directly to the lack of intelligence that provided direction and purpose. Newly minted Lieutenant McClosky would take over an intelligence unit that reported directly to the Chief and his office. Lieutenant Gingold would escape from his exile in the Third Ward to take McClosky's place on homicide.

On Tuesday night, D.A. Peterson, his wife and two kids, along with his office staff, waited for the final election results to come in. It was an unnecessary loss of sleep. Hours earlier it was apparent that Driscoll was a runaway winner for governor. At his news conference just before midnight, the Governor-Elect told a statewide radio audience that he would take an "observe and then decide" approach before making any major changes. He had already decided to retain two high profile public servants. One of them was Attorney General Walter Van Riper, who he commended for his clean-up of the numbers racket in Hudson County.

The reaction at Peterson's office was somewhat unexpected, some would call it weird. He actually looked happy and ebullient. Sensing that Sandra and Johan were crestfallen, he called his kids over for a hug and turned to his wife, who was anything but crestfallen. "I feel free again," she said, stepped forward, threw her arms around her husband and planted a big wet one on his lips.

Just the thought of moving to Trenton had depressed her. The two dinners with the dreary, holier than thou Driscolls, with the promise of more to come, prompted days of anxiety attacks. Now the future would be in her hands. She had all of that Heilman Brewery money behind her, and the international notoriety that Herman had just collected, could provide her with a fresh new future. Why not the U.S. Senate? She would be hobnobbing with the nation's elite, sure most would be politicians, but Huey Long was long gone and there was no way she would ever break bread with any of his ilk.

CHAPTER
FIFTY-THREE

On December 15, Nick and his wife Connie had been back together for more than a month, and they were taking a drive through what passed as the countryside of north Jersey. At first their new sex life was tentative and unsure, but soon Nick discovered a new woman who was now open and responsive. He had awakened her to places she had never been, and once there was more and more reluctant to leave. It could only get better.

Three Jewish fraternities at Rutgers, Tau Epsilon Phi, Alpha Epsilon Pi, and Zeta Beta Tau, had taken up silent vigil at all entrances. They were joined by brother chapters from New York City to provide two lines of silent protestors through which both sides in the M.L. Kraus hearings had to pass.

"Are we ready to put our mysterious Mister Rache on the backburner?" Cisco said. "You comfortable lifting surveillance at the Franke mansion?"

"I've had to detail uniforms to keep watch at the federal building," the Chief said, "and there's only so many to go around. Peaceful so far, but who knows."

By early December, it was apparent that a Kraus settlement was a long way off. The Kraus legal team had undergone a big shakeup with Eduard Siemens replacing

Hugo Manfred Franke as lead counsel. Two other lawyers, both former Nazi prosecutors, were flown in from Germany. The phony collegiality so obvious when the hearing before Judge Hockmeier began, had disappeared completely.

For Jason Tumulty, these developments could not have been sweeter. *Amicus curiae* filed by Dupont and Standard Oil, among others, were thrown into the mix. In Philadelphia, Dilberry, Tumulty & Benson was counting its blessings.

For most of this time, Nick was busy rebuilding family bridges. Angelo Cisco drew his son into the parlor, and making no attempt to hide his tears, wrapped Nick in a bear hug that left him gasping for air. "Nick, you're back. Yes, you were a wife-cheater and I hated that part of you. But you are my son and never, never question my love for you." Another breath-taking hug, a wet kiss on the cheek, and it was over.

Connie and his mother, Angelica, were waiting anxiously in the kitchen. When her husband and son, all smiles and teary-eyed came in from the parlor, Angelica jumped from her chair and smothered Nick with kisses wherever she could find a landing place. Of course, she was bawling like a baby, so was Connie.

For the rest of the family it was quite different. Cousins, uncles, aunts, nieces and nephews had from the beginning made up their mind that Nick was a skirt-chaser unable to keep his zipper closed. It took a lot of work to bring them around. Glass-after-glass of grappa, gallons of homemade Dago red, heated profanity exchanges, enough bocce ball to paralyze your wrist, a round-robin of dinners, dances at the Italian social club still weren't enough to convince some of the family that he was back to stay.

The men in the family knew and appreciated Grace De Marco, and when Nick wasn't around, theorized that after three years with a woman like her, no man could ever be the same.

It was much the same with Connie's family. They were there, had always been there, and it was up to Nick to convince them that he deserved to be there with them. It helped when Connie threw a dinner party at their home on Delavan for her and Nick's parents. Angelica and Anna separated themselves from the men and for almost an hour collected family gossip in Italian. Angelo and Dominic told Nick to get lost and went into the living room, plopped down with a magnum of grappa and proceeded to get tipsy.

For Nick, it was business as usual in homicide, except one thing. Earlier that month, with Mayor Murphy and Chief Riley at his side Nick got his captain's bars and the permanent title of homicide chief. Gingold was turning out to be okay, a little too stiff right now, but he'd come around once he discovered how homicide really worked.

Across the Passaic River in Harrison, Father Peter Majeski was about to say farewell to Saint Casimir's, having already received Father Kaczinski's blessing and bid goodbye to the Franciscan cherubs who replaced him. His two bags were packed, leaving one final detail to be disposed of. Sitting at his desk, he stamped and addressed an envelope bearing the parish return address, withdrew a few sheets of stationery and began to write.

Hi Terry, so you don't get out the bloodhounds and search parties, here are a few lines to let you know what's coming up for Father Ski. My duties here at Saint Casimir have ended and I've decided to retrace my steps. That's right, I'm re-upping, this time with the Army. I'll be at McGuire Air Force Base, and after stops at San Francisco and Hawaii, it's Japan and the Eighth Army Chaplain Corps.

I never really came clean about what was going on with me during my time here in New Jersey. I made a lame attempt when we got together with my old comrade, Samuel. I wanted you to see another side of Father Ski.

I realize that you were undoubtedly puzzled why I drove you across the river to endure all that hypnosis hocus-pocus. I have to say I was surprised myself.

I've been saving newspaper clips, especially those from the New York Herald Tribune, as crib notes on Japan. You might just as well be discussing Germany. It's amazing how we can forgive and forget the atrocities committed by these two countries, all for the greater good. We need authority figures, even those with bloody hands, to help us keep Uncle Joe and the Red Menace at bay.

With Germany it was the gas chambers and millions of lives, and with Japan it was Mitsui Mining and Mitsubishi at the head of a list of companies who used American POWs as slave labor, not giving a damn whether a POW died of starvation, beatings or exhaustion. It's hard to believe even cursory accounts of the horrible, mostly lethal experiments conducted by Unit 731. In exchange for their raw biological data, not one of Unit 731's scientists was brought to justice. Again, all for the greater good.

Getting back to the last two weeks, I visited with my mom and dad and two brothers at their sausage and meat store in the Ironbound. Now here's a greater good I can swear by. GI's returning from Europe with refined tastes means that Majeski's Sausage & Meats has added exotic new flavors to their list of delicacies. I packed some of them for my trip.

You can keep me informed how the Golden Boy of the Newark Archdiocese is getting along by writing in care of APO San Francisco. Blessings and the very warmest from the guy who will miss not being on hand when you get your purple beanie.

Ski

He sealed the letter, collected the newspaper clippings and put them in a manila envelope and inserted it into an outer pocket of one of his bags. The big man arose, grabbed his bags and headed out the door to begin the first leg of his trip to Japan.

Two weeks later and twenty miles from Harrison and Saint Casimir, Connie had no idea that her pleasant mid-December drive with Nick was coming to an end.

"Nick, you've been quiet for a while and I miss my tour guide," Connie said and reached over to place her hand on his thigh. "So, tell me, where the hell are we?"

"Right now, we're turning off Highway 9W, and see that saloon over there, very famous, very famous. The Log Cabin."

"Doesn't look like much. Why is it famous?"

"It's where that skinny little bastard Frank Sinatra got his start, and now he's the swoon king."

"Why that bastard? Yeah, he's skinny, not much to him but he must have something. Certainly not my type, I like more meat on the bone," she said squeezing Nick's muscular thigh.

"We'll go in later for a drink, but first there's something I want to show you," Nick said swinging past the Log Cabin onto a road that paralleled the Hudson River Palisades. In less than a mile, he turned into a circular driveway and stopped. "Connie, come on out, I want to show you something."

"Okay, here I am, what is it?"

"There it is, the novitiate of Saint Michael's, very famous, an architectural wonder. See how it dominates the Palisades. At night when its turrets are lighted, you can see it from the George Washington Bridge and even the skyscrapers in lower Manhattan. The very best for the Sisters of Saint Joseph of Peace."

"I'll say! What is it, two, three, four stories high," Connie said. "Gorgeous. If my sister, Gina, had seen all this when she decided to take the vows, I doubt very much she would be a Benedictine today."

They walked to the front of the Pontiac, and with Nick's arm around her shoulders, took in the beautiful grounds. Their every move was being closely watched from the novitiate entrance.

"Do you see him, Sister Immaculata, do you see him?" Muriel, jittery with excitement exclaimed, at the same time squeezing the nun's hand with all her might.

"Yes, yes, I see him, but I'm not at all sure I recognize him," Sister Immaculata said. She reached inside her apron and removed her bifocals for a closer look. "Yes, now I recognize him."

"He's one of my two best friends. Here's his name, right here," she said pointing to Nick's signature on her cast. "His name is Nick. He's an important police officer. I don't know the lady. But if she's with him, I know she'll be very nice. I've got to go."

The nun bent down and asked, "So, tell me, where are you going?"

"Back to my room for my special yellow dress, and my special shoes and fancy socks. They always bring me luck." She turned and saw that her very special friend had his arm linked with the lady's as they slowly walked down the driveway in her direction.

www.ingramcontent.com/pod-product-compliance
Lightning Source LLC
Chambersburg PA
CBHW060543310726
48982CB00009B/1358/J

* 9 7 8 1 6 4 1 8 4 1 8 1 8 *